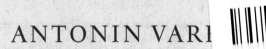

ANTONIN VARENNE

RETRIBUTION ROAD

Translated from the French by
Sam Taylor

MACLEHOSE PRESS
QUERCUS · LONDON

First published in the French language as *Trois mille chevaux vapeur* by
Éditions Albin Michel, Paris in 2014
First published in Great Britain in 2017 by MacLehose Press
This paperback edition published in 2018 by

MacLehose Press
An imprint of Quercus Publishing Ltd
Carmelite House
50 Victoria Embankment
London EC4Y 0DZ

An Hachette UK company

A CIP catalogue record for this book is available
from the British Library.

ISBN (MMP) 978 0 85705 373 2
ISBN (Ebook) 978 0 85705 371 8

10 9 8 7 6 5 4 3

Designed and typeset in Haarlemmer by Libanus Press

Printed and bound in Great Britain by Clays Ltd, Elcograf S.p.A.

RETRIBUTION ROAD

Also by Antonin Varenne in English translation
Bed of Nails (2012)
Loser's Corner (2014)

In 1600, Queen Elizabeth I granted a trading monopoly in the Indian Ocean to a group of English merchants and investors. The first "East India Company" was born. The shareholders in London, and their European competitors, took control of the world's trade.

In 1776, the financial and political elite of the thirteen North American colonies declared themselves independent from British rule. Freed from imperial taxes and laws, the United States of America rapidly became a new economic power. As soon as it became independent, the young American nation began a series of military interventions to extend and defend its commercial interests. In Sumatra, in Ivory Coast, in Mexico, in Argentina, in Japan, in China, in Nicaragua, in the Philippines, in Hawaii, in Cuba, in Angola, in Colombia and Haiti.

In 1850, the East India Company – dubbed by its shareholders "the most powerful company in the universe", with a private army of 300,000 men – imposed its commercial laws over one-fifth of the world's population: three hundred million people.

In the nineteenth century, an American or a British soldier with a yearning to travel could see the world while fighting, moving from country to country.

I

1852

Burma

I

"Rooney! You lazy Irish bastard! Pallacate!"

Rooney got up off the bench, slowly crossed the courtyard and stood in front of the corporal.

"The mare's on her last legs, sir. All the horses are knackered."

"You're the one who's knackered. Now get in the saddle!"

Back bent by exhaustion, head half sunk into the trough, the mare was noisily gulping down gallons of water. Rooney grabbed the reins, pulled the horse's mouth out of the water, and grimaced as he put his foot in the stirrup. He'd spent half the night riding from one barracks to another. His arse hurt, his teeth and nostrils were lined with dust, and the sun was burning his head.

Fifteen miles to the trading post in Pallacate.

The animal shook its head, refusing the bit. Rooney yanked the reins, the mare bridled, and he gripped the pommel to stop himself falling. The corporal laughed. Rooney whipped his horse's ears, yelling: "Giddy-up!"

The mare galloped across the paved courtyard. Rooney passed through the north gates of Fort St George without slowing, whipping the horse constantly. Mulberry plantations flashed past, cotton fields where a few peasants worked, bent over their tools. All along the path, columns of sepoys in their red uniforms walked quickly under the hot sun, kitbags on their backs and rifles on their shoulders.

The garrisons converged on the fort and the port. The villagers, worried by all this activity, had closed their doors and windows to keep out the dust kicked up by the soldiers' boots. The Madras army was on the march, and the countryside had emptied around its path.

Lord Dalhousie, Governor-General of India, had declared war on the King of Burma.

General Godwin, who had arrived from Bombay the day before with ten ships, was mobilising all the regiments.

Rooney had spent the last twelve hours delivering letters all over the region.

Pallacate. His final errand.

Maybe he'd be able to stay there tonight, go to the Chinaman's place and pay for a girl. They were clean, and gin was cheaper there than in St George. The idea of spending the night in the weavers' village gave him wings, but it didn't help his horse, which was gasping like a consumptive.

Rooney, his legs soaked with foam, whipped it hard, again and again. It was wartime: you were allowed to kill a horse.

He passed children on donkeys and peasants in rags. Seeing the first houses of Pallacate, he spurred the horse and entered the main street at a gallop, and women with children clinging to their backs ran for shelter.

"C'mon!"

At the end of the village, he turned left towards the warehouses of the trading post. He'd have the Chinaman's shop all to himself. Same thing at the fort. There'd be no-one left, no more stupid chores to do for weeks. While everyone went off to Rangoon, he'd stay behind and take it easy. The King of St George!

"C'mon!"

The mare shook her head, her strides fell out of time. There was a jolt, as if her legs were giving way beneath his weight. Rooney held on with all his strength and the horse suddenly started up again, accelerating without even the need for a kick in its side, half crazed with heat and exhaustion. In the courtyard encircled by warehouses, Rooney saw the Company's flag waving in the wind.

As he passed the first warehouse, the mare's head sank forward and disappeared. He heard the horse's front legs break – the terrible sound of crushed bones. Rooney went flying straight ahead, six feet above the ground. He held out his arms, but did not feel the collision, did not feel the bones snap in his wrists and arms. His head banged into the ground, he somersaulted forward and his back smashed into the water pump, a cast-iron pillar in the middle of the courtyard.

Sergeant Bowman grabbed his rifle, which was leaning against a root of the large banyan tree, and got up from the deckchair he had positioned in the shade of its branches. The cloud of dust raised by the fall of the horse and its rider was floating slowly over the courtyard. The mare was screaming loud enough to wake the dead and the unconscious messenger wasn't moving at all. The sergeant walked past the animal, which was thrashing its hind legs in the air, put the Enfield across his thighs, and crouched down in front of the soldier.

Crumpled in a heap next to the pump, he opened his eyes.

"What . . . what happened?"

His head fell onto his chest and a thread of blood dripped from the corner of his mouth. His pelvis was smashed, his legs tangled together like bits of cloth. His eyes rolled from side to side, trying to recognise his surroundings. The courtyard, the silk warehouses, the sergeant who was watching him, and the horse lying on its side, its tongue licking the earth as if it were water.

"I can't . . . feel anything . . ."

His eyes looked down at his shattered body. A grimace of panic distorted his face.

"Fuck . . . what . . . happened . . . to me?"

The sergeant did not answer him.

"Help me . . . fucking hell . . . help me."

Again, Rooney looked around. There was no-one else. The horse was whinnying and kicking, but the sergeant just squatted there, motionless. Rooney tried to call out for help, but he choked and spat out blood. Sergeant Bowman moved back a little bit to avoid being splattered.

"You . . . bastard . . . Help . . . me."

The sergeant, stone-faced, tilted his head.

Private Rooney's face suddenly stopped moving, frozen in an expression of panic, his eyelids open and his eyes staring into Bowman's. A bubble of blood formed between his lips and burst.

The trading-post manager came running from his office.

Sergeant Bowman stood up and walked over to the horse, loaded his rifle, placed a boot on the mare's throat and fired a bullet into the side of its head.

The manager crossed himself before opening the satchel that hung from the courier's neck. He took out the sealed letter with his name on the front.

"Bloody ridiculous. To meet your death delivering a message in wartime . . ."

Sergeant Bowman rested the rifle on its butt and and crossed his hands over the still-warm barrel. Sepoys rushed over, forming a circle around the dead man. The Company accountant searched the soldier's pockets, finding his military papers inside his jacket.

"Sean Rooney. Fort St George . . . Well, that's one who won't die in Burma."

The manager turned to Bowman.

"Sergeant, go now. You're expected in Madras with your men."

Bowman put his rifle on his shoulder and headed over to his hut in the shade of the banyan tree. The accountant shouted after him:

"Sergeant! You'll be responsible for taking Private Rooney's body to Madras."

Bowman kept walking.

"I'll leave you the horse."

Twenty sepoys waited in the sun, standing in two columns. Next to the sergeant's horse, an ox was harnessed to a wagon. Inside the wagon, Rooney's body lay covered by the soldiers' kitbags.

Bowman walked past the saluting men and knocked on the manager's door.

"I'm leaving five men here while you wait for Madras to send a contingent."

"Very good. I am not interested in warfare, Sergeant, only in trade. I am not in any danger here. I must admit I am not unhappy to see you leave, Bowman, but it is my duty as a Christian to wish everyone well.

May God be with you, wherever you go."

Bowman mounted his horse and rode to where the dead animal lay. The horse sniffed at the carcass, snorted loudly, and lifted its head. The sepoys passed at a trot, followed by the wagon. Bowman followed them, bringing up the rear.

At Fort St George, Bowman let the sepoys draw breath and asked a guard for the name of the officer responsible for the messenger.

"Rooney? You'll have to see the corporal, over at the stable. What happened?"

Bowman found the stable, where the corporal sat at a table with other tired, dirty messengers, amid the stink of dung.

"What a prick! Killed a horse and himself too! He always was a bit of an idiot, Rooney. And those bloody Irish – they hate being buried far from home! He didn't suffer too much, did he?"

"My monkeys will bring you the body. I'll leave you my horse too."

At the fort's headquarters, Bowman received his orders.

The docks were swarming with merchandise, crates of weapons and ammunition. Mountains of barrels were piled up, over a distance of nearly a hundred feet. Water, wine, rum, vinegar, cages containing chickens and rabbits, squealing pigs. Coolies unloaded tons of food and armament supplies while rowing boats came and went from the seventeen stranded ships of the Madras fleet. The sun hung low over the ocean, and the Company colours, on the immense flags floating above the sea, sparkled in the yellow light.

An endless flood of sepoys and British soldiers were arriving in columns. From the rowing boats could be heard the sound of men singing in rhythm as they pulled on the oars, transporting contingents and cargo.

Seventeen first-class vessels, a thousand cannons and fifteen thousand men at anchor, three-quarters of them sepoys, as they were three times cheaper than English soldiers. The Company's army outnumbered the British army, but its numbers were swollen by indigenous recruits.

The shareholders of Leadenhall Street wanted the Gulf of Bengal for themselves alone. If this armada did not prove sufficient, they would send another thirty thousand men. Pagan Min had to fall before the monsoon season, or the Company would be stuck for another four months while they waited for the rivers to become navigable again. The officers knew it, and the N.C.O.s yelled at the tops of their voices, urging the men forward, urging goods to be moved and sailors to row with greater speed.

Bowman's little troop of soldiers was sucked up into the whirlwind of the port.

For two hours, jostling for position on the docks, they waited their turn to jump aboard a rowing boat. The sun was setting when the sergeant and his men finally started climbing the rope ladder up the side of the *Healing Joy*, the flagship of the fleet.

The sepoys went down to the bottom deck, beneath the waterline, and Sergeant Bowman joined the British contingent on the first deck. Four hundred men searching in the darkness for their places, unrolling the hammocks in which they would fester for the next two weeks.

If the wind was in their favour.

Several hours passed before the sound of cannon fire exploded above their heads and the fleet began to move. On the deck, above the troop, there were whistles and shouted orders, the voices of sailors and the creaking of wooden masts, the vibrations reaching all the way down to the sepoys' hold.

It was midnight. The heat was unbearable.

Surrounded by overexcited men, as the *Joy* listed and soldiers began to throw up, Sergeant Bowman lay in his hammock and closed his eyes, one hand on the Afghan dagger in his belt. Three years he'd waited.

2

A porthole was opened.

Bowman, elbows on the railing, leaned a little further forward.

A body fell into the sea, a white shirt pulled roughly up over its head. It hit the water, sank for an instant, then bobbed back up to the surface. A second followed, and slowly drifted the length of the ship. A grey shape circled the corpses. When a third cadaver toppled overboard, the sea – motionless since dawn – suddenly started bubbling.

Dozens of fins and tails stabbed through the water. Little black eyes appeared in the foam. Huge jaws snapped at arms and legs. The red cloud spread as the soldiers' bodies fell from the porthole like chicken into a vat of hot oil.

Bowman counted eight that morning.

Sprays of pink water splattered the hull, and headless torsos rolled in the frothing sea, tangled up in scraps of shirts. Sharks wounded by their frenzied fellow creatures continued fighting for a piece of shoulder, while others, killed in the maelstrom, floated belly up amid the slaughter.

Bowman looked up. Around other ships, a few cable-lengths from the flagship, the same aquatic frenzy was taking place with figures just like his leaning over to watch. He scraped a match against the rail, protected the flame with his hand, and lit his pipe again.

About a hundred men had died that night, on board the seventeen ships.

Once their feast was over, the sharks moved away and the seagulls swooped down for the leftovers. The sea was red, as if dyed by laterite silt in the estuary of an African river. The current took away the fleet's waste matter, spreading the coloured stain, which grew steadily paler, towards the coast. The morning sun rose above the dark line of the continent, and round-bellied clouds, filled with rain that did not fall, rolled low over the horizon.

Bowman spat in the water, cleaned out his pipe and went back down to the first deck.

After a three-week crossing and three days in anchorage, the *Healing Joy* stank like a zoo. The wind did not blow in the gulf, and the fleet dawdled dismally on a deep swell.

He lifted up the sheet that separated his hammock from the rest of the men and lay down on the mouldy fabric.

On land, Pagan Min's spies could not care less about this immobile armada: they were watching only the sky, waiting for the monsoon to burst. The boredom of the men in the anchored vessels turned to melancholy and more and more of them fell ill. Laid low by fever, stupefied by the ships' slow movement, by the silence and the heat, they lay still all day and all night, amid a constant murmur of groaning and coughing. Under the waterline, where the air no longer circulated, the sepoys were dropping like flies. Of the eight corpses thrown into the water this morning, six were Indians. Piss and shit sloshed over the duckboard, the air was putrid, and General Godwin had forbidden the sepoys to go up to the upper deck: the more degraded the state of the troops became, the more important it was to hide this fact from Min's spies.

This was the second time the Company had gone to war in Burma. The first time, in 1826, Campbell, at the head of the British troops, had won trading posts all along the coast, as far as the kingdom of Siam. He, too, had arrived too late. Rain and fever had killed ten thousand men when he tried to reach Ava by land. His campaign ended in a half-victory and the right to trade in the ports. Since then, the Burmese had regained their strength, attempting to renegotiate the '26 agreement, giving the trading-post managers a hard time, threatening trade in the gulf and on the road to China. Dalhousie had sent Commodore Lambert there at the beginning of the year, on a diplomatic mission. Lambert was no diplomat. The situation grew poisonous and the last recourse remaining to the Company was to declare war. This time, the goal was to put an end to the situation by taking the whole country.

But the wind did not blow, miring the fleet as it waited for the chance to attack. Men were dying before a single cannon blast or gunshot had been fired.

Bowman took a handkerchief from his bag and unfolded it over his stomach. He chewed the last piece of dried pork that he had brought with him from Pallacate, slowly savouring the meat's flavour. He rubbed his teeth and gums with a carefully hoarded slice of lemon peel, then swallowed it.

Supplies were running low. They had not brought enough food with them. Rations were reduced. The fresh water had stagnated, and they'd had to cut it with vinegar.

He sank back in his hammock, cursing the shareholders in London who declared wars without any knowledge of warfare, the officers getting rich in their palaces, the Bengal sepoys who'd been recruited from the more delicate castes and had refused to go to Burma. Bombay and Madras had been forced to supply men, and the Company had arrived later than planned.

Amid the usual moans and other noises of the deck, the sound of raised voices drew the sergeant's attention. Strong words, first of all, which turned to insults. Laughter and jostling. He stood up and pulled aside the sheet.

There were about twenty soldiers surrounding two men who were fighting. A huge, bull-necked blond man was laying into a tall, brown-haired soldier, lighter by about twenty or thirty pounds. The men were laughing, and when the weakling tried to run away, refusing to fight, they pushed him back into the arms of his opponent. The blond man threw him against the hull, his head smashed into a metal girder, and blood spurted from his temple. The men around him laughed even harder. The bull charged at him, the tall thin man evaded the attack, and his opponent collided with the ship's wooden framework. Stunned and angry, he took a knife from the sleeve of his uniform. The spectators stopped laughing, and moved away from the weapon. The weakling raised his hands.

"Stop. This is pointless. I don't want to fight you."

The man with the knife was no longer listening. Forced to defend himself, the tall man took off his jacket and rolled it around his arm, edging back towards the hammocks while never taking his eyes off the blade.

The bull leapt forward. Again the weakling eluded him, tripping over, rolling along the floor and springing back to his feet.

Bowman, leaning against a post, watched with the others. There had not been anything to watch for quite some time now.

In the next attack, the tall thin soldier tried to hit the hand holding the knife. He missed, and the blade whistled through the air in a quick downward arc, slicing through his shirt. He fell to his knees and coiled up like a snake around his wound. As the blond man rushed forward to strike another blow, two hands seized his throat, lifted him from the floor and threw him backwards. He got to his feet, furious, and saw Sergeant Bowman standing in front of him. He blinked, open-mouthed and breathless, and let his knife drop to the floorboards.

Bowman leaned forward over the wounded man. The gash was long but not very deep. He ordered a soldier to fetch the surgeon.

"Why didn't you stop it before, Sergeant?"

Bowman stood straight.

"Throw him in his hammock."

The surgeon arrived a few minutes later, grumbling that he had enough sick men to deal with already without the soldiers slicing each other open. Once he had treated the wound, he stood in front of Bowman's hammock.

"Perhaps you should report this, Sergeant? The men are growing more and more tense. We do not want this kind of incident to happen again."

"I'll take care of it. There won't be any more problems. How's the victim?"

"Nothing serious. I didn't bother with stitches."

The surgeon had an ugly face, eyes red with fever. He stood there, mulling something over, and Bowman waited for him to speak.

"If we stay here too long, I won't be able to do anything. I'm almost out of medicine, and half the Indians are sick. They can't stand the sea."

He looked down.

"Take care of the men, Sergeant. The wounded man is a good Christian. They're all good Christians."

The doctor gave a nervous smile, which dissolved into a look of utter despondency. He was still waiting for something. Bowman cleared his throat.

"I'll take care of them, sir. Don't you worry about that."

The surgeon scuttled off between the hammocks.

Everyone was going crazy, because everyone thought the war had not started yet, whereas the truth was that the first battle – the longest and most fatal battle – was already raging on board the ships: the waiting. Bowman knew that one must first survive the army before surviving the battlefield. He was already at the front.

He picked up his book and opened it to the passage that he always read before going into combat.

Hidden behind his sheet, one finger on the page and his lips moving silently, he deciphered the words.

> But all the silver and gold, and vessels of brass and iron, are conse-crated unto the Lord: they shall come into the treasury of the Lord.
>
> So the people shouted when the priests blew with the trum-pets: and it came to pass, when the people heard the sound of the trumpet, and the people shouted with a great shout, that the wall fell down flat, so that the people went up into the city, every man straight before him, and they took the city. And they utterly destroyed all that was in the city, both man and woman, young and old, and ox, and sheep, and ass, with the edge of the sword.

The Bible was the only book he had ever possessed. Bowman did not even imagine that there could be others as thick as this one, with so many stories inside. He closed his eyes and wondered why God, who made it rain on his enemies, made walls crumble and dried up rivers to help his armies, seemed so indifferent to the fate of the Company. He also wondered why he hadn't stopped the fight earlier, and if the injured soldier, if he'd managed to disarm his opponent or even stab a blade into his belly, would even have asked that question.

All good Christians.

Bowman smiled. The fight had entertained him, and the men, no matter what the quack said, were still ready to fight. That was all they were waiting for.

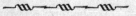

The smell of vinegar rose from the just-cleaned deck, mingling with the scents of lukewarm seawater and the *Joy*'s putrefaction. Bowman stroked the match head against the handrail, and the flame briefly illuminated his hands and then his face as he moved it towards the tobacco. He took a drag, arched his neck and blew out the smoke, chin in the air, emptying his lungs.

To the east, along the invisible coastline, the lights of Rangoon flickered like dying stars. Beneath his feet, the men tossed and turned in their hammocks, hoping that tomorrow the wind would come, that the ship would stop listing, or that the vinegar would be turned into wine. Sentries patrolled the deck, rifles resting on shoulders, while a few officers took the air in the moonlight.

Bowman had recognised some of them during the crossing. Six or seven among the two hundred on the *Joy*. Officers under whom he had fought in the Punjab, in Cavendish's regiment; others he had met at trading-post garrisons where he had been sent during the last three years.

Among the men he had saluted, not one had spoken a word to him. Maybe they were avoiding him, or maybe he had changed since the

Punjab. Maybe not everyone had a memory for faces like he did. He spat in the sea as if to pass on a disease.

"Sergeant Bowman?"

He half-heartedly saluted the deck officer, lifting his pipe to his temple.

"Major Cavendish wants to see you. I must accompany you there now."

"Cavendish?"

"Straight away, Sergeant."

Bowman rebuttoned his stinking jacket.

Cavendish. Second-in-command of the fleet. Heir to the duchy of Devonshire. His family was one of the Company's biggest share-holders. The only time Bowman had seen him was after the palace of Amritsar had been taken, during a promotion ceremony. Corporal Bowman, who had become a sergeant, remembered this well. Cavendish had made a speech. He'd said that the officers were the "spear-heads of the Company". Bowman had thought that a very good expression.

Cavendish was on board the *Joy* and wanted to see him – Arthur Bowman.

Perhaps the attack was about to be launched. Perhaps Godwin was gathering the officers to give them his orders. But Bowman was only a sergeant. He had no business in the fo'c's'le with the general staff, and – unless there was a problem – a soldier like him would never approach a high-ranking officer.

He followed the deck officer, passing sentries and guards, walking through corridors with polished walls where the light of oil lamps was reflected. His guide knocked at a door, and a voice bade them enter. The officer opened the door, moved out of the way, and closed it behind him.

Bowman did not understand where he was. It was not the command room, just a little cabin with one window, a bunk, a map table, two chairs, and a lamp hanging from the ceiling. Behind the table, in one of the upholstered chairs, sat Major Cavendish, looking more or less as

Bowman remembered him. In front of the window, smoking a cigar, was a captain in uniform. He recognised him, even if, back then, Wright had been only a lieutenant. For a second, the sergeant just stood there, before clicking his heels, saluting, and turning his back to the officers and the table.

"Sergeant Bowman at your command, sir!"

A snort of laughter behind him.

"You may turn around, Sergeant."

"Sir! You have not put the map away, sir."

Bowman waited. There was no sound of paper, not even the faintest movement. On a warship just before an attack, N.C.O.s had no more right than a private soldier to see military maps. Glancing at one, even inadvertently, could lead a man to the noose or into the sea with the sharks.

Cavendish spoke to the captain:

"Wright, I have the feeling you've made the right choice this time."

Wright did not reply. In a firmer tone of voice, Cavendish said again:

"Turn around, Sergeant."

Bowman swivelled, his gaze still lifted above the table.

"Sergeant, you are going to look at that map which scares you so much and tell me what it represents."

Bowman blinked.

"I'm not scared of the map, sir. I didn't know I was authorised to look at it, sir."

"Well, you are. Tell me what it represents."

Bowman lowered his eyes, glancing quickly at Captain Wright, then at Cavendish, before resting his gaze on the map.

From where he stood, the map was upside down and he could not read the names, but he saw a sea, a coastline, a large green stain, and in the middle of it the twisting blue line of a river. He tried to focus on the words, but they were printed too small.

"I don't know, sir. But I would guess it is the kingdom of Ava."

"Precisely, Sergeant. And what is that river?"

Bowman lifted his head to the ceiling.

"Sir, I'm not sure, but I would imagine it's the Irrawaddy."

"Correct once again. What could you tell me about that river, Sergeant?"

Bowman gulped.

"I . . . I don't understand, sir."

"What do you know about that river?"

"It's the route to Ava, sir."

Cavendish smiled.

"What else?"

"I don't know, sir . . . It's the route to Ava . . . And the monsoon is coming."

"The monsoon . . . What does that mean, Sergeant, the monsoon?"

Silence again. Bowman felt his legs giving way beneath him.

"Sir! The rain, that means that the fleet can't sail up the river."

Cavendish looked at the map for a moment, preoccupied, then stood up.

"Sergeant, I was told by Captain Wright that you were aboard and he recommended that I meet you. He told me you were a brave fighter, almost . . . How did you put it, Wright? Ah, yes! 'Recklessly bold'. The captain said you fought like a lion under his orders during the attack on the palace of Amritsar. What do you say to that, Sergeant?"

"I beg your pardon, sir?"

"Do you agree with Captain Wright?"

"Sir! It was a hell of an attack, with sabres and bayonets, but I was only obeying orders, sir."

"Ah! That is what I wanted to hear you say, Sergeant. You obeyed orders. And you mounted the assault with your bayonet! Wonderful! So you are a good soldier, and you are brave."

Cavendish paced around the cabin, hands behind his back, then finally came to a halt beneath the halo of the lamp and put his hands on the map.

"Sergeant, I have given it some thought and I am going to assign you this mission. Captain Wright will conclude this interview."

Cavendish went out without saluting or saying another word, slamming the door behind him and leaving Captain Wright alone with Bowman.

Wright took one last drag on his cigar and threw it out of the window.

"It's a stroke of luck that you should be on board this ship, Bowman."

"The kind of luck you don't always get when you want it, sir."

Wright turned around.

"What do you mean by that, Sergeant?"

"Sir! It's a manner of speaking. Nothing special, sir."

The captain observed Bowman for a moment.

"Tomorrow, before noon, a Company dinghy will come here to fetch us, from the *Joy*. You will be under my orders, second-in-command of the expedition. Thirty men, twenty of whom will arrive tomorrow with the sloop, and ten others – ten trustworthy men whom you must choose from among the soldiers on the *Joy*. Be on deck tomorrow morning, kitbag packed, no weapons, ready to not come back."

Wright turned towards the window.

"You are one of the most violent men I have ever commanded, Bowman. You obey orders and you make others obey you. It is for those qualities that I recommended you to Major Cavendish, and that he decided to choose you. I hope you will repay the trust we are putting in you. Not a word to anyone. Dismissed, Sergeant."

Bowman stood stock-still, as if his shoes were nailed to the wooden boards. The cabin spun before his eyes. He tore his feet from the floor, moved towards the door, found himself in the corridor and walked outside. Under the black moon, mouth wide open, he took deep, gasping breaths. The air was warm, humid, stale, too thick to relieve his dizziness.

He did not know why or how it would happen, but he knew he had just been condemned to death. It had not taken place on a battlefield or during an assault on an enemy base, but before a map, a duke too busy to finish his sentences and a cigar-smoking captain. And in place of a sentence, he had been given an order.

He walked over to the railing, leaned his hands on it and stared out at the lights of Rangoon in the distance. He stayed there for an hour, breathing that coffin air, before going back down to the first deck, where he crept between the Company's mercenaries, stretched out in hammocks, their eyes wide open and immobile, clinging to the ceiling like lizards.

Ten men.

3

He didn't sleep a wink. Beneath his feet, sepoys driven mad with fever had spent the whole night screaming. He lifted up a corner of his sheet.

The dawn light filtered in through the half-open portholes. The men were starting to move, giving up on sleep. The galley workers brought in the breakfast rations of rice gruel and rum. The soldiers, holding their mess tins and cups, stood in line. Once they had been served, they went off to eat their ration, devouring the insipid soup and the mouthful of alcohol that, some said, had the power to save a man from fever and toxic air.

Bowman did not leave his hammock. During the slow and pathetic ritual of the soup, he watched the soldiers filing past in front of him. He didn't know any of them, nor did he know anything about the mission for which he would need them.

Wright had chosen him because he was tough.

Maybe he should seek out men of the same stamp?

Besides, what did that mean, a trustworthy man? Wright didn't trust him. He didn't trust Wright. Bowman had never trusted anyone but himself. And yet, the idea of being surrounded by ten men like him disturbed him more than anything.

He had long ago ruled out the idea of choosing any Indians. One never knew what made a native obey orders, nor what might one day make them disobey orders. For him, an order had the same value as a decision he had made himself.

Ten men. Take your pick.

Bowman spotted the weakling who had lost the fight, the one the surgeon had patched up the night before. Standing in the line of soldiers, mess tin in hand, his shirt torn and stained with dry blood, he had managed to get through the night without catching a fever.

"You. Come here."

The soldier followed the sergeant to a quieter corner of the deck.

"You know why I didn't stop the fight before?"

He looked at Bowman.

"Why, Sergeant?"

"Because a fight is like a war: you have to know who the winner is before you can know who was right to start fighting. And sometimes it's the man who didn't want to fight who wins. So he was the one who was right."

The soldier smiled at Bowman.

"God forgives trespasses, as I refuse to fight unjustly or for no good reason. I could have mastered that man, without fighting and without your intervention, Sergeant."

"Bloody hell, are you a vicar or something?"

"Merely a sheep in the flock, Sergeant."

"A sheep who's still standing with a twelve-inch slash in his belly is good meat, I reckon."

Bowman looked around them.

"Is there anyone you trust on this boat?"

The soldier was puzzled.

"What do you mean? Someone I know?"

"Yeah, someone you trust."

The soldier looked at the men who surrounded them, lying or standing, eating or sick, chatting or silent. He pointed at one of them, sitting on his hammock, placidly swallowing his rotten breakfast.

"Are you taking the piss?"

The soldier shook his head. Bowman gave a half-smile.

"Him? You're sure?"

The tall thin man nodded.

"Him."

Bowman walked up to the blond man who had, the night before, tried to cut the sheep's godly throat.

"You."

The soldier jumped out of his hammock and saluted.

"Sergeant!"

"Over here."

When the blond bull found himself face to face with the wounded soldier, he froze.

"Sorry, Sergeant, it was stupid of me. I got in a rage over nothing. I swear it won't happen again."

"Shut your mouth. You, preacher, explain it to him. He has to do the same thing. When there are ten of you, pack your kitbag and meet me on deck. Sergeant Bowman's orders. They'll let you pass. Got it?"

The godly soldier nodded, while the bull said yes without understanding what was happening.

"Names?"

The preacher's name was Peavish. The man he had decided to forgive was called Bufford.

Bowman went over to his hammock, knelt down in front of his bag, and emptied it out on the floor.

He unfolded a uniform jacket that was barely in a better state than the one he was wearing, and on top of it he put his mother-of-pearl powder horn, the almost-empty bottle of rum, his military papers in the little oiled leather pouch, his Bible and his reserves of tobacco, then wrapped the jacket around these objects. At the bottom of the canvas bag, on top of this bundle, he put a pair of new boots and a change of clothes. Then he took his dagger from his belt and added that to the pile.

When he went up on deck, something had changed, though what it was he didn't immediately understand.

The seventeen ships in the fleet, which had not moved for days, were swaying from side to side, the lines of their riggings crossing on the horizon. Small waves lapped against the hulls, the sea turned white and all the men on the deck of the *Healing Joy* felt the wind on their faces. The clouds in the sky were moving east towards Rangoon. On the officers' deck, a sailor hoisted the flags, communicating General Godwin's orders to the other ships.

The wind was blowing in the Company's favour, and the clouds had not burst.

The sailors climbed up rope ladders and on to booms 130 feet above the sea. Godwin and his general staff appeared on the poop deck, their medals and the gold braid of their uniforms shining in the sunlight. Telescopes were turned towards Rangoon. Major Cavendish was there too, staring at the coastline.

The soldiers were sent to battle stations, the sailors to their posts. The anchor chains were pulled from the sea, link by link, the men grunting with the effort. The sails, unfurled, swelled in the wind. The fleet's portholes opened to reveal the mouths of cannons. Thirty-pound carronades, black and stocky, hidden under sail bags, appeared on the decks. The same sounds came from all the ships, ricocheting off the water and carried by the wind: the sounds of armament and manoeuvres.

Amid the general panic, in the middle of the ship's turmoil, Bowman's ten men emerged from the main hatchway, protecting their eyes from the light. They turned around, looking for the sergeant. Peavish, Bufford and eight other soldiers whom Bowman had never seen before. They lined up along the railing, patient as farmers in church, but Bowman did not have time to inspect them.

He could see, threading its way through the fleet's vessels, every sail raised, a three-masted sloop, about 100 feet long, as white as those yachts on the Thames that the rich sail in summer. Except that this one was armed with twenty-pound cannons, eighteen of them, and its decks were populated not only with sailors but with twenty soldiers in uniform.

Captain Wright emerged suddenly from the fo'c's'le, a double-barrelled pistol in his belt and a messenger's satchel strapped across his chest, followed by a sailor carrying his bag. The sloop came alongside their ship and Bowman saw its name, in golden letters on the white hull. The *Sea Runner* dropped its sails, and the sailors on the *Healing Joy* lowered the fenders, threw the hawsers and rolled out the officers' gangplank. Wright went first, jumping onto the deck of the *Runner*, which he quickly crossed before disappearing into the cockpit. Bowman yelled at his men:

"Board now!"

They hurtled down the gangplank, shoved forward by the sergeant, and clambered aboard.

Immediately, the hawsers were cast off, the sloop caught the wind and rapidly moved away, manoeuvring a path through the fleet. A cannon blast sounded. The ships tore themselves away from the water where they had been mouldering and, heading for Rangoon, turned away from the sloop.

The war was starting without them, as if Godwin and God had been waiting for Bowman and his men to leave before setting it in motion.

The *Sea Runner* set a westward course. Bowman remembered Cavendish's map, the drawing of the river in the middle of that green expanse. They were on their way to the Irrawaddy estuary, drawing nearer to the coast.

Land was only a mile off now, parallel to the sloop's course. They could make out details of the forest, beaches and rocks, some trees taller than others, mangrove and coconut trees leaning over the waves; odours reached them from the land, the scented wind sucking their boat in faster and faster. When Bowman turned around, the fleet was already nothing but a line of little white dots on the horizon.

For the men from the *Healing Joy* who had just boarded the *Runner*, the heat of the continent felt like a promise after months spent suffocating in hammocks. A new world, close by, the masts of the sloop leaning towards it like outstretched arms.

The soldiers already aboard no longer eyed the coast with the same curiosity. They had seen enough of it to grow weary of the sight and were aware of what really awaited them there: it was not the promised land, merely the start of an endless jungle, the immense territory where the warriors of the kingdom of Ava lay in wait.

Bowman sat on his kitbag, leaning against the cockpit wall, and looked at the thirty soldiers scattered over the deck.

The ten men from the *Joy* talked between themselves, in groups of two at the bow of the ship. Each of them knew others in the same group, but none of them knew everyone. A coalition of chance and acquaintance. Peavish stood apart and it was Bufford, in the end, who had determined the make-up of the group: sturdy, muscular and probably rather stupid. The man he had chosen, and those who had been chosen after that, were very much in his image. Hard men. The kind of men Bowman would have mistrusted had he chosen them himself, gathered together here by the preacher, with his sheeplike forgiveness and faith.

The men already aboard were in the same mould. Beefy men in frayed uniforms, tattoos on their arms, comparable to Bufford's men in age and appearance, but they stood silent. They stared out gloomily at the coastline or the sea. Two soldiers, scanning the green line of the continent, caught Bowman's eye. One had torn jacket sleeves, with wounds on his wrists from steel chains. The other was barefoot, and like his friend's wrists, his ankles were grazed and bruised, rubbed raw by the touch of metal. Some of the other uniforms had been ripped at the shoulders, where stripes had been removed.

The men from the sloop were prisoners of the fleet, rowdy soldiers and N.C.O.s, taken from the holds where they had been awaiting their sentence, some of them perhaps even the hangman's noose.

Bowman closed his eyes and savoured the cool wind on his face, the smells of the land in his nostrils.

For four hours, the *Sea Runner* sped forward. After the excitement of boarding, his men had returned to the resigned mannerisms of soldiers being transported who knew where, who knew why. The two chain-marked soldiers had ended up sitting in a corner together, postponing their dreams of escape.

Bowman dozed, eyes half closed, surveying the movements around him.

The sailors observed this strange, silent group. The sloop's captain, an old naval officer, stood at the helm on the upper deck, flanked by two Company soldiers, wearing muskets across their chests. The cannons were ready to fire, portholes open, and below deck, Bowman sensed, the rest of the crew was in a state of high alert.

The sloop tacked to one side. The rigging creaked, the sails snapped and the booms swung over the heads of the drowsing men, waking them suddenly. The *Runner* was changing direction, heading towards the coast. It was late afternoon and the sun would soon set. In these latitudes, night fell in the blink of an eye.

Ahead of the ship's bow, the sergeant saw a grey beach: a cove in the shape of a half-moon, quite deep, bordered by two rocky promontories. As the sloop approached, he saw the village and that dark stain that he had, at first, not been able to identify. A large junk in anchorage, with ochre-red sails. In the middle of the beach, a pontoon jutted into the water, some outrigger canoes were drawn up on the sand, and a dozen buildings, parallel to the curve of the bay, backed onto the forest. Wooden cabins with palm-leaf roofs. Fishing lines were hung from bamboo porches. Between these houses and on the beach, patrolling in pairs, were Company soldiers in red uniforms, about thirty of them in total. Ten were gathered in front of the largest building, a sort of temple or communal house, opposite the pontoon, the central point of the village. The soldiers were lined up on the platform of its wide covered terrace, guarding a large closed door. Lobster pots, still-smoking fireplaces, chickens, dogs and little black pigs could all be seen in the village's streets which, apart from the soldiers, looked deserted.

On the captain's order, the sailors lowered the sails. The sloop glided over the calm water, in the silence of this perfect natural shelter, until it reached the junk. Burmese sailors threw ropes to the British sailors and the *Sea Runner* moored alongside the pot-bellied ship. Painted on its bow, six feet above the Englishmen's deck, two red-and-black eyes stared down at them.

Wright came out of the cockpit as soon as the manoeuvre had been completed.

"Tell the men to leave their personal belongings and military papers on board the *Sea Runner*. They'll remove their uniforms and board the junk."

Bowman repeated Wright's words:

"They'll remove their uniforms?"

"They'll get undressed. Uniforms, boots and personal belongings stay on this ship. Tell them they'll get them back when they return. Same thing for you, Bowman."

A rope ladder fell from the junk. Wright took hold of it and climbed up onto the Burmese boat.

Bowman stood in the middle of the deck:

"Round up here! Bags at your feet!"

The men gathered chaotically. The sergeant lined them up.

"Your belongings stay on this ship! On my orders, you will strip off, put everything in your bags and climb onto the junk! Now!"

There were twenty-eight of them, half-smiling and looking at each other. Hands behind his back, Bowman waited. His silence had its effect on the troop, and their smiles vanished. He walked from one man to the next, taking the time to look into their eyes, and stopped in front of Bufford. The blond man glanced at his comrades, then back at the sergeant, and began unbuttoning his jacket. Slowly, the others followed suit.

In underwear, or a shirt tied around their waist, they carefully packed their bags. The sun was going down behind the trees; on land, between the huts, the Company's soldiers were patrolling with flaming torches.

The men on the *Runner* stood in a tight knot in the middle of the deck, their white skin and black tattoos touching. Bowman had watched as a few objects had disappeared into the folds of underpants and shirts. A Bible, a gold cross on a chain, a little pouch of tobacco or a pipe. He saw two knives vanish behind cloth too, and committed the soldiers' faces to memory.

"Board now!"

They climbed up onto the junk, clumsily, hastily, each one showing his white arse and legs to the soldiers below, who laughed, until their turn came to climb the ladder. Bowman, the last man on board the sloop, removed his boots and his uniform. On his belly, under the fabric of his long johns, he slid his Afghan dagger, his tobacco and his pipe, before weighing up his powder horn.

He'd had it made specially in Bombay, after his regiment had returned victorious from the Punjab. The inside coated with rubber-tree sap, the lid watertight, the horn could be plunged in water and still keep the powder dry. Bowman had spent four months' pay on its fabrication and the inlaid silver and mother-of-pearl. It was his reward as a soldier after twelve years of service for the Company. So he could fight even when it was raining.

He packed away his jacket and his boots, crossed the *Sea Runner*'s deck to the steering post and saluted the captain. The old naval officer stared at the trouserless sergeant.

"Sergeant, the sloop has to return immediately. What do you want?"

"Sir, Troop Sergeant Bowman, First Company, Madras Regiment."

"I don't give two hoots for your rank, Sergeant. Board that junk immediately!"

Bowman stood straight, shoulders wide.

"Sir, I want to give you this. It's something . . . It's precious to me, Captain. I want to leave it with you, so it doesn't get lost with the other bags."

Bowman held out the horn.

"What are you talking about? Leave this ship – that's an order!"

Bowman did not move.

"Captain, I need to know your name."

"What?"

The captain of the *Sea Runner* turned to the armed men who acted as his bodyguards.

"Get this man off my ship!"

The two men aimed their rifles at the sergeant. Bowman took a step backwards, crouched down slowly without lowering his eyes, placed the horn on the deck and stood up again. The captain almost shouted:

"Get the hell off this ship, Sergeant, before I have you shot!"

Bowman went down the officers' gangplank and threw his jacket and boots on deck before climbing up to the junk.

On board, under lamps hung from the rigging, the men waited, naked, in a circle around a dark heap in the middle of the deck. Bowman walked closer. It was a large pile of clothes.

"What are you waiting for? Put them on!"

The men picked up old Burmese rags from the pile – baggy fishermen's trousers, too small and stinking of fish, and belted shirts. When they had finished getting dressed, there were still enough clothes for another thirty people. Bowman ordered the rest thrown into the sea.

The Burmese sailors moved into action, raising the battened sails, lifting the anchor, loosing the ropes to release the *Sea Runner*, which moved away towards the pontoon. The sloop was going to pick up the soldiers patrolling the fishermen's huts on land.

The men laughed and swore as they compared their new outfits, which looked like children's clothes worn by adults. Bowman, who had also put on a pair of trousers and chosen a shirt, attached his knife to the cotton belt and turned towards the shore.

A hut was in flames. The soldiers' torches moved quickly from one house to the next and behind them the palm roofs blazed.

The junk's sailors took long bamboo poles from the hold and pushed their boat forward, as the breeze was not strong enough to propel it. They punted with all their strength, glancing back at the village behind them.

The torches converged on the large building. The other houses were burning, sparks rising fifty feet in the air, blown by the wind out to sea and towards the too-slow junk. The flames illuminated the bay in red and yellow, painting the sails and hull of the *Sea Runner*, moored to the pontoon on a sea the colour of lava. On the terrace of the large building, the soldiers threw their torches against the door. The flames quickly climbed up the walls to the roof. The men from the Company withdrew to encircle the building, rifles raised. Screams rose from inside. Naked fishermen ran through the walls of fire, only to be scythed down by bullets at point-blank range. Women, carrying children, their clothes ablaze, also tried to flee, but collapsed in the sand after a few strides, killed by the soldiers. The roof of the building caved in, blowing thousands of cinders into the air where they swirled like a gigantic flight of fiery starlings.

The first scraps of incandescent palm leaves fell on Sergeant Bowman's men. The Burmese sailors screamed as they pushed the bamboo poles. At last, the junk passed the edge of the bay, and the wind swelled the sails, pushing the ship out to sea as it sent a thick cloud of ash down on the men's heads. They covered their mouths with their hands, blocking their noses so they wouldn't breathe in the stench of burnt flesh.

The village disappeared from sight but the fire still lit up the sea and the coastline like a sunset. They saw the flame-coloured *Sea Runner* leave the bay and vanish into the night.

Before the Burmese sailors blew out the lamps illuminating the deck, Bowman saw his men, pale and silent in their fishermen's clothes, start smacking their shoulders and shaking their hair, yanking nervously at their shirts and trousers covered with ash.

4

Lying crammed together on the deck, the men had been awake for a long time when the sun appeared over the forest. The first rays licked the ash-covered ship. Faces grey with ash, black lines in the wrinkles of their foreheads and the corners of their mouths, the soldiers looked like corpses.

A tailwind blew the junk up a river more than a thousand feet wide. The Burmese sailors pulled buckets of water tied to ropes from the sea. The men washed themselves and the deck was rinsed down. Bowman collared a Burmese, asking him where Captain Wright was and who was commanding the junk. The man shook his head, replying in his own language. The sergeant didn't understand a word. He raised his voice:

"Captain!"

The sailor ran off towards the sterncastle, and returned with a fat man in a straight-collared shirt with knotted buttons, holding a switch that he used to swat insects and waft the air. A Chinaman. Here, the Chinese were, after the Company, the ones who did the most trade. Their ships were capable of sailing to Africa, and were well-armed enough to stand up to European vessels. The Irrawaddy, like the other rivers on the continent, belonged to them.

Bowman had not fought in China. When the Opium War ended, he was still in Africa. But he knew that, of all the yellow men, the Chinese were the worst.

The man spoke rudimentary English:

"Me Captain Feng. What you want?"

"I must see Captain Wright. And the men need to eat and drink."

"Captain Wright cabin. You come with me. Men not on deck! Not on deck! In hold! Hide in hold! Not see soldiers!"

"Forget it. I have to see the captain. Now."

Bowman waited for the captain of the junk to give his frightened-virgin act a rest, then to turn on his heel and lead him to the cabins.

They crossed a sort of galley, where ten sailors were eating rice around a table. The Chinaman came to a halt outside a door, gave a nod of farewell, and left. Bowman grabbed him by the sleeve.

"Take the soldiers something to drink."

Then he knocked at the door.

Wright was also wearing fishermen's clothes. Cigar in hand, lying on a bunk, he was blowing smoke towards a window shaded by reeds.

"I didn't ask to see you, Sergeant."

Bowman saw a half-finished bowl of rice on the table, next to some chicken bones with a little flesh remaining on them and a bottle of Gordon's gin.

"What do you want?"

Bowman looked up at him.

"I need to know where we're going. And the next time you burn a village, if I don't know about it in advance, I'd be surprised if I'm able to control the men. I don't even know how we're going to feed them, and for how long. We might encounter Min's troops at any moment: they should be armed, but I'm not sure if that's a good idea, given their pedigree and the atmosphere on board this ship."

Wright sat up on his bed.

"I don't like your tone, Sergeant."

Bowman backtracked:

"I didn't mean to offend you, I just wanted to know what I should do, sir. You know that if the officers don't know what they're doing, the soldiers won't obey them. The baboon who's captaining this ship told me to put the men in the hold. He's giving me orders in front of them, sir. This could end badly, with scum like them in tow."

Wright stood up.

"You're not as stupid as you look, Sergeant."

Bowman's face ticked. Captain Wright stubbed out his cigar in the bowl of rice.

"The men from the *Sea Runner* are indeed criminals whom the Company has promised to pardon. You'll find a way to bring them to heel, Sergeant – that's why I chose you. We'll stay on board this junk for three days, at most, before we can turn back. In the meantime, the men will remain hidden, because this junk must look like a trading boat. There's no point arming them at the moment: Feng's sailors will assure our safety until we have reached our objective. They'll also take care of the food and drink."

Wright swallowed a mouthful of gin from the bottle.

"You may go, Sergeant."

Bowman opened his mouth.

"And what if we encounter one of Min's boats? These sailors won't be enough to . . ."

"I told you to leave, Bowman. Now."

The sky was less cloudy than it had been out at sea, and the heat of the forest rose from the two banks. The junk moved silently amid the murmur of insects and the calls of birds. Monkeys on high branches watched it float past.

"Sit down! Not a single head should appear over the railings!"

The men sat in a group in the middle of the deck, their knees drawn up to their chests. In those too-small clothes, with their ash-grey hair, they looked like a bunch of old prisoners on their way to a penal colony. Bowman had trouble recognising them, though he ended up identifying Bufford and the preacher, the two men who were thinking of escaping, the two who had hidden knives in their shirts, and one or two others from the *Joy*'s group.

"Go down into the hold. And do not come out. We'll reach our destination in three days. The Burmese will bring you soup and water."

He paused, met a few men's eyes.

"Anyone who wants to escape, go ahead and jump in the water now. If you even make it to the shore, I wouldn't give you two days before you're roasting over a campfire. Otherwise you can always swim with the current and in twelve hours you'll reach the sea, except the sharks will have eaten your legs by then. From there, you've got about a six-month swim to reach India."

Smiles and whispers. Bowman stopped speaking and waited for silence.

"The only way to get back from where we're going is on this boat. So get that into your thick heads. And this too: there's no such thing as good or bad orders. You don't know what will save your skin and what will bury you, so don't waste your time trying to think about it. When I give you an order, you obey. Captain Wright does not like being disturbed. If you have a problem, you talk to me."

They were still smiling. Bowman waited.

"Those men who hid knives in their underwear when we were leaving the sloop, stand up slowly now and throw them overboard. You can keep your Bibles and your tobacco, but anyone who brought knives with them, don't wait for me to come and take them from you."

The smiles faded. For a few seconds, no-one moved. The slats in the sails banged against the masts in the ever-weakening wind. Fat Captain Feng had emerged from the fo'c's'le, his switch in his hand, and was watching Bowman. Half the sailors were watching him too, in a rough circle around the troop of soldiers.

One English soldier stood up, hesitated, then put his hand under his shirt and took out a knife. He threw the weapon over the side and tried to look straight ahead, as far as possible from the sergeant.

Bowman moved between the squatting men.

"You won't eat today. Half-ration of water. Anyone who gives him even a grain of rice won't eat for two days. Sit down."

The soldier sat down. Bowman stood above him, staring down. There was another silence.

"You got off lightly, you prick."

He waited for a moment, long enough for the words to get into those thick heads, then turned around to face another soldier – a sturdy, tattooed man, one of those who had not yet stopped smiling. One of Wright's hard men.

"Take that knife out of your shirt."

The man did not blink.

"I don't have a knife, Sergeant."

He was making Bowman's task easier. This kind of example only worked with the toughest men.

"Get up."

The soldier slowly rose. He was four inches taller than Bowman.

"Name?"

"Collins."

"Give me the knife, Collins."

"I don't have a knife, Sergeant."

He smiled.

Arthur Bowman, eyes staring into Private Collins', thought about the horse he'd shot at Pallacate, a month ago. He thought about the mare's big black eye rolling upwards in its socket, about its tongue licking the earth. Then he saw again the messenger, that man broken in two, in the courtyard of the trading post, that man he had watched die, his eyes full of questions. Bowman thought about the charge they had made on the palace of Amritsar, when they had attacked with bayonet and sabre, the skulls they'd smashed, the bellies they'd slit open, the eyes of the Sikhs who fell into his arms, their hot blood flowing over his hands, their sad, surprised expressions, each of them seeking a little comfort in Sergeant Bowman's eyes, before tipping over into oblivion. He saw the mountains of corpses piled up after the battles, which they set on fire and which burned for days, raising columns of smoke all over the Punjab, smoke that stank far worse than that fishermen's village. He saw the blacks in Africa whose hands, arms and tongues he'd cut off, the sepoys he'd whipped, the men he'd beaten to death with his bare hands. Bowman saw the Company advancing ever eastward, him in the lead, a rifle in his hands, shooting at women, children, old people, guarding warehouses of pepper or cloth, taking boats from which, each morning, they threw corpses in the water without a single prayer. The wars and the battles, the bullets that had pierced him, the blades that had slashed him, and still he had moved onward, the "spearhead" of the East India Company, who sliced off ears, branded children with fire, killed men so he could take their women, guarded shipments of tea. He went back as far as the first man he had killed, at fourteen years old, an apprentice sailor on his first ship. Not a battle, just a man who picked a fight with him, had it in for him. A knife in his throat while he slept.

The twenty-seven men around Bowman and Collins did not move a muscle. They had all seen death pass across the sergeant's eyes. They knew death when they saw it. It glided over their heads and turned around Collins in ever-tighter circles.

They had all seen death before, men like that.

Drops of sweat rolled down Collins' cheeks. There was nothing in Sergeant Bowman's eyes now but a great emptiness, and a dreamy smile crept across his face, the kind of smile they put on corpses for funerals.

Collins slipped his hand inside his shirt, then paused out of fear that he was moving too fast. It took him an eternity to find the knife handle and to let it drop on the deck floor. The sound of metal on wood made him shiver. Bowman's smile slowly vanished, and he looked once again like a simple brute, a loud-mouthed sergeant. He seemed to shrink inside himself and took a step back.

"Pick up the knife and throw it overboard."

Collins bent down, picked up the weapon and tossed it in the water.

"No food until you've killed an enemy of the Company. Sit down."

Captain Feng was still there, behind him, watching. The sergeant walked over to a Burmese sailor and slowly articulated:

"Give me your pistol."

The Burmese blinked and turned towards Feng. Bowman held the man's chin in his hand and turned his face back to him.

"Give me your pistol."

The sailor slowly drew the weapon from his belt, held it by the barrel and put it in the English soldier's hand.

"Cartridges."

The Burmese took a case from his shirt containing bullets and primers, then an ivory flask filled with powder. Bowman slipped the gun in his belt, the ammunition inside his shirt, and turned back to his men.

"Hatchway. Everyone in the hold."

Feng had disappeared. The sailors scarpered. The soldiers went down beneath the deck, one after another. Peavish, among the last on deck, walked over to the sergeant.

"Are you happy with the men I chose for you?"

"You only chose Buffalo."

"And you chose me."

"Get in the hold."

Peavish smiled and looked Sergeant Bowman in the eyes.

"I understand why they're so afraid of you, Sergeant. I was afraid too, the first time, when you saved me from Bufford and lifted him off the ground."

"You're in the same boat as the rest of them, preacher. Now go."

"You'll be happy with them, Sergeant."

"Go."

The stink of fish, rotten vegetables and spices rose from the hold. Bowman leaned over the hatchway.

"The one who had a knife and got up when I asked the first time . . . Name?"

From the darkness, a voice rose.

"Private Harris, Sergeant!"

"Harris, you're in charge of Collins. If he swallows a single bite, all you'll get is a knife when we have to fight Min's monkeys."

Bowman closed the large hatch and inspected the gun he had taken from the sailor. It was a French sailor's pistol, '49 model. French weapons were rare in the territories where the English Company had negotiated trade agreements. Either Feng was trafficking with the French or Wright had decided to cover their tracks by equipping the junk with foreign weapons.

The ship's crumpled sails flapped against the masts. Bowman felt a cool gust of air on his skin. He followed the sailors' eyes southward and saw black clouds over the Irrawaddy, moving in pursuit of the junk. The wind was blowing stronger and stronger, and Feng's pilot, clinging to the steering wheel, watched the sky behind him.

If the rain caught up with them, anyone would be able to fall on them without them seeing a thing. Navigating through a monsoon was one thing, defending yourself in a monsoon was quite another. Seeing the expressions on the sailors' faces, Bowman realised they were making the same calculation.

He spat in the water.

The sailors turned around when they heard him say loudly:

"He can go fuck himself."

He checked that the powder was dry, poured ten grains into the barrel of the pistol, pushed the bullet all the way in, placed the primer on the flintlock, and put the gun back in his belt.

At the galley table, twelve sailors were smoking long cigars filled with green tobacco and sipping palm alcohol. They froze when the English sergeant stood in front of them.

"Feng."

The sailors hesitated, then one of them nodded towards a door, the one next to Wright's. Arthur Bowman walked through a short corridor and went in without knocking.

A bunk with pillows, a half-eaten plate of food, an open window through which he saw the river behind the boat, the waves left in the junk's wake and the black clouds moving ever-closer. Feng was lying on the bed, a fan in his hand. Bowman turned around, sensing a presence at his back.

A Burmese child, seven or eight years old, was sitting on the floor, bare-chested, his back to the bamboo wall.

Feng began fanning himself nervously again.

"Not come here! Captain cabin!"

"Where are the weapons?"

The Chinaman stood up, still shaking his fan.

"Not tell. You see Captain Wright!"

The sergeant advanced to the table and dug with his fingers into the rice.

"The weapons."

"Orders Captain Wright! Not see weapons!"

Bowman took the pistol from his belt and put a finger to his lips.

"Shh. Not a sound."

He turned towards the child and beckoned him over.

The child stood up, staring at the gun. Bowman held it in front of him, aimed at Captain Feng's stomach. The little slave did not understand. The sergeant encouraged him with a smile. The child, trembling from head to foot, gripped his fingers around the butt. The weapon was too heavy for the little slave, who held it with both hands, blinking and aiming at the Chinaman's belly. His muscles, tensed by the effort, twitched in the wounds on his back: the whip marks inflicted by Feng's switch, which had torn the skin on his shoulder blades. The sergeant held his palm open above the pistol, signalling him to wait, checking that the child didn't collapse. Feng had put the fan over his belly in a gesture of self-protection. The sergeant spoke softly:

"The weapons. Where are they?"

The Chinaman's eyes moved from the barrel of the pistol to the Englishman's face.

"Under table. Under big table sailors."

"Take some food to my men. Water too."

Feng nodded. Bowman took the gun from the child's hands and, when he stepped back towards the door, the little slave rushed to follow him. The sergeant closed the door, crossed the corridor and stood in front of the sailors, the child clinging to his leg.

"The table."

A hesitation. Bowman waited, giving them time to come to the only conclusion possible: Feng could not help them; the English soldier was disobeying his captain and their only chance was to do the same thing. To make a pact with him. They, too, had seen the village burn and had no illusions over their fate.

One of the sailors looked at the little slave, lowered his head and, in a serious voice, murmured a few words. The sergeant moved his hand slowly towards his pistol.

The sailors stood up, pushed the table aside, and opened a trapdoor hidden beneath a mat. Two of them went down under the floorboards and in their hands the first rifles appeared. Miniés with the letters V.O.C. engraved on them: more French weapons, but supplied to or taken by the Dutch Company. Next from the hiding place they took two thirty-pound kegs of black powder, twenty boxes of forty well-oiled Minié bullets, forty rifles in all, plus another dozen naval pistols, Dutch copper powder-flasks, plenty of primers and a waterproof crate in which Bowman found six small, two-pound fuse bombs.

He walked over to the hatchway, looked at the black sky, which was catching them up, grabbed the child by a wrist and hung him over the hold.

"Preacher! Look after him!"

Hands seized the child by the waist and he disappeared under the deck. The sergeant gripped the ladder and went down in turn. He crouched, pulled his knife from his shirt and, one hand on the pommel, the point of the blade notched in the floorboards, waited. The water of the river splashed against the hull, and in the darkness he made out the men around him, spread out at the back of the hold, tired and starving amid the stench and the dampness.

"Rain's coming. It's going to fall hard. The boat won't be able to go any further, and they're bound to come alongside us. I'm going to hand out weapons."

The men began to sit up.

"There are some on this boat who still haven't understood who I am, but never mind. Once they've got a rifle, they can try to kill me if that's what they want. But there's something else more important that you haven't all accepted yet."

Bowman bent his head and looked at the pale light that fell at his feet from the hatchway.

"We're all going to die on this godforsaken boat. Those who were in chains before they got here and those who weren't. I have only one thing to tell you: I don't want to die here and when I give orders, it will be to get me out of this alive. I never send someone else to do a job I can do myself. If we don't shoot each other in the back, some of us might make it. If you don't listen to me, we'll all snuff it."

He saw some of the men look down, while others met his eye, still mistrustful.

"We'll all snuff it. Including this child."

He stood up, grabbed Feng's little slave by the hair and tore him from Peavish's arms. He held him hanging in the square of light and touched the blade of the knife to his throat.

"That means I can cut his head off right now. Ask Peavish, he'll tell you – it'd be an act of charity."

Faces twitched. Arses lifted from the floor. Some of the toughest were already looking away.

"So?"

Peavish got down on his knees.

Pulling on the child's hair, Bowman lifted him higher off the ground. The child started crying and kicking his feet. He cried out in Burmese, things that no-one understood. The blade pierced his skin when he moved, and blood started to trickle down his chest.

"So?"

One man stood up. The one who had no boots on the *Runner*, the one who had stared silently at the coastline, the canoes on the fishermen's beach, who had eyed the shores since they got out on the river. The one whose stripes had been torn from his jacket's shoulder and who dreamed of escape because he had good reason not to believe Wright's promised pardon.

He stood in front of Bowman. He was the same height and, like half the men in the hold, had the pale hair and eyes of a Viking.

"Leave the child alone, Sergeant. We'll follow orders."

"Name and rank – before they took your stripes."

"Sergeant Penders."

The child had stopped moving. His feet hung limply above the floor. A thread of blood trickled from his throat down to his trousers.

"Sergeant Penders, you're a good Christian. But are you speaking for everyone?"

Bowman inspected the other faces, then turned back to Penders.

"You've got your stripes back. When I'm not there, you're the one who'll kick them up the arse."

He dropped the child, who ran into the arms of the preacher, then lifted his head towards the hatchway and whistled. Two Burmese hurtled down the ladder with a barrel of water, followed by two large bowls of rice in palm mats, two buckets of soup and some mess tins.

"You've got ten minutes to eat. Harris, keep an eye on Collins. Half-ration for you."

The men rushed over to the food, and Bowman climbed back up on deck.

The wind had grown even stronger, driven forward by the rain that was following it. Half a mile downstream, the landscape disappeared behind a white wall. A piston of dark clouds was coming up the river, gaining on them, pushing them towards a bottleneck: ahead of them, the riverbanks were only about fifty yards apart. The water rippled, branches trembled, trees swayed, and all over the forest toads began to croak, so loud you could hear them over the sound of the wind.

Bowman bent down over the hatchway and yelled:

"Rain! Dinner's over! Weapons are coming! Keep the powder dry!"

Crates and rifles were passed hand to hand from the galley to the hold. Bowman oversaw the operation, while keeping one eye on the sky. The banks vanished behind a wall of white mist. The transfer of the weapons was almost complete when the rain fell, as if floodgates had been opened above their heads. The Burmese were hysterical, pointing to the rain, the sky and the rigging. They all started jabbering at the same time, and some of them put the rifles down so they could ease out the sheets and lower the sails.

Bowman yelled again:

"Keep the weapons dry! Move your arses!"

A Burmese standing near the hatchway, a rifle in each hand, fell forward. The noise of the gunshot had been covered by the roar of the rain. The man lay face down on the deck, arms outstretched, the two Miniés still in his hands, his skull exploded by a bullet.

Captain Wright, at the door of the fo'c's'le, his pistol smoking in his hand, now stared at Bowman.

"Sergeant! What are you doing?"

Bowman, at the other end of the deck, started moving towards him. A violent gust swept over the river, and the junk tipped towards port-side. The sails swelled and the boat seemed to make a U-turn beneath their feet, then to start rotating like water going down a plughole.

"I'm arming the men, sir!"

"You disobeyed my orders!

Bowman tensed, ready to dodge a bullet. A yell rose from the cockpit. The two men looked up at the same time. Branches covered with leaves passed over their heads and the junk crashed into something, its whole mass and speed stopped dead. Wright grabbed hold of the doorframe, while Bowman was sent flying against a railing.

The boat's stern had crashed into the riverbank. It began to turn around, gaining speed. The branches swept across the deck, lashing the fo'c'sle, clinging to the masts, the wood creaking and cracking, exploding like grenades, a rain of debris falling on the crew. After completing this U-turn, the bow of the junk smashed into the forest and the whole cycle began again. This time the boat turned around its bow, re-entering the current sideways. The trees tore the sails, the boat gained speed again, and crashed into the shore for a second time. The whole frame was shaken and the central mast, weakened by the mainsail, which they had not been able to lower, broke in half and fell into the woods. After another U-turn, the boat ran aground, side on, and stabilised.

A silence seemed to follow this shock. People stood up slowly, and heads poked out of the hatchway, eyes taking in the wrecked deck and rigging. Bowman lifted himself up on his elbows, his head and back aching. Bufford emerged from the hold with a gash in his cheek. The Burmese moved from sailor to sailor, helping them. The noise of the rain had begun again, after the impression of silence. On the few feet of river that could be seen, the drops made a pattering noise as they bounced back into the air.

Bowman walked over to the fo'c's'le, stepping over the debris. A tree had smashed down the wall and part of the corridor that led to the galley. He moved branches and planks out of the way, found Wright lying there face down, and turned his body over. The captain groaned, a dark wound in his temple.

"Is he dead?"

Bowman turned around. Standing in the ravaged corridor, Sergeant Penders – a Minié in his hand, a Burmese hat on his head – stood watching him. Bowman lay Wright's head back on the floor and stood up. Under the rim of the hat, sheltered from the pouring water, Penders' face was the only clear image in the blurring deluge.

"I won't let you leave like that."

Penders smiled.

"We saved the powder. There are three men seriously wounded, the others will be alright. There are two Burmese missing, including the pilot, and another one is dead. There's a hole in the hull and the hold is filling with water. I want to know if we should abandon the boat or not, and what your orders are, Sergeant."

It took Bowman a second to react, perhaps because of Penders' calm, informal, gentlemanly manners and voice. He looked down at Wright, who still lay unconscious at his feet.

"First we have to find out what we're doing here. The weapons and the food – that's all that matters for now."

Bowman wiped his face, allowing him to see clearly while his eyebrows acted as a dam against the flood of water.

"Send three monkeys here, so they can take Wright somewhere dry."

The sergeant stepped over the captain's body, walked through the wreckage of the galley and the corridor that led to Feng's cabin. The door was open. A tree trunk ran through the room from end to end; it had smashed the edges of two uprights and torn down part of the roof. On the bunk, crushed under the tree, his chest covered in blood, Feng lay with his mouth agape, eyes almost bulging from their sockets. Bowman opened the drawer of the table, but found nothing. Finally, he yanked a cupboard door off its hinges and threw a pile of clothes onto the floor, followed by an opium pipe, some fans, an inkwell and some pens. He discovered a leather-bound book, its pages darkened and covered with Chinese characters, which he tossed onto the table before searching Wright's cabin. But he didn't find any documents there either.

On deck, the Burmese had begun untangling the rigging from the forest, cutting through the intertwining branches with machetes. Bare-chested, hands held together, Peavish was kneeling in front of four bodies stretched out in the rain. Two of the junk's sailors, one English soldier – whom Bowman recognised as being one of the ten from the *Joy* – and another corpse whose face and torso were hidden by the preacher's shirt. Bowman knew it was Feng's little slave, however, because he could see his feet poking out of his trousers. Peavish's lips moved in prayer, though no sound emerged from his mouth.

"Don't hang around there, you'll catch your death. We should throw them overboard."

"We should bury them, Sergeant."

Bowman looked at the corpses.

"In the river. Right now."

He went down to the hold and joined Penders, who was holding an oil lamp. Next to him, a Burmese was shouting and gesticulating.

"I don't know what he's on about, Sarge, but it doesn't sound good."

Water was pouring between several uprights over an area of about six feet, and some of the ribs were broken. The rain was also coming in between the boards of the deck, which had been twisted and pushed up. The water in the hold was already calf-high. The junk was leaning towards the shore, aground on rocks and pressured by the current, which was cracking the hull.

"There are still some watertight compartments on the boat, but the hold is filling up, and even if it doesn't sink, this thing won't be navigable."

Bowman thought fast.

"We'll stay aboard as long as it stays afloat. Put the food and the weapons in the fo'c's'le, where it's dry."

He went back up on deck. The Burmese were busy freeing the rigging. Bufford and Peavish, who had tried to kill each other two days earlier on the *Joy*, were working together to carry the English soldier's corpse to the railing. They threw it overboard. Only the child's body remained. The preacher had sent Buddha's sheep to the sharks, but was still hesitant to do the same with the child. The wind had blown the sheet off his face: his skull was smashed in, and the rain was falling on his dead eyes, filling his open mouth.

"Buffalo! Peavish has scruples, so throw the child in the water. You, preacher, take five Burmese with you and moor the junk to the trees. If the current takes us now, there won't be any food for the worms at all – the sharks'll get us all."

Bowman went back to the fo'c's'le and, before entering, turned around. Bufford was holding the little slave in his arms above the railing. He muttered something as he stared at the child's face, then leaned over him and, before dropping him in the river, planted a little kiss on his forehead.

Arthur Bowman half smiled and almost shivered as he remembered Peavish, on board the *Healing Joy*, pointing to Bufford.

The preacher must be able to see things he couldn't.

Captain Wright was lying on his bunk, a cloth tied around his head. Bowman closed the cabin door and the sound of the rain grew quieter. He bent down to pick up the bottle of Gordon's gin that had rolled onto the floor, took out the cork, drank a mouthful under

Wright's gaze, then put the bottle to his lips. The captain swallowed some and pulled a face.

"Water."

Bowman looked around him, found a flask, and helped the captain to drink.

"What happened?"

"The monsoon. We hit the shore."

"Damage?"

"The rigging's a bit of a mess, but the Burmese are handling it, sir."

Wright tried to sit up, but the pain pushed him back. His face turned grey and he threw up a little bile on his chest. Bowman tore a scrap off the bunk's sheet and wiped it up.

"You disobeyed my orders, Sergeant."

"For the safety of the ship, sir."

"Will the junk be able to keep going?"

"Yes, sir."

"And me?"

Bowman looked him in the eyes for as long as he had to. The officer turned his head to the wall. He was silent for a moment, then looked back at the sergeant.

"You must complete the mission, Bowman. The rain is there . . ."

"What mission, sir?"

"Min's ambassador . . . The Spanish. Buy weapons . . ."

"I can't hear you, sir. What mission?"

Wright's voice shook a little.

"One of Min's ambassadors, on the river. A boat, in two days . . . Or one day. Negotiate for weapons . . . with the Spanish, for the war. The monsoon . . . The war . . . in the next dry season . . . Spanish arms for Min . . . Bowman . . . I'm dying . . ."

Wright gripped Bowman's shirt and looked at him with that expression which he knew so well. The sergeant took the captain's hand in his, unfastened the tensed fingers from the fabric and stood up, taking the bottle of gin.

"Bowman . . ."

The sergeant closed the door, went through the galley and came out onto the deck.

Peavish had gone ashore with a group of ten Burmese. The preacher seemed able to communicate with them, speaking a few words in their language – or in another Indian language that they understood. When the junk was solidly moored to the trees, Peavish came back on board, followed by Feng's sailors, who threw worried glances towards the forest.

Bowman ordered everyone to gather round. Englishmen and Burmese all squeezed into the last free space on the deck, between the fo'c's'le and the large hatchway.

"We're going to build a shelter! Cut the mainmast down, put it on the fo'c's'le, and use the sails to make a roof. Weapons and food will go in Wright's cabin! Peavish, as the monkeys seem to understand you, you're in charge. Dismissed!"

The men were starting to shiver with cold under the rain, and they moved fast in order to keep warm. Bowman led Penders aside.

"We have to make sure we're ready by tomorrow. A boat will pass by then, or maybe in two days. We have to take it."

"How do you know that?"

"Wright, before he kicked the bucket. But it's one of Min's boats, with an emissary or something on board. Wright wanted to stop it. We need that boat, or we'll end up dying here. Would it bother you to throw a captain overboard?"

Penders smiled.

5

Night fell unexpectedly. The rain, masking the sky, had drowned out the hours spent clearing up the junk, dismantling the sails, sawing the mast and laying it on the fo'c's'le. The sails, tied to the railings, now covered the whole deck like a very low mansard roof, and the men had to scurry, bent double, beneath it. The branches had been pruned and the tree trunks on the deck removed, except for the largest, which now served as a gangplank to the shore.

Bowman had authorised fires. Some rocks found on land were used to make hearths in which wood from the boat's broken frame was burned, followed by the scented red wood of the branches. They heated water to cook rice and vegetables. Whenever they had to visit the land, it was in groups of ten armed men, and they would return to huddle inside the big tent as if it were an impenetrable fortress, even though an arrow, never mind a bullet, would speed right through it.

Despite the fire and the smoke, clouds of mosquitoes swarmed around the men, who smacked their own faces and scratched their bodies nervously, well aware that these cursed insects were the ambassadors of malaria, a more deadly enemy than all of Min's soldiers.

In the hold, the water level rose as quickly as the river. Five feet since the rain began.

The Burmese congregated along the railings, where the canvas roof was at its lowest and the air at its least unpleasant. Against the stump of the broken mainmast, against the wall of the fo'c's'le and in the corridor covered by the sails, the rifles were stacked. Extra weapons, ammunition and food supplies were stored in the galley, now free of its large table, which had been chopped up and burned to cook the rice. Penders and three soldiers guarded this improvised floating artillery.

Bowman sat in Wright's cabin and sipped gin from the bottle. The glass bulb of the lamp was broken, but he let the oil burn on the wick, watching the little flame. Hunger gnawed at him, but he made do with regular mouthfuls of alcohol and kept his tiredness at bay by smoking a cigar.

He opened the door to the galley and when he saw the weapons, the three Burmese guards and Penders sitting on the floor, his Chinese hat on his head, he felt like the captain of a pirate ship. Him, Arthur Bowman, with a toff's cigar in his mouth.

He beckoned Penders to his cabin. There, sitting on the bunk, Bowman gestured with his chin to the box of cigars, while holding out the bottle of gin to the ex-sergeant.

"If we complete this mission, you'll get your stripes back. You might even end up a lieutenant."

Penders smiled.

"What about you?"

"Same for me."

"Except Wright wanted to shoot you."

Bowman took the bottle back.

"If we complete this mission and come back alive, we can tell them whatever we want."

"We?"

"You and me. We're not out of here yet, but if we do make it, why would we go back to Rangoon and tell them that we threw Wright in the river when we could be heroes? Men like us never rise higher than sergeant. Unless they accomplish an important mission."

Penders looked at Bowman in a way that irritated him, as if he knew a little more about the world than he did and found it amusing. He reminded Bowman of those lads who have been to school and who have a local rivalry, like the rivalry between a man who works in a factory and another who works in the sewers.

"So what is it, this mission?"

Bowman told him everything that Wright had said before he croaked. The ex-sergeant blew on the embers of his cigar.

"You want to stop one of Min's ambassadors?"

"Well, we need a boat, whatever. And if we go back without having completed the mission, we'll probably be hanged anyway. You saw what happened to those fishermen . . ."

Penders stood up, walked over to the porthole and tossed the cigar out.

"As far as the boat's concerned . . . yeah, definitely. As far as Wright's mission is concerned, though . . . with this rain, I don't think so."

"Well, you'd better think so, because that's what we're going to do."

Penders looked outside: the lights from the junk illuminated a few yards of forest, stained red through the canvas sails.

"You and me, Sergeant, we're not the same. I couldn't care less about becoming lieutenant or being a Company hero. What you said in the hold, with your knife to the child's throat, that's all that interests me: getting out of this alive. And if we find a boat, you can say whatever you like in Rangoon. Me, I'll go somewhere else, somewhere they've never even heard of London."

Bowman sniggered, his hand on the handle of his dagger, ready to jump on Penders' back.

"A corner of the world where the Company doesn't exist? Well, as far as your escape's concerned, we'll cross that bridge when we get to it. In the meantime, go back up to the deck and organise guard duty."

Penders turned around. He wasn't smiling anymore, but his air of superiority had not disappeared.

"At your command, Sergeant."

"And tell them to bring me some food."

In the morning, the rain was still falling. The men had not slept and they lay on the deck, soaked to the bone, shivering with exhaustion, maybe already feverish. With difficulty, they relit the fires and heated some water.

In Feng's cabin, Bowman had found a pair of raffia-soled sandals and a leather jacket that he had put on over his shirt. He went up to the steering post and leaned over to check the state of the hull. The boat was holding up well despite the hold full of water. The hawsers that moored it to the trees were taut as the strings on a fiddle. The river had risen by six feet, and branches and tufts of grass torn from the river-bank sped past the hull. At any moment, a tree trunk might pierce the side of the boat and send them to the bottom of the river.

The sergeant went back down to where the men were dozing. The preacher, having just finished his guard duty, came to give his report.

"Four of the Burmese have left. They must have sneaked out to the shore during the night."

The sergeant looked at the men slumped around him, swore, and kicked over a saucepan full of hot water and rice, scattering the contents all over the deck. The barefooted soldiers scrambled out of the way.

"Men! Attention!"

The Englishmen lined up, and the Burmese imitated them.

"Penders! I want a dozen armed men portside watching the river, six at starboard watching the forest! Three sentries on the bow and three others at the stern! Fifteen-minute shifts! I don't want to see a single eye looking anywhere but straight in front!"

He took a machete from the hands of a sailor and walked along the starboard railing. As he moved forward, he cut the ropes holding the sails in place. The canvas roof slumped onto the deck. Stopping by a hawser knotted around a cleat, he stabbed the machete into the gunwale, right next to the rope.

"A machete for each hawser! When I give the order, I want all the moorings cut at the same time! Peavish, you count the bamboo poles. I need enough for half the crew. If there aren't enough, go on to the shore with your monkeys and five men and find some. If the Burmese try to escape, you shoot them. And ten men with me! Now!"

With the aid of pulleys, Bowman and his team lifted up the main-mast and rolled it into the river, then used axes to chop up the other two masts and threw the rigging overboard to lighten the junk. They cleared out the deck, the holds and the fo'c's'le, made barricades along the railings with anything they could find, creating little holes and spaces where they stood with the poles.

Bowman ordered the sails cut up into yard-long squares of canvas, which were distributed to the men to protect their muskets and powder from the rain.

They managed to remove the tree trunk that had speared Feng's cabin, one team on land pulling on ropes while another pushed from inside. As the trunk slipped out, it took the Chinaman's corpse with it.

By the time the junk was ready, the afternoon was over. The galley was put back in its former place, the stock of arms and ammunition transferred to Wright's cabin. All day long, sentries surveyed the river and the forest, squinting through the grey blur of rain for the slightest movement.

Rice was served, and the men came in turns to devour their ration in the dry before returning to their posts. When they weren't on guard duty, they lay in the middle of the deck, back to back, resting their heads on the little squares of red canvas. Night fell for the second time on their immobile craft. Those who were too sick to do their shift were allowed to sleep sheltered in Feng's cabin.

Penders spent all night outside with the men, the mosquitoes and the forest noises. Howler monkeys growled like lions, and thousands of frogs joined together in a shrill chorus. Bowman slept badly in Wright's bunk, surrounded by guns and bullets.

At dawn, the wind had died down and the rain now fell vertically, producing a softer, waterfall-like sound.

Bowman drank a ladle full of water from a barrel placed under a hole in the canvas, and he felt almost as if he were drinking an enemy's blood.

Men dozed, pressed close against each other. Those on duty, shoulders slumped, let the raindrops roll over their faces without moving. The sergeant made a quick count of the Burmese lying in heaps next to the railing. The sentries, though helpless to prevent a night attack, had at least discouraged the others from attempting to escape. He used his foot to wake up Private Bufford, who was lying on the deck in front of him.

"Buffalo, go to the woods with five men and heat up some water for the soup. You remember the orders?"

Bufford opened his eyes, swollen by mosquito bites, and scratched his beard. Still in good health, Peavish's first apostle got to his feet.

"Fire two shots if there's any trouble, sir."

"And no hunting."

"No hunting, sir."

Penders was on the sterncastle, on guard duty with two other men.

"What do we do if there's no boat today, Sergeant?"

"We turn the junk into a raft tomorrow, leave the monkeys in the forest, and try our luck in the estuary. There must be a way to make this thing float for two days."

Penders lowered his head, tilting his hat, which was beginning to lose its shape.

"In that case, we should tell Peavish to pray that the rain doesn't stop. If it stays like this, we could get to the sea without being seen."

Arthur Bowman nodded, silent.

"But until then, the orders don't change."

Penders looked up.

"Still want to be a hero?"

"Better than being a deserter, don't you think?"

"Bowman, the idea that men like you can become heroes is something beyond my comprehension."

"Because men like you or the preacher make a difference?"

The sound of a gunshot echoed between the trees. The two men turned towards the shore, lifting their guns and cocking the hammers. On the deck, everyone stared at the jungle. As they listened hard to guess what might have happened, the sound of the rain seemed to grow louder.

There was no second gunshot.

Bowman still hadn't lowered his rifle.

"I told those fools not to go hunting. What the hell are they doing? Penders, stay here with the sentries."

He jumped down onto the deck.

"Positions!"

He held his gun in front of him. His men imitated him, aiming the muskets at the forest. They waited like that for a minute, arms trembling under the weight of their weapons. Cheek against the butt of the rifle, Bowman blinked his eyes to get rid of the water that was blurring his view. He turned towards the steering post. Penders had his back to him. Bowman was about to yell out to ask if he could see anything from up there when the former sergeant lifted his rifle upstream, aiming through the curtain of rain, and fired before shouting:

"Sail!"

At the same time, a sentry facing the forest yelled:

"Sergeant!"

Bowman turned.

Bufford and three men were running pell-mell towards them. They clambered onto the trunk that served as a gangplank. Private Buffalo shouted:

"They're coming!"

At the steering wheel, Penders reloaded his gun and the two sentries fired in turn. One of the shots carried, the other failed, the damp powder spurting out in a cloud of white smoke.

Bowman roared:

"Starboard! Fire at will!"

An ear-splitting burst of gunfire swept the still motionless forest. He rushed to the side overlooking the river and stared through a gap between the piled-up crates and bags. A junk was emerging from the rain, sails down, about a hundred feet away. The railings bristled with the shapes of men and muskets.

Bowman threw himself to the ground, and the first round of fire from Min's soldiers hit the deck. Sentries fell, bullets hit wood, whistling as they ricocheted. The second salvo cut down two more men.

Penders had lost his sentries; he jumped down to the deck, abandoning the fo'c's'le because it was too exposed.

"I'll take care of the forest, Sergeant!"

He ran over to the starboard side and organised the first and second line.

"Fire!"

Ten men stood and fired randomly into the trees. They dived to the deck and reloaded while the second line stood up. Bowman had done the same thing on his side and the first English bullets hit the enemy junk. Bufford, his face already black with powder, fell to his knees to reload. Bowman grabbed him by his shirt collar.

"What happened?"

"The monkeys, Sarge! The monkeys who ran away! They came back with soldiers! The powder was wet, we could only fire one shot! They've got bows and arrows and muskets! Harris is dead! I think he's dead!"

"How many are there?"

Bullets hissed like snakes above their heads and they flattened themselves against the barricade of crates.

"Dunno, Sarge! Lots!"

All the men were gathered on the deck, about fifteen on each side. The first arrows and bullets fired from the forest hit Penders' men, just before the impact. Hawsers snapped, and they felt the junk move slightly away from the shore, deeper into the current. It reared up. The water in the hold moved from one side to the other and the weight dragged the whole ship with it. Now it was leaning towards the river. For a moment, suddenly more worried by the prospect of being taken by the current than by the Ava warriors' attack, the men were paralysed, their eyes riveted to the last ropes mooring the junk to the shore.

Above him, Bowman saw the silhouette of a Burmese soldier, a dark shape in the grey rain.

"The fo'c's'le!"

The junk had rammed them from behind, and Min's soldiers had boarded.

Bowman put one knee to the deck and lifted his rifle. The bullet hit the jaw of the first enemy to set foot on his boat.

"Portside with me!"

The men facing the river turned around, aiming up high and shooting the attackers.

"Fire at will!"

Bowman ran to the fo'c's'le, then to Wright's cabin, where he grabbed the crate of bombs. He passed Feng's cabin, where the sick men had taken refuge.

"To the armoury! Load the guns and bring them on deck! Now!"

He opened the crate, picked up a two-pound bomb in one hand and with the other sparked a match, lit the wick and leaned outside through the hole in the hull. He saw the painted eye on Min's junk, arms and muskets above the bow. He waited until the wick was half burned, then threw the bomb, rolling into a corner of the cabin to protect himself, head in his arms.

The explosion shook the entire boat. A few seconds' silence followed, then there were screams and the gunfire started up again. The sergeant lit a second bomb and threw it in the same way. He just had time to put his head back inside the cabin to hide himself: three muskets aimed at him, opened fire, and one bullet pierced the wood and tore open his shoulder. The crate of bombs under his arm, he ran to the door. The second explosion propelled him into the galley.

Bufford and the preacher reloaded their guns, the hot barrels smoking in the rain. Penders fired, Collins yelled as he aimed at the forest, and Feng's Burmese fought like madmen. The Minié bullets of the French rifles caused terrible injuries, lifting soldiers from the ground even when they just grazed them, ripping off arms and leaving holes in bellies, projecting clouds of blood into the vertical rain, which brought them back to earth in a fraction of a second.

Only half of Bowman's men remained.

"Penders!"

Bowman handed him the crate of bombs.

"Bufford! All the men to port with me!"

He put himself at the head of the group.

"Bayonets! All guns loaded!"

The men put the pistols, loaded by the sick men, into their belts, then turned the bayonets round to attach them to the muskets' barrels. Bowman whistled and signalled to Penders, who lit two bombs and threw them over the fo'c's'le.

The two explosions swept the upper deck and corpses fell in front of them, with pieces of wood and scraps of flesh. Bowman screamed at the top of his voice, terrifying his own men:

"Attack! Board!"

Bufford and the other soldiers hesitated, then followed him.

The smoke from the bombs had not completely dissipated. They stepped over corpses and jumped across the bow of the enemy junk, appearing suddenly from the white cloud like demons. Burmese soldiers got to their feet, in shock. The Englishmen executed them at point-blank range. Panic spread through Min's men. Bowman stabbed his bayonet into the first one to drop his weapon and raise his hands in surrender.

On the forest side, two other explosions rang out, and they were caught in a rain of earth and wood. Bowman's men continued moving forward, galvanised by their furious sergeant.

Bowman saw the pilot, up on the enemy fo'c's'le, dive into the water. It was a rout. A Burmese officer fired a last pistol shot, which hit Bufford. Sergeant Bowman grabbed his rifle like a spear and threw it with all his strength, nailing the officer to the door. He picked up a Burmese rifle and loaded it. On the deck now, there were no soldiers remaining but them.

Bufford stood up, holding his belly. The bullet was lodged in his flesh and he smiled as he looked at the massacre. The sergeant turned towards the shore and, with Penders' men on the other junk, fired at the forest.

All the men still standing sprayed the jungle with lead, stripping the bark and leaves from trees, until Bowman heard Penders yell:

"They're retreating! Cease fire! Cease fire!"

Their ears were ringing, their hands trembling. They wiped blood from their faces, unsure whether it belonged to them, a comrade or an enemy. No-one was willing to let go of his weapon yet. Adrenaline was coursing through their veins, and fear was winning out over rage. Little by little, the sounds of the river and the rain returned, mixed with human groans.

Min's boat was theirs.

Bowman ordered Bufford to kill the wounded. He took three men and rushed to the cabins, smashing open the doors one by one. They searched the entire junk, but not a single living being remained aboard, nor was there any trace of Min's ambassador.

Sergeant Bowman returned to the wreck, which was close to being taken by the river. From up on the fo'c's'le, he scanned the deck and the rest of his troops.

Standing, incredulous, bleeding copiously, about fifteen men and five or six Burmese got their breath back, staring at the Ava jungle where the enemy had retreated. With their bullets and bombs, the English had created a clearing about thirty feet long in the forest. The men reloaded their guns, rummaging through their pockets in search of the last ammunition. Peavish was still alive, as if miraculously cured, and he lifted his eyes to the sergeant above him. Bowman stood victorious, invincible, hair soaked with blood, smiling with satisfaction as his gaze swept this rain-lashed world of fury.

Bowman saw the preacher on his feet and his monstrous smile grew wider.

Peavish looked down, turned towards the river and crossed himself.

Bowman turned around.

The only colours in the drowned landscape that surrounded them were two pairs of red eyes, moving closer.

Peavish had a terrifying vision of Cerberus, emerging from Hell through the waters of the Irrawaddy to collect his warrior, Sergeant Bowman, and take him back home.

Two other junks were coming down the river.

6

General Godwin and Commodore Lambert landed at Rangoon on 14 April, 1852 and took the city. Twenty thousand of Pagan Min's men, entrenched on the Singuttara hill, around the great golden pagoda of Shwedagon, surrendered without a fight.

Following the same map that Campbell had used in 1826, the fleet then headed towards the Irrawaddy and made itself the river's master, occupying the estuary. The Company held the shores.

Trapped between the kingdom of Siam to the east (which had no intention of breaking its agreements with the English), China to the north-east (also under the control of the Company), the northern provinces (once again bound to the governance of Bombay) and the coasts to the south occupied by Godwin, the King of Ava refused to admit defeat. Helped by the monsoon season, entrenched in the north in his capital city, surrounded by jungle and largely inaccessible to troops, he stood up to the Company until December. A war without battles, between two enemies separated by nearly 400 miles of forests and mountains.

Rumours were rife in the gulf about negotiations between Pagan and Spain, supported by the French, over the purchase of arms and equipment by the Burmese army. Even if such negotiations did exist, however, the Company was in control of the Irrawaddy, and there was no chance of any aid reaching Ava, by sea or by land.

In Bombay, Dalhousie waited until December and declared the south of the country a Company territory, part of the British Raj. Without any truce, treaty or negotiation, the army of shareholders in London, now masters of the gulf of Bengal all the way to Malaysia, traced a new frontier 125 miles from the coast and took possession of the southern third of the country, leaving Pagan Min cut off in the north.

Pagan's obstinacy and his impossible position led to political dissent in his Court. Having assumed the throne by assassinating all his brothers, the monarch was ultimately deposed by his half-brother, Mindon, supported by Ava's nabobs.

As soon as he had taken control of the kingdom, Mindon Min, a subtler diplomat than his predecessor, initiated a policy of openness with the English, while at the same time negotiating with other European powers to counter the commercial diktats of London. The day of his coronation, in February 1853, he received the Company's ambassadors and, in a show of good faith, announced the liberation of all British prisoners of war.

At the end of March, the monsoon having begun early that year, three Burmese junks entered the port of Rangoon under torrential rain. The three boats docked, unnoticed among the dozens of trading vessels that cluttered the harbour. The gangplanks were lowered and three columns of prisoners disembarked amid general indifference, soaked to the skin, dressed in clothes that were too big for them.

A dozen soldiers and a young lieutenant awaited them on land and escorted them to a Company warehouse, where the goods had been moved out of the way to create space for blankets to be laid out. Behind a little table, another officer sat waiting, with some sheets of paper, an inkwell and a metal pen in front of him. At the back of the warehouse, standing behind little terracotta stoves and steaming mess tins, pitchers of wine and water, three other soldiers watched as the liberated prisoners entered.

Mindon Min had ordered their hair to be cut and their beards trimmed, but that made little difference. If some of them still looked reasonably healthy – those who had spent the least time in captivity – others were in a pitiful state, a succession of stoop-shouldered, jelly-legged puppets walking in line like blind cattle. Some limped, others chewed their lips nervously with their toothless gums. Their eyes were sunk deep in dark sockets, above gaunt cheeks, their skin grey and wrinkled. Beaten down and bent double, they all looked the same height now. Rain trickled from them in front of the little table, and as they filed past, a puddle of water formed, in which they dragged their bare feet. One by one, they gave their name to the seated officer, who slowly wrote down the date and place of the capture, their surname, Christian name, rank, division, regiment and battalion.

The officer had eleven sheets spread out before him, one for each month that had passed since Godwin and Lambert had landed at Rangoon. He chose the sheet on which to write in accordance with the date spoken by the men.

When they had given their names, the prisoners walked between the blankets over to the soup, each hesitating before crossing this wide space alone. They held out their hands without looking at the men who were serving them, staring at their full mess tins, tightly gripping the tin cups filled with wine, sitting cross-legged on a blanket and putting the tins on their laps. Some of them sobbed. The prisoners sat as far away from each other as possible, shooting fearful glances around them like stray cats, ready to flee at the first attack. When another prisoner passed close to them, they leaned over their food and shovelled it into their mouths as fast as possible. Others filled their pockets with it.

The officer at the table raised his eyes, his pen suspended in the air. The man standing in front of him was practically a skeleton, two pointed bones for shoulders; even his skull seemed to have shrunk.

"What date did you say, soldier?"

The man licked his lips. His voice was feeble.

"17 April, 1852."

The officer picked up the sheet for April. No name was yet written on it. He dipped his nib in the inkwell and asked:

"Name?"

The man moistened his lips again.

"Edmund Peavish."

The officer wrote the name on the paper and lifted his head with a laugh.

"Lad, you're the oldest prisoner of this war!"

The soldier smiled, showing a few black teeth, and articulated in his whistling voice:

"God bless you. There are ten of us."

The officer turned his head towards the line and saw other men behind Peavish, men who barely looked like men at all, more like walking corpses or merely ghosts.

On the sheet for April, one by one, he wrote ten names under the same date:

Edmund Peavish
Peter Clements
Edward Morgan
Christian Bufford
Erik Penders
Frederick Collins
John Briggs
Horace Greenshaw
Norton Young
Sergeant Arthur Bowman

II

1858

London

I

On July 1 in Piccadilly, within the walls of Burlington House, the members of the Linnean Society gathered for an exceptional lecture. Biologists, zoologists, botanists and anthropologists waited outside the doors of the main conference hall, their mouths and noses covered with menthol handkerchiefs.

Wallace was going to present his article on the "Tendency of Varieties to Depart Indefinitely from the Original Type", and the rumour had been confirmed: Darwin was not going to be there, stricken as he was by the death of his young son from scarlet fever. Wallace would take the responsibility of reading out Darwin's work: "On the Variation of Organic Beings in a State of Nature; on the Natural Means of Selection; on the Comparison of Domestic Races and True Species".

For months, the scientific community had talked of nothing else but the discoveries of Wallace and Darwin, a veil of mystery surrounding their new theories, which were said to be radical. And yet, standing as far as possible from the draught-proofed windows of Burlington House, those in the know were preoccupied by another subject that day: behind their scented handkerchiefs, they spoke in low voices about the threat of epidemics.

Some reassured themselves by mentioning the latest theories of Snow on the cholera bacteria, transported by water not air, but this had not yet been proved and, faced with the fear of toxic air, Snow's research was widely denigrated while the mass anxiety continued.

Cholera was in the air, there could be no doubt about that.

A journalist from the *Morning Chronicle* passed between the scientists, notebook in hand, questioning them about the risks of contagion and the London sewer system, attempting to get a response to the question that had been on everyone's lips for the past two weeks: when would it end?

While it was easy to explain how it had begun, no man of science dared propose a solution, nor to risk even the vaguest prognosis. The only clue the journalist was able to draw upon to write his conclusion was that the scientists gathered here today were fewer in number than usual, many of them having already fled the capital.

Lyell and Hooker, who had convened the lecture, quickly walked along the corridor. The doors of the main hall were opened and everyone rushed in, hopeful that the stench would be less strong inside.

The journalist stopped writing notes and followed the professors into the sparsely attended lecture hall.

It stank just as badly in there as it had outside.

—ᵐ—ᵐ—ᵐ—

Cesspits were no longer in vogue. For a few years now, the rich had been installing running water and individual toilets in their houses. The water was pumped from the Thames, ran through the pipes, and, once it was dirty, poured out into the sewers, before rejoining the river.

The winter had been dry and the spring warm. By May, the level of the Thames was already alarmingly low. In June, temperatures had reached record highs and the river had begun to run dry. The water that came from people's taps had changed colour and the sewers, too dry, had started to become congested by the influx of all this extra waste. Sinks, bathtubs and toilets were blocked, cesspits had been dug in gardens again, and at the end of June the number of shit-collectors employed to empty these pits – many of whom had been put out of work by the arrival of indoor plumbing – had doubled.

Their carts crossed the streets at night, wheels jolting on the cobblestones, lamps hung on poles casting a meagre light over tired, mean old faces, cartloads of shit, and shapeless men wearing long coats that covered them down to their boots. They passed through the gates of the capital in silence, like the prisoners twenty years earlier who had transported corpses from the great cholera epidemic to mass graves. They emptied their carts in the fields and went back into the city, loading up again and returning to the countryside, and so on until dawn, when the peasants paid them for their work. Two shillings and five pence for a cartload of dung. Prices had fallen as fast as the shit-collectors had got their jobs back. London had so much excrement to offer that the market had collapsed.

The sewers were now so dry that the armies of children searching in the shit for lost treasures to sell, had to dig into the faeces with spades and pickaxes rather than raking them out.

The temperature continued to rise. Waste from factories accumulated in oily, black layers on the surface of this river of putrid lava. Carcasses of cows and sheep from the slaughterhouses, stuck in the mud, slowly passed the new Parliament in Westminster. Skeleton legs poked up in the air as on an abandoned battlefield and crows swooped down to rest on them. It took half a day for the horns of a bull to move from Lambeth Bridge, pass under the windows of the House of Lords, and disappear under Waterloo Bridge.

In certain places, it was said, you could cross the river on foot.

On July 2, the heat was unparalleled and the entire city stank like a giant corpse.

All along the riverbank, windows were blocked up.

The streets were deserted, and there was almost no traffic on the Thames. A few little steamboats still had enough power to advance through the mud, their waterwheels threshing up a foul black spray, but the absence of any wind made it impossible for sailing boats to move. Ferryboats and barques, pushed forward by poles, could still navigate the river, but no-one wanted to take them anymore.

The rich left the city for their countryside homes or went off to the seaside. The courts hurried through their trials: men were judged in a few minutes, receiving unexpected pardons or death sentences for minor misdemeanours from judges who ran through the corridors with handkerchiefs pressed to their noses.

Parliament no longer sat.

In factories, the boilers not only produced sweltering heat but odours that were believed to be fatal. While the price of dung went into freefall, the market for drinking water boomed. Fountains dried up. Clean water from springs or wells, drawn far from the Thames river-bed, transported and sold for a fortune, was now too expensive for ordinary people. Dehydrated workers died in the furnaces of the steel-works.

The Metropolitan police patrolled the empty pavements. London was like a city under curfew or after a revolt, when the troops have charged and the anger has died down and the victims' bodies have been collected. The coppers' steel-capped boots echoed through abandoned streets, replacing the sounds of hammers and weavers' looms. Outside the water board's offices, increasingly large groups of men and women gathered to yell at officials. The police pushed them back to their slums, where the situation was most difficult. In the low parts of town, the sewage rose up through the gutters, seeping between the grilles and filling the side-streets and back-alleys with a vile mud. In cramped cellars where entire families lived, beneath the level of the roads, children in rags waded ankle-deep in the capital's excreta.

Panic gripped the city: how could you escape the air that you breathed?

Along with the unbearable stench and the fear of diseases came bitterness and slander. Scapegoats were sought. The Chinese, people said, were too silent; the Pakistanis smiled too much; the Jews were too good at business. The rich were too rich. The papists were stirring up trouble. The army was going to encircle the slums, it was all part of a plan. There were still parts of London that did not smell bad. The shit-collectors worked for the bosses; at night, they emptied their carts in the poor areas of town, spreading disease.

The only shops still flourishing were sellers of cloth. When their stock ran out, people used wooden planks, mattresses or furniture to block up their windows.

The restaurants and inns had closed.

The factories' production had slowed and almost all activity had ceased in the port of London. The companies' ships no longer went beyond Leamouth and North Woolwich. Goods were unloaded downstream, where the tides were strong enough to permit navigation and dilute the black river's thick current. The dockers were out of work and London's docks were deserted.

In the new port of St Katharine, the empty warehouses were padlocked, but the prowlers, day labourers, thieves and beggars had disappeared. The East End gangs were, like everyone else, waiting for the port to come back to life, for London to be freed from this terror so they could all go back to work.

In this atmosphere of tension and inactivity, all London's police constables had been ordered to appear on the streets and to be on their guard, to nip any minor disputes in the bud. Wherever you looked now, at any hour of the day or night, you would always see a copper. The sound of their whistles could be heard all over the city.

If the Underworld had a smell, it could surely be no different from this one, and this idea slowly gained ground: London really was turning into Hell. This was divine punishment for some buried crime, some monstrous sin. Preachers announced that the Great Stink was only the beginning, that damnation would be eternal and the noxious air merely the first wounds of a more terrifying retribution that would soon be visited upon England.

In London, people prayed, far more than they had done in a long, long time.

The Thames River Police continued to patrol Docklands, just like their colleagues from Blackwall and Waterloo, even though in reality there was nothing left to patrol. Their job was to guard the ships, to oversee the unloading of goods and the activities of the gangs, but the docks they walked along, truncheons in hand, were practically deserted.

In these special forces, funded by the companies, most of the policemen were veterans of the colonies. It was a sort of laborious retirement for deserving or desperate soldiers, who worked for cut-price rates. Recruitment had followed this pattern since the force's creation, and the Metropolitan police had no say in the matter. These coppers had a different reputation and obeyed the orders of the company directors just as much as those of the police administration.

While the foul air was no more bearable for them than for London's other inhabitants, they were at least used to this kind of heat. In fact, for some of them, this pervasive corpse-like stench was quite familiar too. It was simply a question of degree, the smell of the London air redolent of an insanely high pile of disembowelled Indians or Africans on a hot, sunny day in the tropics.

Officer O'Reilly, veteran of the West India Company, heard the bells of Whitechapel announcing the end of his shift and began to walk more quickly on Execution Dock. As he rushed towards the station at Wapping, he passed by the pontoon of the old gallows, not used since the 1830s but left standing here, casting its slender shadow over the thick river.

O'Reilly remembered the last hangings there and the crowds that massed around them when, as a child, he came here to see a pirate dance at the end of a rope. Those guilty of killing English officers were given a short rope. Because they did not fall from high enough, their necks did not break and they died slowly, kicking their legs. These were the hangings everyone preferred.

Children were playing on the pontoon, starving little runts in rags who seemed no more perturbed by the odour than a West India veteran. Beggars, pickpockets, gang messengers, delinquents and orphans, these children were a scourge on the Docklands, the port's inactivity having left them unemployed too. They were parasites – of the river and its trade – whose corpses the Wapping police found about ten times a year, trapped between a dock and the hull of a boat, between the bars of a sewer entrance, or in a fisherman's net. Sometimes they were found covered with knife wounds. These gangs were constantly at war and the settling of scores between them regularly ended in dead bodies.

"Get away from there!"

The children were clowning around on the worm-eaten railings, walking above the mud, pretending to hang their shadows on the shadow of the gallows. They paid no attention to the policeman. O'Reilly took two steps towards them and lifted his truncheon. The children scarpered.

"O'Reilly, you Irish scum!"

"Your arse stinks, O'Reilly!"

"Bloody bobbies, you're the plague!"

"Send the bobbies to the gallows, drown the rich in shit!"

Other guards were converging on Wapping High, all of them in just as much of a rush as the Irishman.

Putting their caps and truncheons on the tables, they sat on chairs in the common room.

Superintendent Andrews was waiting for them, the smoke of his pipe adding to the already unbreathable atmosphere. None of the men bothered opening their notebooks to make their reports. They mentioned altercations, arguments between wives and drunken husbands, citizens who accused each other of emptying their chamber pots in the neighbours' yards. A few thefts and burglaries in shops, a few old people afraid for their safety. Anyone with possessions was worried by those who possessed nothing.

The night shift arrived and the room filled up. Standing in front of these weary, exasperated officers, Andrews gave a speech explaining that the present situation would not last, that things would soon go back to normal. He had learned how to deal with these hot-tempered ex-soldiers who, despite the disadvantages of serving two masters – commerce and the state – were always proud to continue working for the companies. Their pride made him laugh a bit, but at least these men knew how to obey orders and didn't complain too much.

Andrews sucked at his pipe as his gaze swept the room.

"Where's Bowman?"

A few men shrugged.

"Is he on days or nights this week?"

There was no response. He gritted his teeth around the mouthpiece of his pipe.

The church bells rang out over the rooftops. Arthur Bowman emerged from the Corney & Barrow warehouses, swallowed a mouthful of gin, slipped the flask under his shirt and turned right into the deserted Nightingale Lane. People only came out later, after nightfall, when the temperature dropped a little, to buy anything they desperately needed. The shop windows were boarded up with planks or blocked off with wall-hangings, which were watered regularly because it was said that airborne diseases did not pass so easily through water. The shopkeepers, even if they doubted the effectiveness of this tactic, did it anyway once they realised that their customers were deserting them in favour of other, better-watered stores. They filled their buckets from the rotten wells and fountains of London and splashed their storefronts with brown liquid.

Bowman turned into Chandler Street and saw the small façade of the Fox and Hounds at the corner of Wapping Lane, with the lantern lit over its door. Its light was barely visible at this time of day, but it signalled that the establishment was open.

The door was locked. He knocked several times and heard the key turn with a creak. Mitchell, Big Lars' dogsbody, pinched his nose as he stood aside to let the sergeant in. He closed the door behind him and put back in place an improvised portico, made with tool handles and strips of fabric. He pressed this against the doorframe, grabbed a bucket of water and threw it over the hangings.

Lars must be a fan of the water theory, only he had taken it a bit further, presumably deciding that the watering was more effective when carried out from inside the building.

There were half a dozen customers at the bar: the fine few whose thirst was not disturbed by the infernal stink.

"Fucking hell, Mitch! Will you stop throwing that shit?"

Lars, the landlord of the Fox, stood behind the bar reading a newspaper, a damp cloth covering his mouth and nose.

"Rather catch cholera, would you?"

Then, with a movement of his head, he greeted Bowman, who went over to sit at his table. The landlord grabbed a pint glass from the shelf, pumped some amber beer into it, and placed it on the countertop. Mitchell took it over to the policeman's table.

When Bowman had finished it, Lars poured him another one.

Big Lars had been a corporal in the West India Company and had smuggled enough spices and furs to buy this mouldering pub when he retired. An unvarnished wooden counter lit by two oil lamps, four tables and unlit candles, a beer pump, some kegs of wine, behind the counter a trapdoor, on the trapdoor Big Lars, and beneath it a cellar from which not a single free drink had ever been taken.

The place was safe, forbidden to blacks, to Indians, to Pakistanis, to beggars (except those with old military stripes in their pockets), to Mohammedans, Chinamen, bluebloods, redskins, and anyone else Lars didn't like. Hung on the wall above the boss' head was a stuffed fox, its teeth bared, eyes staring at the entrance.

Bowman started his third pint. Sitting at his table, he was mostly in darkness, the light from the oil lamp casting only a few meagre rays towards his feet. Lars' brown ale was just as bad as everyone said, but in heat like this it tasted almost cool. The Fox's landlord, his voice muffled by the cloth that covered his mouth, yelled:

"Mitch, you fucking halfwit! The sergeant's candle!"

Mitchell rushed over, lit the candle on the table without daring to glance at the man known as "the sergeant", and went back to the bar to wait with the other customers.

Lars returned to his newspaper.

It took him all day to get through the *Morning Chronicle*, whose front page he generally saved for the evening, so he could share the information with his customers, who came to hear the news while having a drink. He would spend five minutes squinting at a paragraph, then raise his head and translate it the way he had understood it, and in a way that his regulars would understand. Today, the article seemed to be giving him particular difficulty because Lars was bent over it for a good quarter of an hour, rereading it over and over, his fingertip following the words as he frowned in concentration. Finally he brought the oil lamp closer and held the pages up to the light.

He started with the headline:

"*Lecture at the Linnean Society, in the presence of Professors Lyell, Hooker and Wallace: 'Nature at War!'*"

Heads bobbed up over pint glasses. Mitch blinked and stared at his boss, who went back to reading the article.

"*For an hour and a half, yesterday in Burlington House, Professor Alfred Wallace, biologist, presented a summary of the foundations of a new scientific theory, as well as that of Professor Charles Darwin, concerning the origin of animal species.*"

The silence in the Fox and Hounds was total. Lars' customers opened their eyes wide as the bottoms of bottles.

"What is this crap? Isn't there anything else in the paper?"

Big Lars looked up.

"I already read the rest. Just let me continue, will you? It's the lead article, for fuck's sake!"

"Yeah, well, I don't understand a bloody word of it so far."

"Haven't you got the *Gazette*, Lars? Who got hanged?"

"And what about the sewers, eh? When are they going to unblock those bloody sewers?"

"Shut your mouths!"

The landlord reread the article for another five minutes. Mitch brought back Bowman's empty glass. Lars filled it and put his finger back on the newspaper.

"Ah! There you go!"

He looked back up at his customers, with a satisfied expression.

"The article says that these blokes, at the lecture, they don't believe in God! 'Cos there are birds on islands and some rabbits in Papua and there aren't enough of them to live, so they fuck everything that moves."

There was another silence.

"You sure you read that right?"

"Let me finish! So there still aren't enough rabbits even if they make loads of little 'uns, and that's 'cos nature is at war ... At war with itself! That's what they say."

One of the drunks lifted his nose from his beer.

"I don't see what that's got to do with God."

Lars put his hands on his hips.

"Fucking hell."

He reread a few lines.

"Ah, there you go! It's 'cos nature is at war, and 'cos the animals, between 'em, they get rid of the weakest, and the strongest ones survive."

There were smiles all around, and mouthfuls of beer went down throats.

"So that's their new theory?"

"Well I fucking never!"

"Yeah. I should have been a professor!"

Two customers burst out laughing. Big Lars went on.

"And those ones, the strongest, it's like the rabbit that runs fastest, for example, or the bird that flies fastest to catch the worm."

"I still don't see what that's got to do with God."

"I like the war bit, but the rest ..."

"Fucking shut up!"

Lars finished a paragraph and raised a finger.

"Ah! So the ones that go fastest, they make little rabbits and baby birds that also go faster, 'cos it's hereditary."

One of the drinkers put his pint down.

"Hereditary?"

"It's passed down from parents to children, in the mother's womb. You know, like stupidity!"

"Ah ..."

Lars became animated.

"That's where it's got to do with God, 'cos this Darwin and the other bloke, Wallace, they say that the animals and all the other living beings at war in nature, they keep what suits them best – going fast or having bigger ears than their mates' ears – and that way, they evolve."

The landlord was silent for a moment, thinking that evolution would have a certain effect on his audience. No-one reacted and the customers all waited to hear what came next. In the end, Lars pulled the cloth off his mouth. Suddenly, his voice rang out more loudly and when he leaned forward the customers flinched backwards on their stools.

"Evolution! For fuck's sake, don't you understand anything? That means that the rabbits and the birds, a long time ago, they weren't the same as they are now – they evolved and the species of rabbits changed!"

The silence was punctuated by a few swallowing sounds. Not that the Fox's customers had given up listening, but still, this story was becoming increasingly uninteresting to them. They pushed their empty glasses in front of them and Lars filled them up again.

"I don't know why I bother reading you lot the news."

He placed the pints on the countertop, picked up the newspaper with one hand, and tapped it sharply with the other.

"Don't you get it? That means that Darwin, he doesn't think God created rabbits the way they are today! That he didn't do it in seven days, and that, back when it all started, the rabbits, if He created 'em, they weren't finished properly!"

Lars burst out laughing, and the other drinkers began, hesitantly, to join in. Sensing that his audience was now more attentive, he went on:

"And the journalist from the *Chronicle*, he says that, too – that Darwin, if he didn't come out and say it – he thinks that men, too, back at the beginning, they weren't like us. They evolved!"

All the men, increasingly sozzled, exploded with laughter. This time, Big Lars had them hanging on his words. He pulled a fourth pint for Bowman while he continued to speak.

"They're fuming, on the *Chronicle*! They say that what he said, this Darwin, is that, before, your mother, or your father, they maybe weren't finished people. You know, like blacks or Chinks or Indians!"

The laughter suddenly stopped and some of the drinkers looked worried. Others puffed out their cheeks and looked ready to explode.

"Hang on! Hang on, that's not even all!"

Lars put his nose close to the article again and reread the last lines as fast as he could.

"Yeah! That's it, listen! This Wallace, he says we haven't finished evolving!"

One man, drunker than the others, or less worried about having a black father, began choking with laughter. Lars forced himself not to react so he could continue reading.

"Wallace, he says we're going to keep evolving and we're going to help each other. Help each other! And that, in a thousand years, we'll have a perfect society! With a *Socialist* government!"

The man who was choking fell off his stool, and the others spat the beer in their mouths back into their glasses, producing a head of foam. Lars smacked his thighs, and the old army veterans banged their foreheads against the bar top. They fell about laughing in the light from the oil lamps, as if the idea of having African ancestors, added to this prophecy of a world of justice and solidarity, was the funniest thing they'd heard since the last promise to increase wages. Mitchell, who did not really understand what had been said but liked a good laugh, stood at the end of the bar and watched them with a smile on his face. There were tears in Lars' eyes and he was struggling for breath.

"I'm going to invite that bloke here, that Wallace, so he can make us laugh! He'll teach us how nature is at war, the twat, and how all the nobs in Westminster are going to turn socialist! Oh, fucking hell! I won't even make him pay for his beers!"

This promise of free drinks was the *coup de grâce* for those still able to breathe. Lars turned towards the back of the room.

"Twenty years of studying, and that's what you end up with! Bloody hell, did you hear that, Sergeant? What do you think about it, eh? Nature at war and our ancestors being monkeys?"

Beaming faces turned towards Bowman's table. Lars wiped his eyes with his cloth soaked in brown water. They laughed as they watched Bowman finish his pint, waiting for what he would say, this veteran of the Indies, about all this nonsense, the biggest pile of crap any of them had heard in a long time. Because he had been listening from the start, Bowman, in his corner, but no-one had heard him laugh yet. He wasn't a chatty man, but with something like this, it would be entertaining to hear what he had to say, with his gruff face and his severed fingers that did not invite casual conversation. His eyes were not particularly welcoming either, concealed behind those constantly frowning eyebrows. No-one really knew his story, and people were wary of him even after so many years of his presence. Lars talked about it sometimes. Sergeant Bowman wasn't just a hard man, he was something else: a dangerous man.

But they wanted to hear him too, Bowman, because they had a right to laugh at Darwin and Wallace and their animal war in the nobs' lecture halls, forgetting all the rest for a moment: the real wars and the richest city in the world which stank like a corpse.

He had been listening, Bowman. What did he have to say about it?

Lars was the first to stop laughing, and soon there was only Mitchell, with his halfwit's face, still showing his rotten teeth. The others, slumped on stools, had sunk their mouths back into their glasses.

Bowman was staring down at his table, arms outstretched, hands tightly gripping the edge of the tabletop. His face had swollen above the candle and a line of yellow light ran across his forehead, in the fold of the scar that crossed through his wrinkles.

He stood up, knocking over his chair, and walked across the room, then got his hands tangled up in the portico and the cloths that blocked it up, and ended up tearing the whole thing off the door, before unlocking it and leaving.

Outside, the shadows of the buildings covered the road, ran up the pavements and climbed the façades like black water. Bowman turned on Reardon Street and crossed the Waterman Way footbridge. He drove onwards through back-alleys, until he reached China Court and took a side-street cluttered with sheets hung on washing lines. He shoved these damp cloths out of his way and stopped in front of a wooden crate on which some incense sticks were burning. He knocked on an old wooden door next to these scented twigs.

A Chinaman opened it.

Bowman walked through a corridor, and through half-open doors he glimpsed women sewing, children lying on mats, moon-faces with black eyes, half-naked bodies gleaming with sweat. Doors opened in front of him, and he crossed alleys, then went back through tunnels under buildings until he came to yet another door, guarded by two Chinamen who stood up tall when they saw him arrive. This door was opened for him and he entered the low-ceilinged room, with its rows of benches, bunks covered with mats and carpets, little square cushions, bodies lying close to each other in the heat and the smoke, wide eyes staring up at the ceiling. White wreaths of smoke escaped from open mouths, dry lips that no longer asked for anything to drink; pellets of opium cracked inside pipes. A pot-bellied Chinaman, squeezed into a long white tunic, bowed towards him, his hands joined, and pointed to a bunk. Bowman sat between two other corpse-like Englishmen.

A black-lipped old man, horribly thin, his arse and prick hidden by a knotted cloth, took off his shoes.

The Chinaman in the tunic prepared a pipe and held it towards the policeman. Bowman bit the mouthpiece, sucked in for as long as he could and then closed his mouth. The Chinaman stood up and waved again.

"Sweet dreams, Sergeant Bowman. Sweet dreams."

Bowman opened his mouth wide, but instead of a scream, what came out was white smoke, which he let drift, rising, into the smoke-saturated air of the opium den.

His voice was thick, and it faded as he spoke:

"Fuck off. You . . . bloody . . . Chink."

2

The opium den was deserted and daylight glowed through the curtains. The benches and cushions were abandoned, and in the cold morning light this nocturnal sanctuary looked drab and dusty once again.

The skeletal old Chinaman brought over a teapot and a glass of gin. Bowman sat up on the bench, rubbed his face and slowly drank a few mouthfuls of smoky black tea, then he downed the gin in a single gulp, tossed two shillings on the tray and left the opium den, feeling nauseous.

In the alleys of China Court, children pushed carts full of dirty laundry and pressed themselves against the wall to let him pass. Bowls of water boiled on fires, smelling insipidly of vegetables, the clouds of steam rising through the shadows of the dilapidated buildings. Bowman's stomach contracted. When he passed a table covered with blood and saw a chicken's head roll on the ground, cut off by a Chinese woman wielding an axe, he bent forward and vomited between his feet, right in front of the woman. He wiped his mouth on the sleeve of his police uniform and started walking again. He came out on a back alley in Pennington Street. The agitation of China Court ended here and he found himself once again in the siege-like atmosphere of the city, with its barricaded windows and its empty pavements.

He joined Cable Street and walked to the corner of Fletcher Street, pushed open the door of his building and climbed the three storeys, breathing heavily. His room was in the corner of the building, just under the attic. One window looked over Fletcher Street, the other over Cable Street and the train tracks, while beyond it stretched the district of Whitechapel. A bed, a table and a chair, a little enamel sink, a shelf containing a razor and a shaving brush, a metal jug on the floorboards and a rope stretching between two walls on which hung two uniforms. One was red, the Company's, and the other blue, the Thames Brigade, with the large hooded cape for winter.

Bowman lay down on the bed. The sheet and pillow stank. But at least it was his own stench, not the general stench of London.

It was noon when he woke, drenched with sweat.

On the table, he unfolded a cloth, cut some lard and bread, peeled a clove of garlic.

He remained sitting for the rest of the day, watching the light fade and the shadows lengthen. He did not leave his chair when night fell, did not return to his bed when the nightlights went out in the street, when behind the windows there was nothing but blackness and he could no longer make out the shapes of his hands lying flat on the table, beside the knife.

When the sunlight illuminated his room, he put on his uniform, locked the door behind him, went downstairs and came out into the street.

On Pennington Street, he opened the door of a tavern, ordered a beer and some porridge, then asked for an extra egg, which he broke on the side of the plate and mixed in with the hot oats. He tossed a coin onto the bar and went out again, passing the Fox and Hounds, which was closed at this time of day.

On Wapping High Street, the brick building was bathed in sunlight and, on the other side of the road, the Thames stank worse than ever before. It was seven-thirty and the men from the night shift were returning to the station. Those from the day shift were already there.

Bowman entered the guards' room, looking through the windows at the dried-up river. His colleagues did not greet him. O'Reilly stood in front of him, took the time to glare at him, and cleared his throat as though he were about to spit.

"The superintendent wants to see you."

Bowman waited for O'Reilly to move out of the way and went to knock on Andrews' door, his helmet under his arm.

"You wanted to see me?"

Andrews was cleaning out his pipe with the point of a little knife.

"I heard about an incident on St Katharine's Dock."

"You want me to take care of it, sir?"

The superintendent looked up from his desk and smiled.

"An incident concerning you, Bowman."

Bowman corrected his position as if he had been standing in front of a superior officer in the Company.

"I don't know what you're talking about, sir."

"You and your colleagues are no choirboys, Bowman, but there are limits to what I can tolerate, even if the maritime companies are willing to turn a blind eye to your methods."

"I don't understand what you mean, sir."

Andrews opened a drawer of his desk and took out a sheet of paper, which he pretended to read, letting the silence drag on.

"Two days ago, you had some problems with the supervisor at Corney & Barrow. Some of the warehouse employees say they saw you beat him up. Is this true?"

Bowman rolled his shoulders under his uniform and smiled.

"Is that the problem?"

"What happened?"

"Raymond, the supervisor, was working for a gang in St Katharine's. It was the lads at Corney & Barrow who tipped me off about it. The bosses told me to teach him a lesson. Usual stuff, sir. Nothing more."

"Did Raymond threaten you after you hit him?"

Bowman's smile widened.

"He's got a big mouth, sir, but I have nothing to fear from those quarters."

"Very true, you do have nothing to fear anymore."

"What's that supposed to mean?"

"Raymond is dead. He was found last night, not too far from the Corney warehouses, his fingers cut off and his throat slit."

Bowman blinked.

"I didn't know."

"You would have known if you came here more often to make your reports and receive your orders. Any thoughts on what might have happened to Raymond?"

"Gang members, sir. That's how they do things."

Andrews smiled in turn.

"And you'd know all about their methods, Bowman, wouldn't you?"

Bowman felt the stumps of his middle and index fingers itching.

"I don't see what you're driving at, sir."

Andrews smoothed down the report and let it fall onto his chair.

"Corney & Barrow have asked us to open an investigation."

"What?"

"Into the murder of their supervisor."

Bowman narrowed his eyes, and the corner of his mouth lifted in a half-smile, then fell back again.

"They're the ones who told me to give him a good hiding, sir. It'd surprise me if they wanted anything done about Raymond. It was just a settling of scores, like you get every week. Nobody cares, sir."

The superintendent folded his arms over his belly.

"I don't like you any more than your methods, Bowman. I'm going to clear up this affair. Until then, you're laid off."

Bowman took a step towards the desk.

"You're the one who asked for an investigation. The lads at Corney & Barrow couldn't care less."

"Soon, the companies won't be able to give orders to the Metropolitan police anymore, nor to the Thames Brigade. They've been weakened by the end of the Indies monopolies. Their shareholders can't keep control of Westminster forever. You and your like will be expelled from our ranks, Bowman, and we will have a police force worthy of the name. Your time is over. But if this is any consolation, you're only the first of many. Go home and remain there until the investigation is over."

"You can't do that. I've got nothing to do with this."

"You beat him up in front of witnesses who state that Raymond then threatened to kill you. You are not a man who takes that kind of threat lightly, are you? And don't complain – you'll still get paid for another week. You'll be able to pay for your gin and your visits to China Court."

Bowman unballed his fists and lifted his head.

"Give me two days and I'll bring you the men who killed Raymond."

Andrews stood up and turned his back on Bowman, looking through the window at the black Thames. Crows pecked at the belly of a dead sheep as it drifted slowly downriver.

"This stench will never go away. I think we're going to have to get used to it."

"Sir, you know I'm good at my job. I've got more experience than the other lads put together. We may not always see eye to eye, but you know what I'm capable of."

Andrews stuffed his pipe with Asian tobacco and lit it, and the smell of it filled the office.

"Exactly. And I couldn't care less about your past, Bowman. Your life story doesn't interest me. You are suspended until the investigation is over."

"And who are you going to put on this stupid fucking investigation?"

Andrews did not react to his rudeness, but Bowman guessed from the tone of his voice that he was smiling.

"I haven't thought about that yet."

"It was just a question of time. You've been looking for a reason to get rid of me."

"Yes."

"Let me look for the . . ."

"Dismissed, Bowman."

"Let me do my job. I can't just sit there and do nothing."

"If I have to tell you to leave one more time, you'll be in even more trouble than you are already."

The Great Stink had created the conditions for a massive general strike, and if the protesters' demands had not yet taken form, they were undoubtedly simmering, threatening with each passing day to boil over.

The Lords sitting in the House knew this – knew that they must set the machine in motion once again before it was too late.

The anger grew and the madness spread. Lunatics wandered the streets, surrounded by a world that at last matched their delusions. Their hallucinations had become premonitions, their insanity a form of prescience. The mad – along with the preachers – were now the new prophets of London.

Men still of sound mind collapsed, caught up by their morbid fears, rendered catatonic. They shut themselves up at home, barricaded their windows or chose a solid beam to which they could attach a rope. Among the still silent protest, suicides became more and more common.

Arthur Bowman found his place somewhere between the angry workers, the lunatics yelling that they'd known this was coming for a long time, and the men overwhelmed by terror.

No more shifts, no more gangs to hunt down. A man with nothing to do, no purpose in life.

Sitting at his table, Bowman brooded.

Andrews and his phoney investigation. He should ignore the superintendent's orders. He should find the culprits himself. The men who had murdered the supervisor.

Bowman knew that would do no good. Andrews would find something else. Another pretext.

He bought gin, which he started drinking in the mornings, so he could numb himself, avoid thinking, so he could sleep dreamlessly and calm his anger. His nightmares returned.

This murder case would not hold up. The river would start flowing again and he would get his job back. He'd catch Raymond's killers and throw them in the Thames with a rock around each of their necks. He'd take care of the vermin on the docks. Anything to get his body moving again.

But always his thoughts spiralled back to the same point: Andrews was not going to let him off the hook.

After a week, he increased his alcohol consumption; started buying laudanum. That tincture of opium changed his nightmares into dreams. They were all the same, but at least he could face them without fear. The effects dissipated, and his anger returned. He woke up screaming.

He could bump off Andrews.

He could go and talk to him. Tell him to give him his job back or he'd smash his skull in.

He went back to the Chinamen. The pipes, stronger than the laudanum, kept him calm for a few extra hours.

It was no longer possible to escape sleep. Bowman went round in circles, fighting against the memories that swarmed over his boredom like worms over gangrene. The pains of old scars returned, his back slumped, his legs folded under his weight when he walked to China Court, and it hurt to ball his fists. Bowman had not realised, until now, to what extent this daily routine, the discipline of working for the brigade during the last five years, had been responsible for keeping him going.

He fell asleep with his forehead on the table, collapsed sideways on his bed and woke up covered with sweat, the taste of blood in his mouth because he had bitten his cheeks while he was dreaming.

When he went out that evening, after two weeks of rumination, hallucinations and intoxication, his decision was made. He would go to Wapping. Outside, he realised that it was the middle of the night. That Andrews would not be at the station. That he was very close to China Court.

To the fat Chinaman who opened the door, Bowman threw enough money to pay for four pellets. No dreams tonight. He would go and see Andrews tomorrow, when he felt better, stronger. He would get on his knees in front of the superintendent and beg him to give his job back, give him his life back, to poor Sergeant Bowman who could no longer sleep.

———ᗰ——ᗰ——ᗰ———

At dawn on July 14, black clouds moved towards London, travelling over the Thames from the east. It had been a humid night; warm winds had blown through the city and the sky had clouded over. When the sound of the first thunderclaps echoed overhead, the houses filled with noises. The city was barely awake and already a strange agitation reigned over it.

Bowman, staggering, left the Chinese quarter. He drained his bottle of gin and threw it against a wall. The legs of his uniform trousers were covered with dust, his shirt gaped open over his chest, and a blond beard, scattered with grey, covered his cheeks. His police cap askew on his head, he suddenly stopped dead, balancing on his heels for a moment. Still caught in an opium haze, waiting for the effects of the gin to snap him out of it, he blinked his eyes.

Faces passed windows, doors swung open and crowds of people poured out into the streets, still grey with night, yelling at the tops of their voices. He was startled by something hitting his cap. Arthur Bowman looked up at the sky and a drop fell onto his lips, which he immediately wiped with his sleeve.

Around him, people screamed:

"It's coming!"

Men perched on roofs like lookouts shouted themselves hoarse:

"The rain!"

It seemed to him that he could hear, among some English voices, words that he didn't understand, in a language he vaguely remembered. More raindrops fell on his face and shoulders. His mouth began to move and, amid the yells of the crowd, no-one heard his voice:

"Keep the powder dry."

Lightning flashed, close by, turning the streets and rooftops white, casting pale shadows on the cobblestones. A massive electrical explosion accompanied it, and Bowman threw himself against a wall. The wind was blowing more strongly now in the street. He smiled.

"Pagan's armies . . . they're coming . . ."

A door opened next to him and a woman shrieked:

"The fourteenth of July! The fourteenth of July!"

When she saw the policeman, her face twisted with hatred and delight; she leaned towards Bowman and screamed at him:

"The revolution is coming! It's Bastille Day in London!"

He ran off, trying to regain his balance, pursued by the woman's laughter. As he arrived in Wapping Lane, a bolt of lightning flashed behind the buildings, just above the Thames. It was like a sign, as if God had struck at the heart of the city and its evil stench. The storm hit London and in an instant everything was drowned. Bowman could no longer see more than ten feet ahead. He stopped running, put out his hands, and fumbled for a wall.

Little children ran past, yelling with joy, and disappeared. The noise of the storm covered everything. Gutters filled up and cascades of water began pouring from the rooftops. Bowman walked in slow motion along the brick wall, pushing away the images of red eyes that surged from the rain. Through the bars of sewers, the shit of London rose to the surface, carried upward by the rain and rushing over the streets in torrents, ridding the city of its pestilence, its madness and plots, its theories and science: God the saviour was transformed into God the shit-collector.

Bowman reached the locked door of the building, took his pass from his pocket, entered the police station and walked straight to Andrews' office. The superintendent was not there. Bowman stood for a whole minute inside the room, dripping with rain, swimming with nausea, unable to recall what he had gone there to do. He moved through corridors, into other rooms. The station was deserted. All the constables must be outside, celebrating the arrival of the rain or controlling the flood of people. Dragging his feet, he crossed the guards' room and looked through the windows at the Thames, and the image of that river under the storm made him take a step back. He bumped into a table, then collapsed and huddled up in a corner.

The rain hammered down on the building, rapping at the window-panes. The wind gusted under doors and windows. Bowman buried his head in his hands and cried out to cover up the sound of the monsoon and the screaming of men as their fingers were chopped off, their nails torn away, their skin burnt.

He kept this up until he had no breath left, then stood up, leaning on a table, and puked up all the alcohol in his stomach. He wiped his mouth and it seemed to him that silence had descended again.

Or perhaps it was because his eyes had found something to cling to and his thoughts had been stopped in their tracks, fixed on an image that seemed to belong neither to his dreams nor to reality. A child of about twelve years old, who looked like Feng's little slave.

Yes, it was him, standing in the doorway.

Bowman leaned his head to the side and whispered:

"The sharks in the river . . ."

He smiled at his dream.

". . . They didn't eat you?"

The child moved towards him. Bowman did not understand what he was saying. He was terrified, the little slave, but Bowman was happy to see him again and smiled to reassure him, to apologise for having tossed his corpse in the water, in the river that was flowing there, just behind those windows battered by the monsoon. The boy must have just got out of the water because he was soaked, but he was alive, and the corpse stench in the air was dissipating now. What could he be saying that Bowman did not understand?

"It's in the sewers."

The child had to stop being scared like that. Everything was going to be alright; the sounds of battle had ceased and Feng was dead. There was no need to tremble anymore, there was nothing left to fear. Or perhaps he was remembering the sergeant's knife at his throat and worrying about that. He shouldn't – Bowman wasn't going to hurt him anymore. But what was he talking about?

"It's in the sewers. I don't want to go back."

Bowman leaned his head to the other side.

"What are you saying, child? I don't understand what you're saying."

The child no longer wore his canvas trousers. He had found some boots that were too big for him and a pair of overalls like the ones worn by the shit-collectors.

"Don't be scared, child. Everything will be alright."

Bowman moved forward, and the child took a step back.

"I can't go back there."

Bowman understood: the boy was just afraid of being alive after staying in the water with the sharks for so long.

"You won't go back, don't worry. You'll stay with me. The rain will stop and we'll be able to go back downriver. We'll float to the estuary and then return to Madras. The two of us."

"Sir, I don't know what you're talking about . . . Where are the coppers? Are you a copper or not? It's in the sewers. I don't want to go back there."

Bowman felt a pain behind the scar on his forehead. His stomach contracted again; he leaned forward and threw up for a second time. When he looked up again, eyes squinting, he recognised the guards' room, the tables and chairs, the windows streaming with rain.

What was he doing here? A child stood and stared at him.

"What are you doing here?"

There was shouting in the street. Startled, Bowman turned around. He had to get out of here before his colleagues arrived. He looked at the child.

"Get out of here. Piss off."

The child did not move. He stared at Bowman, and seemed incapable of running away.

"It's in the sewers . . ."

"What? What are you saying?"

"In the sewers. The dead."

Bowman took a step towards him. For a moment, he had thought he recognised him, but it was not his face that reminded him of something, just the fear in his eyes, the retinas staring at images he could no longer wipe from his memory.

"What are you talking about?"

"I can't go back there."

Bowman felt dizzy, and steadied himself. He waited until the whirlwind of blood had calmed down, then approached the little sewer rat.

The child was trembling in his overalls and his foul boots, a skinny little sod, skin covered with smallpox scars, twisting a cap in his hands. He was maybe ten or eleven years old and looked like one of those children who could not survive a life spent working underground. Only the toughest got out alive, from those gangs of half-savages, orphaned or abandoned, who foraged through shit in the hope of unearthing some scrap metal. Down in the sewers, those foragers saw almost as many corpses as the constables did. They did deals with the gangs and sometimes fought against them. Even the police had to negotiate with their bosses, with those children who were no longer afraid of anything.

Bowman knew all about it. He too, at that age, had foraged in the sewers of the East End and survived. At twelve or thirteen, the toughest ones were hired by the companies to work on their ships.

The skinny little forager turned his head away, to escape the gaze of this copper who stank of alcohol and vomit. Bowman took the child's chin in his hand.

"What did you see?"

The child's eyes were wide open and tears trickled down his cheeks.

"What did you see?"

"I don't want to go back."

Bowman put his forehead to the child's and spoke slowly:

"The strongest survive."

"Wh . . . what did you say?"

"It's the war of nature, soldier. You have to go back."

Bowman tightened his grip on the boy's chin, provoking a pained grimace, and drops of water fell between his legs. He was pissing himself.

"Let me go. Please. I told you where it is. Let me leave."

Bowman's grip grew ever tighter. His hand began to move down to the boy's neck.

"You're going to take me down there."

The child closed his eyes and began to sob. He stammered incomprehensibly and Bowman loosened his grip to let him talk.

"What are you saying?"

The boy opened his eyes again and his gaze seemed to nestle inside Bowman's; instead of fleeing, he was now trying to take refuge there.

"It's . . . the sharks? The sharks in the river?"

Bowman let him go.

"What?"

"That's what you said earlier."

"What are you talking about?"

"Is it the sharks in the river that did that?"

The boy wiped his snotty nose on his sleeve.

"I . . . I didn't know there were sharks here, but it makes sense, now you say it. It must be them. Are you really a policeman?"

"Yes. What's your name?"

"Slim."

Bowman pushed open the front door of the station, glanced to either side of the street, grabbed the child's arm and dragged him along the pavement. It had been raining for the past hour now and Wapping High Street had turned into a river.

"Where are we going?"

Slim hesitated. He lifted an arm and pointed in the direction of St Katharine's Dock, then looked at the policeman with a scar in the middle of his forehead.

"I'll tell you where it is, but I don't want to go down there."

"You have to go back. Walk!"

The child advanced slowly, bumping into Bowman's legs. The policeman pushed him on each time, to prevent him from stopping. Bowman continued staring through the curtain of rain. The effects of the opium had almost vanished, but he still half expected to see junks suddenly appear from around the corner of the street.

They walked alongside the Thames, where water streamed over the mud, tearing off patches of accumulated dung, gradually freeing the shores of their braids of excrement. They could make out the figures of people on Tower Bridge: a crowd of people running and jumping, leaning over the river. The corpse smell was still there, as if bodies were decomposing now in a marshland rather than a desert. The torrential downpour slowed to a heavy, regular rain. The thunder sounded more distant, the storm passing over the city and moving westward up the river.

Slim and Bowman walked past the gallows on Execution Dock. Some children were jumping up and down on the pontoon, sent wild by the miracle of the rain. They were singing and dancing, tearing off their rags, when they saw Slim and the policeman.

"Slim's been collared! Slim's been collared!"

"Hang the snitches!"

"Bloody sewer rats!"

Slim walked faster, with Bowman on his heels, as the half-naked children started their hysterical jig again. Gawkers invaded St Katharine's Dock, and the child and the policemen wove their way between them, drawing closer to the water. The little forager's boots bumped into Bowman's steel-capped shoes. The policeman dug his fingers into the boy's shoulder.

"Keep going."

"I don't want to."

Bowman's voice grew softer.

"Go on, boy. You have to go back there."

The child walked forward, lifting his eyes to Bowman, then lowering his head and continuing, repeating the same words over and over:

"The sharks. It's the sharks who did it."

"Shut up, boy. Shut up now."

Their clothes sticking to their skin, their legs touching, they moved forward along the jetty. Slim came to a halt at the top of some steps that descended to the dry port: a layer of thick mud covered by an inch or two of water. They waited there for a moment, Slim's back leaning against Bowman's belly. Bowman felt the boy trembling in his arms. His fingers tightened.

"Let's go."

"Sir, what are sharks like?"

The rain pattered on the jetty and the surface of the water. Bowman closed his eyes.

"They live in the sea, near the coast, and sometimes they swim up rivers to find food. On the Ganges, they attack men who go into the water to say their prayers."

"What's the Ganges?"

"A river in India. Over there, the men dress in long red cloths."

"They pray in the water?"

"Because the river is sacred."

Slim turned towards Bowman.

"But the sharks still go there?"

"Yes."

The child thought about this for a moment and looked at the river before him.

"Is the Thames sacred too?"

Bowman turned to look at it.

"No."

They climbed down the steps and entered a brick tunnel under the jetty, an overflow of the port. At the other end they could see the bed of the Thames. In the middle of the tunnel, a large sewer pipe veered off to the left. Slim entered it.

On each side of the vault, pavements ran alongside the channel where water was beginning to flow again. The sound of the rain had ceased and the heat was there again, imprisoned underground. About a hundred feet ahead of them, there was a well of light, falling from a drain, where the rain poured, vertical and shining and dense. They turned into another subterranean pipe, moving further and further away from the river, deep under the city, going from one drain to another, finding a little light then diving once again into blackness until they reached the next opening. Sometimes, they heard voices, shouts, footsteps on the metal bars above them, which echoed through the pipes. The sewers became gradually narrower, and soon there was not enough room to walk side by side, so Slim went in front, pushed there by the silent policeman.

"Sir, did you see that in India – people killed by sharks?"

Bowman lowered his head to avoid banging it against the arched ceiling.

"Yes."

The drains grew smaller and further between. Touching the stone sides of the sewer, they continued through the darkness, broken here and there by another source of light, to which their eyes clung.

"Did they follow your boat?"

"What?"

"How did they come here?"

Rats scurried between their feet and threw themselves shrieking into the mud as the two humans passed.

"No. The sharks stayed there."

Slim stopped and Bowman felt the muscles in his back tense. The boy turned around. Bowman could not see his face in the darkness.

"It's impossible."

The water was flowing quietly in the sewer; far ahead of them, a little stain of light fell onto the mud. The next drain. The child would not move anymore.

"It's impossible. If there aren't any sharks here, then who did that? You said it was them . . ."

Slim dropped like a sack of potatoes down Bowman's legs and huddled against the stone floor.

Bowman stepped over him and kept walking.

They had gone northward through the sewers. They must be somewhere under Thomas More Street and the district that Bowman had been patrolling for nearly five years.

The raindrops fell on the storm drain. He estimated the distance that still separated him from the light – about sixty feet – and started, involuntarily, to count down his steps. An old soldier's habit, to calculate the distance that separated him from danger. To occupy his mind, as he advanced and the shape that he made out beneath the drain grew more distinct.

3

A ray of sunlight fell on the white sheets. Next to him, on a little bed-side table, there was a bottle of syrup, a tray, a spoon and a bowl of soup. His police uniform, newly washed, hung over the top of a chair back. He rubbed his face and slowly his field of vision grew wider: he saw the long dormitory, the beds and other patients, a young nun helping an old man to drink. His belly ached. Bowman reached out a hand towards the bowl of soup, and swallowed a spoonful, which burned his throat and stomach. All his muscles were stiff. He swallowed some more soup and looked up. The nun was standing at the foot of his bed.

"How do you feel?"

Bowman put the bowl back on the table.

"Where am I?"

The nurse approached him and, with the back of her hand, touched his forehead. Bowman drew his head back.

"You are at Guy's Hospital."

He sat up in bed.

"What happened?"

"Your colleagues brought you here three days ago, after you were found in that sewer."

"Sewer?"

"You don't remember? The day of the rain?"

"The rain . . ."

Bowman closed his eyes. In the darkness he saw a point of light, bright drops falling from a ceiling, a shape. He gritted his teeth to stop himself vomiting up the soup he had just swallowed. The nun made him drink some syrup, a bitter-tasting plant-based infusion that soothed the burning in his stomach.

"You've been raving. You still need more rest. I'll come back to see you."

The nun's gaze lingered on Bowman's chest, and he realised he was not wearing a shirt. He pulled the sheet up over his scars. The nurse looked away.

When she had gone, Bowman sat up and opened the window. Guy's Hospital was opposite London Bridge and, from where he sat, the city stretched out to vanishing point beneath him. The Thames was still dark but its level had risen. Cranes were moving on the docks, and people walked along the shores past vendors. All over the city, the factory chimneys belched out black smoke, and the smell of coal filled the air. The companies' boats were moored in St Katharine's Dock and they had begun their ballet of movements along the river, going both ways around the Isle of Dogs. The curse had been lifted from the capital and Bowman looked out over the rooftops of the city, which had come back to life and was going about its daily business as if everything was forgotten.

But he remembered.

His eyes were fixed on the port of St Katharine on the other side of the river, the warehouses, the sewer tunnels under the buildings.

He drew back the curtain and set his feet on the floor. His legs were weak, his head spun. He put on his clean uniform and his shoes, trying clumsily to move as quickly as possible, as weak as after a bout of malaria. He waited a few seconds – just enough time to get his breath back – then began to walk between the beds.

The young nun appeared at the end of the aisle, her arms loaded with pillows.

"What are you doing? You're in no fit state to leave. You have to stay in bed."

When the nurse approached him, Bowman took a step to the side.

"Please, go back to your bed. You mustn't leave now."

Bowman backed away then turned and ran to a large staircase. He hurtled downstairs, clinging to the banister.

Outside, he was assailed by the sunlight, the noises, the passers-by.

He crossed London Bridge amid a crowd of people who were watching the Thames flow freely again. He walked along the docks, ordering his body to move more quickly.

Arthur Bowman entered like a fury into the building on Wapping High Street, passing guards who stood aside for him, and hammered at Superintendent Andrews' door. At the sound of the officer's voice, he burst in. Andrews dropped his pipe.

"What are you doing here?"

Bowman felt himself waver.

"What I saw . . ."

"What?"

"The sewer . . ."

He took a step forward, bumped into a chair and grabbed hold of the desk to stop himself falling.

"The corpse . . . I know who . . ."

His eyes rolled back in his head. Andrews stood up, and Bowman fell backwards onto the floorboards.

The superintendent ran to the door.

"Two men. In my office now!"

Two guards rushed in and found Bowman lying on the floor, his legs trembling so hard that his ankles were banging against the floor. His hands and his head struck the wood violently too. He bit his tongue and blood, mixed with spit, trickled from the corners of his mouth. They fell to the floor to immobilise him. One of the policemen tried to loosen his jaws so he would stop chewing his tongue, and Bowman almost bit his fingertip off.

When he came to, he was lying on a table in the guards' room. Bowman lifted himself up on his elbows and saw Andrews standing in front of a window.

"You had a nervous breakdown. Who let you leave the hospital?"

Bowman turned around so his legs hung from the edge of the table and held his head in his hands.

"Don't remember."

"What are you doing here?"

"The sewers . . ."

"You're still wearing your uniform?"

Bowman did not understand what he was talking about.

"What?"

"You were suspended. You no longer have the right to wear that uniform."

Bowman looked at him stupidly.

"I don't have anything else to wear."

"What were you doing here when the child found you?"

Bowman got down from the table and tried to stand up. In the end, he grabbed a chair and sat down.

"What child?"

"The one who told us you were in the sewer. The one who went with you down there. That's what he told us, anyway."

"Told?"

Bowman was slowly regaining his wits. He put a finger in his mouth to his damaged tongue. He wanted to spit on the floor, but instead he gulped down a mouthful of blood and saliva. As if the metallic taste of his own blood had set off an alarm, he waited a few seconds before responding:

"I came to see you. To find out what was happening with the investigation into the supervisor's death."

"And then?"

"And then? . . . There was no-one here. I was about to go out when the child . . . I can't remember his name, but this boy turned up. He said there was something in the sewers."

Andrews began walking between the tables, pacing around Bowman.

"There's a lot of talk about this case. The rumours are spreading. No-one has ever seen anything like it in London before and we still haven't been able to identify the victim."

Bowman's mutilated tongue was swelling inside his mouth. He articulated slowly.

"Did you go down there?"

"No. It was O'Reilly who went, along with two other guards. We haven't found the witness."

"The witness?"

"That child who came to warn us – the one you said you met here. He disappeared and we haven't been able to find him."

Andrews turned around near the window and looked outside.

"When you came in to my office earlier, you were about to say something before you collapsed. You have to talk. It's in your interests."

"My interests?"

"Don't play the innocent."

Bowman lowered his head before muttering something. Andrews came closer to him.

"What did you say?"

Bowman cleared his throat.

"Cavendish's mission."

Superintendent Andrews froze.

"Major Cavendish?"

Sergeant Bowman nodded. Andrews' voice had gone high-pitched; now, he attempted to control it.

"The Duke?"

Bowman nodded again. The superintendent stammered:

"What are you talking about?"

Bowman made an effort to open his mouth. He did not want to pronounce the words.

"The corpse in the sewer. I've seen that before. In Burma. In the forest."

Andrews screamed:

"Why are you talking about Cavendish? What is this nonsense about a forest? You're completely mad! Explain yourself before I have you thrown in prison! We found you unconscious next to a corpse in the sewer, Bowman – you are already under a great deal of suspicion. Explain yourself!"

Bowman was paralysed by Andrews' screaming. The images flashed through his head: from the hold on the *Healing Joy* to the fishermen's village, the junk, the monsoon, the attack by Min's soldiers, the line of prisoners being marched through the jungle. The cages and the guards' cries. He wanted to cover his ears so he wouldn't have to hear the superintendent anymore. Instead, he was the one who screamed:

"I know who did it!"

Two guards, who had been standing outside the door, rushed into the room. Andrews signalled the guards not to move, then to leave them alone.

"Bowman, this is your last chance to tell me why you keep saying so many things I don't understand, why you are mentioning the Duke of Devonshire's name in the same breath as that murder in the sewer!"

Bowman trapped his hands between his knees and squeezed them together as tight as he could to stop the trembling.

"I'm trying to. I can't."

"You don't have a choice. This is an order, Bowman."

Bowman took slow, deep breaths, trying to get enough air in his lungs. His head hung down to his knees.

"I was on the *Joy*, Godwin's flagship. We were waiting for the wind to pick up so we could attack Rangoon and the deck officer came to find me. He told me that Major Cavendish wanted to see me. For a mission on the river."

Andrews sent him home, escorted by a guard from the brigade. Bowman found himself back in his room on Cable Street. The chair was waiting for him, in front of the table, facing the window; his sergeant's uniform hung from the line; there were empty bottles on the floor.

Andrews' man remained below on the street to keep watch over his building.

Bowman lay on his bed and slept for twenty-four hours. When he woke up, he felt better rested than he had done for a long time, despite the stiffness in his muscles, worse even than it had been in hospital. It took him five minutes to leave his room, descend the three floors and put a coin in the hand of his landlady, so she would bring him some food. The old woman asked why there was a policeman outside the building. Bowman told her not to worry and to bring him a bottle of gin too.

For two days, he tried to eat regularly and moderate his drinking. He cleaned and tidied his room. The rest had left him calmer: he no longer heard the screaming, but his memory had returned, down to the last detail.

The word circled his head, and surprised him by emerging from his mouth as a whisper, as he sat at his table and looked out over the rooftops of Whitechapel. He saw the letters traced on the bricks of the sewer in the blood from the corpse, barely any darker than the wall.

One word, awaiting him. The killer's signature.

Survive.

When Bowman pronounced it, alone in his room, it was a question. Down there, in the sewer, it was an affirmation.

Had O'Reilly and the other policemen seen it too?

After a week, Andrews knocked on his door. The superintendent was nervous. He sat at the table and took off his hat. Bowman stood near the window, looking down at the policeman outside the front door of the building, and waited for the officer to speak.

"I sent a report, along with your testimony, to the head of the division."

Bowman turned around. Andrews joined his hands on the table and lowered his head.

"I went personally to East India House and checked the prisoner of war register. You and your men do not appear on any list."

Bowman moved towards him.

"What?"

"Yesterday, the head of the division came in person to see me in Wapping. He told me your testimony was a tissue of lies and fantasies.

He made it clear that it was not in my interests to follow this lead. He told me to sniff around the gangs instead."

"You didn't find anything?"

Andrews gritted his teeth and lifted his head. His eyes seemed to shrink in their sockets.

"That mission does not exist, Bowman. Nor do the men you mentioned, nor any trace of your captivity. The chief said he would have my head if I continued asking questions. You know what that means?"

"We're not on the lists?"

Andrews contained himself. He stood up, smacking his hands down on the table.

"This report is going to get me in serious trouble and I advise you not to talk about this story to anyone! The division head wants results quickly and he wants this sewer story to end here. He would be perfectly happy if I brought him some gang member . . . or anyone else, for that matter."

Arthur Bowman no longer heard the superintendent. He was looking straight ahead, suddenly absent, while his superior officer went on:

"We found you next to the corpse. Your reputation for violence precedes you. You are telling stories that no-one wants to hear and everyone knows you are half mad. All my men are already sure that you're guilty, Bowman. Do I have to say anything else, or do we understand each other?"

Bowman crossed the room and lay down on his bed. Andrews stood in front of him. The superintendent spoke more quietly, articulating slowly, separating the words so that Bowman, even in a daze, could hear them clearly:

"You remain under surveillance and you will not leave here until this case has been solved. I won't let you fuck up my career, Bowman, you hear me? If you make any waves at all, I will have you for the murder of the foreman and for the body in the sewer. You know I wouldn't hesitate to do it, and you also know there wouldn't exactly be a crowd of people rushing to defend you in front of a judge."

Andrews put his hand on the door handle and turned around, his gaze sweeping the room.

"You belong in an asylum, Bowman, but if you prefer the rope, all you have to do is go downstairs and utter the name Major Cavendish one more time . . . I'll take care of the rest."

He left the room, leaving the door open behind him.

Bowman walked over to the little mirror above the sink. He unbuttoned his shirt, let his trousers fall to the floor, took the mirror from the wall and put it in front of his body, inspecting the palest lines on his skin. Straight, parallel scars, from his shoulders to his abdomen, passing over his collarbone and his ribs, identical to the ones that ran down his back and his legs. He leaned his head to the side and looked at his eyes in the mirror, examining them for a long time, searching his blue eyes as if they were someone else's, trying to guess what was hidden behind them. He grimaced, pulling a series of exaggerated faces like so many masks. Anger, a smile, sadness, surprise. He opened his mouth to look at his tongue and his teeth.

He pronounced a few words, first in a murmur, then more loudly, observing that face in the mirror, that face that wanted to tell him something he could not yet hear:

"No mission?"

He repeated the question a little more loudly, lifting his mutilated hand and touching it to his lips, feeling the breath of his words when he pronounced them.

He got dressed again, making the scars vanish under the police uniform, and sat at the table while he waited for night to fall, staring out of the window. Then he went out onto the landing, opened the door to a storeroom, grabbed on to the top of the door, lifted up the chimney-sweep's skylight, and hoisted himself onto the roof. At the next chimney, he opened another skylight, let himself down into the stairwell of the adjoining building and came out on Cable Street, heading east to avoid the policeman who was guarding the door to his own building. He turned right on Butcher Row and reached the docks, which he continued to follow eastward, along the Thames.

He walked among a few passers-by, silent figures that he barely even noticed, and lifted his nose as if to sniff the sea, sixty miles from there. He passed Victoria Docks and Duke Shore until he reached Dunbar Wharf, where he slipped between the huts and warehouses, crossing through the darkness over an expanse of dry grass littered with stinking nets, old chains and rusty anchors. He would have liked to pass the Isle of Dogs and go all the way to North Woolwich, where the Thames widened and he might be able to catch the first scents of the sea. But he felt too tired and sat on the docks at the water's edge. The lights of London were dancing on the black surface of the port. He stood up and retraced his footsteps, picking through the litter until he found a piece of rusted boat chain, which he put over his shoulders and wrapped around his neck like a scarf. After that, he walked back to the port, headed straight for the docks and, without slowing down, fell into the water.

When he hit the surface, he opened his mouth. Air bubbles floated up past his body, rolling against his ears. He wished it could be more silent. Keeping his eyes open, he began to sink. He looked down at the blackness below his feet, feeling the weight of the chain on his shoulder, dragging him down deeper and deeper.

There were noises, muffled impacts of wood or metal, that spread through the water. He looked up. A dark shape was swimming towards him.

A shark.

He sucked in all the water he could and repeated the word one last time. A question. *Survive?*

Arthur Bowman opened his eyes. He was lying on the bottom of a small boat. His head was lifted up, the chain unwound from around his neck. A man was yelling as he pushed with both hands on his chest. He shouted but Bowman didn't hear him. There was a dock above the boat, where curious onlookers held lanterns; their light shone between his wet eyelashes. He heard the first words, confirming his disappointment:

"He's alive!"

Bowman coughed, felt the water rise up his throat and come out of his mouth, trickling over his beard. Brackish water, with a muddy taste.

"Hey! Are you alright? Can you hear us?"

The man in the pea jacket, dripping water, leaned over him. When Bowman spoke, water continued pouring from his mouth. There was a silence and someone asked:

"What did he say?"

"I couldn't hear. What did you say?"

The fisherman put his ear close to Bowman's mouth, listened to his croaky voice, and then sat up.

"Shit, I reckon he must have water on his brain!"

"What did he say?"

"He's talking about sharks. He asked where the sharks are."

Three men lifted him up. On the dock, arms reached out and he was laid out on the ground. He shivered. Hands removed his cape.

"Bloody hell! He's a copper!"

"My God, have you seen that?"

"What is it?"

"Scars."

"Shit, did he get caught in a propeller?"

"That was no propeller that did that. They're not new anyway."

They threw a blanket over his body and he felt himself being lifted up again, heard the wheels of a cart on cobblestones. His head rolled from side to side and he lost consciousness.

The flames danced in front of his eyes. Someone chucked a bucket of coals into the stove. Cinders rose into the air and Bowman followed them with his eyes.

"Oh, you've woken up, have you?"

Bowman looked around him. He was lying on some crates in a little wooden outhouse.

"You've been snoring all night. Must be tiring, almost drowning."

On top of the stove, the man put a saucepan of water, then threw in a handful of coffee, which he stirred with the blade of his knife. When he wiped the knife on his hand, Bowman sat up and tried to move away.

"Whoa! What's up with you? Something wrong?"

The man moved closer to him, without letting go of the knife. Bowman rolled to the side, lay face down on the earth floor and tried to crawl towards the door, which opened. Another man came in, dressed in a pea jacket.

"Shit, he's mad as a hatter."

The man who had just entered crouched down next to Bowman, who rolled up into a ball.

"Hey, lad. What's up with you? Don't be scared. We're the ones who hooked you out of the water last night. We're not going to hurt you. Do you want some coffee? You were shivering all night. Drink something hot, and afterwards we'll take you home. Where do you live?"

Bowman moved away from him.

"Cable Street."

"Cable? Is that what you said?"

The man near the stove brought him a steaming mug and said goodbye to the man in the pea jacket, explaining that he was going back to work and would drop in later. Bowman gripped the metal mug between his cold fingers and lifted it to his lips. He took a sip.

The fisherman sat on a crate, coffee in hand, and looked at this man sitting on the ground.

"So you're a policeman, are you?"

Bowman hesitated, then shook his head.

"What was that uniform you were wearing, then?"

Bowman drank some hot coffee and did not respond. The fisherman took off his hat and rubbed his hands.

"I'm the one who fished you out of the water. You fell just in front of my boat. Don't you remember? Anyway, I'm glad you're not a bluebottle. They'd really have taken the piss out of me if I'd saved a copper. What's your name?"

115

"Bowman. Sergeant Bowman."

"Sergeant? Shit, don't tell me I saved a soldier! . . . What? What did you say?"

"East India Company."

The fisherman looked at him darkly and spat on the floor.

"I've got a brother who spent three years in Bombay. What a fucking country. Those bastards in the Company . . ."

Bowman swallowed some more coffee and cleared his throat.

"Madras."

"Yeah? How long were you there?"

"Fifteen."

"Fifteen years? Shit."

In addition to the stove, the sun was now shining through the little window and on the tar-covered planks of the roof. It was hot in the fisherman's hut, filled with canvas bags, nets, lines and lockers. At last, the man took off his jacket and poured himself some more coffee.

"Well, it's none of my business really. I just fished you out of the water. But I do wonder why you wanted to swim with the fishes in that shitty river."

The fisherman waited a few seconds but the sergeant did not reply.

"Is it 'cos of the scars? Something that happened to you over there? My brother, he's had nightmares since he came back. 'Cos of what he saw. 'Cos of what was done to him, or maybe even 'cos of what he did. I don't know, 'cos he never talks about it."

The fisherman smiled.

"My name's Frank. Frankie'

He held out his hand. Bowman shook it. Frank took a small bottle of hooch from his pocket.

"One good thing about this stink is that there wasn't enough water for people to throw themselves into the Thames. Lucky, that, 'cos it sent quite a few of 'em completely mad. We all came close to losing it, I reckon. Like that story in the sewers, that poor bloke who was killed. A real bloodbath, apparently. If you want my opinion, the bloke who did that must have been sent mad by the smell and the heat. You've been through that, haven't you, Sergeant, living in those countries where the sun sends everyone crazy?"

Bowman's chin started to quiver when he tried to speak. His face felt cold when the blood left it, massing in his chest as his heartbeat accelerated.

The fisherman came close to him and offered him a drink.

"Alright. We won't talk about that anymore. Calm down, Sarge. What's your first name?"

Bowman swallowed some hooch.

"Arthur."

"Do you want me to take you home, Arthur?"

Bowman looked at him, incapable of responding.

"Well, let's wait till you're back on your feet, and then we'll see. I'm going to try to find you some clothes. You can't keep walking round in that uniform. Stay here, I'll be back in a minute."

Frank stopped at the door and turned around.

"Don't do anything stupid, Sergeant Arthur. Alright? It's easy enough to snuff it without wanting to. There's no need to do it yourself."

Bowman moved closer to the stove, leaned on a crate and closed his eyes. He fell asleep without realising and when the cabin door opened, he jumped. Frank was back, with a bag over his shoulder.

"You survived then, Sergeant?"

This man smiled a lot.

"I don't have a lord's wardrobe, but I did manage to find a few things that should fit you. My missus gave me an earful, and she's probably right. It's pretty stupid of me, helping someone I don't know. How do you feel?"

Bowman tried to smile.

"Better."

"Well, it's not that I'm a skinflint, but if you could at least give me your trousers, that'd be good."

Bowman put on the clothes – a bit small – then devoured the bread and lard that Frank had brought, along with a bottle of wine. His throat relaxed as he swallowed the food, taking away the taste of salt and mud that he still had on his tongue. He felt embarrassed now he was able to speak again, because he didn't know what to say.

"Thank you."

"Don't mention it."

"I'm going to go home."

He picked up his old clothes, rolled them in a ball and handed them to the fisherman.

"You can use the cape as a blanket."

The fisherman smiled and took the policeman's clothes.

"Yeah, I just won't go out with it."

They shook hands again.

"Come back whenever you want if there's a problem. I'm not going to get all sentimental on you – I mean, I don't even know who you are – but if ever you're in trouble, you can always find me here."

Bowman left the hut. The fisherman stood in the doorway and watched him walk away.

"Hey! Sergeant! Maybe I'm being stupid, but it just occurred to me: you didn't jump in the river 'cos of the Company, did you?"

Bowman turned around.

"What?"

"Shit! Are you the only bloke in London who doesn't know about it?"

Bowman shook his head.

"It was made official yesterday. Lad, you threw yourself under my boat the very day they closed up shop."

"I don't understand."

"Oh! Sergeant, you're pulling my leg, aren't you? The sepoys – haven't you followed any of this? First it was the Hindu soldiers who revolted. Apparently they didn't want to tear the cartridges open with their teeth 'cos there was cow fat on them and they didn't want to eat it! Half of India went to war and the Company got caught with its pants down. The Queen kicked them out on their arses. So, no more East India Company – the Crown has taken over everything.

Your old employer's been sent to the cleaners, Sergeant."

Bowman ran off.

At the corner of Fletcher Street, he checked that the copper was still there, went around the block, and entered the adjoining building. Back over the roofs and into his room. He took his truncheon from the wall, slid it into the knot of a floorboard, lifted it up and picked up the board with his other hand. He put his arm between two joists and took out a padlocked metal box. At the other end of the room, he went through the same steps, lifting up another plank and taking out the key that opened the little chest. Bowman kept forty shillings from what he had saved of his pay and his military pension, before putting the box back in its hiding place. He took his Company uniform from the line and went down to the ground floor to knock on the landlady's door. Bowman paid his rent and gave her an extra two shillings to clean the uniform and another three to get him something to eat and some soap. He also asked the old lady to buy some bottles of wine. Not gin.

When the landlady brought him his purchases, he gave her another penny so that a local child would carry up a bucket of water for him. He opened a bottle of wine and drank the whole thing before eating. Two eggs, which he gulped down, some dried pork, some rye bread, an onion and a candied pear. Then he sat in front of the mirror, cleaned the sink with a bit of water, splashed some water on his face and began to trim his beard. As the razor blade scraped over his throat, he thought back to the black water of the Thames and the coppers who wanted to lock him up.

4

On the bed, Bowman had spread out the shirt, the faded red jacket, and the trousers which, despite being washed, had not regained their whiteness. On the shoulders of the jacket, the sergeant's stripes no longer shone. The outfit was laid out in the shape of a body.

He chewed some bread, washing it down with mouthfuls of red wine, and awaited the courage to put on his old uniform. Sergeant Bowman imagined that suddenly all the soldiers of the East India Company had been vaporised, that from London to Hong Kong, all over the world, in barracks and on ships, there was nothing left but empty uniforms, spread out like his on the mattress. He did not want to believe it.

The Company had existed for centuries. It couldn't just disappear.

Slumped on the table, their leather stiff and folded and covered in mould, his boots creaked when he began to clean them, rubbing them with his old Met shirt. He spread the wax over the dry leather, saturating it with grease, then rubbed until the boots regained a little of their old lustre. When he'd finished the wine, he buttoned up his shirt, chin on his chest, eyeing his fingers, then put on the trousers, adjusting the braces and sliding his arms into the sleeves of the jacket. He put the boots on without socks, buttoned the jacket and looked at himself in the little mirror. He had never put back on the weight he had lost in captivity. Opium and alcohol and his bad diet had made him lose even more. The uniform was loose, the shoulders looking as if they were hung on a coat hanger.

A spectre from an army of ghosts.

He stood in the middle of the room for a minute or so, breathing slowly, then went out and hoisted himself up through the fanlight. On Royal Mint Street, after checking that he was not being followed, he hailed a hackney cab.

"Léadenhall Street. East India House."

The coach driver looked for a moment at the soldier in his worn, old uniform. Then there was the sound of a whip and the horse pulled the carriage at a trot over the cobbles.

"Gee up!"

Bowman lifted the curtain from the little window.

The pavements grew wider, the buildings' façades increasingly white, the windows higher. Women in hats led children by the hand, gentlemen leaning on canes stood talking on street corners; in the parks, in the shade of green trees, couples walked arm in arm. London was clean and serene, resplendent in the summer sunlight. The women's long fingers were sheathed in white gloves; from under their hats, the men gazed distantly. An officer's gaze.

Like Wright's.

Bowman saw the captain again, with the hole in his head, when he had closed the door of Feng's cabin to let him die alone.

Abruptly he let go of the curtain. Mechanically touching his chest, he realised that he had not brought a flask. The wine had not been enough; he had stomach cramps and his nervousness only increased his need.

"East India House!"

The driver pulled on the reins. The horse slowed and came to a halt. The sergeant jumped out of the carriage, paid for his trip and turned to face the building. Lifting his eyes to the six Doric columns of the façade, dazzling in the daylight, he felt so dizzy that he almost fell to the ground. Bowman took a step back, turned on his heel and went down Leadenhall Street to a pub, where he entered and then stood still in the doorway.

The sunlight poured through windows and pooled on the tables and glasses, the coloured enamels reflecting in the ambers of whiskies and beers. Paintings, tapestries and hunting trophies decorated the walls. Bowman remained standing there for an instant, pulling at the hem of his jacket. At the tables, people began to look up at him: men in suits reading newspapers, officers in dark uniforms talking in low voices, waiters placing drinks on tables and walking away bowing. He wanted to leave, but was afraid of appearing even more ridiculous, so he lowered his head in a sort of general greeting and walked over to the bar.

"A gin."

"What would you prefer, officer?"

"What would I prefer? Gordon's . . ."

The barman poured him a glass, which he downed in a single gulp.

"Another."

Bowman paid for the two drinks, the price of a whole night at Big Lars' establishment. He went back up Leadenhall Street, this time passing under the columns without looking up, and found himself paralysed, in the vast lobby of East India House, in front of black lines several yards long stretching out at his feet. Inlaid in black marble in the pale flagstones, the three crosses connected at their bases, the three letters E.I.C. and the motto *Deo ducente nil nocet* (*When God leads, no harm may come*). Cold sweat ran down his back, smelling of whey. His shirt became soaked, and the scent of laundry soap was overpowered by that of mould. Men in suits and redingotes crossed the lobby, the hard heels of their shoes clicking on the marble, the echoes rising up to the impressive, sculpted ceiling. They walked over the three crosses and three letters without emotion and quickly vanished, with folders and briefcases under their arms.

Bowman closed his eyes while he caught his breath, then looked again.

On the walls were huge paintings: boats flying the Company's colours sailing on calm seas. A double marble staircase rose to the next floor, and all about him were busy, rushing men, like an anthill near a forest fire.

Bowman was on Leadenhall Street – that cursed name, which he had heard so many men utter while spitting on the ground when the wages or the post did not arrive, when the rations were too small or there wasn't enough ammunition to attack. Since his return five years ago, he had never once walked past this place. Bowman had imagined something else. The Company's headquarters was an arrogant building, but not a palace or a castle. Officers, shareholders, managers and clerks.

Watching these zealous employees pass through the lobby, Bowman smiled maliciously. He was the only one here to wear the Company's real uniform. Because, with the East India Company's arms stretched all over the world, it had need of dirty fingers like Sergeant Bowman in order to amass its vast wealth. He looked down again at the three black marble crosses. He heard screaming in his head and he did not seek to quieten it. It was only just that Bowman should bring the screams here, even if no-one could hear them and Cavendish's mission did not exist.

Behind a counter, a factotum lifted his head to observe the faded uniform.

"What can I do for you, sir?"

The first person Bowman met at East India House did not even know how to recognise the ranks of its army.

"Captain. Captain Wright."

Bowman was surprised by the tone of his voice – the tone of the drill sergeant he had once been. The man behind the counter stood up tall.

"Excuse me, Captain. How may I serve you?"

"I'm looking for an officer. A naval captain who served in Burma in '52."

"I beg your pardon, Captain?"

"The captain of the *Sea Runner*, in '52."

The Company employee blinked.

"You're trying to find the name of an officer? Is that correct?"

"Yes. Naval captain. At Rangoon with Godwin."

"I think you'll have to ask at the Naval Affairs department, Captain."

"Where's that?"

"The west staircase, on the first floor, sir."

Bowman turned away, walked up the wide staircase to the first floor, followed a long corridor and, before knocking on the door of the Naval Affairs office, wiped his forehead with his sleeve. The door opened on a wide corridor, a high-windowed antechamber with doors opening onto other rooms and, in the middle of this entrance hall, a man sitting behind a desk.

The secretary watched him advance and stood up ceremoniously.

"What can I do for you, Sergeant?"

This one knew the ranks. Bowman felt himself hesitate. He had pins and needles in his hands, as he'd had in Andrews' office before he suffered that fit.

"I'm looking for an officer. Commander of the *Sea Runner* in '52, in Rangoon."

The secretary gave a grimace of irritation.

"Who sent you here? If you don't know the officer's name, I don't see why you are looking for him. Non-commissioned officers do not have access to that information, Sergeant."

Sweat dripped down Bowman's chest, along his legs and into his boots. The two large windows began to change shape, warping, growing rounder, and the light burned his eyes. He took a step forward, his legs gave way and he reached out an arm towards the desk. The secretary rushed over and guided him to a chair.

"My God! What's happening to you? Don't you feel well?"

"Something to drink."

The secretary ran off and returned a minute later with a pitcher of water and a glass, which he filled and offered to the sergeant. Bowman drank the water. The man poured him another glass.

"I'm going to open a window. It must be this heat – you need some air."

He trotted over to the windows and opened one.

"Excuse me, Sergeant. I wasn't very welcoming. It's just that everything is so dreadfully complicated at the moment, with that . . . My God! I'm complaining when you've probably just come back from there. Is that right, Sergeant? You've just returned from there?"

Bowman finished his glass and looked at the little man in his suit.

"There?"

"The revolt, Sergeant. That dreadful sepoy revolt."

The sergeant sat up a little on his chair.

"Yes, I've just come from there."

The secretary turned pale.

"My God. Yes, I can see that you're exhausted. You must have seen some terrible things . . ."

Bowman nodded.

"I do beg your pardon, Sergeant. It's just that we're preparing our move to the Council of India, near the Secretary of State. The whole place is upside down at the moment. And you, coming back from there . . ."

Bowman contented himself with a shrug.

"You're looking for a naval officer whom you don't know? Is that correct?"

"A message for him."

"A letter? From a soldier?"

The water had quenched his thirst. Bowman felt less weak now.

"Yes, that's right. A letter from a soldier."

The secretary joined his hands over his chest.

"That's awful! You have to give this officer the last letter from a . . . a dead soldier?"

"Yes. Dead."

The man put a hand to his forehead.

"A dead soldier. A friend of this officer . . . My God. And you were exhausted, and carrying this letter. What was the ship's name again, Sergeant? Tell me – I'll do all I can to help you."

"*Sea Runner*. Rangoon, in '52."

"Rangoon? General Godwin's fleet or Commodore Lambert's?"

"Godwin's."

The secretary headed towards a door, then stopped and turned around.

"They were friends, is that right? And the dead soldier . . . he didn't have any family?"

"That's right. No family."

The man returned ten minutes later, carrying an enormous register, which he put down on the desk and opened. He turned the pages, his index finger tracing the columns of names and dates, looking up from time to time at the sergeant to smile and apologise.

"We work hard here, of course. But you were over there. And you came back."

"Yes. Just got back."

The secretary tapped a page in the register.

"Ah! The *Sea Runner*. '49, '50, '51 ... '52. Left Madras on January 12. Sergeant, I have your answer. The *Sea Runner* was commanded by Captain . . . Philip Reeves. Captain Reeves is retired. He left the Company in '53, after the Burma campaign."

Bowman stood up from his chair.

"How can I find him?"

"Yes, of course, of course, his address. I shouldn't – we're not allowed normally. But that letter . . . Wait here, I won't be long."

When he returned, he sat behind his desk, took a sheet of paper from a drawer and wrote an address on it, nervously dipping his pen in the inkwell, touching the blotter to the wet ink.

"There you are, Sergeant. You can do your duty now. You're a brave man, to take care of this as soon as you got back."

Bowman folded the paper and slipped it into the inside pocket of his jacket. Before he reached the door, the secretary rushed over and opened it for him.

"Sergeant, may I shake your hand?"

Arthur Bowman gave him his clammy hand.

The secretary watched him walk away down the corridor and Bowman tried to stay calm, suppressing his urge to run off.

Bowman crossed the lobby and came out in the street. Then, his stomach cramping, he walked all the way to the Fox and Hounds. It took him an hour to reach Wapping Lane and when he entered the Fox, soaked with sweat in his uniform, all the conversations came to a sudden halt. The sergeant lowered his head, walked over to his usual table and stared at the wood in front of him.

Behind the bar, a newspaper open in front of him, Lars closed his mouth. The old customers looked at Bowman, wearing that uniform which almost all of them kept at the back of a wardrobe, unless they'd already exchanged it for a drink when times were hard. That red jacket had an unpleasant effect on them, particularly when it was being worn by that angry ghost, Sergeant Bowman, whom they had not seen for weeks and who might just as well have been dead.

Lars pulled a pint and set it on the bar.

"Mitch! You fucking halfwit! Take this beer over to the sergeant!"

Lars served himself a large glass of hooch, pouring a little bit on the floor and downing the rest in one. Then he leaned over his newspaper, glancing up one more time at the sergeant's table, and started to read again.

"Ah! Apparently they're going to move from Leadenhall Street! I bet the accountants are in a tizzy!"

The customers at the bar paid no attention to what Lars was saying. He himself was not fully focused on the words in the paper. Over their shoulders, everyone was watching the sergeant. In a voice that lacked conviction, while continuing to fill glasses, as Mitch walked to and from Bowman's table, Lars read the article in the *Morning Chronicle*, which explained how and why, because of a gang of sepoys in India, the Company had been ripped off by the Crown. The Fox and Hounds seemed filled that evening with a group of orphans, in mourning for the Company and cursing it the first chance they got. Behind the smiles and the weak jokes, there was a guilty sadness that they were now veterans of something that no longer existed. Their old enemy was dead and at the table in the corner, its ghost was drinking enough beer to make his belly explode.

Bowman downed pints for an hour and, at nightfall, went home. He collapsed on the landing when he jumped from the roof through the skylight, then crawled over to his bed. The beer was not strong enough to send him to sleep, not strong enough to end the screaming.

*

Reeves lived in London. In Westminster, near St George's Fields, by the Thames.

From his chest under the floorboards, Bowman took a few shillings, then made his usual escape over the rooftops, walked to Royal Mint Street and hailed another hackney. This time, he did not watch the passers-by through the carriage window. The cab dropped him outside a recently built two-storey house with a white façade. One side of it faced the river, the other Grosvenor Road and the park. A wooden gate opened onto a small, well-kept garden. Bowman crossed this and knocked on the door. A middle-aged woman opened it, wearing a headscarf and an apron.

"What's it about?"

"Is Captain Reeves here?"

"He didn't tell me he was expecting anyone. Who are you?"

"I don't have an appointment. Tell him that I want to see him."

"Son, I can smell the beer on you from here. I think you must have the wrong address. And what's that moth-eaten uniform you're wearing. Who did you nick that from, eh?"

Bowman climbed the steps to the front door. The maid stepped back into the house and tried to close the door. He put his hand on the doorframe.

"Go and tell your master that I want to see him. Sergeant Arthur Bowman. Go and tell him now."

A voice rang out inside the house.

"Dorothy? What's happening?"

Bowman leaned forward and spoke more quietly.

"Tell him that Sergeant Bowman wants to see him. Tell him I was on his boat when the village burned."

"Let go of the door or I'll scream."

Bowman let go.

"Go and tell him."

He walked back down the steps and waited for Reeves to appear at the door.

His face was the same as the one in Bowman's memory, standing behind the helm of the sloop, only older and more wrinkled, his hair now completely white. He no longer had a beard, just two thick sideburns that went down to the bottom of his jaw. The straight-backed, solid captain Bowman recalled was now a slope-shouldered old man. One hand on the doorframe, the other hidden behind it, Reeves watched him anxiously.

"Who are you?"

The old captain narrowed his eyes and seemed to have trouble with his vision. Bowman took a step forward in spite of the weapon that Reeves was undoubtedly hiding behind the door.

"Stay where you are."

"You don't remember me? Sergeant Bowman. On the *Sea Runner*. I boarded the junk."

Reeves squinted even harder.

"What did you say?"

"I was there when the village burned. I gave you something."

The captain's face tensed. Bowman put his foot on the first step and spoke more slowly.

"I was there. So were you. You can't have forgotten. Sergeant Bowman."

Reeves clung to the door.

"Sergeant Bowman?"

The old man let go of the doorframe and put his hand in his pocket, drawing out a pair of glasses that he placed on his nose. His eyes appeared suddenly huge, leering at the sergeant in his baggy, worn uniform.

"You were dead . . . They told me you were all dead."

"Not all of us, Captain."

Reeves opened the door wide. In his right hand he held a loaded pistol, but he seemed to have forgotten this.

"Come in."

Bowman looked at the gun, and the old man stammered:

"I beg your pardon, I thought something was going on. I couldn't understand what Dorothy was saying to me."

The old captain put his gun on the sideboard in the entrance hall.

"Follow me, Sergeant."

They walked through the living room to a semi-circular solarium on the other side of the house with windows overlooking the Thames. The masts of little boats moored outside the house swayed gently in the sunlight. Bowman stood facing the windows, keeping as much distance as he could from everything: the polished furniture, the embroidered chairs, the flower pots; if he could, he'd have removed his feet from the carpet. Souvenirs of Reeves' travels hung on the walls: African masks, muskets and swords, spears and daggers. Lit by the low sun, six paintings of Company ships. The vessels that the captain had commanded. One of the frames was smaller than the others, the wood plain, no gilding, and the picture inside showed an elegant white sloop. The *Sea Runner*.

"Please, sit down. Would you like to drink something?"

"What?"

"Something to drink?"

"Coffee."

Reeves went off to the kitchen, and Bowman heard him speaking to his maid; the woman protested in a whisper, advising Reeves to put this man out on the street. Reeves told her to calm down and bring the coffee into the solarium.

"Please, Sergeant, do sit down."

Bowman took his eyes from the painting and sat in a chair without putting his hands on the armrests. Reeves sat facing him. The old officer, sitting on the edge of his seat, his eyes enlarged by the lenses of his glasses, was observing him intently.

"What . . . what happened to you?"

Bowman looked away, to avoid the old man's probing eyes.

"We came back from Wright's mission. Only ten of us."

"Wright . . ."

"He died on the river. We were taken prisoner."

"They told me there were no survivors."

The sergeant lowered his gaze.

"No-one knows anything about Wright's mission anymore. That's why I came. It was the Naval Affairs office at the Company who gave me your address."

"Wright's mission?"

Bowman looked up.

"The ambassador, on the river. We were supposed to intercept the ambassador's boat. But that's not why I came, Captain. It's for something else."

"What then, Sergeant? What . . . what do you need?"

Bowman turned towards the river, and tried to moisten his dry tongue.

"It's about that murder. The murder in the sewers, a few weeks ago."

The two men jumped and turned around: Dorothy, the maid, was standing in the middle of the living room, her hands open, a silver tray at her feet, the cups broken and the coffee pot overturned.

"Mr Reeves, tell him to leave! Tell him to leave!"

The old captain stood up, took the maid by the arm and tried to reassure her.

"Clean this up and leave us, Dorothy. Go home. I won't need you this evening."

The servant protested. She did not want to leave her employer alone with Bowman. It took Reeves a few minutes to lead her to the door. Outside, the sun was setting, turning the Thames yellow and splashing golden reflections on the hulls of the boats. Reeves took a bottle of whisky and two glasses from a sideboard and placed them on the coffee table. He poured a glass for Bowman, who raised it. The old man stared at his severed fingers.

"Help yourself to more, Sergeant, please. I heard rumours about that horrible story, but why have you come to speak with me about it?"

Sergeant Bowman poured himself a second glass. This was perhaps the best whisky he had ever tasted, but it was no stronger than ordinary tavern gin and he needed more alcohol to calm down.

"I'm a policeman now, in Wapping. I have to find the murderer. My colleagues think it was me, and they'll frame me for it if they get half a chance."

"What are you talking about?"

"I found the corpse in the sewer. They think I'm mad. I'm not mad. It's just . . . it's just the nightmares. Since we got back to England, it's been better. But I don't sleep well at night, Captain."

"What nightmares, Sergeant?"

"The forest. What they did to us."

"I don't understand. You have to tell me why you're here. Sergeant?"

Bowman was silent for a moment. He pulled on his shirt collar because it was making it hard for him to breathe and the top button went flying.

"We came back, ten of Wright's men. The murderer is one of the prisoners who was with me. I gave the list to the superintendent, but the Company said there was no mission, that we did not exist. And now the Company doesn't exist. You understand?"

"You're looking for a former prisoner?"

"The murderer."

Captain Reeves smiled to encourage Bowman and took a sip of his whisky, which he hadn't touched up to now.

"Tell me."

Bowman finished his glass, and turned towards the windows and the almost black Thames.

"When we boarded the junk, we went up the Irrawaddy to intercept Min's ambassador. The monsoon began and we ran aground on the bank. We didn't see them arrive. We fought against the first boat . . ."

Reeves listened to Sergeant Bowman's story for an hour, sunk deep in his armchair, without interrupting or making the slightest movement. Bowman told him everything. How the boats carrying Min's prisoners, those starving ghosts, entered the port in Rangoon. Their repatriation to Madras. Then what happened to Bowman afterwards – becoming a Company copper in Wapping, the discovery of the corpse,

Andrews' visit to his room, his subterfuge at East India House, and his arrival here.

Night had fallen. Reeves got up, lit some candles, and gradually light returned to the room again. The bottle was empty. The old captain lit a match and brought it up to his pipe. His tired face was illuminated, his eyes replaced for a moment by the reflection of the flame in his glasses.

"I have nightmares too, Sergeant Bowman."

"What?"

"The village, Sergeant. The women and children."

The light of the candles danced on the paintings that hung on the wall. The *Sea Runner*, in Reeves' living room, was the same colour it had been that night, under the cloud of cinders.

"It was war, Captain. Orders. We had to . . ."

"What war, Sergeant?"

"Against Pagan. The ambassador . . ."

"The rubies."

"Huh?"

The old man let his head fall backwards. He looked tiny in his large armchair.

"What happened to you had nothing to do with the war. Not Dalhousie's war, anyway. It wasn't the Company who sent you up that river – it was some of the fleet's officers, Cavendish and a few of his friends. Of whom I was one."

Bowman's shoulders trembled under his uniform. He stared at the windows, which now revealed nothing but the flickering candlelight, and tried to see what might lie beyond the glass. Reeves' voice, shaky with age and fatigue, spoke slowly:

"Wright was a Company spy. A brave man, but above all an ambitious man, who became close to Cavendish's inner circle. His mission was to draw up a list of Pagan Min's forces before Dalhousie's declaration of war. As he was seeking this information, he found out that the king was already preparing for defeat, well aware as he was that he could not defeat the Company. If war broke out, his plan was to flee, and take his treasure with him. Do you know Mogok, Sergeant? It's a small town of no interest, about fifteen miles from Ava, in the middle of the jungle. But it also has the best ruby mines in the world. When Bombay declared war on the kingdom of Ava, Pagan filled chests with those jewels and sent them by boat up the river, so he could safeguard them before he fled. Wright told Cavendish what he had discovered. Together, with the help of other trusted officers, they decided to mount that expedition. In the middle of the war. That's why you were chosen, Sergeant, you and the dregs of the fleet who were waiting to be sentenced. There was no ambassador aboard those junks, only rubies. Burning the village and its inhabitants was not a Company order, it was a precaution to ensure our plan remained secret. Your superintendent did not lie to you: that mission never existed. Despite our precautions, the Company's managers ended up discovering what we had done. It put them in a difficult position. There was no question of allowing the news to break: they could not let the future Duke of Devonshire be seen as a brigand, a sordid jewel thief. Thanks to the patronage of Cavendish, we were protected. The Company suppressed the affair for us – much more effectively this time. While the loss of Captain Wright was regrettable, no-one cared about the disappearance of a bunch of criminals and a few soldiers. You could spend years searching for it, but you will never find any record of your mission in East India House. And now that the Company no longer exists, the Crown will take charge of everything. Our secret is safe."

Reeves took a drag on his pipe, but it had gone out and he sucked in only air.

"It's rather ironic, but in fact it was Wright's death that saved you. If the mission had been a success and you hadn't been taken prisoner, you would have been executed upon your return."

Bowman got up from his chair and staggered, knocking the candlestick from the coffee table. Reeves did not react. The dead pipe hung from his lips. The candles began to burn the varnish on the wood. Bowman went over to the sideboard and took out a bottle without looking to see what it was. He tore out the cork and drank some sweet, strong port from the bottle. It burned his throat and made him even thirstier. He dropped the bottle, which rolled across the floorboards and came to a halt next to an armchair.

Ship's lanterns, hung in the rigging, passed outside the window of the solarium. The sound of a steam engine reached them and made the windowpanes shake. Reeves stood up, left the room and returned a moment later. He put a sheet of paper, an inkwell and a pen on the coffee table, then relit the candles.

"I'm listening, Sergeant."

Bowman's voice was mournful:

"What do you want me to tell you?"

"The list, Sergeant Bowman. Give me their names. I'll find them all for you."

"Why would you do that?"

"There will not be any truth, Sergeant. There will never be any truth. But it's . . . a sort of duty."

"A duty?"

"That man who committed murder in the sewers, he has to know. You must find him, Sergeant Bowman."

"I don't know what you're talking about. That's not how it has to be. There's no point explaining anything to the man who did that. He has to be killed."

Reeves smiled and Bowman wanted to smash his head against the sheet of paper.

"I hope you'll have time to understand before, Sergeant. Now, give me their names."

Bowman unbuttoned his uniform jacket and his shirt, and began, his face gaunt in the candlelight, to slowly recite the names, as if each letter was part of a face that he was remembering.

The old man had drained his memory. Bowman could barely stand straight, and Reeves had to lead him by the arm, taking small steps, a candlestick in one hand, to the front door. The old captain asked him to wait there for a moment, then put the candlestick on the sideboard in the entrance hall and disappeared. He returned from the living room and stopped six feet from Bowman. He took off his glasses, slipped them in a pocket and stood facing the sergeant, who was pointing the pistol at his chest.

"You deserve your nightmares. We don't. You're scum."

"There's nothing you can do about that, Sergeant. You are who you are, now. The only choice you have – you said it to me yourself – is to find your old comrade. You can kill me later if you still feel the need."

"It's too easy."

"Yes."

The old man raised his hand. He was holding a scrap of those coloured cloths that Bowman kept in Madras, made by the village weavers. Reeves unfolded the cloth. The mother-of-pearl and the inlaid silver sparkled in the candlelight. Bowman slowly put down the pistol and opened his hands. Captain Reeves put the powder horn into them.

"I never thought you would come back for it, but I kept it all the same. I didn't forget you, Sergeant."

Bowman gazed at the horn, caressing the mother-of-pearl with his fingertips.

"Come back in a week. I'll have found your men."

Bowman walked through the garden, stopped at the pavement and looked around him. The street was empty: no passers-by, no lights. He crossed Grosvenor Road and disappeared under the black trees of St George's Fields, holding the powder horn close to his belly.

5

Bowman drank alcohol and took laudanum until he lost track of the days. Curled up in a ball on his bed, he watched the bits of iridescent shells change colour in the light, caressed the silver inlays, opened the watertight leather lid and held the horn to his ear so he could listen to what it had to say. He told it everything that had happened to him since their separation, apologised for having abandoned it on that boat, reassured it that everything would be fine now they were back together.

Bowman waited for it to respond. As the horn remained silent, he continued speaking to it.

He sent the landlady out to buy him drugs, while outside on the street, Andrews' men took turns to guard him. Beneath the floorboards, the chest was almost empty: he had spent most of his savings.

"Why should I be the one to find their killer, eh? Why don't they deal with it? They're the ones who sent us there. Leave them be. All ten of them! They should leave us be or do it themselves."

The neighbours came to knock at the door when he started shouting to his horn. Bowman screamed at them and scared them away. The coppers who guarded him did not intervene. Bowman was mad, there was no doubt about that now.

He woke up and did not recognise his room. He fell asleep thinking he was on the junk, in a hammock on the *Healing Joy*, or in his cage in the middle of the forest.

"It wasn't the war. They sent us there for rubies. We had no powder or ammunition left when the other junks arrived. I kept fighting, but there was no point: there were too many of them. I tried to cut the hawsers, so we could drift away in the current, but it was too late for that. Back then, I didn't know why I was fighting. I know now. I know why we were kept for months inside those cages."

He spent his days looking out of the window. The women coming out of the shops, the Wapping guards who accosted them, the children carrying buckets of water on their heads, the grinders with their millstones that sent sparks flying when blades touched them, the open door of a forge and the sound of hammers on anvils.

"With a horn like this, I could throw myself in the Thames without getting my powder wet."

He laughed sometimes too.

When he had finished a bottle of laudanum, he saw Burmese fishermen in their baggy trousers out on Fletcher Street, Company officers in full uniform parading past along the pavements, four-masted ships with their portholes open moving up the train tracks on Cable Street.

With the horn to his ear, he listened to the sound of the sea muffled by rubber-tree resin.

"Can't you hear the screams? That's Clements, when they burned his ear. And Peavish, the first time they took him away. Can't you hear them?"

Ten days had passed. Bowman had forgotten all about Reeves when, one morning, his forehead glued to the window, a spectator to the life of the street three storeys below, emerging from a nap that he'd begun either last night or five minutes ago or two days before, he saw a carriage stop outside his building. A man in a long coat and a top hat descended from it. Some children went up to the horse, a handsome beast, and the driver cracked his whip over their heads. The children scarpered. The man in black was no longer there.

"That one was an executioner. I recognise them."

There was a knock at the door.

"Piss off! Leave me alone!"

Another knock, and then he heard a voice on the landing.

"Sergeant Bowman?"

He walked across the room, opened the door and staggered backwards.

Captain Reeves, in his long black coat and his shiny hat, walked past him like a ghost, the folds in his clothes unmoving, his footsteps making no noise. The captain looked pale and drawn, a hundred years older than when Bowman had gone to visit him.

Reeves dropped an envelope on the table, in the middle of some bottles, and turned around. When he stopped in front of him, Bowman sniggered.

"Get fucked. Why don't you just find him yourself, that whoreson you sent to the river?"

He spat in Reeves' face. The old man wiped his eyes with a gloved hand.

"Unfortunately for you, Bowman, you survived things a normal man would not have borne. You should have killed yourself a long time ago, but if you haven't, that's because there is something stronger in you than what you suffered. It is now up to you to choose what you will do in order to keep surviving. Remember that the man you are looking for is like you, but that he is perhaps not as strong as you."

Reeves put his hand on Bowman's shoulder.

"I am sorry, Sergeant, for what happened to you. To you and your men."

Bowman shoved his hand away. The old man lowered his head, concealing his face under the brim of his hat, and left the room. Bowman caught him on the landing and shouted:

"I tried to die and someone saved me! Why did I have to be saved, eh? What does that mean?"

Reeves turned around in the stairwell, his hand on the banister, face still hidden beneath his hat.

"That your life no longer belongs entirely to you, Sergeant Bowman. You should leave here as soon as possible. I couldn't obtain this list without people finding out. It won't be long before they're here. Farewell, Bowman."

Reeves walked down the stairs. Bowman remained on the landing until the sound of footsteps faded to silence. He went back to his room, grabbed the envelope and tore it open. He took out a sheet of paper, saw some neatly written words, and from the folds of the letter fell five ten-pound notes. A year's pay at the Thames Brigade.

He dropped the list of names and addresses so he could pick up the cash, and a second sheet fell to the floor. Bowman knelt down and retrieved the document. A bank's insignia and address. A bearer bond in his name, to the sum of five hundred pounds.

Bowman rushed over to the window and opened it. The carriage was rounding the street corner. He turned around when he heard sounds coming from the other side. Five Wapping coppers, led by O'Reilly and Superintendent Andrews, were walking along Fletcher Street towards his building. For a few seconds, Bowman watched them, incapable of moving. Then he ran to his sink, shoved the three fingers of his left hand down his throat and puked his guts out. The adrenaline that was running through his bloodstream sharpened his mind and his eyes. He didn't even put on his shoes, just put the money and the list, the bond and the powder horn into his pockets, then went out on to the landing and pulled himself up through the skylight. He crawled over the ridge of the roof to the neighbouring building. Then, his feet bleeding, he ran through back-alleys, stopping at every corner to make sure that no other coppers were waiting for him. Keeping a wide berth around his district, Bowman crossed through China Court, his lungs on fire, and ran ever faster eastward towards Limehouse.

He didn't stop until he reached the hut, his whole body cramping. With a shoulder barge, he smashed the door open and rushed inside. After running two miles without slowing down, his body refused to go any further and he collapsed on the earth floor. His stomach heaved as his mouth opened wide, gasping for air, and his head felt as if there were a leather strap being tightened around it, crushing his skull.

—⁂—

He lit a fire in the stove. Wedged against some crates, Bowman struggled to stay awake. When he opened his eyes, night had fallen. He didn't have time to get up – his body was too stiff and aching for him to move. The door opened and two men entered. One of them held an oil lamp, the other a bludgeon. Bowman lifted one hand to protect his eyes from the light and with the other he fumbled in the darkness until his fingers touched an iron bar, which he held up to defend himself.

"Shit!"

"What's he doing there?"

"Don't come any closer," Bowman warned them.

"Bloody hell, Sergeant! It's us. You scared the shit out of us."

Bowman recognised the fisherman's face.

"Frank?"

"Jesus, who did you think it was? What are you doing here?"

The fisherman saw Bowman's clothes and laughed.

"Where did you find these old rags?"

The other fisherman had remained standing at the door, the club still in his hand.

"This bloke's dodgy, I told you before. We should get rid of him."

"He won't give us any problems. Will you, Sergeant?"

Bowman looked at the two men.

"I won't make any trouble. I just need a roof. Not for long."

"I told you before: this is your home. What happened to you this time?"

The other fisherman put his hand on Frank's shoulder.

"Frankie, you shouldn't. You'll end up in deep shit. And this time, I won't help you."

"I'll take care of this. You go home."

Frank's colleague took one last look at Bowman, then left the hut and closed the door behind him.

"Don't worry. Stevens is always like that. He's not very trusting, but he won't make any trouble either. I know him."

The fisherman hung the lamp to a ceiling beam.

"Are you going to let go of that iron bar?"

Bowman put the piece of metal back on the floor.

"I won't stay long. Just a few days. I've got money."

Bowman took a ten-pound note from his pocket. Frank whistled with surprise.

"Shit. How did you get all that money? Oh, Sergeant, maybe my mate was right . . . How can you be on the street with that much cash in your pockets? What have you done?"

"It's my money. I didn't steal it."

"This isn't about money. What I want to know is, why have you come back? And don't give me any rubbish."

Bowman crumpled the banknote and put it back in his pocket.

"The coppers are after me."

"What have you done?"

"Nothing."

"Oh, really?"

"They think I've killed someone."

"Have you killed someone, Sergeant?"

Bowman lowered his head.

"I killed dozens of people when I was a soldier. Women, old people and children. But I didn't kill this one."

Frank pulled the little bottle of hooch from his pocket and drank half of it without stopping for breath. He wiped his lips and put the bottle on a crate next to Bowman.

"Well, I didn't think you'd spent fifteen years in India just counting sheep, Sergeant, but what difference does that make, what you're telling me?"

Bowman picked up the bottle.

"The killer, the other one . . . I have to find him. You won't have any problems with me, but I need your help. I'll pay you. I've got more money. Enough."

"You have to tell me more, 'cos otherwise you've already told me too much."

"I didn't kill that man."

"You're not going to go crazy and attack someone, are you, Arthur? Or throw yourself in the river again?"

"I have to find that man."

6

The first name on the list was Edmund Peavish. The preacher. With an address in Plymouth.

Bowman dipped his pen in the inkwell and put crosses next to four addresses. Four of his former men, out of the nine, lived in or near London. Peter Clements and Christian Bufford, known as Buffalo, recruited by Bowman on the *Joy*. Frederick Collins, the corporal with the knife, and Erik Penders, the one who wanted to escape – both of them Wright's men. John Briggs, another man from the *Joy*, lived in Bristol. Norton Young, one of Wright's recruits, lived in Southampton; Edward Morgan and Horace Greenshaw, two of Bowman's soldiers, in Birmingham and Coventry. Most of the entries were followed by the words "Last known address". Still ghosts, all of them, as on the Rangoon list when they had been liberated.

The addresses in London could be the most likely, though really he had no idea. Just because he hadn't moved for years didn't mean that the others didn't travel. They had to live. Move to wherever they could find work.

Squinting at another piece of paper, he copied down Peter Clements' address. 16 Lamb Street, in Spitalfields.

Then he opened the door of the red-hot stove and threw his old Company uniform inside.

Standing in front of a shard of broken mirror placed on the shelf, he shaved his beard, washed himself in a bucket and put on the new clothes that he'd asked Frank to buy for him. High-quality shoes, a pair of wool trousers, solid and comfortable, a shirt, a herringbone tweed jacket, a leather cap lined with soft wool, and some underwear.

Bowman had not been this well-dressed since they gave him his first soldier's uniform. He hadn't worn clothes that actually fitted him for a long time either. He couldn't see this in the little mirror, but the fact of wearing a new suit made him stand a little straighter.

He slipped a flask of gin into the jacket's inside pocket, put the cap on his head, and walked away from Dunbar, heading towards the north of the city. A cold wind blew and Bowman pulled up the collar of his jacket. On Commercial Street, he asked a passer-by for directions. Like many inhabitants of the East End, Bowman didn't really know his way around the rest of London, just a few names he'd heard people mention, including Spitalfields Market, which he reached one hour after leaving the hut.

He walked through the market, with its silk boutiques and its weavers' workshops. Half of the stalls sold imported Indian cotton. At the corner of Commercial Street and Lamb Street, he unfolded his sheet of paper and checked Peter Clements' address.

Spitalfields had been a refuge for Protestant weavers fleeing France. The whole area was devoted to fabrics, and trade had boomed until the market was invaded by Indian products. The people who Bowman had, ever since he was a child, heard referred to as "the Silkers", were a bunch of poor beggars, of no higher standing than those from the East End.

The brick buildings on Lamb Street were all occupied by shops with storefront windows on the ground floor, with run-down apartments above them. The street swarmed with carriages and porters, sellers and beggars, who clung to his legs. Bowman pushed them away without understanding what they wanted. He was not yet used to his new clothes or to the reactions they provoked. People moved out of his way and greeted him politely.

He stood for a moment on the pavement facing number 16. The door leading upstairs was in a narrow gap between two shop fronts, its door gaping open, without a bolt or a handle. On the first floor, he chose a flat at random. A fat woman opened the door and took a step backwards. A man dressed like him, knocking at the door . . . It had to be bad news. Bowman asked where Peter Clements lived and the woman appeared relieved that misfortune had simply got the wrong floor.

"The Clementses? They're on the second floor, on the left. Are they in trouble?"

Bowman went up to the next floor and stopped outside the door. Sweat dripped under his armpits and his arms moved, fists tightening on emptiness, searching for a weapon that wasn't there. Earlier, they had just been names on a scrap of paper; now he was standing at this door. Peter Clements might be inside. The strongest of all the men who had boarded the *Sea Runner*.

Bowman knocked and bent his knees, ready to bolt. A girl of about ten opened, a skinny little thing, in a patched-up pair of overalls. Her blonde hair was as pale as her face, her fingers brown with dye; she had worker's hands, incongruous at the end of those spindly little-girl arms. She looked at the well-dressed man, her eyes too tired to express the slightest surprise, and Bowman lost his composure. So even ghosts had children . . .

"Peter Clements?"

The girl left the door open and trudged back into the apartment.

In the narrow entrance hall, Bowman saw a tall, stooped figure. Peter Clements stopped at the threshold. He had the same white-blond hair as his daughter, and his right eye was deformed by scars, the cornea whitened and swollen by hot metal. The eyelid was stuck to the arch of the eyebrow and did not move at all.

"Sergeant?"

Bowman had not imagined that Clements would recognise him – in these clothes, without his uniform, but particularly in his emaciated state. He realised that, for the men on the list, Bowman would always be a skeletal figure trapped in a cage. That the only man to retain a memory of the old, strong Sergeant Arthur Bowman was he himself.

"Sir? Is that really you?"

Clements' lips trembled. His right eye began to shine.

"You're alive?"

The sergeant stood before him, but Clements asked him the question anyway. A succession of emotions appeared and then mingled on his face. When he smiled, his forehead wrinkled with pain; when his eyes lit up with happiness, the corners of his mouth fell and his chin began to quiver.

"Say something, Sergeant. Please."

"It's me, Clements."

"What are you . . . what are you doing here?"

"Looking for you."

"Me, Sergeant?"

"And the others."

"The others?"

"The ones from over there."

"They're alive too?"

Bowman loosened his lips and swallowed some air.

"I don't know."

Clements lowered his head.

"He doesn't know."

"I have to talk to you, Clements."

"What?"

Clements put his hand through his hair and lifted his head.

"What do you want to tell me?"

"Not here."

"Do you want to come in?"

He withdrew into the room without taking his eyes from Bowman's face.

"Come in, Sergeant. Come inside, if you need to talk to me."

The cap reduced his field of vision; Bowman took it off and put it in his pocket before following him. Clements had lost weight. He even looked less tall, with his stooped, humped back, which Bowman followed into the little kitchen. The room was six feet square, with a stove next to the open window, a saucepan warming on it. Clements' daughter stirred the contents with a spoon, and a smell of porridge filled the air. Clements grabbed a bottle from a shelf.

"You want a drink, Sergeant?"

The old soldier was still looking at him doubtfully. Bowman turned to the little girl, then to her father.

"Tell her to leave, Clements."

Peter Clements looked startled and then sad. He leaned his head sideways as he looked at the sergeant.

"Why should she leave, sir?"

"Do as I say."

Clements gently spoke to his daughter.

"May, go out for a walk, would you? I have to speak to the sergeant. You understand? You have to leave us alone."

The girl observed the man in his new clothes, let go of the spoon, and left the kitchen.

There was no chair or table in the kitchen; through the door to the living room, the only other room in the apartment, Bowman saw two beds pushed close together, mattresses lying on the floor, rumpled blankets and a pile of clothes.

Clements took a gulp from the bottle, forgetting to offer some to the sergeant.

"She's gone. You're right, Sergeant. It's better if it's just the two of us."

He drank again. His limbs moved jerkily, as if his joints had been broken, as if his arms and legs moved from position to position like a rusted piece of machinery.

"I always wondered if you were alive. And the others? I haven't looked for them, Sergeant. I mean, I wanted to, but I didn't know how to go about it, where they lived."

Clements' voice grew more emotional, his nervousness increased, but the strangest thing was that he didn't seem to be speaking to Bowman at all; as if he were in the habit of talking to people who weren't there.

"Why didn't you want my daughter to hear what we're talking about, Sergeant? My wife and my son are at work. I don't have a job at the moment. It's difficult. How did you find me, Sergeant? It's . . . it's good to see you. Really. You're here and I don't have to imagine it. You understand? Because it's hard to imagine. When I think about it, I feel so bad. I can't talk about it. It's not a nice thing and I don't want my children to hear that. That's why it's better for her to leave, my little May. So she doesn't hear. My wife and my children, they get woken up at night when I think about it in my dreams. They don't understand."

Clements advanced towards Bowman. He leaned forward so the sergeant could hear him, his face drawn with the fear that he would not be understood or that his interlocutor might suddenly disappear.

"I had trouble working when I got back. They offered me my old job back at the slaughterhouse, where I worked before I went to India. My son was three years old back then, and the little 'un had just been born. They were eight and five when I returned to England. The pension isn't really enough to live on, and I couldn't work in the slaughterhouse anymore. I just couldn't. I tried, because we needed the money, but it made me sick to my stomach. I just kept puking. So they gave me the sack and I looked elsewhere. My son started working and my wife and the little 'un too. We get by, just about, but it's better when I can find a job from time to time. But there are so many things I can't do. Because of the headaches, and sometimes the fatigue that comes over me. I shake all over and bite my tongue. The others don't want to work with me anymore, because I never know when it's going to happen. So I keep getting sacked. It's not that I lack courage, I just have no strength left. You see, Sergeant?"

For a moment, he seemed unable to speak or move. His burned eye stared straight ahead, the other down at the floor.

"I try, Sergeant. Every day, I go out to look for work, sometimes pretty far – into the countryside, so I can work in the fields during harvest time. But it means leaving my family behind. I don't like to leave them alone. I don't like being alone, Sergeant. It never lasts long, though. Because of the pains that make me collapse, and when I wake up I don't know where I am."

Bowman could no longer bear to look at Clements' deformed face. In a single breath, he asked:

"Have you tried working in the sewers?"

Clements did not react, continuing in the same dejected tone:

"I can't. I wanted to. I asked, and even during the stink, that horrible time, I asked the sewer workers, but it was that smell, Sergeant, the smell of shit, like, like . . . in the c–c . . ."

He could not get the word out. He stammered as he tried to talk about the cage. His whole body started to shake and he almost yelled as he moved towards Bowman:

"The shit, it's like . . . my smell, over there."

Bowman thought that Clements was about to collapse at his feet in the kitchen and have one of his fits.

"You don't understand, Sergeant. It's as if I fear that I can't stop, finding myself back there . . . You, you're not afraid. You were never afraid. On the river, and then, there, afterwards. You don't know what fear is."

Bowman retreated towards the entrance hall.

"I have to go, Clements."

The former soldier stopped talking and suddenly looked terribly sad.

"I understand. You have things to do. You look like you're doing well – you're nicely dressed, you must have a job. You have a family waiting for you, Sergeant, and you have to look after them. I understand. When you're alive, you have to do those things – look after your family and work."

A smile lit up his face under the burned eye, the gaze fixed and milky next to the sad, living eye.

"I'm glad that you're here."

Bowman was at the door.

"You're leaving already?"

Bowman rummaged through his pockets and took out a one-guinea coin, which he handed to Clements.

"Oh! No, Sergeant. There's no need, I'll be fine, it's nothing, just a tricky moment, but it'll pass. You don't have to worry about me. Even if it's nothing to you, because I can tell you must have a good job."

Clements tried to push away the coin, but in the same movement he caught hold of Bowman's hand.

"For the girl, Clements. So you can buy her something. For your children. I have to go now."

"That's very good of you, Sergeant. Very good. But you must come back to see me and we can talk some more. My wife'll make us a nice meal and you'll stay longer next time, alright?"

Bowman withdrew onto the landing. Clements still hadn't let go of his hand.

"We could also visit you, Sergeant, and your wife could talk with mine, and your children could meet mine. Like friends. We hardly ever go out, you know how it is, but we could come and see you if you don't live too far away. Where do you live, Sergeant? In Westminster, next to the park, I bet! We could go for a walk there. The children would love that. With what you've given me, I could buy them some nicer clothes, and a pastry to eat in the park. Is that where you live, Sergeant? Am I right?"

"I have to go, Clements."

The former soldier released Bowman's hand, and tears rolled from his eye.

"Thank you, Sergeant. Thank you for coming. And this money – I don't need it, I'll be fine, but it's so kind of you. You're taking care of me. Like you did over there, eh? You haven't forgotten us, have you, Sergeant? You're coming to find us, aren't you? To take care of us?"

Bowman descended the first step on the staircase. Clements' voice was getting louder and louder.

"How you looked after us over there! You're right, Sergeant – it's better that my daughter isn't here to hear us. How you looked after us, with the little boy, when you put the knife to his throat! It was so we'd understand, wasn't it, Sergeant? That's right, isn't it?"

Bowman moved away from him without turning his back, holding on to the banister and walking backwards down the stairs. Peter Clements yelled:

"So we'd understand what it is to survive! Eh, Sergeant? That not everyone would get out alive and that we had to follow your orders! Bowman's orders! So we wouldn't die in the jungle! So we could go home! We had to kill the monkeys, Bowman! Kill them all and come home!"

Bowman hurtled downstairs.

Clements' yells pursued him all the way to the ground floor.

"We were afraid, Sergeant! You don't know what that is! But we came back! You're going to come back to see me, Sergeant! Are you going to come back?"

Bowman slammed the door of the building behind him and stopped on the pavement, where he drained half of his flask of gin. On the pavement opposite, in her patchwork overalls, with her gaunt, exhausted face, Clements' daughters watched him. The child continued to stare at him, a pale, filthy, little ghost straight from one of her father's nightmares. Bowman wiped his mouth and walked away from Lamb Street.

By the time he got back to the hut, night had fallen. He took off the jacket, unbuttoned the shirt, and threw himself at the supplies that Frank had brought him. He pushed away the food and uncorked a bottle of Gordon's.

7

The last known address for Private Buffalo – Christian Bufford – was near Walworth.

Bowman got dressed, discreetly left the cabin and wove his way between the warehouses of Dunbar. He took a series of back alleys through Wapping, making a detour to avoid the docks and the streets patrolled by Andrews' men, then turned towards the Thames and crossed London Bridge. He found himself on the south bank, in the broad streets of Southwark, and stopped outside a shop window displaying headless mannequins wearing hunting outfits. Inside were other mannequins, leather and oilcloth jackets on crossbars, fox-hunting uniforms, riding boots, rifles hanging on wall racks and a collection of daggers behind a window. The shopkeeper let him walk alone around all these items, while he took down weapons to show to a gentleman in a coat. The man held the rifles one after another and, legs slightly apart, eye glued to the sights, turned in a circular movement, aiming the gun all around the store. Startled by the sight of the rifle's double barrels pointed at him, Bowman bent down and hid behind a display case of shoes. The aristocrat laughed and lowered his weapon.

"Don't worry, it's not loaded!"

The shopkeeper laughed too. Bowman stood up, grimacing as he tried to smile, and an assistant approached him.

"How can I help you?"

Bowman pointed to a dagger behind glass, a straight blade with a false edge, about eight inches longer.

"This one."

"A very good model. We have some slightly less expensive straight blades of equal quality, sir, if you prefer . . ."

"This one."

The assistant opened the glass case and showed Bowman the knife.

"The handle is cherrywood, the guard and pommel are nickel silver, and the blade is tempered steel. The knife is from one of the best armouries in the country, and the engravings were made by a master craftsman in London."

Before handing him the knife, the assistant said:

"This prestige weapon costs six pounds sterling, sir."

The handle was just the right size for his right hand. Bowman passed it to his left hand. Even with two fingers missing, he had no problem holding the knife, which was light for a dagger of this size, nicely balanced and with a perfect edge.

"I'll need the sheath too."

The assistant remained suspicious until Bowman took ten pounds in coins from his pocket.

Bowman put the weapon in his belt and looked at the racks of rifles.

"That last one the gentleman was trying . . . can I see that?"

The assistant took down a rifle and showed it to him.

"This weapon, sir?"

"What is it?"

"I beg your pardon?"

"I don't know this model."

"It's new. An American rifle."

Bowman took it in his hands. It weighed almost nothing.

"How does it work?"

He handed it back to the salesman who put a box of ammunition in front of Bowman and gave him a demonstration. The bullets were copper, about an inch and a half long, finished with a lead point. Bowman turned one between his fingers.

"The bullets are central percussion, coated with a copper sheath. The primer, the charge and the bullet are assembled. You load it like this."

The assistant moved the lever, positioned under the butt, half cocked the hammer, slid the barrels forward and pushed the cartridge into the chamber in less than three seconds.

"What kind of range does it have?"

"With a .44 calibre, you can hunt small game. At a hundred and fifty feet, the accuracy is excellent. It will go through a half-inch plank from up to sixty feet. It does not have a very long range, but this new technology is proving very popular. The ammunition too is imported from the United States by the Wesson company."

The assistant gave the rifle back to Bowman. He lifted it, leaning the butt against his shoulder, and pressed his cheek to the wood. Through the sights, he aimed at a headless mannequin dressed in fox-hunting gear: red jacket and white breeches.

"Is sir interested? You may try the weapon if you like."

Bowman did not move, the barrel remaining aimed at the manne-quin's red torso. The rifle was loaded. His index finger stroked the trigger.

"Sir?"

As he stared at the jacket, the target blurred and his eyes stung. He opened his fingers: the sweat left damp traces on the wood.

"No need."

When he left the shop, his hands were still trembling. He saw Bufford again, on the *Joy*, when he'd tried to cut open Peavish's belly. The presence of the dagger against his hip reassured him a little bit. All the men on the list might be as mad as Clements, but they wouldn't all be as skinny. Bufford was dangerous. Bowman tightened his maimed hand around the knife's handle.

When he found Searles Street, he thought to himself that he must have made a mistake; that he must have misread the address or got the wrong district. The address was that of the largest house on the street. A garden behind ten-feet-high railings, a forged-iron gate, ten windows on every floor, with curtains, flowers climbing up the façade of the building, six huge chimneys, sculpted stone bondings, a front door that was wider than Frank's hut, and, along the side of the house, a drive-way, sealed off by another gate leading to the carriage door.

Bowman crossed the street, paused for a moment outside the gates, hesitant, frustrated, then left again. Passing the carriage gate, he saw a boy in an apron, holding a pail and shovel, scooping up dung from the cobbles. Bowman looked around him and whistled to the stable boy.

"You there! Is this Christian Bufford's house?"

"What?"

"Bufford."

The child, from the other side of the railings, looked suspiciously at Bowman, who took twopence from his pocket.

"There's only his wife."

"His wife? She lives here?"

The boy turned towards the house, then back to Bowman.

"Well, yes."

"I have to see her."

The boy frowned.

"You can't, sir."

Bowman dangled two more coins in front of him.

"Go and tell her that there's a friend of her husband's outside. Someone who knew him a long time ago, in India."

The child scratched his head, took the coins and went off towards the carriage door. A few minutes later, he reappeared at the end of the driveway and, standing next to a servant in a black dress and apron, pointed to Bowman. The woman walked up to the gate.

Bowman touched his hat with his fingertips.

"I didn't mean to scare the boy. It's just that I know Mr Bufford, and I need to see him."

The servant stared at him for a moment, frowning.

"I don't know who you are, sir, but my husband is dead. Please leave."

Bowman burst out laughing as he realised his mistake.

Bufford's wife turned her back on him and began to walk away.

"Wait! I didn't know. I must talk to you."

She stopped and came back towards him.

"My husband is dead. I don't want to talk to you. I don't know who you are."

"Sergeant Bowman. I was with Bufford on the *Healing Joy*. We were together. In Burma."

The woman put a white hand on a bar of the railings.

"Bowman? Is that what you said?"

"Arthur Bowman. I was with your husband."

"I remember your name. He spoke about you."

Bufford's wife was pretty, with dark eyes and smooth skin. She looked tired but healthy, and her teeth were good. Her hair was tied in a bun.

"I have to talk to you. It won't take long."

The woman turned back towards the house.

"My master and mistress have gone out, but you mustn't stay too long."

Bowman followed the woman, watching the movements of her dress as she walked. Her hips swayed attractively under the fabric. The servants' quarters were on the other side of the house, at the end of another garden, as big as a park. A long, single-storey building, adjoining the stable. A brick cottage with five doors, with two little windows between each one. Bowman could make out figures behind the curtains, watching him and Bufford's widow as they passed.

She took a key from the pocket of her apron, opened one of the doors and told him to go inside. On top of the warm stove was a kettle. The woman made tea. The place was in perfect order. Two doors opened onto the main room. Two bedrooms. And the kitchen facing the large garden. At the back, behind the trees, a pergola was visible on a large terrace: the masters' house. If Bowman had tried to describe the woman and her home, he would have said that they were the exact opposite of Bufford, who had been dirty, coarse and brutal.

She poured the tea into a cup and placed it in front of Bowman, with a sugar bowl and a little spoon.

"I didn't know about Bufford. I didn't mean to disturb you."

"Please, don't speak too loud. You can hear everything through these walls."

Bowman looked stupidly at the wall.

"Alright."

Then he observed the woman's face again and lowered his gaze to the cup. He didn't know what to do with it.

"What happened?"

She broke down in sobs. In an instant, her pretty features grew distorted. She took a handkerchief from her sleeve and brought it to her nose.

"Elliot . . . Elliot died in June."

Realising that he hadn't taken off his cap, Bowman hastened to put it on the table.

"Elliot?"

"Our son."

"Oh . . . I didn't know about that either."

She blew her nose. And even that, Bowman thought, she did prettily.

"He was eleven. He drowned in the garden well, during that dry spell this summer. They had to open it up because there was no more running water. Christian . . . Christian was angry because he said that the well was too old and dangerous, but they needed someone small to go down there.

Not knowing what to say, Bowman drank a mouthful of tea, which he had to spit back out.

"The wall collapsed. Elliot was trapped at the bottom. Christian – and the others, everyone – we didn't know what to do. He drowned almost in front of our eyes."

Snot ran from her nose. Bowman took the flask from his pocket and offered it to the widow. She shook her head. Before putting it back, Bowman drank some.

"Christian, he couldn't get over it. He said it was his fault. He went mad. He also said it was the master's fault that Elliot was dead, for wanting water to wash in when we were dying of thirst. They hired some stonemasons to rebuild the well, and at the same time they brought his body out . . . The rats, sir. There was hardly anything left of him because of the rats."

This time she made animal-like moans, which choked her throat with sobs. Bowman wanted to stand up and leave, but she kept talking and grabbed his arm.

"You knew him, my Christian! You were there with him. You know how hard it was to come back, don't you? He wasn't like that before he went away. He always had a bit of a temper, but not like that. He said he would come back from India with money, that I wouldn't have to work here anymore, that Elliot would be able to go to school. That was why he joined the Company and left us behind. But when he returned, he had these dreams, these nightmares. And these scars, my God, what they did to him . . ."

She would not let go of Bowman's sleeve. The knife in his belt was digging into his side, but he couldn't extricate himself from her grip in order to put it back in place.

"He went mad with grief after our son's death. He was too fragile. You knew him. You understand what I'm saying, don't you?"

Bowman remembered Bufford, at his side, attacking the junk, yelling savagely, sticking his bayonet into Burmese bellies, screaming with joy in the pouring rain.

"I knew him, ma'am. A good lad."

"He couldn't bear it. With the heat and that terrible smell, he left."

Bowman leaned forward.

"Left?"

"He left us to join Elliot. You were with him in that forest, weren't you? You fought together. You know he was a good man. If he left us, it's because he couldn't bear it anymore, because it was better that way. It's a sin, to take your own life, I know. But if he chose that, it must have been the right choice. Don't you think?"

Bufford in a cage, fighting another prisoner to the death so he could steal his rice. Biting his ear and spitting the bits out. Or maybe he even swallowed them.

"It was for the best, ma'am, I'm sure it was."

"He has to be forgiven, doesn't he?"

"How did he . . . leave?"

"The simplest way, sir. To join Elliot, he took the same path."

Bowman gulped.

"The well?"

She collapsed on the table, holding Bowman's arm tight against her cheek, wiping her snotty nose and her eyes on his new jacket.

"And the rats, those vile beasts . . ."

Her fingernails dug into Bowman's arm.

"There was nothing left of my Christian either. The master and mistress refused to pay for his funeral, because it was a sin. A pauper's grave for him who'd taken care of their house for so long, their house that had already taken our son."

Suddenly she let go of him, shoved her chair back, lifted up her apron and buried her face in its white cloth. Bowman got to his feet, cap in hand. She apologised, without being able to stop sobbing. She tried to wipe Bowman's jacket with a cloth. He told her it didn't matter, took four pound notes from his pocket – his change from the purchase of the knife – and put them on the table.

"That's for Bufford and your son. For a grave. Or some other kind of monument. Whatever you want."

As with the money he'd given to Clements, the result was catastrophic. The widow collapsed again on the table and started sobbing even harder.

"Pardon me, ma'am, but Bufford . . . did he leave before or after the rain?"

The widow lifted her head. The question had interrupted her tears.

"What did you say?"

"Your husband, Bufford, did he leave before or after the bad smell ended?"

The question, rather than seeming absurd or out of place, seemed to light up something in the woman's dark eyes.

"Before. He died in the middle of that stink, sir. That's what took him away!"

Bowman thanked her and left her sitting there at the table, straight-backed, her eyes wide open and shining. He put on his cap and walked as fast as he could across the park. When he crossed London Bridge, an image came to his mind, an image that stopped him in his tracks. Maybe it was the widow with all her misfortunes and her pretty face, but his eyes were smarting. Even though he knew Bufford was a rough brute of a man, even though his wife was sending flowers to heaven when he was in hell, fighting over a bit of tripe, that image still brought tears to his eyes. It was the image of Private Buffalo, on the deck of the junk, soaked by rain, with the corpse of Feng's little slave in his arms. Bufford embracing the child's dead body as he thought of his own son on the other side of the world. Little Elliot, drowned in his masters' house.

He crossed the street, pushed through the gate and knocked at the door.

When he asked the maid – all in black, with a headscarf on her head – if he could see Captain Reeves, she broke down and started to scream that it was all his fault, that he had brought misfortune to this house and she was going to call the police. Bowman ran away through the gardens and did not slow down until he had left this posh district and returned to the port. He wondered if Reeves had croaked of old age or if the captain had, after bringing him the envelope, blown off his own head with a pistol. Bowman thought about this for a moment, as he was crossing through the tunnels of China Court in order to keep out of sight of the Wapping guards.

But, in the end, who cared? However it happened, old Reeves was now six feet underground, and he'd lived long enough anyway.

Inside the hut, he relit the stove, put a pan on top of it and threw in a slice of butter, four eggs and some lard, then put some potatoes to cook in the embers and slowly drank a few mouthfuls of wine. He ate quickly, and crossed Bufford's name off the list. Unable to sleep, Bowman put his cap back on and went out walking until he reached Dunbar Port, where he strolled along the docks, looking out at the black water and the black sky.

Another seven names still to go. Two in London, and then he would have to leave this city to find the others.

8

Bowman stirred the coffee on the stovetop. Frank came closer to the fire and rubbed his hands above it.

"It's really freezing now."

The fisherman looked around him.

"Looks like you've made yourself at home."

The hut was tidy. Bowman had piled up the crates and tools on the shelf, put the nets in a corner and spread the blankets over the floor near the stove. On another crate, the fisherman saw the inkwell, pen and papers. Bowman grabbed his jacket and threw it on top of them. Frankie blew into his hands as he stared at the long dagger hanging from the former sergeant's belt.

"How's your search going?"

Bowman filled a cup and handed it to Frank. They cut the coffee with hooch and drank it in silence.

"Well, I'd better leave you be. Need to catch the tide."

Bowman stopped him before he left.

"Don't ask. It's better that you stay out of it."

Frank smiled at him.

"You look in better shape, Sergeant."

He waved goodbye and closed the door behind him. Bowman got ready.

Collins' address was in Millwall, on the Isle of Dogs. Bowman went out of the cabin and into the cold air. He had started counting the days again. Today was September 13 and it already felt like autumn. After the summer heatwave, the temperature drop seemed very sudden.

He left Limehouse and walked to Canary Wharf, going deeper into the peninsula – West India Company territory – until he reached the construction site of the Millwall basin. Hundreds of men at work; columns of cattle pulling carts full of earth; cranes and hoists; ditches spanned by bridges on stilts, on which stood groups of engineers, looking through theodolites mounted on tripods, making calculations and shouting orders. The excavated mud was poured into the channels, where it mixed with the water pumped into the Thames and came out further downstream on the peninsula's wastelands. Navvies, covered with mud, standing knee-deep in earth, pushed the waste from the building site away from the mouths of the pipes, where black water poured in a continuous flood. The port was hundreds of yards long, its dimensions equalled by the number of men bent over their shovels and pickaxes. The Port of London was constantly growing and, as during the construction of St Katharine's Dock, the houses in the area had been razed to the ground to make space for the Company's plans, pushing the dockers and their families to its edges, all crammed into the overcrowded little buildings on the docks.

Bowman crossed the building site, watching the labourers slave away, and without realising what he was doing, he began to study their faces, wondering if Collins was somewhere among them, digging in the mud. He saw flour mills along the shore and the masts of boats in dock, where they were unloading their cargos of corn and wheat. He walked along the bank, keeping his distance from the workers and the noise of the steam pumps. He went past the shipyards. In the large holds, on the loading ramps, half-built ships and the same muffled sounds, the shouting of men mixed with hammer blows and the grating of saws. He passed between mountains of wood, piles of planks and beams higher than houses, vast hoists and men pulling on chains, squinting in the clouds of sawdust raised by the wind. When he was a child, the Isle of Dogs had been a place full of farms and fields, the closest countryside to Wapping, where Bowman would sometimes go to steal fruit and vegetables.

He continued walking through the narrow parallel streets of Millwall, each named after the docks to which they went. Ferry Street.

Empire Wharf Road. Caledonian Wharf. Mariners Mews. Glenaffric Avenue.

In Sextant Avenue, a few houses were built of brick, but most of the buildings were wooden. Extra floors and extensions, recently built, added on to the older, shaky constructions. These shacks only seemed to stay up by leaning on each other. Bowman stopped outside the building whose address he had noted. An old man opened the door, chewing like a cow, his toothless jaws rubbing together. He had a thick Cockney accent, rendered even more incomprehensible by his lizard's mouth.

"Collins?"

The old man spat on the front steps of his house.

"I ain't seen that piece of shit in months! Don't even want to know where he is! Just look round the pubs in the port. If he ain't in prison, that's where he'll be!"

The old man swore and slammed the door in Bowman's face. The former sergeant headed towards the docks. At the end of the streets, each block of houses ended with a few shops, at least half of which were taverns. Some of these were nothing more than a door with a little sign above it or even just some letters painted on the walls.

He entered one of these pubs at random, one of the largest. It was, like the rest of the area, practically empty. A few drunkards and old men sat in front of pints of stale beer, pushing their pieces around a draughts board or holding some worn, old playing cards in their twisted fingers. Bowman ordered a beer and waited for the barman to get used to his presence before he asked his question:

"Collins?"

As with the old man in Sextant Avenue, the name did not provoke much enthusiasm.

"What do you want with him?"

"Nothing. I'm just looking for him."

"Looking for Collins? I'm not sure that's a good idea. Anyway, you won't find him in here. He's banned. I haven't seen him for months."

"Is he still in the area?"

"Could be."

"Any place round here where he's not banned?"

"No idea. Try the Greenland. Maybe those bloody Irish still serve him."

"Where's that?"

"Follow the gutter. You'll find it."

Of all the pubs he had seen, the Greenland had the narrowest façade and the most rotten door, painted green like the name of the establishment.

He went through a dark corridor, reluctantly breathing in the odours of piss, cold tobacco and beer-soaked floorboards. The room was badly lit, too. At the back, two windows offered a view of brick walls and a little interior courtyard that never saw the sun. A few candles on the tables, an oil lamp hung from a beam, another on the wall behind the bar.

Collins had not lost weight. As if he had wanted Bowman to find him easily, he was sitting with his back to one of the windows, in the sole ray of natural light in the entire pub. At his table, three men sat with him, with dockers' arms and shoulders. Two other tables were occupied by card-players. The Greenland was a gambling den. The men were playing faro. Coins were spread out in front of them, with a few banknotes tucked under pint glasses. They played for tobacco, too; one of the men had even bet his pipe. Two customers were drinking at the bar, one at each end, their backs turned to the room. The barman, arms crossed over his chest, was looking over at the tables. At Collins' table in particular. So were the other players, over their shoulders.

Bowman approached the bar. One of the men next to him drank a mouthful of beer and muttered into his glass:

"He's pissed. He'll start losing soon."

The barman, a man who was taller than Bowman and twice as wide, rubbed his ginger moustache.

"Shut your mouth."

Bowman did not have time to order a drink. There were noises behind him. In this order: a hand banging on the table, then a voice in a thick Irish accent saying "Spades"; a silence; a chair scraped over the floorboards; a deeper silence; and footsteps coming towards the bar, making the wood creak beneath them. Bowman saw the landlord uncross his arms, his chest swelling as he took a deep breath.

Collins put his hands on the counter, just next to Bowman, opposite the man with the moustache.

"No luck today. Give me a beer."

"Shall I put it on your tab?"

"Why'd you say that?"

"No reason."

"Don't bloody mention it, then!"

Bowman turned towards Collins.

The last time he had found himself facing him, they had been standing on the deck of the junk and Collins had been hiding a knife under his shirt. Bowman tried to control himself, but it was too late: the fear had already flashed in his eyes.

"Who are you?"

Bowman was paralysed. Collins' eyelids opened wide, the lines in his face deepened, and his head leaned towards the sergeant.

"Bowman?"

From the corner of his eye, Bowman saw the barman move behind the counter. A growl rose up through Collins' throat:

"Bowman?"

Collins lifted his hands from the bar. The two customers on either side of him moved too. The hands rose towards Bowman's throat. The sergeant could not move a muscle. They wrapped around his neck, his windpipe crushed by the pressure of those fingers. Then there was a strange sound, like a wooden bell hit with a mallet. Collins' eyes crossed, then rolled back in his head. His hands loosed their grip and he collapsed at the sergeant's feet.

A club in his hand, his face still swollen by the effort needed to make the blow, the barman watched Collins slump to the ground. Hands grabbed Bowman by the shoulders and pushed him away. The customer at the other end of the bar leaned over the counter and grabbed a second club. The landlord had come around the bar. The two men stood over Collins, who, still cross-eyed, was groggily touching his bloody head. The two clubs were raised at the same time. The barman yelled:

"For O'Neil, you bastard!"

Bowman just stood there, watching the cudgels beat down on the former soldier, who managed to lift his hands at first, to protect his head. Then his broken arms fell and the blows continued to rain down. His jaw hung loose. His face swelled up in a few seconds and exploded. Blood spurted onto the bludgeons. The other drinker had come over too, also armed with a club. The three Irishmen insulted Collins, hitting him as they shouted their friend's name:

"For O'Neil!"

When they stopped, Collins was still alive. Air came whistling through his broken, almost torn-off nose, popping little bubbles of blood. At the tables, the card-players watched in silence. The three dockers sitting with Collins had got to their feet. One of them spat on the floor.

"Got what he deserved."

Another lifted his glass.

"We told you not to come back."

The landlord and the two other men, still holding their clubs, turned towards Bowman.

"Why did that bastard want to strangle you?"

Bowman rubbed his throat. He couldn't speak. He looked at Collins and his fingers that were silently scratching the floorboards.

"What did he call you? Bowman, is that right?"

Bowman nodded.

"Why did he attack you?"

Bowman spoke in a feeble voice:

"The army. Together in the army."

The landlord of the Greenland turned back to Collins, who was lying on the ground.

"Yeah, that cunt was always going on about how he'd gone to war."

He spat on Collins' chest.

"And what a warrior he was! The stupid bastard!"

One of the men at the bar nervously asked what they were going to do. The barman came a bit closer to Bowman.

"Why did you come here?"

"To look for him. Had a score to settle."

The man rubbed his blood-covered hand over his moustache.

"A score to settle?"

"Yeah."

"Looks like we did it for you, eh?"

"Been looking for him. A long time. Didn't know where he was."

The barman stared at him for an instant.

"This cunt's been in jail for a year. That's all he got for stabbing an Irishman to death. We told him not to come back. You turned up just in time, Bowman. A bit later and you'd have missed him."

The barman smiled. Bowman looked down at Collins. His eyes were half open beneath his smashed brows. He looked at Sergeant Bowman and his lips moved silently in his shattered jaw.

"What are you going to do with him?"

"You didn't come here, Bowman. We never saw you and you won't come back. Get out of here. He's no longer your problem."

———————————

Feeling too tired to walk the seven or eight miles that separated him from Battersea, Bowman hailed a carriage. The driver asked him which way he wanted to go.

"South bank or north bank?"

"The shortest way."

"Chelsea Bridge, then. It's just opened. But there's a toll, sir. On top of your fare."

"A new bridge?"

The driver took the north bank, and Bowman let the jolts of the carriage rock him into a doze. Half an hour later, the driver shouted that they had reached the bridge. He made comments about Queen Victoria, who had come in person to inaugurate it. They went alongside Battersea Park, almost as new as the bridge, and the driver continued to give his tourist commentary. It was a quiet place, and the vegetation acted as a sort of barrier to the smells of the factories on the shore.

Bowman paid his fare when they arrived at Kennard Street.

"Would you like me to wait for you, sir? Out here, you won't find anyone to take you back."

Bowman told him he could go.

The street was lined on both sides with recently built houses – low brick terraces, all identical, lined up like a long family of Siamese twins. Kennard Street was a cul-de-sac, ending in a loop, like a long interior courtyard. The place was inhabited but strangely lifeless, as if it were still so new that its inhabitants had not yet made any impression on it; or maybe it was the other way round, and the place had not yet made any impression on its inhabitants. Bowman walked down the street, counting the house numbers until he reached 27. Here, he entered the little garden. An old woman opened the door.

"Erik Penders?"

The old woman smiled at him.

"He doesn't live here anymore. Can I help?"

She made some tea, which Bowman drank unsweetened.

"My husband and I bought this house six years ago. He was working at the porcelain factory in Battersea. When he died, I had to rent out a room. Mr Erik was my first tenant. He came in the autumn of '57. He worked at the factory too. He stayed almost a year, but then he quit his job and left, and I haven't heard from him since. You were with him in India, is that right?"

"In Burma."

"He used to talk about that period sometimes, his army days."

"Do you know where he went?"

"No. He didn't talk much. He was a discreet young man. Very friendly, even if he didn't say much. He just mentioned his travels two or three times, and I didn't ask him any questions. Other than that, it was just the usual conversations. Oh, except for books."

"Books?"

"He read a lot. And I love books too."

She smiled.

"I was a schoolteacher. He read all the books in the house. Sometimes, he would lend me his. Travel books, mostly. Not my favourites, but some of them were amusing. When we talked about books, you couldn't keep him quiet!"

"When did he leave?"

"This summer, after the terrible drought. The smell wasn't too bad out here. We're far enough away from the Thames, and we have the fields. But still, it was difficult, especially for people like Mr Erik who worked in the factories on the riverbank. He told me one morning that he'd quit his job and he wouldn't be renting the room anymore."

Bowman peered between his fingers to the bottom of his empty cup.

"I'm sorry, Mr Bowman. There's nothing else I can tell you."

She poured him more tea. Bowman sipped it.

"Did he go into the city?"

"Quite often, yes. To visit bookshops, and he liked to walk, too. Almost every Sunday, he'd set off on foot and he wouldn't get back until evening. Sometimes he'd tell me what he'd seen. Even during the drought, he would go off for his walks. He said he'd been through worse than that, but that he'd never seen an entire city transformed in that way. Like it was a prisoner to the smells. That's how he described it, I remember it well. It made a big impression on me. The city as a prisoner."

Bowman felt a shiver down the back of his neck, as if the air had suddenly grown colder.

"I'm not sure how to say this, but I wanted to know if Mr Erik was . . . Was he alright? Was he normal?"

The former schoolteacher gave him a surprised, almost angry look.

"I beg your pardon?"

"He stayed here a long time. Did you notice anything strange?"

"Strange? What are you talking about, Mr Bowman? Mr Penders was a perfect tenant."

"That's not what I mean, ma'am. It's just . . . The colonies, it's not always easy, and some of them who came back weren't quite right. Because of what they saw over there."

"Aren't you actually talking about yourself, Mr Bowman?"

Bowman rolled his shoulders under his jacket and lowered his gaze.

"It's not always easy."

The old lady's expression softened as she looked at Bowman's hands crossed on the table and noticed his severed fingers.

"Mr Erik did sometimes have nightmares, it's true. He never talked about it and I never asked. Well, you can't, can you? Almost all of the time, he was fine. But sometimes he slept badly and left the house without eating breakfast. I've seen enough men come back from the war to know, Mr Bowman. I understood what happened to him. Mr Erik was a very good young man, but he had bad dreams."

"When exactly did he leave?"

"My Lord! It was just after the rain. In July."

"After the rain. And he left just like that, without warning?"

"Yes, he left quite suddenly. I asked him if there was something he didn't like here. I even asked him if he'd met someone. He said it wasn't that, he just needed to leave."

"Met someone?"

The old lady blushed.

"A woman, Mr Bowman."

Bowman thanked her, and the old schoolteacher accompanied him to the door.

"I'm sorry you haven't been able to find your friend, Mr Bowman. I have the impression it was very important to you."

Bowman put on his cap and half smiled. The old lady put her hand on his arm.

"I don't know where Mr Erik is, but if you asked me what I thought, I would guess that he's gone far away."

"Far away?"

"Yes. He read so many books about . . . Oh, but wait! Please, just wait here for a moment."

She walked quickly across the living room and returned with a package, tied together with a string of coloured cloth.

"It was a book I'd ordered for him, a present to celebrate the anniversary of him coming here. A story about a country he used to talk about a lot. Perhaps he's over there now."

She blushed again.

"The parcel arrived after his departure. I kept it, thinking perhaps he'd come by one day. But I don't think he'll be back. Please, accept it. You're his friend – I'd like to give it to you. And if you ever need a place to live, Mr Bowman, don't hesitate to come and find me. If . . . if you find Mr Erik, tell him I'm thinking of him."

Bowman took the packet. He didn't know how to respond. The old lady smiled at him from the doorway, waving her hand as she watched him walk away.

From out here in the fields, it was a three-hour walk to his hut, and his legs refused to carry him. He walked to Battersea Park and sat on a bench by the lake. The sun shone softly. His eyelids were heavy with fatigue. He drank a bit of gin and took the parcel from his pocket, undid the string and removed the wrapping paper. *A Tour on the Prairies* by Washington Irving. Bowman turned the book in his hands, put it on the bench and watched the swans and geese moving past on the lake, as if blown by the wind. The park was immense, but deserted. There was no-one on this side of the Thames, and on the other side, in Chelsea, the porcelain workers were not going to pay the toll for the new bridge just to come over here and watch ducks on a pond. The place was beautiful but useless. Bowman felt better amid this greenery, without another living soul in sight.

He picked up the book again. Apart from the Bible, it was the only one he had ever opened. And, tracing the letters with a finger, murmuring the words under his breath, Bowman began to read.

In the often-vaunted regions of the far West, several hundred miles beyond the Mississippi, extends a vast tract of uninhabited country, where there is neither to be seen the loghouse of the white man nor the wigwam of the Indian …

His eyes grew wide. He kept reading, bent close over the printed letters until dusk. When it was too dark, he lay down on the bench and rested his head on the book. His mind drifted far off, without alcohol or opium, towards the banks of the Arkansas and the Red River. He fell asleep thinking of Penders, whom he hadn't found, and this gift he'd left behind him.

He was woken by the cold of dawn. On the way back, he stopped in a tavern to eat. Refreshed, he walked all the way to the hut, staying on the north bank, far from Docklands, before crossing the Thames on the Canary Wharf ferry. He wanted to get back to his stove and his blankets, to open the book again.

When he arrived, the first thing he saw was the list on the crate, next to the pen and the inkwell. He sat in front of it, looked at the names, dipped the pen in the ink, and his hand hung suspended above the paper. Black drops fell onto the page. He put one line through Penders' name, then a second, and kept going until he had crossed it out completely.

Next to this blackened name, he drew a question mark, going over and over it until he tore a hole in the paper.

John Briggs lived in Bristol. This meant he had to take a train and leave the city. Another journey.

Bowman put the old lady's gift next to the list, wrapped himself up in the blankets, and uncorked a bottle.

9

At Paddington Station, Bowman paid for a second-class ticket and then waited for an hour on the platform for the train to depart. The sun poured through the glass ceiling of the main concourse, illuminating the smoke of the locomotives. The platform was busy with porters and travellers, families and workers, shopkeepers and businessmen, aristocrats leaving to visit spa resorts on the West coast.

In a shop, Bowman bought some Virginia tobacco and a new pipe. He smoked while gazing absent-mindedly around at the immense steel and glass tunnel of the station, the pigeons nesting in the girders that curved above the travellers' heads, flying down to nibble crumbs before taking off again, their wings skimming the tops of people's hats. The ticket-seller for the Great Western Railway had assured him that he would arrive at 12:35 precisely. Bowman still couldn't believe that Bristol – which had seemed another world, far out of reach, in his childhood memories – was now only four and a half hours from London.

Aboard the carriage, and before anyone sat down on the seat next to him, Bowman took a large gulp of gin. His clothes were beginning to look dirty, but he was still presentable enough to sit in this second-class compartment. Rather than a gentleman of means, he now looked like someone possessing only one set of good clothes. When he sat down, the belt of his trousers felt tight around his waist. He had put on a bit of weight. There were whistles on the platform, the train began to shake, and very quickly the suburbs of London disappeared and the train sped through the countryside beyond.

Despite its incredible speed, the journey was monotonous. Bowman smoked during the entire trip and regretted not having taken the book with him. The sky was cloudy over Temple Meads Station. Bristol did not look very different to London. From the train, he had seen a river, ships, factory chimneys and docks: life here seemed to be organised in the same way, with identical rhythms, smells and sounds. The only notable difference between Bristol and London was in the air, which, here, carried a hint of the sea.

The sergeant whistled for a cab and unfolded the map on which he'd written the address for John Briggs – the man whose ear Bufford had eaten. The driver looked at him in surprise.

"Stapleton? The prison or the hospital?"

Bowman said he had no idea and hid himself inside the carriage, closing the curtain on the window. He did not see the rest of the city, but the journey seemed long to him. Stapleton had to be at the other end of Bristol. The driver finally came to a halt outside a wall a good fifteen feet high with a gate designed to keep people out – or in. Bowman contemplated this mass of brick and iron and felt oppressed by its size and austerity. On either side of the reinforced metal doors, two soldiers stood guard. Bowman explained to them that he was looking for someone.

"This is the prison. The hospital's the other gate, a bit further on."

Bowman walked fifty yards along the wall. A guard in a sentry box wrote down his name in a notebook and let him enter. In the middle of a park stood a sort of manor house or barracks with a belfry, built in dark stone. The trees were still young and the architecture modern. He had to pass through one reception area, then another office, occupied by secretaries too busy to direct him where he wanted to go. On the way there, he overheard words, and gradually realised which part of the institution he was being directed to.

"Isolation" . . . "Maximum security."

Bowman passed male nurses with burly shoulders, guards with bunches of keys and truncheons hanging from their belts, and finally came to another office, in a corridor protected by thick iron bars, where he introduced himself to a guard in a white coat.

"What is the purpose of your visit, Mr Bowman?"

"I've come to see someone."

The guard smiled.

"Well, I guessed that. No-one comes here alone to be locked up. The patient's name?"

"Briggs. John Briggs."

The man looked surprised.

"Are you family?"

"No. Actually, I just need to know how long he's been here."

The guard stood up.

"You don't look too well. Is everything alright?"

"The journey. It was tiring."

Big drops of sweat rolled down Bowman's face. The odour rising from the cells behind the iron bars made him feel nauseous.

"Where have you come from?"

"London."

The guard raised his eyebrows.

"To see Briggs? Or not to see him, in fact? That seems very strange."

"Just need to know."

The guard put his hands on his hips.

"You know Briggs, you come from London to see him, and when you get here, you don't want to see him anymore?"

"Exactly."

"You just want to know how long he's been locked up?"

The man seemed very keen to make sure, in his lunatic asylum, that things were clear.

"You're the first visitor Briggs has had since he was locked up here. I'm not going to let you leave until you've seen him."

"What?"

Bowman blinked. He stared down the long, dark corridor, going cross-eyed as the iron bars blurred and doubled.

"There's no need. Just tell me . . ."

"I'm not going to tell you anything until you've seen him!"

The guard's voice echoed down the corridor, provoking a few reactions in the cells, like the yaps and howls of a doghouse.

"Where do you know Briggs from? Because we don't know anything about him. And even though it probably wouldn't really change much, it'd still be good to find out a bit more."

Bowman wiped his hands on his jacket.

"How long has he been here?"

The guard did not reply. He turned the key in the lock.

"Follow me. And don't worry – the bars are solid."

Bowman hesitated before passing through the barred gate, and shivered when the guard closed it behind them. There were a few openings at the tops of the walls, but they did nothing to dissipate the heat and the stink. He walked in the middle of the corridor, staying as far as possible from the bars of the cells, which were no bigger than cages. Curled up in the corners, men in torn, filthy pyjamas drooled into their hands. Most of the patients did not seem to even see them as they walked past. They had the eyes of opium smokers – presumably because they were sedated with laudanum – lost in the labyrinths of their thoughts. The guard paid no attention to the madmen, going on in the same loud voice:

"All we know is what he says when he's babbling. Especially when we come to fetch him for the shower. He's pretty aggressive, but the doctors say it's fear, that we shouldn't take it personally. All the same, we do have to defend ourselves quite often. We don't wash him as often now. I'm telling you that so you won't be surprised."

Bowman lowered his head, following behind the man in the white coat.

"Apparently he thinks we're soldiers who want to hurt him – Chinamen or something. He hurts himself sometimes too. All his scars, according to the doctors, are self-inflicted. No-one's ever managed to speak with him. They've tried everything: hypnosis, drugs, cold baths . . . nothing works. One of our first clients. He's been here almost since the hospital opened. Three years."

The guard stopped and Bowman almost walked into him.

"You've come this far, so say hello to Briggs!"

Bowman took a breath, gathering all his strength just to prevent his legs collapsing beneath him, then looked inside.

It was Briggs. Exactly as he had been in the bamboo cage. Skeletal.

Terrified. Shit-stained trousers, bare scar-covered chest, his ear torn off by Bufford's teeth. His face was swollen and bruised.

The guard looked at Bowman.

"He tried to bite me yesterday."

Bowman moved slowly over to the bars and clung to them.

"Careful. Don't get too close."

Bowman was not listening.

"Briggs?"

The man turned around, jumped when he saw the guard and held his head in his hands. Bowman called out his name again. Through his fingers, Briggs looked at him.

"It's me. Sergeant Bowman. You recognise me, Briggs?"

The old soldier's eyes opened wider and he stared at the sergeant.

"It's me. Shit, Briggs, what's happened to you?"

Briggs began to shake his head and mutter:

"No . . ."

That distress. That grimace of helplessness and supplication, when they came to fetch them. That terrible feeling that it was starting again, that nothing could be done to stop it, not fighting, not screaming, not begging for mercy. Briggs began to yell, swaying back and forth:

"No!"

Bowman slid down the bars until he was on his knees.

"Stop, Briggs. It's over. It's over . . ."

The yells turned to screams:

"NO!"

Bowman clung to the bars.

"It's just a nightmare. Stop. It's over, for fuck's sake. It's just a dream, Briggs. You have to snap out of it now. Snap out of it!"

Briggs covered his head in his arms, blocking his ears, and continued to scream while Bowman begged him to stop.

"Briggs! Stop, for God's sake! You have to stop that! It's over! You're not there anymore! We came back! You're not in the forest anymore!"

The cries of Briggs and Bowman woke the patients in the other cells. The sound of a lunatic choir began to swell in the corridor, like a pack of hounds chasing a wounded animal. The guard started yelling too, telling them to shut their mouths. Then he took a whistle from his pocket and blew it with all his strength.

"Briggs, let's go home. They're not there anymore. There's nothing to fear now, Briggs . . ."

Other guards ran towards them. Briggs stood up and, with all the momentum he could muster in the tiny cell, threw himself against the wall. His head rebounded and he collapsed. Sergeant Bowman rolled on the ground, his body stiff as a plank, and his heels started to drum on the floor. Slobbering, he swallowed his tongue, and his head bounced against the tiles, his eyes rolling back in their sockets.

"He's waking up."

"You feel better?"

Bowman opened his eyes.

"Where am I?"

"At the hospital in Beaufort. You had an epileptic fit."

A man in a suit was leaning over him. Bowman saw the man's fingers move towards his eyes, felt his eyelid lifted up.

"You look much better."

Bowman could not move. He was lying on a bed. As well as the doctor, there was a male nurse in the corner of the room. Bowman thought he recognised him.

"You're in the infirmary. Don't try to sit up."

"What am I doing here?"

"You came to visit one of our patients and you had a fit. Not a simple fit. Your condition is serious, sir . . ."

The doctor turned to the nurse.

"What's his name?"

"Bowman."

"Your condition is serious, Mr Bowman. You need to be treated. What do you remember?"

His muscles were stiff and aching. He raised an arm, but it fell back before it could reach his face.

"Bristol. I took the train . . ."

"Had you been drinking, Mr Bowman?"

"Huh?"

The doctor turned back to the nurse.

"Given the colour of his eyes, not to mention the smell of his breath, he'd obviously been drinking. Keep him under observation, I'll drop by later. How is Briggs?"

Bowman heard the nurse's voice as if through a door.

"Not too good. He really smashed his head this time."

The doctor sounded amused:

"Probably the best treatment for him."

The nurse laughed.

"What shall I give this one?"

Bowman closed his eyes.

"Nothing for the moment. I'll see about that later. Let him sleep. What was he saying, when he was talking to Briggs?"

"I didn't really understand. But he did seem to know what had happened to him. He kept saying it was over and they'd come back. Something like that."

"Interesting. The same delirium as Briggs."

"Yeah, and that's not all."

Bowman felt hands on his chest. He kept his eyes closed and let them do it. They opened his shirt.

"Fascinating! Exactly the same mutilations."

The nurse added: "We found this on him."

"Why would he come here with a weapon like that?"

"No idea."

"Keep it somewhere safe. I want to know more about this man."

"Alright, Doctor. Shall I put him in a cell?"

"We'll decide that later. He can stay here for now."

Bowman heard them leave the room, waited a few seconds, then opened his eyes.

He rested for a moment, just long enough to collect himself, tentatively moving his arms and legs, one after another. The muscles responded a little better. He rolled onto his side, letting his feet fall from the bed, and sat up. He put his hand to the back of his head, felt a bump and looked at his fingers, which were stained with blood.

He had to get out of here.

Bowman put his hands in a bowl of water with bloody gauze pads floating in it. He splashed water onto his face, and drank some, which tasted faintly of his own blood. His tongue was swollen where he'd bitten it, and the water brought the pain back.

He walked over to the door and turned the handle as slowly as possible. A long corridor swam before his eyes. No-one around. He sneaked out of the infirmary, walking until he reached another corridor and soon became lost, wandering around the hospital with the peak of his cap over his eyes, trying to hold himself straight whenever he passed any guards or nurses. He ended up opening a door that led outside, and found himself in the park. He walked around the building until he reached the main entrance and the driveway that led to the gates. The man in the sentry box stopped him, looked for his name on the register, wrote down the time and looked up.

"Well, you don't look too good. It's really something, that place, isn't it? Every day, I see people coming out of there looking like you do now! You want some advice? Have a drink – it'll make you feel better."

—ııı—•—ııı—•—ııı—

Three days later, Arthur Bowman was at Euston Station, boarding a North Western Railway train to Birmingham. For this trip, he had bought a leather bag, which he had filled with food and a bottle of wine, along with the book that the schoolteacher had given him.

> *Pursuing our journey, as we were passing through a forest, we were met by a forlorn half-famished dog, who came rambling along the trail, with inflamed eyes and bewildered look. Though*

nearly trampled upon by the foremost rangers, he took notice of
no-one, but rambled heedlessly among the horses. The cry of
"Mad dog!" was immediately raised, and one of the rangers
levelled his rifle, but was stayed by the ever-ready humanity of
the Commissioner. "He is blind!" said he; "It is the dog of some
poor Indian, following his master by the scent. It would be a
shame to kill so faithful an animal."

Bowman read all the way through the journey, not stopping until the
train arrived four hours later. His head cleared by wine, his stomach
settled by the food he'd eaten, Bowman took a cab through the city.

Morgan was from this particular area of Birmingham, and though
he was no longer living at the address that Reeves had located, Bowman
found him a few streets away. The neighbours knew him and told
Bowman where to find his new lodgings.

Morgan had not left his bed in nearly a year. He was dying, his body
poisoned, after four years spent working in a foundry where they made
cutlery, lead wires for stained-glass windows, and ammunition for the
British army. His wife explained that many other employees from the
factory had the same illness, and that it was caused by the lead vapours,
which entered the body and never left it. Her husband's body was
twisted by cramps, his fists permanently balled. His teeth had fallen
out and his skin was peeling off. He lay there groaning, incapable of
saying a single word.

He was the first man on the list not to recognise Bowman. The
illness had weakened him to the point that he no longer even recognised his own wife and children. Bowman made up a story for their
benefit: that he had worked with Morgan years ago, that he was passing through the area and happened to remember him. His family
survived thanks to money from a charitable organisation. Bowman left
them two pounds, and for the first time the money he gave away seemed
to serve its purpose. The woman thanked him at great length.

After the encounters he'd had up to this point, the visit to Edward
Morgan's deathbed came almost as a relief. But the poverty in this

house and the rotten stench of this still living body weighed heavy on his heart. He drank some wine, just enough to make him feel better, and hailed a cab to take him to Coventry, twenty miles away. Bowman hoped that his meeting with Horace Greenshaw would be as simple and uneventful as this one.

Only a few fields separated the factories in the suburbs of Birmingham with those in the suburbs of Coventry. The city was expanding at a phenomenal rate, and there were whole muddy streets in the process of being built, rows of brick houses rising from the ground as they were around all the cities in England now.

When he found the address, it was indeed occupied by the Greenshaw family. They were peasants who had recently moved to the city, and they looked at Bowman, descending from the horse-drawn carriage in his suit, as if he were a captain of industry. They got rid of the children by smacking them, cleaned off the kitchen table, and invited their visitor to sit in the best chair. Bowman was given a glass of wine, which he didn't even touch, then he asked them where he could find Horace. The family seemed disappointed that this visit was for their cousin. They hesitated, fearing that Bowman would leave straight away, then pointed out the cemetery to him. Horace Greenshaw, the cousin who had been a soldier, had been buried there since 1856. When Bowman asked how he died, they replied that it was progress that had killed him. He had fallen into a steam-powered combine harvester.

"All that came out was some dung that smelled of booze."

Back in Birmingham, Bowman managed to catch a evening train. Sitting under a lamp in his compartment, he started to read again, taking refuge in the words of Washington Irving in order to forget Briggs' screams and the stink of Morgan's poisoned body.

> *Several Osage Indians, visitors from the village we had passed, were mingled among the men. Three of them came and seated themselves by our fire. They watched everything that was going*

> *on round them in silence, and looked like figures of monumental*
> *bronze. We gave them food and, what they most relished, coffee;*
> *for the Indians partake in the universal fondness for this beverage*
> *which pervades the West.*

Irving wrote of the Indians with sympathy. Bowman remembered the stories told by Big Lars, who had met some and said they were like all the other savages in the world: dirty, stinking thieves whom you should never turn your back on. But there were several different tribes. The Osages, who drank coffee with Irving, and the Pawnies, whom he and his troop avoided like the plague. Bowman doubted that the indigenous tribes of America were any better than those of Asia, but the way Irving recounted his voyage aroused a longing in him. Especially the landscapes he described.

When he arrived in London, he had not slept for twenty-four hours, but he did not feel tired. From Camden, he walked to Limehouse, his travelling bag slung over his shoulder.

The next morning, after a few hours' rest, he unfolded the list and crossed off another two names. He only had one journey left to make – to the south, this time. Norton Young, one of Wright's men, whose address was in Southampton, and then the last man on the list, Edmund Peavish, the preacher, whose address was in Plymouth.

Bowman looked at the page with all its crossings-out. When he had seen it for the first time, the idea of searching for all these men had seemed an impossible task. A few weeks later, there were only two names left. Bowman remembered what Captain Reeves had told him. That there would not be any truth and that it would take him time to understand.

And already time was running out. Soon there would be no-one left to look for and the certainty that he would not find some*one* but discover some*thing* was slowly penetrating his head. If Young was not the killer in the sewers, he could not imagine that the preacher would have murdered anyone in that way.

Bowman felt profoundly depressed, though he did not understand the – too subtle – difference from the despair he usually felt. He did not feel like reading, so he sat on the wooden crate, pulled the inkwell towards him, smoothed out a sheet of blank paper and dipped his pen into the ink. With his hand in the air, hesitating, he tried to remember the first lines in the book by Irving. In small letters, at the left-hand top of the page, he traced the first words.

> *Arthur Bowman. London. 1858.*
> *26 September.*
> *I have found seven addresses.*
> *Another two to go.*

He paused to look at the words, impressed. He could continue if he wanted to. Write down everything that went through his mind. He thought some more, and realised he'd written today's date when, in fact, it had all begun long before that, and he had to tell all of that too. He wanted to cross out the first words, but in the end he decided to leave them and continued below.

> *It was Wright and Cavendish who told me to find ten men on the*
> *Healing Joy.*
> > *The first one I found . . .*

Bowman crossed out the word "found" and replaced it with "chose", though he wasn't sure how to spell it.

> *The first one I chose was the preacher and now he's the last one*
> *on Reeves' list. But I didn't find Penders.*

The lettering was clumsy, the page full of crossings-out and (he felt certain) mistakes, but he leaned back a little bit and proudly observed the two lines he had written. He reread them several times, not knowing what to write next. He thought for a long time, drank some wine, shovelled some coal in the stove, and looked out of the window at the wasteland between the warehouses. Then he went back to the crate and picked up his pen again.

The list is almost finished and I don't know if I'm going to find anything. Or what I'm going to do if I don't.

Bowman folded the page and carefully put it away with his belongings: the mother-of-pearl powder horn, the book, and his clothes. He took the money and the bond from their hiding place, buried under the hut's earth floor. Of the original fifty pounds, he still had two ten-pound notes and three pounds in change. He had spent half of it in barely a month, but he still had the bond, a veritable fortune.

The next day, he would prepare his last journey.

10

Bowman had not bought another knife. The weapon, hanging from his belt, had disturbed him as much as it had reassured him, and the one time it would have been useful to him – when Collins had attacked him – he had not been capable of using it. On the way to Waterloo Station, he wondered if it was worth writing this: that he was going off to find Norton Young and Edmund Peavish, unarmed.

An employee of the South Western Railway told him that there was a line to Southampton and another one to Plymouth, but that the train line between the two cities was not yet finished. He would either have to come back to London or travel from Southampton to Plymouth by carriage or boat. There was a regular boat service and the journey took twenty-four hours. Bowman bought a one-way ticket for Southampton and decided to make his decision once he was down there.

The train reached its destination in less than three hours.

In Bristol, he had only smelled the sea's presence; here, he found himself facing it. The station was on the docks, at the end of the bay. As the travellers left the terminal, they came out into the middle of a trading port. Bowman asked a station employee for directions to Hamble.

"It's pretty far off, sir. You have to take a ferry, which'll take you over the Copse, and after that you have to go through Weston, then West Wood, and then keep going until the Hamble estuary, where all the canneries are. After you've taken the ferry, you'll be able to get a carriage on the other side. Otherwise, it's a good six or seven miles on foot."

Bowman put the strap of his bag over his shoulder and started walking towards the landing stage for the ferry. He paid three shillings for the crossing and, once he'd reached the other shore, decided to walk.

He walked past the docks, seeing four-masted ships and steamboats going up and down the bay. Sometimes he moved away from the sea, taking little side streets, walking among workers' houses that backed onto fields and marshes. He stopped on the way to have a bite to eat. The earth here was mixed up with the water from rivers and the sea. Hundreds of birds gathered and, in the cool September air, stuffed themselves with food before their long journey south. Bowman remembered their arrival, in October, over the African coast. He started walking again, a little faster now. The afternoon was passing and he wanted to get there before nightfall.

He reached the canning district after a three-hour walk. At the address for Norton Young, there was no response; the house was empty. Bowman knocked on the door of the neighbours' house. A man opened and looked suspiciously at Bowman's clothes.

"I'm looking for Norton Young. Do you know him?"

The man had huge hands and a blotchy sailor's face.

"I don't know where he is."

"Does he still live here?"

"Why are you looking for him?"

Bowman did not react to the man's aggressive tone. He lowered his gaze, then turned towards the street.

"I know him. I'm looking for him."

"Well, I don't know where that bastard is. You'll have to figure it out yourself."

"I don't want any trouble, sir, but I have to see Young."

"Round here, knowing Young means trouble. Don't come back here."

Bowman crossed the road to a tavern, from where he could see Young's house. The place was empty when he went in and he sat at a table near a window. He ordered a beer. As night fell, the tavern filled up. Workers on their way home dropped by for a pint. When there was no room left at the bar, they sat at tables, and the last arrivals remained standing.

Bowman listened to their conversations. They kept glancing over at this well-dressed man, whom no-one seemed to know, sitting alone with his beer. Amid the hubbub, he heard some men shouting louder than the others. Something about a strike in a canning factory. Wage cuts, six-day weeks, ten-hour days. Trays of beers were carried over heads and as the night went on, the voices grew more raucous, the yelling more aggressive. He observed the drunken crowd, discreetly checking out everyone who entered and left, but he did not recognise Norton Young. He continued watching the street, on his guard, and finally saw a figure sidle up to the house, open the door and disappear inside. Bowman waited a few minutes. No light came on in the windows of the house across the street. He finished his beer and left the tavern.

He knocked three times, without a response, and at last called out: "Young? Norton Young?"

Behind him, he could hear the noises of the tavern.

"I know you're there. Open up! It's Bowman. Sergeant Bowman."

There was a light on in the house next door. He saw a corner of the curtain lifted up, glimpsed a silhouette behind the window, and called again:

"Young?"

He hammered at the door and listened. More noises from behind him, and then a very quiet voice. Someone was answering him, someone who did not want to be heard.

"What is this shit? Who's there?"

"It's Sergeant Bowman."

There was a silence. In the neighbour's window, the curtain twitched again, and the silhouette disappeared. The voice came again from behind the door:

"Bowman? Is that really you, Sergeant?"

"It's me."

"Ah, this is bullshit. Who is it, for fuck's sake?"

Bowman said, in a quieter voice:

"I was with you on the junk, with Collins and Penders and the others."

The door quickly opened.

"Come in. Fucking hell, don't just stand there."

Bowman walked into the dark entrance hall and felt a body brush past him. The door closed and the lights of the street vanished.

"Come this way."

Bowman followed the footsteps ahead of him. They passed a door. He bumped into some furniture, a chair and a table, then there was another door and a glimmer of light. In a tiny room at the back of the house, a candle was burning on a shelf. Young stood aside and smiled, a lead cosh in his hand.

"Bloody hell! Is that really you, Sergeant?"

Young was tense as a bowstring. He kept hopping up and down.

"It's bloody good to see you!"

Bowman, unsure how to respond, tried to smile.

"What are you doing here, Sergeant?"

"And you?"

Young burst out laughing.

"It's heating up here, Sergeant! It's all going to blow up soon. I just came to fetch a few things and then I'm out of here."

"What's going on?"

Bowman's eyes were adapting to the dark. He turned his gaze away from the candle flame to avoid being dazzled. Young kept looking over his visitor's shoulder, to the other room and the window that looked out on the street.

"I work for the blokes at the cannery. There's been a strike there going on for weeks. The lads don't want to give up. It's war, Sergeant!"

"What?"

"I work for the bosses. I've got a team, Sergeant, like you had! Brave soldiers. They hired me to break the strike. I couldn't care less about any of that crap, it just makes me laugh. We have to find the ringleaders and beat the shit out of them, and protect the lads who want to keep working. You know what the workers call us?"

Bowman slowly put his bag down at his feet. He did not take his eyes off the cosh.

"What do they call you?"

"*Yellows!*"

Young laughed.

"Like the monkeys! Fucking yellows! But what are you doing here, Sergeant? Eh? You looking for work? The bosses'd definitely be interested in a bloke like you. Sergeant Bowman! I bet you could get those bastards back to work in less than a day."

"I'm not looking for work. Why are you hiding in here with your bludgeon, Young?"

"'Cos they want my guts for garters, what do you think? It's the same thing every time. But they're not going to get me. We've been through worse than this, haven't we, Sergeant? Eh?"

"Put the club down, Young."

"What? Oh, yeah! You want a drink, Sergeant?"

He placed the cosh next to the candle. They were in a sort of box room. Young rummaged through the contents of the shelf and opened a bottle, which he handed to the sergeant.

"Let's have a drink, and after that we need to get out of here, alright? Not that I don't want to have a good talk with you, Sergeant – I'd love to, in fact – but we don't want to hang around here."

Bowman lifted the bottle while keeping an eye on Young.

"Get down!"

A window exploded behind Bowman. He fell to his knees.

"What's going on?"

"They're coming, Sergeant! They're attacking!"

Another stone, followed by a shower of small rocks, which smashed the glass to smithereens. Out in the street, the men were yelling, calling out Young's name and threatening him with a whole list of horrors. He crawled over to Bowman, a pistol in his hand.

"Come on, Sergeant, we have to get out of here! Follow me."

Bowman picked up his bag and grabbed the bludgeon on his way out. Young, bent double, pushed a chest of drawers away from the wall. In the candlelight, Bowman saw a hole in the bricks, knocked through with a sledgehammer, big enough for a man to pass through.

"Go on, Sarge!"

Bowman felt bare earth under his hands when he emerged on the other side. Young followed him and pulled the chest of drawers back in front of the opening. They heard bellowing, then the front door being smashed down and the drunks from the tavern rushing into the house.

"This way!"

They were on the other side of the street, on a dirt path that ran behind the houses. Young was already running ahead of Bowman, yelling, his words muffled by laughter, that it was all going to kick off soon. Bowman ran forward and banged into something, or something banged into him, and he found himself rolling on the ground. Instinctively, he raised his legs and, when he felt the weight of a body against them, he kicked it away with all the strength he could muster. He glimpsed someone get back up and charge towards him. Bowman hit out randomly with the cosh and heard a crack, followed by a groan of pain. The figure wavered in front of a lit-up window, and Bowman recognised the neighbour, the one who had sent him packing, and had sneaked out into the path to ambush them.

Inside the house, the workers, furious, were destroying everything they could lay their hands on. They soon found the opening in the wall. Norton Young had disappeared. The neighbour started to shout:

"They're here! They're . . ."

Bowman threw himself at the man and flattened him against a wall, the club crushing his throat.

"Was Young here on July 14?"

"Huh?"

Bowman pushed harder on the club.

"Young! Was he here in July?"

"Who the fuck are you? What are you on about?"

"Tell me!"

The man, his nose broken, stammered as his throat was crushed:

"He didn't leave. He was here, for the strike . . ."

Bowman released him and the man, half asphyxiated, fell to the ground. Hearing shouts from the house, Bowman ran away as fast as he could. When he was out of breath, he slowed to a walk. He kept turning, taking random roads between factories and houses, and ended up on the path he had taken on his way here. He reached the landing stage for the ferry on the River Copse, curled up in a ball in a small boat moored to the pier, and waited, wide awake, for daylight.

He didn't sleep on the train either, and when he got to the hut he drank a whole bottle of wine, then finally picked up his pen and bent over the sheet of paper.

> *I found Young. He was mad too.*
> *I ran away and I hid in a boat all night scared that the workers would find me.*
> *There's only Peavish left.*

Bowman wrote another line that he thought about crossing out, but decided in the end to leave as it was.

> *It's a bit worrying because he's the last one but at the same time I'm looking forward to seeing the preacher again.*

—◇◇◇—

> *He then descended from his roosting-place, mounted his horse, and rode to the naked summit of a hill, from whence he beheld a trackless wilderness around him, but at no great distance the Grand Canadian, winding its way between borders of forest land. The sight of this river consoled him with the idea that, should he fail in finding his way back to the camp, or in being found by some party of his comrades, he might follow the course of the stream, which could not fail to conduct him to some frontier post or Indian hamlet.*

Bowman closed the book. He only had a few pages left for the return journey.

Millbay Station, on the edge of Plymouth, was not one of those buildings made from stone, metal and glass, but a simple wooden construction. It was like an unambitious outpost, built not to last but merely as a staging post for a future conquest, on the periphery of that other outpost on the sea, which was Plymouth itself. On the square outside, Bowman asked a coachman where Herbert Street was and, seeing him hesitate, the driver offered him a good price. Bowman got into the carriage.

The city was lively in this late afternoon, the air still warmed by the sun. Bowman was lost in his thoughts as the driver told him about the city, taking seriously his role as ambassador to this visitor from London. He explained about the buildings under construction, the names of streets, the way to the port where steamboats and large sailing boats would set off for Europe and the Americas.

It took them twenty minutes to reach Herbert Street, a wide, peaceful, sun-soaked road. Bowman paid the driver and waited until the carriage moved away before crossing the lawn to the little chapel.

The interior was dark and bare. The altar was made of wood, and above it was a cross without any ornament. Through the windows, like long arrow slits, without any stained glass, just enough light filtered that visitors could see their own hands, know where to kneel.

A young boy was sweeping between the pews.

"Peavish – is he here?"

The child, who had a hunchback and one leg shorter than the other, looked like a halfwit.

"The pastor?"

"Peavish."

"He's at home, sir."

"Where's his home?"

"Well, here. But over there. Behind."

The boy showed him a door behind the altar. Bowman walked over to it and knocked. A voice answered him:

"Have you finished cleaning?"

Bowman opened the door without a word.

Peavish hesitated for a second before this apparition, then his smile widened, illuminating his face. He had no incisors left in his upper jaw; two yellow canines ended the smile at each corner of his mouth, framing his pink tongue.

"Sergeant Bowman."

Peavish crossed himself, closing his eyes for a moment without ceasing to smile, and then opened them again.

"The man who has been in my thoughts for such a long time."

The preacher still had the same voice and the same puppy-dog eyes, and he still spoke like a visionary; he had not changed a bit, even when the Burmese had smashed his teeth out with rocks. They, too, had ended up sick of the sight of that smile.

Bowman glanced around the little room: a chair and a table, a Bible, a bed pushed against a wall, an iron bowl and a pitcher.

"Hello, preacher."

Behind the chapel, there was a garden encircled by a low wall, with a tree and a bench. Peavish invited him to sit down.

"What are you doing here, Sergeant?"

"Why did you say you'd been thinking about me?"

Peavish smiled.

"It is my duty to go towards those who are in need. And to seek out those who are most in need. To recognise them, I think of you, Sergeant."

"Your bullshit won't work on me, preacher."

"And yet you've changed, Sergeant. I can see that clearly."

Bowman stared at Peavish and his toothless smile.

"You always thought you knew me, but you don't know anything."

"Then why did you come here, Sergeant?"

"Because there was a murder in London."

Peavish stopped smiling.

"That's awful, of course, but it shows how much you've changed, Sergeant. Before, you were not the sort of man who worried about a corpse. Why have you come to speak to me about it?"

"Where were you in July?"

"I beg your pardon?"

"Answer the question."

Peavish looked amused again.

"You mention a murder, then you ask me where I was in July? You're not being very tactful, Sergeant."

Bowman put his hands on his thighs and lifted his head.

"Just tell me where you were, Peavish."

"I was here. Do you need witnesses? Ask anyone in my parish. To be honest, I even wonder why I'm answering you, Sergeant. And I still don't understand the reason for your visit."

Peavish looked at Bowman, his eyes as tender as a saint's, his smile as patient as a martyr's.

"Yes. You have changed, Sergeant. You remember what I told you the first time I ever spoke to you? I remember it perfectly, but I never thought that, all these years later, it would seem so prophetic. If you'll pardon the expression."

"I'm not pardoning anything, preacher. I have no idea what you're talking about."

"I asked you why you didn't stop the fight earlier, aboard the *Healing Joy*."

"And what prophetic conclusion do you draw from that?"

"You replied that one never knows who was right to go to war. And that it is sometimes he who did not want to fight who wins. You recognised, Sergeant, that there is no such thing as a coward, and without meaning to, you admitted that you didn't believe in courage."

Bowman tried to smile, but his body tensed up. Peavish's voice sounded as assured as if he were preaching.

"You changed because you discovered fear, Sergeant. Perhaps now, you will learn true courage. Why are you looking for a murderer?"

Bowman got up from the bench and took a step away from Peavish.

"Because in London they think it's me and they're trying to hang it on me."

"You want to prove your innocence?"

The preacher's tone was ironic now. Bowman gritted his teeth.

"You killed men too, Peavish."

"But I'm not making the mistake of thinking myself innocent. Why are you looking for that murderer?"

Bowman stood in front of him, his face pale.

"Because it's one of us."

"Us? Is that a metaphor?"

"Don't get clever with me. You're the last one on the list."

"The list?"

"I found them. All of them."

"All of them?"

The colour had drained from Peavish's face and his hands, joined in prayer, were visibly trembling. Bowman leaned towards him.

"They were all mad. And as far as I'm concerned, you've always been crazy. I'm not going to believe you're any different to the others just because you've got a chapel and you act like a saint. Bufford threw himself down a well because his child drowned. Collins . . . well, it wasn't him either, but I saw some blokes smash his skull open because he'd spent too long looking for the knife that would finally slit his throat. Clements lives like a ghost. Briggs is locked up in a lunatic asylum and he thinks he's still in the cage and they're coming to get him for . . . for what you know about, Peavish, for what we all have under our clothes, even your stupid fucking priest's dress. Morgan, I didn't actually speak to, but he was dying because he'd been poisoned, and if you want to make that a metaphor, then go ahead. Greenshaw got so drunk that he fell in a farm machine. Young is completely crazy: he risks his life and laughs about it, and he's just waiting for the same thing. There were ten of us, Peavish. Those ten – who else do you think I could mean by 'us'?"

Bowman stifled a laugh between his cheeks and his teeth.

"Changed? Is that what you think, preacher? I don't even blame my colleagues in Wapping for thinking it's me, because I thought I could have done it. Some nights, I even wondered if it *was* me. When you've lived your nightmare in reality, Peavish, you can explain to me how you tell the difference between what's in your head and what's actually happening. But you should know that, given that you've always lived in a fucking dream. I remember something I told you once too, you know: that you're in the same boat as the others. You're arrogant because you believe you're sitting next to the good Lord and that you can whisper words into His ear while you wait for Him to get you out of the shit you're in. You want blasphemy, preacher? I'll give you some. Something I saw in a sewer tunnel when the whole city was dancing in the rain."

Peavish closed his eyes and did not react when Bowman grabbed his collar and shoved his fists under the preacher's chin.

"It was a child who led me down there. Are you listening to me, Peavish? Open your eyes, for fuck's sake!"

The preacher opened his eyes and looked at Bowman's face, planted right in front of his.

"The others, I couldn't talk to them about it, but you, preacher, you who pardon everything, you get to hear about it. I never believed you were capable of such a thing, but you at least deserve to know. I haven't forgotten a single detail. We'll see how well you get through it. Don't close your eyes, you'll need them too."

The two men remained silent for a long time, sitting on the bench in the little garden. Bowman was drained, his rage all used up, and Peavish filled with all the horrors that the sergeant had poured into his ears. Night was approaching and they were getting cold. Edmund Peavish finally stood up and walked on the grass, following a beaten path, a little circle around the tree, with his hands crossed behind his back. He came back to Bowman and stood still.

"Bufford is dead?"

"And Collins, Greenshaw and Morgan too. Briggs won't last much longer."

The preacher lowered his eyes.

"And your friend, Sergeant?"

Bowman looked up at him.

"Who?"

"You haven't found them all. You didn't tell me about your friend."

"Who are you talking about?"

"Penders. Where's he?"

"I dunno. The woman he was staying with said he'd gone. Maybe to America. Why did you call him that?"

"Your friend? Because he was probably the only one – along with me, perhaps – who understood you a little bit and was able to talk with you."

The preacher sat down next to him.

"Whether it was courage or not, without you, no-one would have emerged from that forest alive. I was unfair to you earlier. I won't ask you to pardon me, just to excuse me."

"Forget it, preacher. It would have been better for us if we'd all died out there."

"But we are alive."

Bowman looked ahead of him at the little wall surrounding the garden.

"There was something else in the sewers."

Peavish looked troubled, as if he had an itch that he was trying not to scratch, an itch that made him writhe about on the bench.

"I think I've heard enough, Sergeant."

"After what I've told you, it won't make much difference. The man who did it, he wrote a word in blood on the bricks of the sewer wall."

"A word?"

"*Survive.*"

Silence fell over them, then the preacher articulated slowly:

"Are you going to continue to search for him?"

Bowman turned to face him.

"Penders?"

"Who else?"

Bowman stood up.

"I have to go."

Peavish offered to let him spend the night in the chapel. Bowman declined the invitation with a smile. Together, they walked through the dark building, and the pastor opened the door for Sergeant Bowman.

"Peavish, what would you have done if I'd come here to confess, and I'd told you it was me?"

The preacher smiled.

"Is that the question you're asking yourself, Sergeant? What you'll do if you find him?"

Bowman put the strap of his bag over his shoulder and adjusted it.

"I don't know."

"Me neither, Sergeant."

"Goodbye, preacher."

"Come back whenever you want, Sergeant."

The next train did not leave until dawn. Bowman took a room in a hotel facing the station in Plymouth, and ate dinner in the little restaurant, surrounded by travelling salesmen talking in loud voices.

In the light of his bedside lamp, he finished the book he'd been given by the old schoolteacher.

> *The next morning I returned, in company with my worthy companion, the Commissioner, to Fort Gibson, where we arrived much tattered, travel-stained, and weather-beaten, but in high health and spirits. And thus ended my foray into the Pawnee hunting-grounds.*

II

Bowman worked for two months with Frank and his partner, Stevens. He learned how to be a fisherman.

It took Stevens a while to accept Bowman. And Bowman kept an eye on him. He had grown stronger again, and he wasn't afraid of hard work – nor of working long hours. Stevens, though more taciturn than Frank, was not a bad bloke, just more wary. For several weeks, he left Bowman to fend for himself, but in the end he grew to appreciate his stamina and discretion, and was happy to help him out with advice. When they were on board the boat, Bowman was a calm, disciplined presence. After a few weeks, Sergeant Bowman's past was forgotten; he had a dark side, just like so many other men on the port had, but it was never brought up again.

After the New Year celebrations, Stevens, Frank and Bowman went back to the hut. Bowman had warmed up the stove and bought a nice bottle of wine. The two fishermen clinked glasses with him in a gloomy silence, and then explained the situation to him. The boat was too small for three men. The pollution of the Thames by London's factories was forcing them to head out further towards the estuary, with diminishing returns. Bowman deserved to earn a wage, but they couldn't afford to pay him, not in those conditions, because it would mean their families going hungry. Bowman asked what they could do. The two men shrugged. What they needed was another, bigger boat, a sailing dinghy that was capable of higher speeds, of going out to sea. What they needed was fifty pounds, and no-one was going to lend them that sort of money.

Bowman went to the Peabody & Morgan bank, which had issued Reeves' bond. He received a hundred pounds in cash and another bond for four hundred. He offered to pay for half of the boat, without his name appearing on the purchase deed, and promised his partners that he would never mention it. They quickly found the vessel they were looking for, at a cost of one hundred and thirty pounds. After selling their old boat, Frank and Stevens had to borrow twenty-three pounds, paying the loan back at six shillings each per month. Bowman paid for the necessary work to be carried out on the sailing dinghy, so that they would be ready to start work in February.

Rigged up and renamed the *Sea Sergeant*, the boat lived up to expectations. Frank, Stevens and Bowman went on voyages that lasted two or three weeks, in all weathers, and came back with the hold full of fish, which they sold at auction in Limehouse or to the workers at the Millwall basin. In the estuary, they caught trout and smelt, and they returned from the Channel loaded up with sea bass, herrings and mackerel.

Bowman did up the cabin, changing the door, repairing the window, patching up the roof. He bought a bed and a wardrobe, where he hung his suit, which he had now swapped for work clothes and a pea jacket. He let his hair and beard grow, though he trimmed them regularly. He controlled his drinking when they were fishing, making do with some wine that they brought with them and a bit of hooch once the hold was full and they were heading back upriver. At home, he continued to drink heavily. While the days were easier now, he could not get through the nights without numbing himself with gin. On the *Sea Sergeant*, Bowman felt better. There was always something to do, and he was so tired when he went to bed that he slept well for hours. His insomnia accommodated itself to the rhythm of the shifts and the work. When he was on land, he only ever left the hut to meet up with his partners in the port, and occasionally to go into town to buy a book.

After six months of work and sailing, all that remained of those weeks spent tracking down the men on the list was his appetite for reading. This appetite was only strengthened by his solitude. His two companions he did not consider friends, but simply as men he needed in order to keep going, along with his books and his bottles. He also retained the memory of a woman he often thought about as he was falling asleep, and whose beauty was mixed with grief. And the memory of a man he hadn't found, and whom Peavish had called his "friend"; though the meaning of this word was uncertain to him, that did not alter its possibility. Lastly, he guarded the memory of a soldier and a copper that he no longer was, not entirely, but which – like the screams and the nightmares – he could not escape completely.

Sometimes they would sail to Wapping with the *Sea Sergeant*, and when they did, Bowman would pull his hat down over his eyes as he watched the police station pass, trying to glimpse figures behind the windows of the guards' room. When he walked the streets of London, he kept away from that area. He never went back to the Chinaman's opium den, though he did sometimes buy a little laudanum – when it rained and he was afraid to fall asleep.

In the springtime, at the mouth of one of the Thames' tributaries, Bowman and his partners caught two big salmon. These fragile creatures had deserted the filthy river during the past twenty years. Frank, Stevens and Bowman decided to keep these fish for themselves. Frank suggested they all eat them together, along with their families. Bowman refused this invitation. The next day, Stevens brought him some of the salmon, which he ate alone in his cabin.

During summer, the fishing was good, and it was even better in the autumn. When winter arrived, Frank and Stevens talked about hiring a ship's boy, some child from the port who wanted to learn the job and work aboard the *Sea Sergeant*. Bowman thought for a moment of going to fetch Slim and bringing him onto the river, but it was impossible. In the end, it was Stevens's nephew, a solid lad of thirteen, who was hired.

In December 1859, wearing his city suit, Arthur Bowman entered the Mudie bookshop on New Oxford Street. He had accepted Frank and Stevens' invitation to eat Christmas dinner with their wives and children. Bowman was nervous at the idea of this meeting and, for several days, though not daring to believe in the scenario he imagined, he had thought about Bufford's widow. In addition to the toys he'd bought for his partners' children, the presents he'd got for their wives, a nice jacket for Frank and a new pea coat for Stevens, he also wanted to find something special for the widow, so he went to the bookshop. Even if she didn't agree to go with him, he still didn't want to turn up at her house empty-handed. A bookseller asked him what he was looking for, but Bowman didn't know if Mrs Bufford read books.

"It's for a woman."

The bookseller suggested books on cookery or dressmaking. When Bowman asked for a novel, the bookseller seemed surprised.

"A novel for a woman? Well, there's *Jane Eyre*, of course, by Mrs Brontë. I think we have one copy left. It's a sort of romance."

Bowman weighed up the volume in his hand.

"A woman wrote it?"

"Yes, though initially with a male pseudonym: Mr Bell."

The bookseller hesitated:

"I don't know if it's an appropriate book for . . . for a woman."

Bowman bought the copy of *Jane Eyre* and asked for it to be wrapped in paper with pale blue ribbon. Before leaving, he asked about new travel books. He was shown a book by Sir Francis Burton, the account of an expedition to India. Bowman shook his head and asked if there were any new books about America. The bookseller said no, but in desperation suggested some newspapers.

"We receive copies regularly. The news is a little old, of course, but if you're interested in America, you'll find a lot of things in there. Though they're not books, obviously . . ."

Curious, Bowman bought two month-old copies of the *New York Tribune*, and finally asked the bookseller what all those people were waiting for in front of the main counter. There had been about twenty bourgeois people standing in a queue since Bowman entered, all engaged in a lively discussion.

"It's because we are expecting a delivery, sir: a work from the Murray Press that is causing quite a stir. A scientific treatise."

The bookseller gave Bowman a small printed sheet, an advertisement announcing the book's publication.

"If sir is interested, we could put you on the waiting list."

Bowman left the bookshop and, on the pavement, read the advert.

Written by Professor Charles Darwin, published by
John Murray: *On the Origin of Species by means of
Natural Selection, or the Preservation of Favoured Races
in the Struggle for Life.*

He crumpled the sheet of paper up in his hand and tossed it in a gutter.

Back in the cabin, Bowman mused. He could never invite the widow here.

As he had the means, he decided to find some decent lodging as soon as possible, somewhere close to the port. The fishing was going well. With all the money that remained to him, he could begin to plan a future. If he didn't spend too much, he could even live on what he was earning.

He turned the gift-wrapped book between his fingers, trying to remember every detail of the face of Bufford's widow. He carefully placed the present on the table, next to his own few books, the inkwell and some sheets of paper. He had not written anything since his visit to the preacher, one year earlier.

Bowman walked over to the mirror and took a good look at himself. His body was now the way it had been before his captivity. He was muscular, heavier, and his face had grown rounder and softer with the years. The scar on his forehead looked more discreet, his skin lightly tanned from his work at sea. He stretched his lips in front of the mirror, in training for Bufford's widow, and saw that he had a pleasant smile. His teeth had been solid since childhood. Fifteen years of being well-fed by the Company had given him teeth able to withstand a year of famine in the forest, and his alcohol and opium consumption had only slightly spoiled them. He was thirty-six years old.

When Frank knocked at the door of the cabin the next day, he found Bowman sitting on the floor, surrounded by empty bottles. When he spoke to him, the sergeant did not respond. His face was white and his eyes blank. Frank crouched down in front of him but Bowman did not seem to see him.

"Arthur?"

III

1860

New World

NEW YORK TRIBUNE
A Funeral in Reunion

by Albert Brisbane
21 November, 1859

*Readers, friends, brothers and sisters. In this column, devoted
for so many years to the most wonderful of accomplishments,
we, associationists, heirs and reformists of a dream born in
countries too old for it and now being built on the earth of our
new nation, we, the people of tomorrow, have never hidden
any of our goals, our hopes or our difficulties. It is a question of
trying to change Man. Think of those governments, incapable,
for all their power, of harmonizing relations between their
fellow citizens, and then think of us, with nothing but our ideas
to help us succeed. It would be dishonest of us to claim that we
have not known failure. But we are not giving up, absolutely
not, because we believe that it is possible for mankind to be
happy. Freed from the yoke of sterile work, of an education
that prepares one only for duty and obedience when responsibility and free will shall be, with our passion and our creativity,
the only guides we acknowledge in a world at peace.*

*It is here, in this newspaper, for a long time now, that we
have told you about this new world. With more and more
believers.*

*And yet today, if not a failure, we must tell you about some-
thing shocking, something deeply sad.*

*It was five years ago, on the banks of the Trinity River in
Texas, very close to Dallas, that 300 men, women and children,
led by our friend Victor Considerant, had come from France,
Switzerland and Belgium to build a new town, Reunion, the*

first step towards the city of our ideals. They, too, encountered difficulties, because, in addition to the problems that confront all this country's pioneers, they also had to face up to those of a land that was still uncultivated and of a humanity in the process of transforming itself. Their hearts are pure and their determination is magnificent.

Among them, in this town of Reunion where everyone is good, Mr Kramer merited the name of gentleman. The most gentle of the gentle.

It was at the heart of their dream that the thunderbolt struck, on their lands, open to all, and in their houses built to welcome everyone. With them, today, we are in mourning. For the death of our dream? No. Because we are not giving up. But for the death of a man who represented what we love.

It is the hope that Mr Kramer carried within him that was murdered.

A murder of indescribable violence, as if the killer had known that, with this man, it was not the body that had to be destroyed, but his spirit. What was inside him and could not disappear with his earthly remains.

The monster failed. Because we remain. Let us celebrate the spirit of Mr Kramer today, and continue to keep it alive.

The murderer, on the run, left behind a message. He signed his vile crime. Not with his name – no, he did not have the courage for that! But with a word, one single word, written in the victim's blood, and on which we must meditate.

Survive.

Is this message addressed to us? I don't think so. Because we live for a greater dream, we fight for a better life.

This word reflects the human beast that committed this crime. Because an individual capable of such things does not live, he merely survives, at a level of humanity so far below the one we wish to reach. While we are climbing, step by step, towards a superior state, this murderer is at the foot of the ladder. An animal, without a conscience, that seeks only to survive.

He leaves behind him a shocked, saddened community, but a community that will still be there when the memory of his crime has long since disappeared. Mr Kramer was buried in the earth of his dreams, and there will still be someone there to visit his grave when the animal responsible for his death dies in some deserted corner of the world. Let him dig his own hole and vanish down it! We will remain beside the gentleman, Mr Kramer.

We are not in mourning for our ideas, and our sadness will soon fade before the happiness that we are building. Let this column, today, be an opportunity for us to gather our thoughts, readers and friends, and to regain our strength so that we may continue. The dream is not destroyed.

I

"He scares me."

Frank put on his pea jacket and his hat, standing in the entrance hall of the apartment.

"All you have to do is take him some food. You don't have to talk to him."

"That's not the point, Frankie. You know I don't like him."

Mary had thrown a shawl over her shoulders. In her hand she carried a basket of food for her husband. The *Sea Sergeant* was stocking up for a week-long voyage.

"Just go to the hut once a day, leave the food there and check that he's alright. That's all."

Mary lowered her head. She was upset.

"I don't like it when you go away for a long time, and now you're asking me to look after him. You're the only one that can't see he's not normal. He's going to bring us trouble."

"Arthur's not a bad bloke, he's just had a few bad experiences. He's been through things we can't even imagine. Anyway, don't forget he paid for half the boat. We don't have to worry anymore, and that's thanks to him."

His wife handed him the basket, and he kissed her on the cheek.

"What does the pastor say to you when you go to church, eh? That you should help others, right?"

"If he's suffered, it's because he made other people suffer. He's a bad man."

Frank looked at her reproachfully.

"You're judging him, Mary. That's not like you."

"He scares me. There's nothing I can do about it."

Frank was becoming impatient. Stevens must already be waiting for him at the port.

"I'm going to say it one last time! Just leave the food and check that he's alright. He hasn't spoken a word for two weeks anyway. He doesn't even hear people when they talk to him. If you can't do it for him, do it for me. If it wasn't for him, we'd still be counting our money at the end of every week."

Mary's face flushed.

"Alright, I'll do it. But I don't like it."

Frank kissed her on the cheek again and opened the door.

"Frankie! Go and kiss the children!"

Groaning, he turned on his heel, kissed the children, who were sitting at the kitchen table eating soup, and dashed back through the entrance hall. Mary watched him go downstairs, forcing herself not to wish him good luck. She didn't hold with these sailors' superstitions, and wanted every time to tell him to be careful, to wish him good fishing and a swift return. But she bit her tongue and listened to his footsteps thunder down the stairs until he reached the ground floor. In the still-dark kitchen, she watched the children eat, her shawl wrapped tight around her. Bowman had only been here twice. The first time was when he'd started working with Frankie and Stevens, more than a year ago. He had been thin, with a sickly complexion and shifty eyes. The second time was a few weeks before Christmas, when he came to say he that he accepted their invitation for the New Year meal and to ask if he could bring someone. A woman. This time, Bowman had been sturdier and healthier-looking and he'd looked less ill at ease. He was tall and strong, silent, and still disturbing.

She dressed the children for school and waved goodbye to them on the landing, listening to them walk downstairs. Then she put on warm clothes, filled a shopping bag, and went outside. She walked through the streets of Limehouse in the direction of the port, turned towards the warehouses and headed down the path – through the tall grass, yellowed by frost – traced by the comings and goings of Stevens, Frank and Bowman. A few puffs of smoke escaped the hut's chimney. She knocked and, receiving no response, entered. At first, unable to make out anything in the darkness, she advanced carefully to the shelf and placed the food there. The ex-soldier was lying on his bed, rolled up in blankets. His eyes were open and he was staring straight ahead, showing no reaction to her presence. Mary retreated to the door. Outside, she crossed herself and walked back home. All day, she felt guilty for not having added coal to the stove and for not having asked Bowman how he was. He might even have been dead, the way he was staring like that. That evening, she was in a foul mood. She yelled at the children, who were playing up, and sent them to bed early.

The next day, she went back to the hut. The fire was out and it was cold inside. Bowman had not touched his food. This time, she walked up to the stove, keeping as far away from the sergeant as she could. The coal started to crackle. The light from the flames flickered on Bowman's immobile face. His pale eyes still stared fixedly, while in his hands was the famous powder horn that Frankie had told her about.

"I'll come back tomorrow, Mr Bowman."

And she did come back the next day. This time, Mary waited a longer time for the hut to warm up. She did some tidying, hoping that her activity would catch Bowman's attention. But it was no good. He remained prostrate on the bed, blind to her presence. He still hadn't eaten anything. By her fourth visit, Bowman had moved. He had drawn closer to the stove, presumably to keep warm when the fire died down. He was lying on the floor, wrapped up in his blankets, and he had eaten a bit of bread. Mary watched him for a longer time, sitting on the bed just across from him. It was so strange, this man who was alive and dead at the same time, who did not see her at all. The whole port of Dunbar could have passed through the cabin and he wouldn't have moved a muscle. The stove grew too hot and Bowman got up, slowly, like an old man with an aching back, and went to his bed. Startled, Mary got out of his way to let him lie down and took refuge in a corner of the room. Then she came close to him again.

He stank. His shirt collar was unbuttoned and she could see some of the skin on his shoulder. Mary bit her lip. She wanted to see those scars Frankie had told her about.

Holding her breath, she lifted one side of the shirtfront, revealing Bowman's shoulder. She almost cried out. Her hand covered her mouth. But she was at least as curious as she was horrified, and her other hand brushed the line of the scar, descending from the back of his neck to the end of his shoulder. Bowman shivered. Mary leapt backwards and rushed out of the hut. That night, she prayed for a long time.

Frank's wife believed in the world as God had created it. She believed in good and evil, in the battle and the balance between them. Only saints suffered out of pure injustice, and Bowman was no saint. Perhaps he was no longer the man he had been, but those marks on his body were the proof that he had been a monster. After her prayers, after dwelling on these dreadful thoughts until late at night, she fell asleep and the next morning she refused to believe in her dream.

Mary did not dream. Or only about the day she had just lived through, or sometimes the next day and what she had to do, like someone making a grocery list. This dream was completely different.

Before going to the hut, she went to the local church and asked to see the pastor. She told him about her dream, explaining the situation: a sick man she didn't like but who she had to look after. The pastor told her she was a good Christian and that her dream was good, perhaps even a sort of vision.

"But that man scares me."

"Your dream is telling you to help him. It's an order from God."

At the hut, she did nothing except leave the food near the bed and take care of the stove before going home. The next night, Mary had the same dream, even more detailed and disturbing this time. When the children had left, knowing that she could no longer ignore this divine injunction, she prepared herself, exactly as God had asked her to. She heated some water, got undressed and washed herself in the kitchen, combed her hair, put on a clean skirt, a white blouse with a high collar, and the bustier that Frankie had given her for Christmas. She hid her clothes under a large winter coat and quickly walked through the streets.

Bowman was sitting on the bed, the horn on his lap, watching the last embers in the stove. He'd eaten a few mouthfuls of food. His face, this morning, was marked by an expression of deep sadness, and his eyes had an anguished look. Mary shovelled coal into the stove and opened the air door as wide as it would go. Her movements were nervous. She murmured to herself:

"Don't be scared, my girl. You have to do what you did in the dream. It's the good Lord who wants this. Don't seek to understand, just do it and that's all."

Outside the hut, rainwater dripped from the roof gutter into a barrel. Mary used a stone to break the ice and filled some buckets with water, then she put a kettle on to boil and got a bowl ready.

"Do what the pastor told you. Don't think about it."

Inside the wooden cabin, the temperature was rising. She stood in front of Bowman, controlling her breathing. The bustier felt too tight: it was not the most practical thing to wear for this kind of activity. Her dream was stupid, from beginning to end. Her voice sounded weak. She started again and tried to clear her throat.

"You're not going to hurt me, Mr Bowman?"

Bowman did not react. He was staring at the mother-of-pearl powder horn.

"The pastor said it was a duty. So you're not going to hurt me, alright?"

Mary began to unbutton his shirt, sliding the sleeves over his arms and taking it off. She felt troubled by a feeling of *déjà vu*. Repulsed by the smell of his body, intimidated by his scars, she stood up straight.

"We have to wash them, Mr Bowman. Wash your wounds."

Mary knelt down, dipped a cloth in the warm water, wrung it out and rubbed a bar of soap against it. She began with one of his shoulders, barely daring to press down, then, little by little, her maternal instinct took over and she washed his arms, his chest and his neck. She talked to herself as she cleaned his skin:

"It's because you did something bad, but the pastor said I had to wash you."

Lifting up his arms, she rubbed his sides, then his belly. Beads of sweat formed at Mary's temples. She took off her bustier and put it on the bed. When she leaned over him to wash Bowman's back, her breast, beneath the fabric of the blouse, brushed against his scar-striped shoulder. She shivered.

There was another part of the dream that she had not told the pastor.

Drops of sweat ran from her scalp down to her neck. She unbuttoned her collar and wiped her face with the back of her hand. The heat was making her head spin. Her brisk motherly gestures were becoming slower and slower. She bent down and traced, with the damp cloth, the lines of the scars running over his shoulder blades and down his back, her breast pressed firmly against Bowman's arm.

Delicately, she picked up the horn from Bowman's lap and put it on the bed. Bowman followed her movements with his eyes.

"You're not going to hurt anyone anymore, Mr Bowman. Not me, not Frank, not anyone. I'm going to wash you, and after that you'll leave."

She put her hands on his shoulders and gently pushed him back until he was lying on the bed. Then she undid the buttons on his trousers and pulled them off.

Mary knelt against the bed, turning her eyes from Bowman's penis, and began to clean his feet, his calves and his knees, which were covered in scars. Then she rubbed his thighs.

His penis too was scarred.

Mary soaked the cloth in the water. Bowman's face was blank. As Frank's wife touched his penis, it grew erect. She closed her eyes. She felt a tingling between her legs. Letting out a little cry, she stood up, threw a blanket over Bowman's body and stepped back from the bed. She wiped the sweat from her forehead and undid a few more buttons on her blouse. When she had woken this morning, her hands had been gripping her breasts; her fingers followed the same path they had followed in her dream, between the open folds of her blouse, caressing her hot skin, down to her breasts.

"I'm going mad."

Her fingers played with her hardened nipples and she pinched them until they hurt. She breathed in deeply and then exhaled, hollowing her belly, and her other hand moved down under her skirt. Her legs were giving way beneath her. She touched herself, squeezing hard, then jumped as if someone else had done it. Both her hands moved to her face and she covered her mouth with them. She turned back towards the bed, crouched down and dipped the cloth in the water to wash Bowman's face.

"You are in purgatory, Mr Bowman. And so am I. You're going to leave now. You're washed. Just like in my dream. You're going to leave and so am I."

Feeling sure that he couldn't hear her, she continued speaking, as if to herself:

"In my dream, I washed you. And then . . . there was this love. Not God's love, but . . . a woman's love."

Mary, kneeling on the floor, pressed her breasts against the edge of the bed, squeezing her legs together.

"But I can't. I mustn't."

She was no longer holding the cloth. She caressed Bowman's face with her hand.

"That woman . . . the one who was supposed to come to our house. If you want, I can go and fetch her."

Mary pulled at the blanket that covered Bowman. She leaned her head down and put her cheek on his arm.

"I can go and fetch her."

She was speaking more and more quietly.

"Perhaps she will give you that love. Because I can't."

Tears welled between her eyelids.

"I'm scared of you. I judged you. That was wrong of me. It's my punishment to look after you. I'll go and fetch that woman for you. After that, you'll leave."

Mary caressed her own neck and Bowman's at the same time. She was whispering now, as she hoisted her skirt up over her thighs, pulled her knickers down and slid her hand between her parted legs. She kissed the sergeant's shoulder, then his belly, her mouth moving down towards his crotch, her tongue touching him ever more firmly. She had never done this to Frank. Bowman did not move. Only his penis was hard between her lips. As in her dream, she felt herself about to climax and tried to stop it, all the while rubbing herself with her fingers and masturbating Bowman with her other hand and swallowing him whole. She climbed on the bed, pulling her skirt over her head so she wouldn't see him, biting the fabric, and sat on him. Bowman's voice made her shudder. Mary fell backwards onto the bare earth floor, her legs and breasts exposed. She couldn't stop herself coming now, closing her eyes and squeezing her crotch with both hands, as if to muffle the cry that was about to come out. Bowman feebly repeated the same words, which she didn't understand. She bit her hand while she got her breath back. The sweat on her back turned cold. On her knees, she advanced towards the bed, pressing her ear to Bowman's mouth.

"Peavish. Pastor Peavish. Peavish. Pastor Peavish. Peavish . . ."

Mary started to cry out. Foul drops were leaking between her legs. She spun around like a dervish in the hut, grabbing her clothes and getting dressed as she wept, throwing the coat over her shoulders and running out of there.

The next day, trembling with fever, Frank's wife went back. Bowman was asleep on the bed, his face against the wall, his back to her.

"Mr Bowman? Can you hear me?"

She stayed close to the bed, unmoving.

"You mustn't say anything about what happened. It was nothing, just a moment of madness. I didn't know what I was doing . . . I was scared. Are you going to leave?"

Bowman did not reply. On the shelf, next to the food, she saw an envelope. A letter addressed to the pastor of the chapel in Herbert Street, in Plymouth. Mary crossed herself, picked up the letter and left with it, swearing never to come back.

*

When Frank returned from his fishing trip, he found his wife in bed with a fever. She told him she had caught a cold because she had to walk to the cabin in the wind and rain. Mary told him that Bowman had not moved, that he had eaten almost nothing, and that he had written a letter that she posted for him.

"A pastor?"

"In Plymouth."

Mary was tired and didn't want to speak anymore. Frank insisted:

"In Plymouth? I think he did go down there, before he started working with us. Didn't he say anything?"

"Let me rest. I did what you told me. I don't want to go back there. I won't ever go there again. Let me sleep now."

Frank left her in peace.

In the days that followed, he and Stevens took turns to go and see how Bowman was. The sergeant seemed a little better. Sometimes he looked up as they came in, answering their questions with a yes or a no. He was no longer the ghost of the first weeks, but he seemed to be waiting for something else before he fully came back to life.

Mary stayed in bed for a long time, but she too regained her strength. She never asked about Bowman.

———✺———✺———✺———

At the end of January, a pastor arrived at the port in Dunbar, looking for two fishermen, Frank and Stevens, owners of the *Sea Sergeant*. He was led to the place where the boat was moored. He introduced himself to the two men and asked where he could find Arthur Bowman. The two partners, hats in hands, explained the way to the hut and watched as the pastor disappeared between the warehouses.

The man knocked at the door of the hut. Bowman looked at the white collar around the man's neck, then his face.

"Who are you?"

"I am Pastor Selby. I received your letter to the chapel."

"Where's Peavish?"

The young pastor moved closer to the stove. Bowman watched him.

"I've taken over the Herbert Street congregation from him. May I warm myself for a moment before I answer you? I can't feel my fingertips and it's difficult to speak."

Selby rubbed his hands over the fire.

"I apologise that I am not the visitor you were expecting. I also apologise for having opened your letter. It's just that Pastor Peavish would never have received it. After reading it, knowing that he would not be able to come here to help you, I decided to make the journey in his stead."

"Where is he?"

Pastor Selby smiled.

"Pastor Peavish left England more than a year ago now."

"Left?"

"Excuse me, Mr Bowman, but in your letter it said something about a murderer, a killing in London and another in America. I didn't understand what it meant, but your letter worried me."

Pastor Selby moved towards him.

"That is why I decided to come here. You see, Pastor Peavish has followed the teachings of our founding father, John Wesley, and has taken the same path as him. He left for America to preach the Methodist faith. And as you mentioned a murder over there, I thought it was important to come."

Bowman sat on the bed.

"What did you say?"

Selby, with his smooth chin and his slender hands, couldn't be more than twenty-five years old. He was pale, tired from his journey, and wore a worried look on his face.

"Pastor Peavish left for the United States of America in September last year. You must tell me what this is all about, sir. I gathered, reading between the lines of your letter, that you and the pastor knew a murderer. Is Pastor Peavish in danger? Please, tell me what's going on."

"September?"

Bowman looked up at the young pastor.

"Just after my visit?"

"Your visit?"

"He left just after?"

Selby sat next to Bowman.

"I know I shouldn't have opened that letter. I still feel badly about it. But at the same time, I think it was a good thing. There is no way of knowing where Pastor Peavish is now. You said you needed his help. He isn't here, but I am. You can count on my discretion, sir. But please, answer me. Is your friend, Pastor Peavish, in danger?"

When Stevens went to visit the hut, Bowman was no longer there. His belongings were, but the room was in a state of disorder, overturned in a fit of rage. The bed and the furniture had been knocked over, clothes thrown all over the floor.

The next day, it was Frank who passed by. The hut had been tidied up, but Bowman was still not there. On the table was a pile of wrapped presents, each with a name handwritten on the paper. For Stevens, his wife and their children, and for his children too, and for him. Next to this pile was an envelope, addressed to Stevens and to him.

Frank took the gifts and the letter, put them on the kitchen table and handed the letter to Mary. Frank didn't know how to read. Mary was pale, and the page trembled between her fingers as she began to read it out:

> *The boat is yours. I leave you my share.*
> *I don't know when I'll be back. Everything in the hut is for you too. And the presents, which I'd bought for Christmas.*
> *Arthur*

Frank collapsed onto a chair.

"What the hell is going on?"

Mary was silent.

"He left? Just like that? Bloody hell, it's because that pastor came!

He smashed everything up, and after that he left . . ."

Frank searched his wife's eyes.

"Do you understand any of this, eh? He didn't say anything when we were at sea? About the letter to the pastor?"

"He didn't speak a single word the whole time you were away. One morning, I found the letter, so I put it in the post. That's all."

Mary rummaged among the presents and found a little packet tied with a blue ribbon. She weighed it in her hand, stroked it with her fingertips. A book. Written in ink on the paper: "For Mary."

Frank was horrified.

"You're sure he didn't say anything? You have no idea where he might have gone?"

Mary's voice went up an octave:

"Stop questioning me. I don't know any more about it than you do! And if he has gone, it's the best thing that could have happened for everyone!"

She left the kitchen, furious, taking the book with her. Frank remained sitting at the table, head in his hands.

2

Bowman entered the vast lobby of the Peabody, Morgan & Co. bank, on Commercial Street. The clerk recognised him and asked him to wait for a moment. He returned with another bank employee holding a leather briefcase under his arm.

"Everything is ready, Mr Bowman."

The employee opened the briefcase and inventoried its contents.

"The letters of credit to Duncan, Sherman & Co., our partners in New York, as well as the list of other American banks with whom we work. Your ticket for the Cunard Line, and your train ticket for Liverpool. A carriage will be waiting for you at the station, and your room is reserved for tonight at the Atlantic Hotel. And, lastly, the sum you requested in twenty-pound notes. Is everything to your satisfaction, Mr Bowman?"

As with the previous day's visit, the employee did not know how to behave with this man who looked like a common worker but was leaving for America with a small fortune, dressed in a suit that had seen better days. It had taken a while to explain to this Mr Bowman, who was obviously rich but ignorant, how letters of credit work, and to make him understand that, with the equivalent sum in dollars of what he was taking over there, he would be able to build a ranch, buy hundreds of acres of land and pay for the livestock that went with it. Bowman left with two thousand dollars in letters of credit, which he put in a travelling bag worth about six shillings.

At Euston Station, he climbed into a second-class train carriage. When, one hour later, as the train was speeding northward, the conductor pointed out to him that he had a first-class ticket, Bowman ignored him and remained where he was. Then he opened his bag and the little briefcase, disturbed by the idea that the Peabody employee had also bought him a first-class ticket for the ocean crossing.

He had asked for a third-class passage and the banker had almost choked with surprise.

"We don't sell those, sir. Moreover, only first- and second-class tickets will spare you the customs and sanitary formalities at Liverpool and at your arrival in New York."

A second-class ticket for a private cabin on board the *Persia*, a Cunard ship, leaving 27 January, 1860.

Beneath the printed drawing of the boat – a long, two-masted steamer – he was struck by the Cunard company's motto: *We never lost a life*.

Bowman reread this strange sentence several times, and the idea came to him that the East India Company could have used it too, for recruitment purposes. As if crossing an ocean in a ship was as safe as going off to war.

He took a flask from his bag and quickly drank half of the contents.

Having nothing else to read, he went through the documents they had given him. The list of American banks, the letters of credit, which he hid from other travellers, and the Cunard brochure. The *Persia*, said the pamphlet, has held the Blue Riband, the world record speed for a transatlantic crossing, for the past four years, having accomplished the journey in nine days, sixteen hours and sixteen minutes. When Bowman came back from Madras, after his liberation and his transfer to India, it had taken him four months to reach London.

The *Persia*, at nearly 400 feet long the biggest ship in the world, was also the first entirely built in steel, giving it a weight of 3,300 tons, which was able to speed through the water at 13 knots. To reach this incredible speed, the *Persia* was equipped with a 3,000-horsepower engine, consuming 150 tons of coal during each day of the crossing. Bowman imagined 3,000 horsepower harnessed to the hull of a little fishing boat, propelling it over the crests of waves.

Two hundred first-class cabins and fifty second-class. There was no third class on board the *Persia*. The pamphlet continued with a description of New York, the modern capital of the New World. The city seemed to be a paradise for those who wished to do business there, a city equipped with all the latest technological advances, filled with opportunities, inexhaustible economic resources, a clean and beautiful city where, every day, taller and taller buildings were being constructed to house companies and immigrants from all over the world. Engravings of the port of Manhattan and the Hudson River illustrated the text. Another of Broadway Avenue accompanied an article promoting tourist activities, dance and theatre shows, concerts and exhibitions. Trains left the city in all directions, towards Philadelphia or Chicago, taking you there in a few hours. Others went west, to St Louis, or south, to New Orleans. From St Louis, whether by a Mississippi riverboat or by stagecoach, those who wanted to could explore the Wild West. After that, there were a few lines about the grand plains and the Indians which, if they were not copied word for word, nevertheless seemed to have come straight from one of Fenimore Cooper's books, which Bowman had read in England. He read the pamphlet all the way to the end, without finding even the smallest mention of Texas.

Bowman finished his gin and looked outside. It took him a moment, after all these images of America, to recognise the cultivated fields and the cold, gloomy landscape of the English Midlands.

He saw houses flash past, and recognised Birmingham Station when the train entered it. After a two-hour stopover, during which most of the travellers left the carriage and were replaced by others, the train headed northwards. It arrived in Liverpool four hours later, as night was falling. A driver in uniform was waiting at the exit of the station, holding up a blackboard with Bowman's name drawn on it in chalk. Bowman climbed up into the horse-drawn carriage. When he got out, in front of the hotel, he could not believe his eyes. The Atlantic was illuminated by dozens of lamps hung from the façade, and the front door was ten feet high, made in shining copper and glass. At the reception desk, blushing with shame, he muttered his name and the hotel employee, just as surprised as he was, confirmed his reservation. He gave Bowman the key to his room on the second floor.

The room was so huge, he could have fitted not only his old hut in here but the entire wasteland it sat upon. In the doorway, petrified, he stared at the decorations, the immense bed with its embroidered blankets, the cast-iron radiators that warmed the room, the large mirror hung over a gilt-painted sideboard. The idea came to him that he should count his money again, just to be sure that the bank still had something to give him after paying for this carpeted castle. By the bed, a cloth cord hung from the ceiling, with a tassel at its end. Bowman grabbed hold of it and pulled. The cord was attached to a spring, and it rose into the air on its own. Bowman looked around him, as if a secret door was about to open, but nothing happened. He sat on the bed, facing the mirror, and looked at himself without understanding what he was doing there. He was startled by a knock at the door. They had found him out. It was all a mistake: his hotel was further down the street, on the port, a simple inn he could afford.

When he opened the door, a young man in uniform, with a little hat on his head, asked him what he wanted.

"What?"

"You rang, sir. What do you desire?"

Bowman looked at the cord on its spring.

"I didn't know what it was."

The boy, curious rather than irritated, observed Bowman.

"That's alright. So there's nothing you want?"

Faced with this badly dressed client, the boy had adopted a more casual tone. Bowman hesitated:

"Is it possible to get something to eat here?"

"Of course. I'll bring you a menu."

"A menu?"

The boy raised an eyebrow.

"There's meat in sauce, with vegetables. Would that suit you?"

Bowman felt ridiculous, but said yes to the meat.

"And a drink."

"Wine, sir?"

"Yes, and gin. Is there any?"

"A bottle, sir?"

"A whole one?"

"You think these gentlemen drink out of thimbles? I carry up crates of the stuff every night, sir. And if you want my advice, ask for a bath. It comes with the price of the room."

The boy walked away through the carpeted corridor, leaving Bowman standing in the doorway.

One hour later, he slid into a hot, scented bath. He ate on the bed, trying not to get sauce all over the covers, then, having eaten his fill, lit a pipe and opened the bottle of gin and watched the candle flames dance on the sideboard, reflected in the mirror. Unable to sleep, he finally took the inkwell and pen from his bag, unfolded the sheet of paper and read through what he had written on it.

> *Arthur Bowman. London. 1858.*
> *26 September.*
> *I have found seven addresses.*
>> *Another two to go.*
>> *It was Wright and Cavendish who told me to find ten men on the* Healing Joy.
>> *The first one I chose was the preacher and now he's the last one on Reeves' list. But I didn't find Penders.*
>> *The list is almost finished and I don't know if I'm going to find anything. Or what I'm going to do if I don't.*
>> *I found Young. He was mad too.*
>> *I ran away and I hid in a boat all night scared that the workers would find me.*
>> *There's only Peavish left.*
>> *It's a bit worrying because he's the last one but at the same time I'm looking forward to seeing the preacher again.*

He did not understand. In his memory, he had recorded all his research, all the things that had happened to him, but in fact he had only written about twenty lines, which didn't say very much at all: a terse summary of the last two years of his life.

He thought for a moment, then sat on a chair in front of the side-board and dipped his pen in the inkwell.

> *I found an American newspaper and inside they wrote that another murder just like that one had happened in a city in Texas.*
>
> *After that, I don't remember much.*
>
> *Frankie's wife came in the hut when I was having a break-down. She washed me and then she said she wanted to fetch a woman for me and at the same time she touched me. I couldn't move and she told me to go away.*
>
> *I wrote a letter to Peavish and she was the one who took it. Another pastor came to the hut and he told me that Peavish had gone to America after my visit to his chapel.*
>
> *Peavish lied and I thought I was looking for Penders. Now I don't know if it's him or the preacher.*
>
> *I left a letter to Frank and Stevens to say that the boat was theirs and that I'd come back.*
>
> *I left the Christmas presents and the Bufford widow's book for Frank's wife.*
>
> *Tomorrow I'm taking a boat that goes to New York and it scares me to be at sea and to go there.*

When he had finished writing, he reread it several times, lying on the bed.

At dawn, long before the departure time, Bowman was waiting in the cold outside the Cunard landing stage. He was not the first in line.

They had spent the night on the quay: a crowd of men, women, old people and children. Blankets thrown over their shoulders, babies hidden under coats, they had got up, silent, in the grey dawn, shivering with cold in the falling sleet. Sleepy-eyed, they stood in a line in front of the entrance to the Cunard offices reserved for third-class passengers. Three or four hundred people, all huddled together, holding suitcases. They shuffled forward, inch by inch, nervous and exhausted, breathing out clouds of steam.

Bowman walked past them and entered the building through the second-class door. He did not have to wait in line. An employee checked his ticket then asked for his name, and his date and place of birth.

"Arthur Bowman. Eighteen twenty-one. London."

Before arriving at the counters, the third-class passengers went past tables where Cunard employees sat, along with doctors who examined them. Teeth, ears, hair. They made the passengers cough and listened to their lungs. Every ten or fifteen passengers, a doctor nodded, and the passenger picked up his suitcase and went back the way he had come, head down, accompanied by his family, if he had one.

Bowman asked the employee who was writing his name in the register:

"Is there a risk of illness?"

"The American customs fine the shipping companies a hundred dollars each time they bring in sick immigrants. So we check them before they board. But don't worry, sir, you won't be travelling on the same ship as them."

Bowman went out through the other side of the building and found himself on the landing stage. The *Persia*, with its black steel hull, seemed to turn its back on the other Cunard ship: a wooden four-masted vessel that had seen better days, similar to the slow, pot-bellied ships of East India. The third-class passengers were boarding this sailing ship. At the bottom of the gangplank, they walked between sailors armed with crop sprayers, who squirted them from head to foot with disinfectant. The passengers coughed and wept. The Cunard employees also sprayed the contents of their luggage. Once they were on deck, the third-class passengers went down into the hold where they remained, in cramped conditions, for five or six weeks. Bowman guessed that the mortality rate must be the same as it was for the sepoys in East India. One in ten. Children excluded.

We never lost a life.

The *Persia* was still empty. At the top of the gangplank, Bowman showed his ticket to a company officer, who whistled for a ship's boy. He was the first passenger on board, having arrived four hours before the ship was due to depart. He followed the child in his too-short sailor's uniform, passing by the foot of a large red-and-black chimney from which billows of smoke escaped. Under the steel deck, he felt the vibrations of the idling engine, the pistons pumping every few seconds, beating as slowly as a bull's heart. His cabin was one of the lowest on the ship, with a porthole just above the water line. A bunk, a table, a wardrobe and a washstand.

Bowman put his bag on the bed and gave twopence to the boy, who was waiting by the door with a smile on his face.

"So it's like a hotel, this boat, eh?"

"Yes, sir, it's a floating hotel."

"Can I take my meals in my cabin?"

"I don't know if that's allowed for second-class passengers, sir. But I can ask."

Bowman observed him for a moment, then gave him another coin.

"I want to eat here twice a day, with a bottle of wine. Is there a bar on board?"

"Course, sir."

"Go and get me a bottle of gin. I don't want to see anyone else. You bring me my food. You'll get more money at the end of the voyage."

The boy ran off, and Bowman locked his door. The walls, painted white, were also made of steel and he could feel the engine, very close by, vibrating through them. The cabin was already hot. The porthole, looking out at the tresses of seaweed stuck to the legs of the landing stage, could not be opened. Bowman sat at the little table, placing the pen, inkwell and sheets of paper on it, along with the copy of the *New York Tribune*. He unfolded the Cunard pamphlet, then folded it back together in a way that allowed him to see the little map of New York printed inside. The city was built on an island, at the centre of a network of great rivers, inlets and bays. Other names of cities, illegible on the reproduction, surrounded New York in that interlacing of water and earth. The complexity of this maritime network worried him. The port of New York was in the middle of a labyrinth whose dimensions he could not guess.

He took off his shoes and his jacket, lay on the bunk, and drank the rest of the gin from the bottle he'd bought at the Atlantic. One hour later, he heard noises above him, then in the corridor outside. The other passengers were boarding. Two more hours passed before the *Persia*'s foghorn sounded. The engine started up, shaking the entire hull. The noise of the pistons, connecting rods and gears was impressive, and the temperature in the cabin soon went up by several degrees.

The ship began to move. Bowman twisted his neck to look out through the porthole. He saw the quay, the four-masted ship still moored to the docks, and the sky full of black clouds rushing inland, over Plymouth. The waves started to lap at his little window. The visibility was poor, but he could glimpse the coastline of England, about twenty miles away. Within a few hours, the *Persia* was past Ireland. Away from the shelter of land, the swell grew, and every ten seconds or so the cabin's porthole would be plunged into darkness. Bowman lit the oil lamp hung from the ceiling.

There was a knock at the door. The ship's boy had brought him a bottle of gin.

"Bring me something to eat. Bread, lard and fruit. Bring a lemon, too, if you can find one."

"Sir, there's everything you could ever want on this ship."

The boy left again, sprinting without difficulty down the passageway while the *Persia* swayed and rolled with increasing violence, slamming into the sea like a battering ram on a castle's portcullis. This was not just the usual ocean swell. The steamship, engine roaring at full power, had entered a storm.

The boy came back half an hour later with a bottle of wine, an entire loaf of bread, some cheese, an orange and a lemon, all of it wrapped up a large tea towel.

"What's your name?"

"Kit."

"How old are you?"

"Twelve, sir."

A resourceful child with quick eyes, bitten nails and long legs. In the middle of a growth spurt, by the looks of it.

"What's it like outside?"

"There's a storm, sir, and I've heard that it's likely to last for most of the crossing. The passengers are all in their cabins and half of them are sick. The dining saloon's empty. I often come down this passage, so if you need anything, just trap the towel in the door, and I'll stop by and see you. And in ten days, when we get there, you'll give me a pound."

Bowman took a penknife from his pocket, cut the orange in two and handed the boy half of it. The child refused.

"There's no lack of food on board, sir! Hang the towel from the door if you need something."

Bowman sat at the table, reread his notes, dipped his pen in the ink and adapted his movements to those of the ship.

> *I am on the boat.*
> *The first battle in a war is knowing how to wait.*

Then he cut up the bread, swallowed a few bits of lard, sliced the lemon into quarters, bit into the pulp and rubbed the peel against his gums before swallowing it.

The boy came back in the evening, and Bowman ordered some extra food.

"How can I go up on deck without seeing the other passengers?"

"If you really don't want to see anyone, go left down the passage, and take the second staircase, not the first one. That comes out below the front mast, sir, on the bow of the ship."

"Can you find me a pea jacket or a raincoat?"

The boy thought for a moment.

"Well, that depends, sir."

Bowman gave him three shillings. Kit brought him an oilskin coat. It was on the small side, but good enough. Bowman put on his shoes and his cap, slid the letters of credit into his inside pocket and then put on the oilskin.

The deck of the *Persia*, long and wide, with its lights fixed to the masts, looked like a fragment of a city – a deserted street or boulevard – floating in the middle of the ocean. Sea spray swept the deck like rain sweeping a pavement, and lightning illuminated the white crests, throwing the hollows of the waves into dark shadow. The ship seemed to be moving forward without a crew or any passengers.

Bowman made his way around it, holding on to the railing. The sails had been taken down, and the engine was battling alone against the storm. The machines occupied one third of the vessel's length, and when Bowman walked over them, in the cold and the gusts of rain, he felt their heat beneath his feet.

He went back down the same set of stairs. In the lit-up corridor, he smiled. There were towels hanging from almost every door handle. The ship's boy must be making a small fortune.

Bowman put his clothes to dry on the wall that was heated up by the engine. He washed, letting the water pour over his scars for a long time, then he lay down naked on his bunk, a bottle of wine in his hand. The combination of the alcohol and the noise of the machines – the regular rhythm, the volume loud enough to fill his mind – did him good. Bowman slept for several hours, a heavy, dreamless sleep.

He went on deck at dawn or at dusk, when he was sure that he would meet no-one on the deck. The sailors, used to seeing him patrol the ship, greeted him familiarly.

On the fourth day, the storm grew calm, giving way to a sluggish swell that did no damage to the *Persia* but still discouraged the other passengers from going up on deck. Bowman spent hours up there, watching the sea and smoking his pipe. When the weather really improved, he decided not to leave his cabin anymore. Passengers would go out to take the air at all hours of the day, leaving their cabins one after another, straight-backed but still pale, to parade around on deck as if in the streets of Westminster. Women in hats even walked their dogs on leashes, turning away as their pets vomited all over the boat. Men smoking pipes or cigars greeted one another, striding along and chatting about the speed of the *Persia*. They went out to retake possession of this ship, which had mistreated them for four days. Its 3,000 horsepower was theirs for the nine days, sixteen hours and sixteen minutes of the crossing, just quick enough for the business that they would be doing in America.

Bowman did go out a few times in the middle of the night when he couldn't sleep, and found, once again, his empty street afloat in the middle of the Atlantic.

Every day, Kit brought him what he needed, keeping him informed about the steamship's speed.

"We'll arrive tomorrow, sir. The storm caused a few delays. Normally we disembark at noon, so everyone can come and see the *Persia*. But this time, we'll be arriving at night, just before dawn."

Bowman made one last order for food and drinks – enough to take with him when he landed at New York. When Kit came back a few hours later, Bowman gave him his wages. He put the pound coin in his hand:

"Good crossing?"

The boy laughed.

"There's nothing better than a bit of bad weather for me, sir. Here, I nicked this from the restaurant. They always have a party there, the night before we arrive."

Kit handed the bottle of champagne to Bowman. Then he made a sort of military salute, trying to click the heels of his shoes together.

"Good luck, sir!"

And he scarpered, his pockets heavy with all the coins that Bowman had found at the bottom of his own. Bowman sat on the bed, untied the wire from around the neck of the bottle, and pulled at the cork. The explosion of the champagne made him jump. He drank a mouthful from the bottle, his eyes stung by the bubbles, and looked at the label, written in a language he did not understand. He knew that champagne was a French wine, so he tried to guess what the words might mean. Then he drank some more and belched. The bubbles burned his stomach. He put the almost-full bottle on the table and lay flat, incapable of sleeping, listening to the roar of the engine, waiting for the foghorn to sound.

When the hull of the *Persia* bumped against the dock, in the middle of the night, Bowman was fully dressed, sitting on the bed, his packed bag pressed against his legs, his heels nervously drumming the steel floor.

—⁓⁓—⁓⁓—⁓⁓—

Having been first on the ship, Bowman was the last one off it.

Never before had he travelled this far, only to land in a country that was just as cold as England. The lamps of the *Persia* projected a halo of yellow light into the mist, and the ground was covered with a thin film of frost. The windows and doorways of the Cunard ship were lit up too. Behind it, the city was invisible, drowned by night and fog. Bowman pulled up the collar of his jacket and followed the lanterns leading to the customs offices. He went to a counter. A man in uniform asked him for his name.

"The purpose of your visit to the United States, Mr Bowman?"

"The purpose of my visit?"

"Business or immigration, sir?"

"I've come to see someone."

"Someone?"

"Family."

"Does your family have American nationality?"

"I don't know."

"Do you wish to obtain American nationality, Mr Bowman?"

"What?"

"If you fill out a form now, to prove your arrival on American territory, you will be able, five years from now, to present that document at any courthouse in the country and ask to become an American citizen."

The Cunard employee looked up at him.

"Do you wish to fill out this form?"

"I'm not going to stay five years."

"Alright. Then please be aware that you may, at any moment during your stay here, obtain this document from the authorities. Welcome to the United States of America, Mr Bowman."

He signed next to his name on the register that the employee showed him, crossed through the building, and came out in the street, amid a crowd of porters and travellers diving into carriages. The trunks and leather suitcases were loaded onto trolleys; the first-class passengers, irritated by this unceremonious nocturnal arrival, gave terse orders for them to be taken far away from here as quickly as possible.

Bowman stopped a porter.

"John Street?"

"Yeah, the Methodist church."

"No idea about the church. But if you follow South Street, you'll cross John Street after about five or six blocks. To the left. But if I were you, I wouldn't go too far down that way at this time of night."

He didn't have time to ask why, because the porter went back to his work.

Bowman followed the pavement and disappeared into the mist. It was daybreak. A grey glimmer was visible in the east. The street ran by the docks of a vast port and he could glimpse the silhouettes of moored ships, their masts rearing up in the fog. To his left were the façades of locked warehouses, letters painted on brick spelling out the names of trading companies.

Having lost count of the streets, Bowman finally turned left, advancing into the city without any idea where he was going. He could not see more than fifty feet in front of him, as he passed buildings whose upper storeys were invisible. Working men appeared out of the fog. It was the time of day when labourers would be hired. With caps on their heads and hands in their pockets, they walked quickly, the dawn air cold on their necks, their shoulders hunched. Bowman turned again at a street corner, and then at another, and found himself on a wider boulevard where the visibility was slightly better. He walked past the metal fence surrounding a park. Bare trees, ghostly figures, reached out with twisted fingers towards the light of the sky, their trunks still concealed behind a soft, milky veil. There was no-one on the pavement. He read one of the signs hung to the fence: *City Hall Park*.

Bowman was walking aimlessly now, waiting for the city to reveal itself to him. Clouds of steam escaped his mouth, dispersing in the mist as if in the breath of the city itself, the city that was still sleeping. In fact, he could hear it breathing, a distant murmur, like the rustle of fabric or a stream. The unreal atmosphere and his lack of sleep must be playing tricks on him. Bowman stopped to listen more closely. No, he wasn't dreaming. The sound grew louder. He walked to the middle of a deserted road and turned towards the side of the street from where this strange murmur was coming. A dark mass surged out of the fog, occupying the entire width of the boulevard. Bowman ran back to the fence.

Women were walking down the road, elbows joined, their clothes and their light footsteps mingling to produce that dreamy swishing sound, filling up the silence of the city. As they advanced towards him and came into the light, Bowman saw the procession. There were hundreds of women. Maybe even thousands. The flood of black clothes, arms invisible, but bristling with heads, seemed to go on forever. Their faces were serious and pale, and they wore coats over their dresses. Working women.

Bowman turned around and fled from this silent flood, walking fast. Increasing the distance between them and him, he found himself alone in the lightening mist, pursued by an ever-louder chorus. Hundreds of gentle voices combining to become one giant voice, rumbling like thunder.

"To City Hall!"

"To City Hall!"

"Strike! Strike! Strike!"

Bowman kept following the fence, trying to find the entrance to the park. Another sound rose in the distance ahead of him. But this time he recognised the noise. About sixty feet away, he saw a line of soldiers moving towards him. A troop of men marching in time, their boots beating rhythmically against the ground, the barrels of their rifles pointing above their heads and mist-wreathed bodies. Bowman was trapped between the soldiers and the protesters. He quickly crossed the road and dived down an alleyway. The echo of slogans and boots ricocheted from the walls around him. Holding his bag tightly, he kept running until he heard an officer yell an order:

"Halt!"

He stopped and retraced his footsteps. The boot heels struck the ground as one, making a noise like a gunshot. The voices of the women went silent and the rustle of the procession slowed and quietened. A hundred feet separated the protesters and the soldiers. The silence lasted for a few seconds. The breaths of the troops and the workers, warmed by the march, rose in little clouds like the bodies of horses before galloping away in the cold. The women had rosy cheeks and frowning faces and they stood with elbows joined. The soldiers, straight-backed and immobile, did not look at them. Their eyes stared at a point above the crowd.

Bowman knew nervous men when he saw them. Perhaps they weren't afraid of these unarmed women, but they certainly didn't feel at ease, faced with these workers of all ages. Old and young women, adolescent girls, some pretty, some fat, some rebellious. There were a few black women too. Perched on some of the women's shoulders were small children.

Bowman did not recognise the uniforms of this army, nor the rank of the officer who advanced, passing between the rows of his men.

"The strike must end! There will be no more negotiations! If you advance, we will open fire!"

A woman's voice rose from the procession in reply:

"Our children are starving to death!"

Another woman spoke out:

"We want to see the mayor!"

"Yeah! Let Mr Wood come out of his palace – we've got things we need to tell him!"

And the shouting began again:

"To City Hall! To City Hall!"

The officer stepped back behind the rifles of his men.

Bowman, from his alleyway, watched the other side of the boulevard. Behind the fences of the park, in the last patches of fog held in place by the trees and plants, figures were moving quickly. Other soldiers were taking up positions on the side of the protest march, hidden behind trees and benches. The women were trapped between the fences on one side and the buildings on the other, and the troops were barring their way. The slogans gradually fell silent again. A woman in her forties, her hair in a bun, walked towards the soldiers.

"The men will be joining us soon! The steelworkers have voted to strike! You can't stop us advancing!"

She took another few steps towards the young soldiers.

"Soldiers! Soon it will be your wives and children who'll be starving to death! These are your mothers out in the street today! What are you doing here? Eh? Go home or march with us! You and your families are dying of hunger too and you're slaving away for less money than you need to live! Soldiers, join us!"

The first rows of the women chorused this, and soon the whole procession was chanting:

"Soldiers, join us!"

"Soldiers, join us!"

"To City Hall!"

Bowman, used to hearing orders even under the racket of gunfire and heavy artillery, heard the voice of an officer amid this riot of voices:

"First line! In position!"

Twenty soldiers knelt on the ground.

"Second line! Take aim!"

Forty rifles were pointed at the protesters' chests. In the park, too, the soldiers took aim. Cries arose from the procession, near the fences, swallowed up by the slogans:

"They're in the park! They've got us surrounded! We have to get out of here!"

Bowman took a step back and pressed his body against the brick wall of the alley.

In the front rows, some women closed their eyes while others wept and trembled, held upright by their comrades. They took a step forward. The procession began to move. The soldiers' rifles shook. The officer yelled:

"Fire!"

The first salvo seemed to make no noise. Because no-one really believed it was happening, or because the cries of the women were as loud as the gunshots. A cloud of smoke filled the space separating the two groups. When it dissipated, there were screams of terror, drowned out by the slogans still being chanted by the crowd behind. The front rows, pushed forward by their comrades, tripped over corpses and tried to turn around. From the park came another salvo. Bullets whistled through the bars of the fences and smashed the windows of the buildings opposite. This time, the chorus of slogans stopped, turning to shrieks and screams as panic took hold of the entire protest march.

Bowman covered his head with his arms. It took several minutes before the women stopped running in all directions and bumping into each other, before the flood of workers turned around and began to flee. During this time, there were five more bursts of gunfire. The alley was invaded. Women ran past Bowman, screaming, helping the wounded, carrying children. The soldiers were now shooting at will. The boulevard emptied and the screams of the workers grew more distant.

"Bayonets! Forward march!"

The troop advanced down the boulevard, stepping over bodies lying across the road. Bowman watched the soldiers pass the alley. When they had gone far enough, he came out and walked in the middle of the street, amid the clouds of smoke and the smell of powder. The bodies were lying on their backs or bellies, faces humiliated by death, muscles tensed by the impact of bullets. Torn dresses revealed grazed legs and white bellies. Long hair, unpinned, flowed over the ground, soaked with trickles of blood running in straight lines between the paving stones. Bowman stood there, unmoving. In the park, the last soldiers were dispersing.

Someone called out to him:

"Help me."

At his feet, rolled up in a ball, a young woman was looking up at him.

"Please. Help me."

He turned her onto her back. She was holding her stomach with both hands. Bowman pulled apart her fingers, lifted up her clothes, and examined the wound.

"Help me."

He put an arm under her head and another under her legs. She weighed almost nothing. Just a child of fifteen or sixteen. Blood dripped onto Bowman's jacket, steaming in the cold air.

He leaned her against a wall in the alleyway. Her face was white and her lips dry. Bowman rummaged through his bag, but found only a half-empty bottle of gin. He stood up, turned around, wondering where he might find some water and knowing that it was already too late. He pressed down on the girl's stomach to slow the blood loss. She put her hands on his.

"I need a doctor. Please. It hurts."

She looked around her, then back at this man she didn't know. She begged him:

"My parents. You have to find my parents."

Her eyes did not leave Bowman's. She squeezed his fingers with her hands.

"Please."

She sat up, grimacing with pain, and clung on to him. Her voice grew weak:

"My parents . . ."

She bit his shoulder to avoid crying out. The blood was no longer dripping on Bowman; the wound was drying up. She held herself tight inside his arms, as if he were a mother, her jerky breath slowing. Her head fell backwards, into the man's hand. Her neck muscles no longer held it up. Bowman could feel the skull heavy in his palm. She was still looking at him.

She was too young to be able to die peacefully; the fear, stronger than anything, of dying alone without knowing why.

"There's nothing I can do for you, child."

Her heart was still beating and she begged him to say something before she could no longer hear. Bowman moved his hand towards her face, and the girl, seeing his fingers touching her eyes, started with panic.

"Shh. I'm not the one you need to look at. Don't be scared. It's your time, child. Breathe. There's nothing else. Just a bit more air."

Her body relaxed. Her chest rose slowly, then Bowman felt the air from her mouth on his hand, a little lukewarm puff of air, which stopped when the body, like a balloon, had stopped emptying. His fingers slid down her face, closing the eyelids. He freed himself from the corpse's grip and lay it on the ground.

On the boulevard, soldiers were picking up the workers' bodies and throwing them on carts. The wounded were lined up on the pavement, without any medical aid or even blankets. Day had risen over New York. Arthur Bowman, covered in blood, walked down the narrow alley, repeating a question to himself, with a sour smile on his face. He wondered if the girl, lying in the alley, had chosen to fill out the form to become an American citizen.

John Street Church was a simple building in black stone. Almost square, its façade was embellished only by a triangular pediment with straight mouldings. Two high, narrow windows flanked the front door. A sort of monolith trapped between two residential houses that plunged the little church in their shade.

The interior was dark too. Candles burned on both sides of the nave, while on benches old men and women were praying. In front of the altar, a pastor was talking to a young couple. The pastor was elderly, his head bald but for a few last white hairs. He smiled as he listened to the couple.

Bowman waited near some candles, overhearing a few words of the conversation and gathering that the couple were preparing for their wedding. They were organising a ceremony with the pastor, who was answering them in reassuring tones.

When they walked away, Bowman approached the old man.

"Can I speak to you?"

"Of course, my son. What's it about?"

"Pastor Selby in Plymouth gave me this address."

The old pastor smiled.

"I don't know Pastor Selby, I'm sorry. I'm Pastor Ryan. You've come from England?"

Bowman was about to reply, but Ryan was looking at his jacket, bending forward to examine it.

"My Lord! Is that blood? Are you injured?"

Bowman looked down at his clothes.

"Not mine."

"What happened, my son?"

"I picked up someone who was injured."

Ryan put a hand on Bowman's arm.

"Follow me."

They walked around the altar and went into a room at the back of the church. It was not a lodging, just a little study cluttered with buckets and brooms, a little table and three chairs. The light came through one narrow, barred window.

"Sit down."

Pastor Ryan grabbed a pitcher and two glasses from a shelf and poured some water for Bowman, who drank it willingly. The water was cold and hurt his teeth.

"What happened?"

"I got trapped in the middle of a protest march."

"You were over there? How is the wounded man?"

Bowman drank a little more.

"It was a woman. A girl. She's dead."

Pastor Ryan crossed himself. Often Bowman found this gesture ridiculous. But the old man had not done it pityingly, nor in a mechanical way. More as if it were a thought he didn't like translated into a polite gesture, suggesting that all of this, in the end, was a sick joke.

Bowman opened his bag and put the bottle of gin on the table.

"I need a drink. Help yourself."

Ryan sat opposite him and poured a little gin in the bottom of a glass.

"My son, it is not to be mean that I'm taking so little, but because my liver has been terribly painful for some time now. About twenty years, if you really want to know."

Ryan lifted his glass.

"Do you have a change of clothes?"

Bowman nodded.

"Do you have a place to sleep?"

Bowman said no.

"Give me your things. I'll get them washed and you can stay here."

"I'm not in need. I can pay for a room."

"But you'll be better off here."

Bowman got to his feet. Without even thinking, he took off his jacket and his shirt, and stood bare-chested in front of the little table. Pastor Ryan crossed himself. What a joke.

3

"May I ask what happened to you?"

"It was a long time ago."

"You don't want to talk about it."

"Seems like for a while now, the only people I've met have been pastors who want to make me talk and madmen who want to shut me up."

The old man lowered his eyes and turned his glass in his hands, as if unsure whether to poison his liver a little more.

"There are cases where I don't believe in confession, Mr Bowman. Often, talking about something painful just brings back the suffering. Whoever you are, I don't think you have anything to reproach yourself for regarding those wounds."

Bowman stuffed his pipe with tobacco and lit a match by scraping it on the table.

"I wouldn't be so sure about that."

The old pastor smiled.

"Do you want to ask God for forgiveness?"

"Or I could piss in a violin and wait for it to play music."

The old man's smile grew wider.

"Good Christians are not always the ones you think, my son. You tried to save that young girl. Most of us would have just run away."

"There was no-one else there. And I couldn't save her."

"Chance is something I have learned to mistrust. I ought to tell you that it is God's work, but I suppose you don't believe in that?"

"I didn't do anything. I just picked her up."

"Did you say anything to her?"

"What can you say to someone who's dying?"

Pastor Ryan had pushed back his chair and was observing the man in front of him. Bowman met his gaze.

"Why did they shoot at those women?"

"You don't seem to be a man overly encumbered with illusions, Mr Bowman. If you still have any regarding this country, this should be enough to cure you. The United States is not a young nation, but a flourishing trade in human beings. Those in Washington who are currently debating the emancipation of the slaves are the owners of the factories where those women work. It was they who ordered the striking workers shot. In the South, a white man who kills a negro does not go to prison, but a white man who helps a slave escape will rot in a cell for a long, long time. The arithmetic is set down in law, Mr Bowman. There are too many poor people, so they must not be allowed to unite. The textile workers have been on strike for three weeks. The steelworkers were going to join them. So the negotiations were ended. If an honest count were kept of the protests, strikes and revolts that break out here every year, not a single politician would dare to talk about prosperity for fear of getting stoned. And when there isn't an economic crisis, like this one, which has been going on for three years, they always find a way of starting a war. The factories go to work to supply the army with weapons, food and trains."

The old pastor leaned over the table.

"But you already know all that, don't you?"

"I don't care about politics."

"Are you sure you couldn't have said anything to that young woman?"

"When you die, you're alone. All the rest is bullshit."

"And I suppose you, Mr Bowman, are not afraid of dying alone in this country where you have just arrived and know no-one? Is that right?"

Bowman filled his glass, and then the pastor's.

"I know someone. That's why I'm here."

"Do we have a mutual acquaintance, Mr Bowman?"

"I'm looking for Pastor Peavish. It was Selby, in Plymouth, who told me that he might have passed through here."

Ryan pushed the glass away, fighting his desire to drink.

"Yes. Peavish."

"You know him?"

"He stayed only a few days."

"Do you know where he is?"

"I don't have the faintest idea. When we go away to preach, we don't keep in touch. We simply go where we are needed. In towns that are sometimes just tents beside a river and the church a wooden crate under a tree, standing on top of which anyone who can read can become a pastor. Peavish left here more than a year ago. He might be in California by now, or buried by the side of a road in Utah. Would you tell me why you're looking for him?"

"I think he was in Texas in November. In a town called Reunion."

"How do you know that?"

"Is there a church there?"

"I told you: what you call a town, which existed four months ago, might have disappeared today. But I don't know that place. Do you know what Pastor Peavish was doing there?"

"It's a town that's not like any others. An ideal community. Utopian."

Ryan smiled.

"Lots of people try to found communities in the West. People who think they can find virgin territory there, without any religious or political authorities. But the ideal does not last long round here, Mr Bowman. The theorists, the dreamers and the visionaries are usually robbed, unless they have a good army like the Mormons. What do you know about Reunion?"

"It's in Texas."

"And?"

"There was a murder there."

The old pastor thought for a moment. His smile was frozen in place and his forehead crinkled.

"Mr Bowman, I would like to ask you a few questions, so that things are clear between us. I am not asking you to make confession, just to trust me."

Bowman leaned back in his chair. Ryan crossed his hands on the table.

"Did you make this journey to kill someone?"

"Yes."

"Are you looking for Pastor Peavish in order to kill him?"

"Dunno."

"Do you want to kill him or not?"

"I don't know if it's him. Peavish or someone else."

"Those scars . . . Are you looking for the man who gave them to you?"

"No. But he has the same ones."

Ryan was pale.

"The murderer in Reunion, Mr Bowman . . . Are you saying he went through the same hell as you?"

Bowman gritted his teeth.

"The same."

The pastor began to make a gesture, but did not finish it, as if he had wanted to cross himself but realised it was pointless.

"All the pastors who leave for the West go through St Louis, in Missouri. That is also the route you must take to get to Texas. I'll give you the address of the Methodist church and the name of a pastor there, who might have met Peavish. I'm going to make up a bed for you, and tomorrow I will bring you back your clothes. I'll also bring you some food."

The pastor stood up, holding his back with both hands. Bowman got up at the same time.

"I'll pay you for all that."

"You will make a donation to the parish, Mr Bowman."

A choirboy unfolded a mattress on the floor and gave Bowman some blankets. He brought him bread and stew, and a bit of rum and water. The child told him he was locking up and he would be back at dawn.

Bowman walked around the church, a blanket thrown over his shoulders. He went up to the front door and listened to the street sounds on the other side. He paused by the candles, warming himself on their flames, and took two back with him to his cubbyhole. Sitting on the mattress, back to the wall, the blankets covering his legs, he smoked a pipe and drank some rum while he watched the candle burn down.

The next morning, Pastor Ryan found the little room empty. On the table was a letter, held in place by some English coins.

> Pastor, if you can find the parents of the girl who died, the money is for them and her burial. If not, it's for the church.
>
> I don't know if it's Peavish. Because there's another sergeant and I'm looking for both of them. We all came from that hell you talked about, and what's sad is that monsters like us are alive and children are dying in the street.
>
> I might send news here or tell you when I return.
> Arthur Bowman

Ryan crossed himself, folded the sergeant's clean clothes and tidied them away in a wardrobe.

—⚏—⚏—⚏—

He bought a new jacket – tweed with leather-lined shoulders – and matching trousers, some fur-lined boots with flat heels, a pair of bison-skin gloves, and a long black coat. All he kept of his old clothing was the leather cap.

Entering the Duncan, Sherman & Co. bank, at 48 William Street, Bowman looked like just another customer. At the counter, he asked for two letters of credit to be paid out. They gave him the two hundred dollars in gold and silver coins, inside a leather purse stamped with the bank's initials. He asked how to get to St Louis and they answered, as if it were obvious:

"New York Central Railroad. You'll be in Chicago in two days. From there, it's another day by train to St Louis. The best line in the country, sir. You should take a carriage: the station is at the other end of town."

Bowman set out into the flood of pedestrians, walking down Broadway Avenue, past the City Hall Park. Bowman did not recognise the place now it was packed with people, the road cluttered with horse-drawn carriages and cabs. People were strolling in the park, families and merchants walking the pavements, donut sellers and shoe-shines. No trace remained of the shooting.

He deviated from his route, pushing past a few shoulders and stopping at the entrance to the alley. At the foot of a wall, he found an ankle boot with the laces undone. He picked it up and turned it in his hands, then tossed it on a pile of old rags and went on his way.

The city was designed like a military camp. Straight lines and numbers. He left Broadway and continued on Park Avenue for another mile, until he reached the junction with 42nd Street.

Inside the Grand Central Depot, you could have fitted Plymouth's wooden train station three times over. For thirty-one dollars, he received a second-class ticket for Chicago; a train was leaving in two hours.

"You should buy another ticket once you get there. Several companies go to St Louis, without any changes of train or driver."

"Are there changes for Chicago?"

"Three, sir."

In the station's shopping mall, Bowman took a seat on a restaurant terrace, under the arch of the main concourse, ordered some meat and beer, and sat watching the other passengers. He bought a newspaper from a vendor. The front page announced the candidacy of Abraham Lincoln, Republican, for the next presidential elections. Bowman put the paper down, too distracted to read any more. He had no idea how far Chicago was from New York. Calculating that the trains travelled at the same speed as those in England, he thought that the trip must be thousands of miles long. Then it would take another day to reach St Louis, the final staging post before the start of Irving's West.

Bowman felt dizzy when he realised that the United States was as big as India and that he was searching for two men who were hiding from him. But in places as vast as this, public transport was rare, particularly when the territory itself had not been entirely colonised. Anyone who wanted to travel far had to take the same routes. So, despite the sheer size of the country, it was still possible to find a man. Sitting in front of his steak, in his new clothes, Bowman also realised that his fortune would soon no longer be of any use to him, that he would have to abandon his bourgeois suit. Penders and Peavish had no money. He must travel like they did, go through the same places, with the same means, if he was to have any chance of finding them. Because he felt sure now that they were surviving somewhere far from any city.

He boarded his train and only felt better once it had left the city limits behind, when the track began to snake between hills and lakes, passing over rivers swelled by rain. Bowman watched the landscape rush past until nightfall – a world of dark, snowy forests – without glimpsing any of the tall grass described by Irving. The second-class seats were made of padded leather; after an initial sensation of comfort and a few hours of travelling, however, the passenger started to toss and turn in all directions to try to avoid aches and pains in their backs and behinds. It was cold in the carriage, and the train shook as it rounded corners, the carriages in front and behind banging into it. The noise was as loud as in his cabin on the *Persia*.

His mind filled by this din, Bowman began to doze off, wrapped up in his coat, holding his bag tight against him. When he woke up, it was still night, but the train was slowing down. They entered a station lit by three lamps, in the middle of nowhere. A conductor passed through the carriages, announcing that all passengers had to change trains. Bowman waited on the platform, where an icy wind blew. Twenty minutes later, another train stopped at a second platform. A man walked past pulling a trolley filled with blankets for sale. Bowman gave him twenty cents and covered his shoulders. Then, feeling the thickness of the cotton, bought a second one, which he haggled down to ten cents.

"Why are we changing trains?"

The blanket vendor blew into his numb hands.

"Because you're changing company, sir. And as they all have different width tracks, that means you have to take a different train."

"I only paid for one ticket, though. Do I have to buy another one?"

"No, sir. Because all the companies belong to one big one, in fact – Vanderbilt's New York Central. The Central has bought all the companies in the north-east, but they haven't remade the tracks yet, so you still have to change trains."

There was no change in the quality of the seating, however. Bowman folded a blanket on the bench, wrapped himself up in the other one, and fell asleep again. The next day, the train sped through pine forests all morning, interrupted only by a few woodland shacks. Bowman had left without any food. The conductor told him they would soon be stopping at Rochester to change trains, and that he would be able to eat something there.

The train line went past a vast, iced-over lake for several miles. Whirlwinds of snow flew over the ice, and cold gusts of air blew some snowflakes through the cracks in the carriage doors. In Rochester, Bowman had time to buy a few things – some food and a bottle of bourbon. All afternoon and evening, this third train followed the shore of the lake. They filled up with water and coal at the station in Buffalo. In Cleveland, after another change, he climbed aboard the last train – to Chicago – and, at the end of the day, got off the train and immediately bought a ticket from the St Louis, Alton & Chicago Railroad. He left again a few hours later and travelled through the night without seeing anything of the land he was moving through as the train took him south.

Bowman had hoped St Louis would be a quiet little town, but it was even more frenzied than New York, despite weather so cold that the ground was rock-hard. The station was a rail hub the like of which he had never seen before. The trains were loaded with goods. Drivers shouted and whips cracked as lines of connected carts carrying crates and barrels were pulled by teams of twelve or sixteen mules. The station was built on the bank of a brown river, as wide as the Ganges or the Irrawaddy, where dozens of boats as big as houses were moored, like some enormous three-storey steam barges, surrounded by gangways. The goods passed from trains to boats and from boats to trains. The streets were made of bare earth, criss-crossed with ice-hardened ruts over which the carriages skidded and bumped. Bowman had never seen such turmoil. It was as if all the goods in the country were arriving here at the same time, and the inhabitants of St Louis, panic-stricken, were rushing around trying to get rid of them before they were engulfed. To make themselves heard in this chaos, everyone shouted. The horses were noisy too, whinnying as they were whipped, their hooves caught in ice. He threw a blanket over his shoulders and covered up his head, crossing the street to a saloon from which the hubbub of conversations could be heard on the opposite pavement.

At the entrance to the Two Rivers Saloon, a sign announced: *Buy a drink, get a free meal.* In spite of this offer, everyone inside was busy drinking, and there were few plates cluttering up the tables. The crowd was like that of a Bombay market. It was hot and the smoke-filled air was unbreathable. A hundred people bellowed and laughed. Bowman shouldered his way through to the counter, where a barman asked him what he wanted.

"Bourbon."

"You want a meal?"

He waited to taste the five-cent bourbon before deciding. When the barman placed a tiny glass in front of him, he asked where he could find the Methodist church of St Louis. The barman burst out laughing without answering his question, then went to serve some other customers. Bowman downed his drink and left, following the plank pavement – a sort of bridge over the flood of icy mud – and went into a shop, the Rovers' General Store. The display cases and shelves were filled with food, clothing, tools, tobacco, ammunition and alcohol. In a glass-fronted wardrobe behind the counter, Bowman saw weapons for sale, new and second-hand, rifles and pistols. He waited his turn and approached the till. The manager, a bald man with a plug of tobacco swelling his cheek, asked him what he wanted without looking up.

"I need some tobacco."

"How much?"

"Half a pound. And a bottle of bourbon. Not the cheapest, but not the dearest either."

Bowman paid for his purchases.

"I'm looking for a church. A Methodist church, in St Louis. You know anything about that?"

This time, the manager looked at him and smiled.

"The Methodists. They must be in Manchester with all the others. Personally, I don't really have time to go, but I have to say that I regret that. If you're looking for a preacher, just go over there and kick a tree. Three or four'll fall on your face."

"Manchester?"

"It's about fifteen miles away, an encampment outside the city. If you want, I can arrange transport there for you."

"You do that too?"

The man seemed surprised.

"Of course! And if you want a boat, I can get that for you too. The only thing you won't find in my store is girls."

He laughed loudly.

"For them, you have to go and see my brother-in-law, on the other side of the street."

Behind a workhorse with an arse the size of a locomotive, a tilbury was harnessed, just big enough for two people to sit side by side. The driver looked as if he might be related to the shop manager, hiding his bald head under a fur hat, his cheek also swelled with a plug of tobacco.

"Are you the English man? Did my brother tell you the fare? You have to pay right away."

Bowman paid for half of the fare.

"Are you always a suspicious bastard or is it just my face you don't like?"

"Bit of both."

The driver burst out laughing and snapped the reins.

"Walk on, Lincoln!"

"Is that his real name?"

"No, but this nag's a real politician. He answers to any name you call him. I just called him Lincoln to make you happy. You look like a Republican."

The driver grabbed his whip and cracked it against the horse's rump.

"They never pay what they should."

He laughed again and the tilbury jumped into the air as it went over the ruts, behind the horse which trotted along at its own pace, indifferent to the whipping or the driver's yells. When the driver tried to pull the reins to slow it down, the animal lowered its head and the man was thrown forward from his seat. He put his hat back in place and spat black tobacco juice at his nag.

"Piece-of-shit horse! Maybe he is a Democrat, then, after all? Do you have them in England?"

The countryside was flat, the fields empty and the trees huddled in orchards, looking like frozen old people. On the gravel track, the horse trotted at a good speed. The driver had drunk more than half of his flask of rum and was dozing by the time they reached Manchester.

On each wooden shack, its windows draught-proofed by cloths, was hand-painted the name of a congregation. Evangelists, Baptists, Adventists, Bible Students, Lutherans (Reformed or Universal), Catholics . . . all the representatives of the Lord's trade were gathered here. An outpost with smoking chimneys, improvised stable, one-room schools and these chapels differentiated from coal holes only by the painted letters on their walls; all around, canvas tent flaps snapped in the wind, and swaddled figures rushed to find shelter. In the middle of these little shacks, the chapel of the Methodist Episcopal Church stood tall: the sole brick building, painted red, with a pediment of columns and a white belfry. The Methodists were well-established in this temporary village and the absence of any draughts in their building seemed likely to give them a certain spiritual success. Bowman elbowed the driver, who opened his eyes and yanked hard on the reins.

"Whoa, Victoria!"

Bowman climbed down from the tilbury with his bag.

"I won't be long. Wait for me here."

"At your service, Your Majesty."

Fifteen minutes later, when Bowman came out of the chapel, the driver had taken refuge under its pediment and was stamping his feet on the steps to warm up. In the tilbury, Bowman wrapped himself in the blanket, took out his bourbon and drank a quarter of it without pausing for breath, watched attentively by the Rover brother.

"How do I get to Texas from here?"

"Well, you've either got the boat to New Orleans and then Houston, or you can take the Butterfield line that goes to Fort Worth."

"The Butterfield?"

"The postal service. They also take passengers on their stage-coaches."

"Is Fort Worth far from Dallas?"

"Not as far as I know."

"And is it far from here?"

The driver looked at Bowman.

"What do you think? There's at least six hundred miles between us and Texas."

"What's the fastest way?"

"Are you really in a rush to get there?"

The carriages of the Butterfield Overland Mail left twice a week from St Louis, and the next scheduled departure was the following morning. Opposite the Rover brothers' General Store, their brother-in-law's whorehouse rented rooms for a dollar a night, with dinner and break-fast thrown in if you paid for a girl or bought a bottle. The Rovers' sister, who worked the till there, was not bald and did not chew tobacco, but she was just as ugly as her brothers. Bowman was entitled to his free meal after ordering a bottle of bourbon, the same brand he'd bought at the store, though for twice the price. The ground floor was a large room with a bar, similar in every way to the Two Rivers Saloon except for the curtains on the windows, some cushions on the benches and far fewer people. The girls looked more like waitresses than dancers, their work consisting in encouraging the customers to consume alcohol rather than leading them to the bedrooms. Besides, you'd have had to do a lot of drinking before setting out on such an adventure. While they were perfectly friendly and polite, it was better not to make them smile. They had the bad teeth of the very poor and the sad complexions of mothers who have lost their children. In comparison to this, the Chinaman's whorehouse in Pallacate was a palace filled with princesses. Bowman sat on his own to eat, rejecting the girls' commercial advances under the landlady's disappointed gaze.

The bedroom was clean, the bed sagging, the air warmed by a coal fire. He lay down in bed and a few minutes later the landlady knocked at his door. Given that he insisted on sleeping alone, she agreed to a substantial reduction and offered to send him a good-looking girl to keep him warm tonight. Bowman asked her if this girl was a member of the family, and the Rover sister slammed the door and left. The only company Bowman kept in bed that night was his travelling bag and his letters of credit.

At the church in Manchester, the pastor remembered Peavish. He had passed through one year earlier, and had then returned to the camp twice for short stays. The last time he had been was about five or six months ago, during the summer, before he went off to Colorado. According to the pastor, Peavish had not gone south to preach but had spread the good word in Oregon. He added that Peavish was a tireless traveller, however, and it was possible he had gone to Texas without him knowing about it.

Bowman tossed and turned in his bed, trying to fall asleep. The night went on, and as more alcohol was consumed downstairs, the upstairs bedrooms began to fill up. With the creaking floorboards and the noises coming through the thin wooden walls, it was all quite similar to the train in the mountains or the *Persia* on the waves.

4

Advise to travelers on the Butterfield Overland Mail

The consumption of alcohol is forbidden on stagecoaches, but if you must drink, please share your bottle.

If ladies are on board, gentlemen must not smoke cigars or pipes because the smell offends women. Chewing tobacco is permitted, but please spit downwind.

Bison skins will be distributed in the event of bad weather.

Do not sleep on your neighbor's shoulder. Do not snore too loud.

Firearms are permitted but may be used only in emergencies. Do not shoot for pleasure or at wild animals, as gunfire may frighten the horses.

If the horses bolt, remain calm. When descending from the stagecoach, you risk injury and being left at the mercy of the elements, hostile Indian tribes and hungry coyotes.

Forbidden subjects of conversation: attacks on stagecoaches and Indian rebellions.

Any men behaving in a cavalier fashion with ladies will be expelled from the stagecoach. It's a long walk back. Let this warning suffice.

Four other travellers were seated in the waiting room. A young, well-dressed couple, their bags at their feet, sitting in silence. A round little man, ruddy face under a bowler hat, wearing a second-hand coat, reading a newspaper. And, lastly, an older man reading a book, his elbows resting on his suitcase. From where he sat, Bowman could not make out the book's title. The driver, a fur thrown over his shoulders, was armed with an automatic rifle similar to the one Bowman had seen in the armoury in Walworth. His name was Perkins and he announced that the stagecoach was ready. The man in the bowler hat, who obviously knew him, shook his hand.

The benches in the carriage were barely wide enough to seat three people, and with the bags of mail at their feet, they all sat with their knees up to their chests. As the journey to Texas lasted six days, some of the Butterfield line's recommendations were far from superfluous. Bowman sat next to the old man and the man in the bowler hat on one bench, their backs to the road ahead, while they left the other bench to the couple. Pieces of cloth were stretched over the windows, blocking the view but failing to stop the wind that always blew in St Louis. As soon as the passengers were on board, Perkins cracked his whip and the stagecoach set off through the city.

The little fat man's name was Ernst Dietrich. He bought and sold livestock, and he was going to Fort Worth to purchase a herd of six hundred cattle that had to be delivered to St Louis in the spring. Dietrich was chatty and, despite the rules, wishing to reassure the lady, told her that, on this part of the track, there was no risk of attack. Since the army had pushed back the redskins into the reserves, the country was at peace. The last Cherokees and Choctaws who lived in the Fort Smith region worked for Butterfield, supplying food for people and animals, and sometimes serving it too. As for attacks from bandits, there was nothing to fear there anymore either. The bands of outlaws mostly worked in New Mexico these days. And, proud of himself, Dietrich opened his bag and took out a revolver.

"And if there was a problem, I'm fully prepared. Remington .44. Here you go, sir, feel how light it is."

Feigning admiration, the young husband weighed the revolver in his hands. He clearly knew nothing about firearms. This couple, the Bradfords, were not travelling all the way to Fort Worth, but stopping at Fort Smith to see family and visit inland. Mr Bradford planned to cultivate saffron. This spice, imported from Africa and Asia, would, he said, acclimatise perfectly to Arkansas. And no-one had thought of doing it yet. His wife, her good looks ruined by her severe expression, listened without a word, a bourgeois lady convinced that this project was part of God's great design, already calculating how many children she would bring into the world per number of hectares planted. Dietrich, loud and jovial, continued to take care of the civilities, turning now to the old man in glasses.

"And you, sir, where are you headed?"

The old man looked over the rims of his glasses at Dietrich and smiled.

"To Dallas. I run a school there. Alfred Brewster."

The old teacher was a thin man, and Dietrich had to push himself hard against Bowman in order not to crush him. Now, the livestock trader turned to the sergeant.

"And you, sir?"

"Dallas too. Or a town near it. Name of Reunion."

Dietrich rubbed his chin.

"Reunion? I've never heard of it. Mr Brewster, do you know it?"

The old man looked up from his book and shook his head.

"What are you going to do there, sir?"

"I'm going to see someone."

"Business or family?"

Bowman was about to tell him to shut his mouth when the old man interrupted:

"Are you comfortable, Mrs Bradford?"

Her husband responded for her:

"We're used to it, Mr Brewster, don't worry about us."

The track was smooth and the driver kept the horses galloping, in spite of the rain. The leather suspension creaked, the wood rattled, and water poured through the makeshift curtains. Dietrich rummaged about in his bag again and this time came up with a bottle.

"Mrs Bradford, I hope it won't disturb you if we have a drink. With this cold, even a New York doctor would advise a sip or two of this Kentucky bourbon."

The lady blushed and her husband refused to partake.

"Really? Well, you're a strange kind of farmer, Mr Bradford!"

Dietrich, who knew his manners, also took a glass from his bag.

The old man drank a little bit, then Dietrich served a glass for Bowman, who downed it in one. Dietrich had already been quite merry before he boarded the stagecoach. When he had finished the bourbon, he collapsed onto the old school teacher and started to snore.

After six hours of travel, Perkins stopped at the first inn. In the badly heated log building, they ate some porridge and some watery meat, and drank coffee. When the horses had been replaced, the new ones set off at a gallop half an hour later. After five minutes, Mrs Bradford stuck her head out of a window and vomited, taking care to do so downwind. The old teacher, Brewster, took a flask of syrup from his pocket and offered her a drink.

"It's made with plants. Nothing contra-indicated in your condition, ma'am."

Mrs Bradford looked at her husband. Brewster smiled at them.

"Your wife is expecting a child, isn't she? I'm a herbalist too. This syrup will do her good, don't you worry."

Dietrich, determined to celebrate the arrival of a new American, took another bottle from his bag and insisted that Mr Bradford take a sip. His wife drank a little bit of Brewster's potion, and a few minutes later was snoring as loudly as the livestock trader.

At night, there was another change of horses, though the passengers did not leave the stagecoach. At dawn, they stopped at another Butterfield inn and were served the same fare, this time under the guise of breakfast.

Inside the coach, when Dietrich was not going on in great detail about the expanding market for meat, with the Pikes Peak mines to supply, and the cities of the East growing in number every day, Bradford would describe for them the infinite virtues of saffron. They also talked about money, neither of them wishing to be outdone, each increasing the amounts he was likely to make as the conversation went on. Bowman had finally made out the title of Brewster's book. On the cover was an engraving of a wood cabin, with the title and the author's name printed below: *Walden; or, Life in the Woods* by David Henry Thoreau. He would have liked to ask the old man what the book was about, or chat with him about the books he himself had read, but didn't dare in front of the other passengers.

After three further changes of horses and as many stops at inns, all five passengers wrapped in damp, stinking bison skins, the Butterfield stagecoach reached Fort Smith. They said goodbye to the Bradfords and the driver announced that they would depart again at midnight, as they first had to wait for the mail to arrive from Memphis. There was a hotel near the company's offices, he said, where they could eat, drink and even rent a room to sleep for a few hours.

Bowman dined alone in the hotel restaurant, ordering a shot of hooch to end his meal, and old Brewster, who had eaten at another table, asked if he could join him.

"I noticed you were interested in my book. Are you a reader, Mr . . ."

"Sometimes, yeah. Bowman. Arthur Bowman."

"May I ask why you are going to that town you mentioned – Reunion?"

"I have to see someone."

"Yes, so you said. You're English, aren't you? Have you come all this way just to see someone?"

"That's right."

"That person must be very dear to you."

Bowman finished his glass of alcohol, which tasted like fermented rocks and rodents.

"You could say he's my only friend."

The teacher gave a brief smile before standing up.

"I'm going to rest for a while before we leave, Mr Bowman. I'll see you later."

Bowman remained at the table, continuing to drink. When he got back in the stagecoach, fairly well oiled, at midnight, Brewster and Dietrich were already sitting there. There were no new travellers, but the mailbags occupied all the free space on the benches. With the rain still falling, Perkins had put his entire cargo under shelter. Bowman fell asleep as soon as the coach's wheels jolted over the first rocks on the path.

Midway between Fort Smith and Fort Worth, the stagecoach came to a halt in a mile-wide valley. The track followed a river bordered by willows and poplars which ran between hills covered with dry grass, brown rocks and stunted sage. Perkins stopped the carriage in the middle of a ford, in a bend of the river. The horses plunged their heads into the water and the passengers got out to relax and enjoy the sun that had finally risen. The driver remained perched on his seat, rifle in hand. Dietrich offered him a drink and asked if he could try shooting his Remington. The driver, curious to see the brand-new revolver in action, told him he could take a few shots. His legs planted firmly, both hands on the butt of the pistol, the little man aimed at the trunk of a poplar. The echo of the gunshots ricocheted across the valley. After emptying an entire cylinder, he had lodged only a single bullet in the tree's bark. The livestock trader looked disappointed, explaining to the others that he was not yet used to this weapon and had not spent long training with it. Perkins had a go. From sixty feet away, he put two out of four bullets into the trunk, handed the Remington back to Dietrich, declared that it was an excellent gun and even offered to buy it from him. Dietrich, embarrassed, refused.

"Mr Bowman, would you like to try?"

Bowman watched him reload the cylinder – six bullets in a few seconds – then took the pistol and weighed it in his hand.

"I haven't shot anything for a long time."

Perkins smiled.

"There are plenty of people round here who carry guns but have no idea how to use them. I've seen men shooting at each other in the street, standing fifteen paces away, and hit nothing but a few windows in nearby houses."

Bowman took off his gloves, stood sideways on and, with his right hand, arm extended, aimed at the trunk. He took three shots. Each time, he sent the bark flying. He moved the pistol to his maimed left hand and missed with his first shot. Then, concentrating, he closed one eye and put the next two bullets straight into the tree.

During the next two hours, inside the stagecoach, Dietrich bored Brewster and Bowman with tales of gunfights, gunslingers and bank robberies.

They reached Fort Worth the next day in the late afternoon, barely one hour later than they were supposed to, according to the Butterfield timetable. They had just driven seven hundred miles south. The sky was blue and the temperature much milder than in St Louis, as if they had gone from winter to early spring. Dietrich bade farewell to his travelling companions, assuring Bowman that, if he needed anything, he would be in Fort Worth for the next week. He also congratulated the former sergeant on his shooting prowess and even asked him if he would like to buy the Remington from him. Bowman refused this offer and asked the driver how to get to Dallas.

"There are often convoys leaving from here. If not, you can rent a carriage, or even a horse. It's about twenty miles away. You won't find anything tonight, but tomorrow there's bound to be someone headed that way."

As Bowman walked off in the direction of the nearest hotel, old Brewster caught up to him.

"Mr Bowman, someone's coming to pick me up in town. We leave tomorrow morning. If you like, we could make the journey together."

"Could you take me to Reunion?"

"We wouldn't even have to make a detour. I'm going there myself."

"To Reunion?"

The old man smiled.

Fort Worth was a trading post. About twenty buildings, all standing close together, separated by a wide, unpaved street. The town was constructed on either side of a track heading straight from east to west, like one big way-station. General stores, shops selling grain and agricultural equipment, a Texan government land vendor's office, a Butterfield inn, a farrier, a saloon and two hotels. Other buildings were under construction at either end, increasing the size of the nascent town. Almost all the shops displayed signs offering rooms to rent. Brewster took a room in the same hotel as Bowman.

"Would you like to dine together, Mr Bowman?"

The place was clean, the furniture relatively new, and the bed comfortable. Bowman lay down for an hour, his back aching from the long trip. When he came out again into the passageway, he saw Brewster sitting at a table in the restaurant, speaking to a woman. Bowman could not see her face, which was hidden by a man's wide-brimmed hat. She was wearing a dusty black dress and a canvas work jacket. Bowman walked past her as he went downstairs. She did not look up, but he caught a quick glimpse of her face and a few strands of red hair escaping from her hat.

Brewster drank a beer, the foam sticking to his grey moustache. The table was set for three.

"Why didn't you say you were from Reunion, when we were in Fort Smith?"

"Because I wanted to know a little bit more about you."

"Do you know more now?"

Brewster smiled, took off his glasses and cleaned them with a hand-kerchief.

"Not much, except that you are an excellent shot. Perfect military style. Which army did you serve in, Mr Bowman?"

He put his glasses back on and peered at Bowman.

"India Company."

"West or East?"

"Africa and India. Why did you wait till we were here to tell me?"

"Mr Bowman, the town of Reunion is not universally beloved. What exactly do you know about the place?"

Bowman ordered a beer for himself.

"Nothing. Just an article I read, by a journalist called Brisbane."

Brewster put his glass down and wiped his moustache with the back of his hand.

"An article by Brisbane?"

"From last November."

The old man grew pale.

"To my knowledge, he has only ever written one article about Reunion. The one describing the death of Mr Kramer."

"That's the one."

"Who are you going to see in Reunion?"

"What makes you say that the town isn't loved by everyone?"

"Answer my question."

"I don't owe you an explanation."

Brewster's face was white as a sheet. His head trembled on his narrow shoulders.

"Why have you come here?"

He had raised his voice. Bowman looked around him at the other customers sitting at tables.

"I won't stay long, if that's what you're worried about."

"Mr Bowman, if you don't answer me, I will not take you to Reunion."

"I'll get there anyway."

Brewster stood up, offended.

"We will forbid you to enter our territory, Mr Bowman."

At the other tables, faces turned towards them. Bowman gritted his teeth and spoke in a mumble:

"Sit down, for God's sake."

Brewster sat back down on the edge of his chair.

"Did you know Richard? Is that why you've come?"

"Richard?"

"Mr Kramer."

"No. I'm searching for his killer."

Brewster turned his head and looked up. The woman was standing there, smiling, but her expression changed when she saw the look on the old man's face.

"What's the matter?"

She had put on a clean, figure-hugging dress and her hair was done up in a bun. At the other tables, men stared at her.

"Alfred, what's going on?"

She glanced at the man with the scarred forehead. Bowman stood up.

"If you don't want to take me there, I'll get there myself."

He moved away from the table, sat at the bar and ordered a drink. He downed several glasses while watching Brewster and the woman, deep in discussion. Then he left the hotel and walked over to the saloon, a smoke-filled room echoing with merry voices. He drank some whiskey, and asked the barman if there was a convoy leaving for Dallas the next morning. The barman pointed to a table occupied by two men.

"They're from Guadalupe Salt."

Bowman approached the men.

"Can I get you gentlemen a drink?"

They were already drunk. It struck them as a tempting proposal.

The mines of the Guadalupe Mountains were next to El Paso, and the men had come four hundred miles with two carriages filled with blocks of salt, through a desert that, apparently, gave a man a terrible thirst. Bowman paid for a third round. They were filthy and they stank, they laughed a lot, and kept looking around them at the other customers; the kind of men who think an enjoyable evening should end with a good brawl.

"You know Reunion?"

"The community? Yeah."

"Loonies."

"They share everything and they all take turns doing chores, men and women. Or they did, anyway."

"Yeah, 'cos there's hardly anyone left there. There were three hundred of them to start with. How many are left now?"

"Twenty or thirty."

"Yeah, at the most."

"They bought shitty land and none of 'em knew how to plough a field."

"They're better at explaining the mysteries of life than feeding their children."

"And then there was that incident."

"A man who got bumped off."

"Half of the ones who were still there took off after that."

Bowman negotiated the price of his journey and agreed to meet them the next day. Then he went to the bar and bought a bottle.

"You know the men in the convoy?"

The barman answered him without looking over at the table:

"We see them pass through occasionally."

In the hotel restaurant, a few customers were still sitting at tables, drinking alcohol. Others were finishing their drinks at the bar. Brewster had left, but the woman was still there, sitting with a well-dressed man of about twenty. She looked about Bowman's age, perhaps a little younger. Bowman remained at the counter with the last of the stragglers, his back turned to the room, observing her in the large mirror on the wall. She leaned forward and whispered something to the boy before getting to her feet. Bowman turned around. She walked past the bar, glancing over at the tall Englishman, a wry smile on her face, her eyes tired from drinking. The door of her bedroom opened onto the passageway. Bowman watched her go inside. Her departure seemed to be the signal for the restaurant to close. The customers disappeared, the young man included, and the waiters cleared tables, then set them ready for breakfast and turned off the lights. The bar was shut up and only a few nightlights were left on in the entrance hall.

The young suitor returned ten minutes later, discreetly pushing open the door, passing under the nightlights and climbing the stairs. He knocked at a door. In the dim light, Bowman saw the figure of the redhead in a dressing gown. The boy went in and she closed the door behind him.

Downstairs, hidden in darkness, sitting on a chair in the restaurant, Bowman smiled and raised his bottle of bourbon.

He ate steak and eggs, accompanied by a pot of coffee. Old Brewster came down from his room, carrying his suitcases, handed his key in at the reception desk and approached Bowman's table. Bowman was slowly chewing the last piece of his steak.

"I found a convoy. Told you I'd get there anyway."

Bowman bent over his plate and cleaned it with a hunk of bread.

"Mr Bowman, if you are looking for Richard's murderer, you may as well drive with us to Reunion. If you have questions, we will try to answer them. In exchange, we would like to know why you have come here."

"We?"

"Mrs Desmond and I."

"Mrs Desmond?"

"The woman you saw yesterday. She is the one who came to fetch me."

Bowman finished his coffee and stood up.

"When do we leave?"

The carriage, pulled by an old mare, left the hotel stable. The woman had put her work jacket back on, along with her wide-brimmed hat and her wool dress. Brewster was sitting next to her. Bowman threw his bag on the flatbed and sat on the back seat.

The track was straight and flat, amid a backdrop of prairies scattered with thorny trees. Pale, round hills rose on the horizon; cattle – little dark specks in the distance – sought what little succour there was in the yellow grass. Ravines traversed the prairie: the dry beds of seasonal rivers. Although the air was still cool, the sun shone down from the blue sky, heating their heads and making them thirsty. They travelled seven or eight miles, or so Bowman guessed: it was hard to be sure of the distance in this unvarying landscape. Ahead of them, to the east, a dark line appeared.

The mare was breathing hard as it jogged along. When they came within sight of a thicket of trees in the middle of the scree, Mrs Desmond turned off the main path and followed some tracks leading to the small, leafless trees, white-limbed and knotty. There was a muddy waterhole, fed by a spring that flowed unevenly. The mare headed towards the brown water. The woman helped old Brewster to descend, and he went to sit down in the meagre shade of a tree. She brought him a flask and some bread. Bowman stretched as he looked at the path to the west, arrowing towards Fort Worth. There was a dust cloud behind them: maybe the Guadalupe Salt convoy, catching them up. He sat close to the old man, accepted the flask, and drank a few mouthfuls of water. The woman remained at a distance, next to the spring.

"Mr Bowman, I hope you didn't take my reaction last night the wrong way. The local authorities did not try very hard to find Mr Kramer's murderer. The idea that a stranger should come from England to get involved in the affair, after all this time . . . that is enough to disturb us. That horrible incident was a shock for our community."

Bowman picked up a stone, turned it between his fingers and began to rub the dust off it.

"It's not the kind of thing that's easy to forget."

The old man turned towards him.

"What did you say?"

Bowman held the stone in his fist, watching the dust cloud move closer to them on the path.

"I'm here because the man who killed Kramer did the same thing in London. Nearly two years ago now. I searched for him over there, but I never found him."

"The same thing?"

"It was me who found the body."

The old man's voice sounded hollow:

"When we were in Fort Smith, you said . . . that you were looking for a friend."

"There's no point me telling you that part of the story. It goes back a long way."

"Do you know who did this?"

"Maybe."

"Why didn't you talk to the American police about it?"

Bowman dropped the stone and kicked it away.

"I can't."

"That man must be arrested, whether he's your friend or not."

"I can't because the police in London think I did it."

Bowman stood up. He could now make out the shape of a carriage on the track. The sound of shod hooves and wheels clattering against stones reached their ears. Mrs Desmond walked over to the old man and the Englishman. Bowman used his hand as a visor.

"What do you do when you meet someone on this path?"

She seemed to have to force herself to reply.

"Normally, there are no problems here."

"Do you have a weapon in the carriage?"

"Why?"

"Those men were at the saloon last night. I don't trust them. Are they going to stop?"

"The Trinity River is only eight miles away, but convoys often stop here at the spring to rest their horses."

"Stay here."

Bowman unbuttoned his coat, shoved his hands deep in his pockets, and walked towards the track. The two men from the saloon were each driving a covered wagon pulled by four horses, rifles lying across their legs. They did not deviate from their course, remaining on the main path and nodding to Bowman as they passed, without slowing down. Bowman waited until they had passed into the distance before turning around towards the woman and the old man.

"You should be armed."

They got back on board the carriage, and the woman took the reins.

"You said you didn't trust those men? I wonder what impression you made on them."

Two hours later, they reached the first trees bordering the Trinity River – the dark line they had been able to see since Fort Worth. They turned onto a secondary track running alongside the river to the north. The lands on the shores of the river were irrigated and cultivated. As far as Bowman could tell, it was a good place for farming, a flow of green amid the arid surroundings. The carriage followed another path and began to move away from the water. When they passed between the first buildings in Reunion, they were already two miles away from the Trinity.

Half-collapsed fences encircled plots of sandy land where nothing but rocks grew. The town was a pile of ruins. Some of the houses had been abandoned during construction: four posts and some rafters blown down by the wind. Doors and windows banged in draughts, and the façades were so dusty they had turned the colour of the earth. The streets were not like those in other American towns that Bowman had seen. Instead of being parallel and perpendicular, they all converged on a central point, a large building whose outline he could just make out. Bowman guessed the shape of the unfinished town from the stakes planted in the ground and connected by string. The project had been imagined and designed, begun and then abandoned, just like the empty fields surrounded by fences. The carriage stopped outside a house. Alfred Brewster turned towards him.

"The people who lived there left at the start of winter. There's enough left for you to move in. We have to meet the other citizens of Reunion before we can decide what to do with you."

"What to do with me?"

"We can't make the decision without them."

Bowman got down from the carriage and watched as it moved away. The inside of the house was covered with dust but otherwise in order. A table and some chairs, three beds without mattresses, a brick chimney, and – next to the blackened hearth – a brick bread oven. Draughts blew through the planks of the cladding where the nails had come out. Bowman put his bag on the table and went out again. Behind the house, he found a pile of wood – shingles that had fallen from the roof – and gathered up an armful. Near an empty vegetable garden, he snapped off branches from a bush for kindling. He lit a fire and, when the shingles began to burn, he went out again. Using a rock, he nailed back the planks that were falling off. A bell was ringing. He saw men and women – some alone, some in pairs, some holding their children by the hand – come out of their houses and converge on the central building.

The chimney did not draw well and the room filled with smoke. He took one of the beds apart and threw the bits of wood in the fireplace. The chimney stones began to heat up and the fire burned more easily. He sat on a chair and uncorked the bourbon.

Brewster knocked on the door one hour later. The old herbalist was holding a lamp and a basket. Bowman brought another chair close to the fire and offered him the bottle. Brewster politely refused.

"I brought you some food."

The old man rubbed his eyes as he sat near the flames.

"Mr Bowman, your arrival was the subject of a lively discussion. The citizens of Reunion would like to know how long you will be staying."

"No idea. One day. I might even leave tomorrow. All I have is a few questions. I don't expect to find much here."

"The others do not wish to speak with you, but you can rely on Alexandra and myself."

With the toe of his boot, Bowman pushed another plank onto the fire.

"Alexandra?"

"Mrs Desmond."

"Does she live here with her husband?"

"The Desmonds arrived from France with the first citizens of Reunion. Mr Desmond died three years ago, of malaria. Like many others. The winters are cold in Texas, but the summers are suffocatingly hot and the banks of the Trinity are infested with mosquitoes. We also suffered badly with a lack of food. Jerome Desmond was already in a weak state, and he didn't survive the fever."

The old man paused.

"How will you find the man you are looking for?"

"Everything I know ends here. After this, I don't know where I'll go."

Brewster looked at the bits of bed burning in the hearth.

"Every time I look at a fire, I think the same thing. That a person's first memories are always of campfires when they were children, and that when they come towards the end of their lives, old people pull their chairs close to the fireplace so they can remember them."

The old man smiled, lost in his thoughts.

"Do you know Charles Fourier, Mr Bowman?"

"Who?"

"He's a French thinker, a philosopher. It is his books and his ideas that led us here, to found this town. What Newton called 'universal gravitation', the fundamental law of the universe, Fourier imagined as a human law, which he called 'passionate attraction'. A force that rules over the relations between men. Our passions and our natures are finite, and a society is a combination of those natures; individuals too. By identifying and cultivating them, we can choose the life that will most truly fulfil us. Find the job that we love, find our lifetime companion. One condition for harmony and happiness is the avoidance of repetition. If a job no longer satisfies us, we must change jobs, and the same thing applies to our partners. Fourier called this the 'butterfly passion'. A pretty expression, don't you think?"

Bowman wondered if there was a connection between this butterfly passion and the red-headed woman in her dressing gown at the hotel in Fort Worth.

"Why are you telling me all this?"

"Because I've been thinking about it since you told me about that murderer."

Bowman swallowed some bourbon. It was strong and it burned his throat.

"What's the connection?"

"You say you've been searching for him for a long time. That you have made the same journey as him and that in England, you were mistaken for him. Passionate attraction, Mr Bowman. The connection that exists between you and him."

With the flames reflected in his glasses, Brewster reminded Bowman of Captain Reeves in his living room by the Thames.

"What a load of bull. It doesn't exist, this attraction. Anyway, you said it was a force for building towns."

"Harmonious cities, yes."

Bowman and Brewster watched the fire, perhaps playing with the idea of thrusting their hands into those embers, so full of memories.

"You said there was another murder in London. As if this murderer had an attraction to horror, a passion that drove him to start again. You, his pursuer, perhaps you have a complementary passion?"

The old man waited for the Englishman's reaction, but Bowman did not reply.

"The news that you bring, Mr Bowman, is that there will be no new world. Because, here, the freedom to become oneself is also available to monsters like your friend. And, faced with people like that, we are not sufficiently armed. That is a battle for men like you, and as long as you exist, we will remain mere utopias. You are an objection to our project."

The old man stood up, the light from the flickering flames deepening his wrinkles.

"I understand why you are reluctant to tell your story. I have seen that fear in your eyes, Mr Bowman. The fear of being thought a monster. But you should not be afraid. No-one knows what you will become here, what sort of free man you will be."

Brewster opened the door. An icy gust of air blew through the room and flattened the flames in the fireplace.

"We will help you tomorrow. But please, once we have answered your questions, you must leave."

Bowman watched the wood being consumed as he sipped at his bottle. Then he took apart the other beds in this abandoned house until there was nothing left to burn.

5

"He doesn't feel well. His journey to St Louis tired him out."

She took a step back on the porch.

"He asked me to take his place."

Bowman had not slept. His face was gaunt and drawn, his eyes sunken. He put on his cap and went outside without a coat. Reunion, under a blue sky, still had the same desperate appearance: a ghost town, an abandoned dream. The men and women who passed in the street had skin the same colour as the earth and the houses, grey figures with pale faces; even the children, who had lost the desire to play, and dragged their feet as they walked behind their parents between deserted shacks. Brewster and his dreams of the perfect city had made an impression on him, the previous night, by the fire. In the cold light of day, the gap between his theories and the reality just seemed laughable. Bowman had seen villages in Africa filled with half-naked negroes that seemed more desirable than this place.

The woman stopped outside a house with closed shutters.

"This is where Richard lived. And where we found him."

Bowman looked at her.

"What accent do you have?"

"If you wish to enter, please go ahead. I'll wait here."

Bowman turned to face the house. It was one of the most solid and best-designed buildings in the town. With its log walls, it was the only one that would resist an attack for more than a few minutes. It was also the only place in all of America where Bowman knew either Peavish or Penders had come.

"Who found him?"

"Someone who has since gone away. Back to France."

"You speak good English. I don't know any other languages. Except a few words I learned from the monkeys."

Alexandra Desmond looked at Arthur Bowman.

"The monkeys?"

"The natives in the Indian army."

Bowman stared at the door of Kramer's house.

"I'm going to take a look."

Though covered in dust, the inside was still fully furnished. Glasses, plates, kitchen utensils, a rug under the dining table, framed pictures on the walls of engravings of plants and city streets. On the table, a plate of dried fruit covered with a blanket of mould. There were two doors in the opposite wall, on either side of the fireplace. He opened the one on the right, entered a smaller room, opened a window, then pushed open the shutters. The bedroom. The bed was neatly made, the quilt and pillows grey with dust. There was a wardrobe full of clothes, a book on the bedside table. Everything he touched became marked with his fingerprints. There was another door in the bedroom. Bowman entered the third room – an office this time – and in the light from the window discovered a bookcase, filled with books of all shapes and sizes. He read a few titles on the spines. Scientific works: chemistry and mechanics, botany, agricultural handbooks. On the desk were papers, notebooks, letters, pens, and an inkwell, which Bowman touched with his finger. The bottom was dry and black. In the office, another door led back to the main room. The house had been constructed around the large fireplace.

In the living room, Bowman opened the two windows overlooking the street and saw Alexandra Desmond on the other side, watching him. Her pale dress and red hair stood out against the black-painted doors of a barn behind her. They exchanged a look, then he turned around and moved towards the fireplace.

Bits of rope hung from either side of the wooden lintel, attached to large roofing nails. Bowman crouched down by the hearth. The stones were black with soot and the floorboards burnt by flying embers.

No.

There were other stains on the stones. And the floor was dirty, as if a cooking pot that was warming over the fire had been knocked over. The blood had dried and blackened a long time ago. But there were still these traces of it, on the stones of the fireplace. Signs. Letters. Black on black. He deciphered the first few. *S. U. R. V . . .* Bowman stood up and looked again at the bits of rope on the lintel: for holding the arms outstretched.

He came out of the house and bent double to vomit. Outside the black barn, the woman watched him. Bowman walked over to her, his legs like jelly, his vision blurred. He opened his mouth to ask where he could find some water, because he was so terribly thirsty, when his entire body prickled with pins and needles and his hands, dangling heavy at the ends of his arms, seemed to swell up. He couldn't speak. The street grew wider as he crossed it. The woman took a step towards him, with her hair red as flames. He wanted to slide his fingers through it, to feel its heat. Dizziness overcame him and he lost his balance, rolling over in the dust.

When he opened his eyes again, she was leaning over him. She had dragged him to the shade of the barn and leaned his back against the wall. His mouth was full. He spat. From his slack lips, a thread of saliva and blood trickled down over his jacket. Clumsily, he wiped it on his sleeve.

"Can you hear me?"

He couldn't speak.

"What happened to you?"

Bowman managed to articulate:

"Too much light."

"What did you say?"

"Too much light. It hurts."

Bowman closed his eyes and let himself be swept away by another spell of dizziness.

Brewster made him drink a decoction of plants, a cloudy liquid, thick and bitter, that turned his stomach. Slowly, the tingling in his limbs faded and he came back to his senses. He was slumped on a chair.

The redhead was there, with Brewster sitting on a chair next to her.

"You should eat, Mr Bowman. You need to get your strength back. Mrs Desmond will take care of you. I'll drop by later."

The old man waved to Alexandra and left. Outside, night was falling. Bowman's travelling bag was on the dining table, along with his coat. A saucepan was warming on a stovetop, and a sickening smell of soup rose through the air. The windowpanes were covered with steam. She was busy in the kitchen, her back to him, and Bowman guessed that she was doing all this to avoid looking at him. His tongue was cut and swollen.

"I've had these fits for a while."

"How long?"

"Two years."

She put a plate on the table and looked at him with a mixture of mistrust and indifference.

"I didn't think you were so sensitive."

"Sensitive?"

"There's nothing left in Richard's house."

"You don't understand. It's because I've already seen it."

She opened the drawer of the stove and the fire started purring.

"Alfred explained it to me. That thing in London – I don't believe a word of it. I don't know who you are or why you have come to Reunion, but what happened to Richard has nothing to do with you. You're lying. There's something else."

It was growing hotter and hotter. Bowman could feel the sweat beading on his forehead. His head fell backwards against the headrest of the chair. Maybe it was Brewster's plants, or that floating sensation – his body still weak after the fit – but he felt good.

"You don't understand. I've seen it dozens of times."

She turned around. Her eyes were the colour of those grey pearls that you found in the oysters of the Indian Ocean.

"What are you talking about?"

"Over there, they didn't do that to kill us, although half of my men died from it. And all the Burmese. They killed the Burmese more quickly, but they were all my men."

Bowman rolled the words around his mouth, like those little round stones that the soldiers used to suck during long marches to fight off thirst. She was sitting at the table, her hands on her thighs. Strands of hair fell over her frowning brow. She listened.

"I was the toughest sergeant in a fleet of ten thousand men, maybe in all of the Indies. That's what Wright said, and that's why he chose me, so the Company would win the war against the Burmese king. It was a lie. Captain Reeves told me that. And a man who burns a village, with women and children, is a man you can believe. The river mission failed. We were taken prisoner, in a camp in the middle of the jungle. It took us days to walk there, getting further and further away from the coast, where the Company's troops were stationed. There were twenty of us, including the monkeys. We walked to a village with houses on stilts, a little river, women in red clothes and children. Min's soldiers evacuated the village and we were left alone with them and a few peasants who looked after the camp. For a year. First, they wanted to know what we were doing on the river, if we were spies, if other boats were going to arrive. After that, we had nothing else to tell them. We didn't know anything, in any case. But they didn't stop. By the end, there were only ten of us. The man who killed Kramer, he was in a cage next to mine. That's where he learned it. By seeing what the guards did to the others and what they did to him. It's true that there's nothing left in Kramer's house. Nothing at all. As if it was just a nightmare, all in my head, a hallucination. That's the worst part. Because I have to remember it all – the forest, the cages and the sewer – to know that I'm not mad. I look at my scars to be sure they're still there. And sometimes I don't know what they are anymore. I wonder if they're decorations, like the marks the negroes make in their skin to show that they're warriors. Once, I thought they looked good, after Frank's wife cleaned them in the hut. The man I'm looking for, it could have been the other way round. Like Brewster said. Passionate attraction and all that. It could have been me who killed Kramer, and a pastor sitting here, or the other sergeant, Penders, with his smile. We could do like you did with the young lad in Fort Worth, like butterflies of the night. Change roles when we got bored of being the same person."

Bowman smiled, ecstatic.

"Then we could make a perfect town together. Like this one. A ghost town in the dust."

He closed his eyes and a smile remained on his face. Before falling asleep, he had an image in his mind of the little opium den in China Court and the dreams he used to have there. Maybe there was opium in Brewster's potion, or other plants that had the same effect. He had forgotten how good it felt to smile at the monsters in his memory.

Alexandra Desmond approached the English soldier, who was still muttering and mumbling incoherently, pursuing his delirium in a world of dreams. She pulled back the blanket, unbuttoned his shirt and pulled it open.

———⅏——⅏——⅏———

The next morning, she prepared a meal for two. Bowman, sitting opposite her, observed his surroundings with apprehension, unable to separate his dreams from what he had said and done. The woman's attitude had changed. Her hostility had given way to a cautious attentiveness. Instead of ignoring him, she kept pacing around him. They ate in silence, then she pushed her plate away.

"Richard Kramer was a friend. An intimate friend. But he was also a difficult man, who struggled to find his place in the community. Some people are more complicated than others when it comes to living together. If you're feeling better, I can show you around town. What's left of it. And explain it to you."

Bowman stood up when she did. Despite the sunshine, he put on his coat, feeling too weak to face the cool air. She walked next to him, following his rhythm, stopping whenever he needed to rest. She wore only a skirt and a blouse. Her hair hung loose. He could see freckles on her cheeks and nose.

"The land was bought from France by Victor Considerant's company. We all gave money and one of the company's partners, here in America, took charge of the transaction while we prepared for our journey. Considerant had come here himself to negotiate for the land, but his emissary was conned by the representatives of the Texan government, who receive bonuses for every acre of land they sell and every immigrant they bring in. They keep the best land for themselves and their friends. When we arrived, the plots of land were not those we'd been promised and we discovered that the prices were far too high. The soil is like clay, unfit for cultivation, and the land is nearly three miles away from the river. Part of it was marshland, infested with insects. We did some drainage work, but nothing grew well, and the owners of the land along the Trinity refused to let us irrigate our fields or to sell us a few farmable hectares. We dug wells, but they didn't give enough water. For three years, we had droughts and harsh winters. When the situation became difficult, conflicts arose between us, and with the company directors. Alfred was in St Louis to meet a lawyer; we are still trying to assert our rights for the land Considerant agreed to buy during his visit."

Bowman stopped in the shade of a building to get his breath back. She waited for him. When he started walking again, she continued her story:

"Almost all of us came from towns. Some of us were artisans, people full of good will, but who knew nothing about rural life. Richard Kramer was a chemical engineer. A brilliant man. Faced with our difficulties, he told us that we had to stop talking and act, that the town would die if we didn't do something. He was looking for a way of enriching our soil, hoping that would solve our food problems. He was looking for a solution for everyone, but at the same time he rejected the system that we wanted to set up. That was his contradiction. More and more often, he would go to Dallas, to sell his services as an engineer and bring back some money for the community. Considerant's company, which was also in debt, finally agreed to reimburse those who wanted to leave Reunion. Many people went back to Europe; a few remained in America to try their luck elsewhere. By the beginning of last winter, there were only about sixty citizens left. After Richard's murder, half of them went away. Those who are still here are preparing to return to Europe. The land was bought in our own names; we live together, but each of us owns his own land."

They walked between empty houses; whenever they passed someone, Alexandra Desmond exchanged a smile and a greeting. The citizens of Reunion reminded Bowman of those plague colonies he had seen in Asia: monsters who fled the presence of healthy people, staring at them with a mixture of curiosity and fear.

"Was there a preacher here?"

"The community is open to all cults. There were several priests to begin with. The last one left after Richard's death. He was an old Frenchman. He went back to France. After your fit, you talked about a pastor . . . Is that the man you are searching for?"

"An Englishman. My age, more or less. Were there any British people here, at the time of the murder?"

"No."

"A former soldier? A man about my height, blond like me?"

"No, there was no-one who fits that description."

She took a few more steps and her face darkened.

"Richard's murderer was not an inhabitant of Reunion. We are on a busy road and Dallas is only two miles from the other bank of the Trinity. As I told you, Richard had been going there more and more often."

They arrived outside the large central building. She explained that it was their meeting place, where they organised communal activities, marriages and baptisms and parties, when there had been any. It was also where they provided teaching.

"Anyone with knowledge of a particular field would share it with the children, and with adults too. This building is a temple, the centre of government, a school and a meeting place."

They were walking away from the town now, heading towards the dark line of the river. Bowman was feeling better. The air was refreshing and he threw his coat over his shoulder. They walked slowly, their footsteps raising little clouds of clay dust.

"I've never taken a walk like this."

"Like this?"

"In London, I walked all the time. But I did my patrols alone. I've never walked with a lady."

Alexandra Desmond gave a little smile, which quickly faded.

"I haven't been for a walk in a long time either. Not since Jerome's death."

Bowman waited a few seconds before asking his question:

"Why did you come here with him?"

"Because we'd read too many books."

"You read books?"

"Shouldn't women read?"

Bowman blushed and the words came tumbling out of his mouth:

"I bought a book once for a woman. A book written by a woman."

She looked at him again.

"I can't imagine you with a book in your hands."

He hesitated.

"Before, I only read the Bible. When I was a soldier. And then an old lady gave me another book, about America . . ."

He stopped mid-sentence.

"Go on. I like this story."

Bowman turned back towards the town, a few hundred yards behind them.

"That book, it was a gift for one of the Englishmen I'm looking for. All my stories come back to that."

And by "that", Bowman seemed to include the grey outlines of Reunion's houses.

"Mr Bowman, when you fell asleep, after your fit, I looked at your scars."

Bowman felt a hot flush wash over him. Mrs Desmond's grey eyes were staring into his.

"You said that you once thought they looked good. After a woman had washed you."

"I said that?"

"That's what I heard."

She started walking again and Bowman followed her.

"We came here to live the life we dreamed about."

Bowman lowered his head.

"I'm not the sort of person who could live here. Not like your husband."

"I don't think so either."

She came to a halt.

"And yet you are here."

She looked at him strangely.

"Would you take my arm and walk with me to the river?"

Bowman, intimidated, lifted his arm, unsure whether he was going to accompany Mrs Desmond or whether she would support him.

"You also said that we were just ghosts. Perhaps that is true. And when we have all left, you will inherit this town, Mr Bowman. But there was another image that you used, one that I preferred."

"An image?"

"Butterflies of the night. Moths."

He didn't remember. The woman's hand lay lightly on his arm.

"We think we know moths because they circle around lamps, but the truth is they live in darkness. When they are drawn to the light, they are no longer themselves and they go mad. Perhaps this community is one of those lights, a deceptive brightness, and the truth is in darkness, where we cannot see. Mr Bowman, you are a strange kind of lamp, a lamp that gives out shadows instead of light. I don't like the night. But I like your image."

It was dark when they got back to Reunion. Bowman sat in the chair with a blanket. Alexandra Desmond slept in the next room. He fought against sleep, listening to the creaking of the house as it cooled down, wondering if it wasn't the sound of footsteps on the floorboards.

The next morning, they ate in silence. When she had finished her breakfast, they began their conversation again as if the night had never interrupted it.

"Actually, I don't really believe that we read too many books. The problem was that we were surrounded by people who hadn't read enough of them, people as uncultivated as this land. If we were naïve, it was in believing in the word of businessmen, more than in our ideas. If there was a place somewhere, where I could be a free woman, where I could read or write books, take part in political life, teach others what I know, speak when I want to and choose the men I want to live with, then I'd go there now."

As if there were an intimacy between them that Bowman knew nothing about, Alexandra Desmond gave him a look that embarrassed him.

"I didn't sleep much. I was wondering where you would go. For a moment, I thought about going to see you. To ask you to stay."

She stood up and smiled at him.

"But that's not possible. Your scars are not beautiful yet. You are still that soldier, that man with whores on every continent, and you wouldn't be happy with a woman like me. Did you know that in certain Indian tribes in this country – those people you call 'monkeys', or 'yellows', or 'redskins' – when a woman no longer wants her husband, she puts his things outside the door of their house in the middle of the night? When the husband finds them the next morning, he picks them up and goes away to find another house and another wife."

Bowman looked for his bag and his coat. They were not in the room anymore.

"I'll drive you to Dallas. That's where you should continue your search. You are not obliged to reply to me. Just because I've been open with you, that doesn't mean you have to be open with me, and anyway I think you've already said a great deal. If you can bear this silence, then accept it."

His mouth was dry.

"Silence. That's what I'd like."

Alexandra Desmond opened the door for him. His belongings were neatly stacked on the doorstep.

Bowman went to say goodbye to Brewster. The old herbalist gave him another flask of that potion, advising him, if he could, to take a spoonful before a fit came – if he felt it coming – and to drink two spoonfuls afterwards if he wasn't able to prevent it. The old man was in a bad way. He was falling to pieces just as his town was, and soon he would die along with it. Brewster did not even mention Bowman's search for the killer, and watched him ride away on the carriage with the same expression he'd had when he was looking at the flames: that nostalgic, almost senile absent-mindedness.

The carriage left Reunion and, half an hour later, Mrs Desmond stopped it on the outskirts of Dallas.

"I won't go any further. I hate this city. But you're nearly there."

She shook his hand and did not let go.

"You probably came for nothing, but your arrival brought back all my sadness, Mr Bowman, and with it the hope of escaping it. We should be glad about that."

Bowman understood nothing of what she was saying, but he didn't want to let go of her hand. He got down from the carriage. Alexandra's knees were at his eye level. He wanted to put his hand on her leg, but he hesitated, and, stupidly, his fingers touched the wood of the carriage instead, grazing against the fabric of her dress. She smiled, and snapped the reins, and the mare snorted.

He walked past the sign for Dallas, a rapidly growing Texan city where it was forbidden to carry firearms and whose population, in this year of 1860, was 678 souls. He did not turn around to watch Alexandra drive back to Reunion.

———— ⚊⚊ ———— ⚊⚊ ———— ⚊⚊ ————

That evening, after asking around in Dallas' stores, he descended from a trailer filled with timber at the entrance to the Paterson ranch. Barns and fences were being built around a new, two-storey house, about sixty feet long. The buildings were multiplying before his very eyes, as if the ranch were growing in perfect synchrony with the dilapidation of Reunion, on the other side of the river. The Paterson foreman was supervising the hoisting of a gable for the barn, moved by horses and men with pulleys. Once the structure had been put in place and made stable, Bowman approached the foreman.

"I heard in town that you were hiring."

The foreman, who had to be as expert in construction as in the raising of livestock, looked him up and down.

"You know what to do?"

Bowman turned towards the building site and the land where cattle grazed.

"I can learn. But if you need someone to give thirty blokes a kick up the arse, I already know how to do that."

"Oh, you want my job, do you? What's with the hunting jacket?"

"I didn't have time to get changed. And I don't want any problems. I don't mind orders, as long as I'm paid right."

"You know the Patersons?"

"They're the bosses."

"And they didn't get where they are today by letting a bunch of servants screw them over. Where else have you worked?"

"Fifteen years in India. I was a sergeant."

"I'll put you in charge of the team that supplies the ranch with materials. They can't be bothered to turn up on time. Eight dollars for a six-day week, bed and food included. If everything goes well, you'll get sixteen dollars a week after two weeks. There are eighty lads working on this ranch. Out of all of them, there are bound to be three or four who'll take the piss out of your British accent. You will not beat up anyone."

Bowman held out his hand.

"Bowman."

"Shepard."

He asked where he was to sleep.

"That big hut over there. Talk to Bill – he'll find you a bed."

Bowman picked up his bag.

"How much does a horse cost here?"

"Depends what you want it for. You want to attack a bank or you just want an old nag who'll wait for you by the water trough of the local saloon?"

"I want to visit the area."

"To carry a man like you around in the hot sun, a twenty-dollar mustang should be enough. If you leave it on the ranch, it'll 'cost you fifty cents a week."

Bowman took five dollars from his pocket.

"If I'm still here in a week, you can take five dollars out of my pay. Will that be enough of a down payment for me to take a tour of the region?"

"I'll even throw in a saddle. A word of warning, though: I wouldn't go around telling everyone that you've got here with your pockets full of money. Go and get changed."

"Bill?"

"One of the lads who doesn't like the English."

"There won't be any problems."

The foreman burst out laughing.

"That bastard's from Ukraine. You can put him in his place if you have to."

Bowman walked off towards the workers' building.

"Bowman!"

He turned around.

"If you see anyone from Hollis Ranch or Michaeli in town, and they offer you better wages, come and see me before you clear off."

6

In the Patersons' workers' building, the men were divided into two categories: those who looked after the cattle and those who looked after everything else. It was like a barracks where rank was unclear, where discipline was limited to working hours, and where people resigned as often as they were hired and fired. The atmosphere was good and, like everything that Bowman had seen in this part of the country, temporary: it had the feel of something people did in passing, while waiting to make bigger dreams come true. The cowherds were saving money to buy their own farm, the craftsmen to start their own business, the cooks to open their own restaurant. And while they dreamed, the Paterson ranch grew. Having begun with 7,500 acres that soon became 12,000, it now comprised a hundred square miles, all of it along the banks of the Trinity River. Bowman learned that, in Texas, with two thousand dollars, he could buy almost as much land as the Patersons. The problem with a ranch of a hundred square miles was all the money you needed afterwards to turn it into something good.

By putting aside five dollars a week, a cowherd would have to work for two years to buy some land, a few cattle and four planks to build a house. If there was still land for sale by the time he'd saved that money. At those prices, entire pieces of the country were being bought every day.

Everyone talked about the King Ranch, near the Rio Grande, which was close to 200 square miles. King had crossed the border to hire entire villages of Mexicans. The names of all these rich owners explained why all the restaurants, stores, farms and ranches that people talked about over dinner were going to be built "in the West". Over there, where no-one yet lived, opportunity still awaited. There was fertile land – all you had to do was choose it and take it – as well as rivers, game, the most beautiful wild horses in the country, and vast forests. To go West, you needed a carriage, a pair of cattle, enough food to last you the journey, a rifle and ammunition; then you had to find yourself a wife and wait a little longer, until the army had finished with the Indians. Consequently, as the dream was always delayed a few months, a solution opened up for everyone, this one a quick, safe and painless solution: go to Colorado in search of gold. Those who talked about the big mining companies swiping all the lodes and getting rid of the little gold-panners were jeered at and called cowards. To become rich in Colorado, you just needed balls and a bit of luck. In the evenings, among all these men bragging ever louder that they were right as they gradually realised they were wrong, there were about fifteen who said nothing: those who had no plans, for whom the West ended in Dallas, with its 678 souls; the lads from the food-supply team.

Once the cowherds and the construction workers had been hired, followed by anyone who knew how to do anything at all, the three big ranches had no-one in town left to employ, except a few loafers and losers. Which explained why Bowman had been hired on the spot, and why the food-supply team was so useless. They were mostly big, tough men who had quite a bit in common with their mules – but definitely not the spirit of self-sacrifice.

On Bowman's first two days at the ranch, no-one made any comments about his accent, nor did they laugh at his strange work clothes: a fisherman's pea jacket and trousers. The ranch was located eight miles north of the city: an hour and a half by horse, twice that long with a fully loaded carriage. The wood bought in Dallas arrived either from the great Northern lakes – by boat on the Mississippi, then on mule convoys from Vicksburg – or from Pennsylvania to the port in Houston, on the Gulf of Mexico, after sailing southwards over the Atlantic. Two merchants in town divided up the northern and southern networks. To build in stone, all you had to do was take a pickaxe to the Patersons' land, but the stonemasons took too long. For the past five years, the ranch had doubled the size of its herds every year, and convoys of wood arrived in Dallas in a continual flood. The city was like a swarm of bees hanging to the branch of a tree in the middle of the desert.

While the men who transported the supplies were not particularly motivated workers, there were also problems with the suppliers themselves. The three big ranch owners – Paterson, Hollis and Michaeli – were in competition for the spring sales, with each trying to build the biggest ranch in the region. In wood merchants' offices, bribes were a daily fact of life, and when Bowman encountered his counterpart at Hollis, he understood why Shepard had hired him. The leader of the Hollis Ranch team was a big, not very likeable man who bribed and threatened the suppliers. His name was Brisk but no-one laughed at his German accent or his broken English. When they went to Dallas for the second time, accompanied by Bowman, his men watched him take Brisk aside and talk to him in the middle of the street – and that was the end of it. From that day on, Brisk had not given them any trouble at all. Bowman's mule-drivers and porters also suddenly started working harder.

One Sunday, after eight consecutive days of work, Bowman saddled up a mustang in the ranch's stable. Shepard had chosen it for him, with a half-smile. It was a stallion, of an average size for these wild horses, like a slightly shorter and stockier version of an Arabian-Andalusian breed. A muscular, eight-year-old chestnut, with black feet. The horse had been broken in by Paterson's cowherds, but it was too nervous to work with cattle: a common character trait among mustangs who have lived too long in the wild before being tamed. Captured at three years old, Bowman's horse had a hair-trigger temperament. He liked it though: there was something about its faraway gaze. He had imagined that, once he was in the saddle, no-one would come too close to them, that they would make a good pair. The mustang had not been saddled for several months, and it was upset by the touch of the leather. Bowman stayed with it for a while in its box, sitting on a fence and smoking a pipe as the animal kicked at the wooden walls. Little by little, the horse came closer to smell the tobacco smoke. Bowman waited until it touched him first, then gently struck its neck, promising it a bullet in the head if it tried to throw him from the saddle. Hearing his voice, the horse had stepped backwards and its ears had pricked.

The mustang had no name; if it returned alive from its first trip to Reunion, Bowman would give the matter some thought. He let it follow the track from Dallas without touching the reins, observing its reactions as it passed a leafy copse or when they encountered another horse-rider or a horse-drawn carriage. The mustang did not even seem to see other horses. When it passed food, its ears rotated towards its rider, but it did not slow down or turn its head. It was waiting to find out more, as if it had understood that these slack reins on its withers were a kind of trap. As they approached the ford in the Trinity, Bowman urged the horse to a trot. The mustang maintained a constant speed without him having to use his spurs. It was a clever horse, and Bowman concluded that it was not, in fact, too nervous to work – it simply didn't want to. Coming out of the water, Bowman dug his heels into its sides. Its legs cooled down by the river, the mustang went into a quick, supple gallop that spared Bowman quite a bit of pain. The horse might not have been saddled for months, but it had been more than six years since the sergeant had been on horseback.

They entered Reunion at a trot. This time, the mustang became agitated, turning its head from side to side when the doors of the abandoned houses banged in the wind. Perhaps the horse also sensed its rider's nervousness.

Alexandra Desmond came out of her house as she saw Bowman approach.

"Back already? You're braver than I thought, Mr Bowman."

She smiled.

"Come in, please."

She served him tea, apologising for her bourgeois formality, and Bowman did not understand why she said that. She listened as he told her in a few words about being hired at the Paterson ranch and his first visits to Dallas as the leader of the supply team.

"And what did you say to him, in the middle of the street?"

"Nothing. I just acted like I used to when I was a sergeant. I look them in the eyes and think about whatever passes through my head, and no-one messes around."

"And this Brisk stopped causing you problems?"

"Yeah."

She was amused, as if he were a child telling her about his adventures. Bowman didn't care.

"I had an idea, an image, when I arrived at the Paterson ranch. It was as if their barns were being built up at the same time as your town, here, was falling apart."

Alexandra Desmond lowered her eyes. Bowman no longer amused her.

"Another two families left this week."

Bowman looked at her slender hands, barely misshapen by work, curling around the cup of tea.

"And you? How long will you stay here?"

She did not reply. Bowman spoke more gently:

"Will you go looking for that place? The one that will be better than Reunion?"

Alexandra stood up and took a book from a shelf, then put it on the table in front of him.

"You said you sometimes read books. I think this one might interest you."

Bowman picked it up and traced the engraving on its cover with his fingertips.

"This is the one Brewster had in the stagecoach."

"I lent it to him. Let me know what you think of it. And if you have to leave, take it with you. I'll be the second woman on this earth to have given you a book. I'll be content with that, but only because I'm younger and more beautiful than the first one."

Her freckles glowed slightly on her pink cheeks. Bowman's heart pounded, making his pulse beat noisily in his temples.

That night, Bowman, lying in his bed, separated from the rest of the dormitory by a hung sheet, opened Thoreau's book and began to read.

Economy

When I wrote the following pages, or rather the bulk of them, I lived alone, in the woods, a mile from any neighbor, in a house which I had built myself, on the shore of Walden Pond, in Concord, Massachusetts, and earned my living by the labor of my hands only. I lived there two years and two months. At present I am a sojourner in civilized life again ... I require of every writer, first or last, a simple and sincere account of his own life, and not merely what he has heard of other men's lives; some such account as he would send to his kindred from a distant land; for if he has lived sincerely, it must have been in a distant land to me.

He lay there for two hours and, when he closed the book, after thinking about the pages he had just read, he fell asleep with a smile on his face.

———ᵕᵕ——ᵕᵕ——ᵕᵕ———

The next week, the foreman raised his weekly wage to sixteen dollars, and asked him to take charge of the ranch's supply of food and equipment for the livestock.

"You're the Patersons' man in Dallas. Everything that comes here goes through you. I'll take care of the work. It's your job to make sure that everything we need gets here on time. If it continues going well, we'll look at your wages again. And, Bowman, the next time you go into town, buy some clothes. The ranch will pay for them. If no-one else is going to, I'll have to start taking the piss out of your fisherman's rags."

Once the mustang had crossed the Trinity, it set off at a gallop without Bowman even having to spur it on. He pulled lightly on the reins and the horse turned right onto the path to Reunion. This was not his day off, but Bowman had finished his business in Dallas and, if he rushed, he could spend an hour here before going back to the ranch for the night.

Alexandra was not at home. The horse, still nervous in the streets of this ruined town, let itself be led to Brewster's house. She was there, in the shack full of books and flasks, the rooms dark behind closed shutters. The old man was in bed and Alexandra was looking after him. Bowman talked with her a little bit, then tried to exchange a few words with Brewster, who was pale and silent. The old man was dying. He did not seem to be suffering from any particular ailment, rather a general exhaustion, as if the air around him had grown thinner. Alexandra remained with him all day long, listening as the last warm heart in Reunion was slowly extinguished. Brewster did not recognise Bowman, who wondered if his arrival had finished off the old herbalist. His place was not at this man's bedside.

"I have to get back to the ranch."

Alexandra accompanied him outside.

"Mr Bowman, you look more and more like an inhabitant of this country, with your horse and your new clothes."

She was weary. In the dim light of dusk, even her hair was turned the same grey as the town. Bowman untied the mustang, which buried its nose in the woman's hair, inhaling litres of her perfume in a single breath.

"He's called Walden."

She smiled and squeezed his hand. Bowman mounted the horse.

"If you're here, I'll come back on Sunday."

Passing in front of Richard Kramer's house, Bowman felt a shiver run down Walden's spine. As he left the town, the horse set off at a gallop along the black path.

> *Where I Lived, and What I Lived For*
> *At a certain season of our life we are accustomed to consider*
> *every spot as the possible site of a house. I have thus surveyed the*
> *country on every side within a dozen miles of where I live.*

"Bowman, Mr Paterson wants to see you. He's expecting you."

Everett Paterson was simultaneously younger and older than

Bowman had imagined. Back from his trip, he received Bowman in his office. He threw his city clothes on the ground, putting on a horseman's outfit that was folded on the back of a chair.

"Shepard told me about you, Mr Bowman."

Behind Paterson, hung on the wall, the full-length portrait of a severe-faced man glared down on the room. Paterson's father had sharp features and sunken eyes that the artist's skill could not soften. The son had the same tiredness, the same aged and lightless expression on his face. Like the father's eyes, sunk beneath heavy brows, Everett Paterson stood in the shadow of the portrait, his back bent beneath a sickly, invisible load that was turning him prematurely old. Bowman could not tell what ailed him, but the pain had long ago withered his skin and deepened the dark rings under his eyes. Bowman imagined him as an insomniac, spending his nights in a chair, eyes half closed, building dreams in order to forget his suffering.

Everett Paterson's eyes lingered for a moment on Bowman's wide shoulders and straight back. He probably knew how to judge the strength of a horse, a bull or a man in a single glance, this man who remained standing only by dint of his force of will. Bowman was impressed by his look, that spark of pride which forbade the pity inspired by his broken back and sloping shoulders.

"Shepard keeps telling me what excellent work you do. The ranch needs men like you. I wanted to tell you that personally. What's more, I've just come back from New Orleans and the situation is becoming difficult. Washington is trying to impose its law on the southern States. The abolitionists are leaping at the chance to discredit us, and we are close to breaking point. The South will not bow down, you can be sure of that. Your military experience will be useful to us. A veteran of the English colonies knows what it takes to protect the interests of commerce. If you wish to stay, be assured of your place and your future at the ranch."

Bowman wondered how long the Paterson heir had left to live. When it came down to it, what he said about the future made no sense.

"For the moment, I don't have any other plans, Mr Paterson."

The boss smiled and sat down in the chair.

"Very well. Then I wish you good day. I'll be seeing you again."

Bowman saluted him and walked across the office. Before leaving, he turned around and saw Everett Paterson, grimacing with pain as he put on his boots. The owner of the land that ran alongside the Trinity, the man who had refused access to the water for the citizens of Reunion . . . it was him.

When his working day was over, Bowman saddled his horse and rode along the river, following the bank until he came level with the ghost town where Alexandra Desmond was nursing old Brewster. He let Walden trot between the poplar trees, thinking about the fortune that Reeves had left him. He would not return to the workers' building until late that night.

> *The traveller on the prairie is naturally a hunter, on the head waters of the Missouri and Columbia a trapper, and at the Falls of St Mary a fisherman. He who is only a traveler learns things at second-hand and by the halves, and is poor authority.*

The following Sunday, Bowman left the ranch before dawn. He rode Walden at a trot for almost the entire trip, launching into a furious gallop only after crossing the Trinity. They arrived at Reunion under a barely risen sun still yellow from the night. Outside the old herbalist's house, the last remaining citizens of the town were gathered. Bowman stopped a few yards short and remained in the saddle, watching as the coffin moved past. A rough box made from planks of cladding; Brewster would enter the earth amid the ruins of his harmonious city. Bowman took off his hat as the funeral procession passed. Alexandra Desmond came over to say hello and Walden put his nose on her shoulder.

"You can wait for me at my house."

She returned half an hour later. Brewster's funeral had been a brief affair. The community lacked the strength to face up to this new bereavement; the ritual had been cut short and Alexandra Desmond's weariness was turning to melancholy. She made coffee, and they sat in their usual places on either side of the table.

"I came home last night – for an hour, if that – to prepare a meal. He was dead when I got back to his house."

She paused.

"When you look after a sick man, you have to do that too, even if it scares you."

"Do what?"

"Leave them alone. In case he wanted to go out on his own. It's an idea we have – that it is better to die surrounded by people – but sometimes the dying prefer to be alone. I didn't go out for very long."

"In the forest, when people were dying, no-one looked at them. Maybe they wanted to be alone, but they couldn't be. So we turned our eyes away. For those who didn't want to die alone, there was nothing we could do. We were in cages and we weren't allowed to speak. Peavish, the preacher, always said a prayer, but not out loud, just moving his lips. If a woman like you had been there, they wouldn't have died in such an ugly way."

"Why are you still alive?"

Bowman's maimed hand passed over his face, brushing the scar on his forehead in an embarrassed reflex.

"Because I'm tough. Because I was lucky."

"Do you really believe that pursuing that murderer is your only reason for living, Mr Bowman?"

"What do you mean?"

"Is that enough to give your life purpose?"

He looked down.

"I dunno. For now, yeah. Afterwards, if I find him, I don't know what will happen."

"That was my question."

She said this ironically. Perhaps she was thinking about her own fate as she interrogated him, but Bowman felt the blood rush to his head.

"And what about you? Now that your town is in ruins and you've lost your husband, now that Brewster is dead, what meaning does your life have?"

Mrs Desmond responded calmly:

"Don't get angry. I was just trying to understand you. As for my life, I'll be fine. But I am curious to know how a man like you can answer that question."

"A man like me?"

"A man of action."

"A thug?"

She looked at him reproachfully.

"Don't be ridiculous."

"I'm not an engineer and I haven't read as many books as you, but I know that no-one can really answer your question in just a few words. There's what we do now, and what we hope for afterwards. That's all."

"So you're working at the Paterson ranch. Nothing else."

"For now."

"In that case, what are you hoping for afterwards?"

Bowman had to force himself to listen to her. He wanted to leave the widow's house and forget this sickening conversation.

"That's not how it works. Not for me."

"So you have no more hope, Mr Bowman? Is that what you mean?"

He balled his fists.

"Shit, you know perfectly well that I think about things. But that's not how it works. I can't just do what I want anymore. And you . . ."

"And me?"

He stared at the table, wanting to throw it across the room.

"I'd better leave."

"Are you angry?"

"Stop."

"Because I don't want you? Because you stay here without knowing why and because you might leave any day to find my lover's murderer?"

Bowman's anger died out and he was filled with an incomprehensible sadness.

"Why are you doing this?"

Alexandra pursed her lips. She lifted her hand in the air and Bowman did not react when she slapped him.

"You think a woman will save you from your condition, Mr Bowman? That it's our job to close our eyes to what you are? I'm not talking about a love of that kind, servile and old-fashioned. There are greater loves. What you have are not hopes, they are pathetic fantasies."

She lowered her head and rubbed her hand, which was red where it had slapped his face.

"You don't even know if you're seeking an honourable death or an honourable life, Mr Bowman. You'll have to choose in the end, but until you do, you will not belong here, or anywhere else on this earth."

Bowman waited for her to look up again, but Alexandra did not move. He went out of the house, leaving her alone, and spent the rest of the day following the course of the Trinity southward, before going back to the ranch along the other bank.

When he arrived at Paterson, night had fallen. One after another, sprawling in carriages, the employees returned to their quarters after getting drunk for the whole of Sunday in Dallas. With half their savings spent on alcohol and whores, their departure for the West had just been delayed for another week. Bill the Ukrainian, as usual, had made a Mexican-style bean soup, though all this really meant was adding a few handfuls of chilli peppers to liven up the flavour and to help sweat out the whiskey before everyone went to bed.

Bowman gave up trying to read. A final group of cowherds had just arrived, noisy and drunk, demanding their ration of soup. Bowman listened to them rail and carp. He stood up and pulled back the sheet hung by his bed. The men stopped speaking as soon as they saw him appear: big Mr Bowman, with his bulging eyes.

—⫘—⫘—⫘—

Reunion was silent and deserted. There was not even a breeze to blow shut the gaping doors of the abandoned houses. Ten people were still hiding out there, scattered in various shacks across the town. The horse snorted, as if to rid its nostrils of the sad air in this place. Bowman lowered his head as he headed towards the widow's house, his face shadowed by his hat brim from the low rays of the morning sun. She was standing on the porch, shoulders hunched in the cold of dawn. She understood even before he had set foot on the ground, even before noticing the full saddlebags and the travel bag strapped to the saddle. She entered the house and left the door open. Bowman followed her, sitting at the table while she put water to heat on the stove.

He spoke quietly, forcing himself to pronounce the useless words:

"I had some news. Some men from the ranch were talking with mule-drivers in a convoy from El Paso. It happened in Fort Bliss. I've resigned from Paterson."

She put cups, sugar and spoons on the table.

"Are you sure about this?"

"Maybe it's not connected. In London, after the murder, when people talked about it, there were so many different versions. People invent stuff. So, no, I'm not sure."

She sat across from him.

"You know perfectly well that that's not my question."

He turned his head to the dust-covered window. Through the dirty pane, he could see the distorted outlines of empty houses.

"There's no point starting this again."

"I'm not asking you to stay. All I'm saying is that you're not obliged to pursue this."

Bowman gathered all his courage, still looking outside.

"And if I did stay?"

She poured the coffee.

"After your arrival, I sent a letter to New York. The Victor Considerant company has agreed to pay for my return to France."

Outside, Walden was waiting. He stamped and snorted noisily. They remained silent for a moment, bent over their cups. Bowman covered his mouth with his hand, as if to hold back the words.

"And if I came back after finding him?"

"You don't know if you'll come back."

"If I had a reason, that would change everything."

She stood up and, as on the first day, when he woke up to find himself in her house after the fit, she turned her back on him.

"There's no point to all these conjectures. You know as well as I do that the whole thing is absurd."

He took the letters of credit and a wad of ten-dollar bills from his pocket and placed them on the table.

"You said you didn't want to be sad anymore. As for me, all I know is that I'm still alive."

She turned around, looked at the letters and the banknotes without any emotion, and then looked at Bowman.

"What do you want to buy with this money?"

"Nothing. All I've done with it so far is pay for the funerals of people I didn't know. Maybe you could do something better with it."

"I don't need it."

Bowman clung to his idea.

"I know one thing. There's nothing left for us in France or England. You could look for your new place."

She held her arms tight around her chest, as if to prevent herself breathing.

"Stop."

"I'll come back. Even if you're not here anymore. I'll have nothing else to do."

She sat down and put her hands on the table, halting her movement before she touched him.

"I can't stop you doing that."

"When are you leaving?"

"In a few weeks, when I've got everything organised. Mr Bowman, you have the right to hope, even for something impossible. That is what we came here to do. You shouldn't force yourself not to."

"What good would it do?"

At last she moved her hand forward and placed it on his arm.

"It's just an image, Mr Bowman. A bit of light for the butterflies of the night."

Bowman looked up and saw her sad smile, her grey eyes welling with tears. He managed to return her smile.

"When I was preparing my things, last night, I thought about something. Soldiers always say they have a woman waiting for them. The most beautiful woman in the world. Those are lies and dreams that mustn't be broken, otherwise they're no good anymore. But, for me, for once, maybe it's true."

Alexandra Desmond's fingers tightened around his arm. Bowman gently placed his maimed hand on hers and they remained there like that, in silence, until the strength to enjoy this moment abandoned them.

Bowman got back in the saddle. She walked up to Walden. The horse gloomily placed its head on her shoulder.

"It's always regrettable to have to say it, but I'm sorry."

Bowman pulled his hat down over his head.

"That money, it's the Company's. Do something good with it. There'd be no better way of spending it."

He pulled on the reins. Walden began to trot away and the sergeant did not turn around. When he passed Kramer's house, he did not need to spur the horse; it set off at a gallop on its own.

He reached Fort Worth in two hours and, before continuing on the road to El Paso, stopped at a general store to buy food and equipment.

He had kept two hundred dollars for himself. Now he had to make it last as long as possible. The balance he had to find lay somewhere between his own survival, his horse's survival, and the weight that Walden could bear. A horn-handled dagger, more rustic and much cheaper than the one he'd bought in London; twenty yards of hemp rope; a hatchet; a gallon of oats for his horse and a cloth bucket that he could flatten and put away in the saddlebags; two others in leather, each holding three pints; a pound of lard and two pounds of cornflour; coffee; a tin plate and saucepan; a firebox containing a steel lighter and two flints, a small reserve of tinder and some matches. He exchanged the clothes and shoes he had bought in New York for a long raincoat, a good blanket, some tobacco and a bottle of whiskey, and he swapped his pea jacket and fisherman's trousers for two pens, a small bottle of black ink and a block of paper. The last thing he bought, for twice the price of his horse, was a .44 Henry rifle with a sixteen-bullet magazine, and enough ammunition to go hunting for twenty days. When he paid his bill – a total of fifty-eight dollars – the shopkeeper threw in a holster for his rifle, a small bottle of oil, and a bottle brush to clean it.

"That's a lot of stuff. Where are you headed?"

"Fort Bliss."

"If it's your first trip out West, don't worry. A whole heap of people died out there for you. Now, it's just a question of patience. The only thing that can kill you, apart from the rattlesnakes and a few Comanches, is the food they serve in the Butterfield inns."

For a lone horseman, the inns were two days apart. Up to the Pe'cos river, the land was well-irrigated. The only arid part was between the Guadalupe Mountains and El Paso, on the last hundred miles of the track. Like all the main roads in the West, the shopkeeper said, it was an old Indian track.

"The redskins know about springs that we haven't found yet. They even make the journey on foot. But that doesn't mean it's any easier with a horse. Those savages don't drink any more water than lizards and they're capable of running all day long under the hot sun."

Bowman walked back to Walden. The horse was in the hotel stable, where it had eaten its fill of feed. Bowman filled the flasks with water, loaded up his new equipment, and walked alongside the horse until the outskirts of town, enough time for the animal to digest its lunch before he tightened the girths over its belly.

Fort Bliss was six hundred miles west: a two-week trip if all went well. Behind him, Reunion was still only twenty miles away. Walden snorted when he jumped into the saddle.

"I might lose a few pounds by the time we get there. That's about all I can do for you."

The sound of his voice was strange to him, as if he hadn't heard it for a long time. It hadn't changed, though; it was just the fact of speaking to himself. The sun was directly ahead of him; he lowered his head and let himself sway in time with the shoulder rolls of his mount.

After leaving Fort Worth in early afternoon, Bowman travelled about fifteen miles before leaving the track and moving away from it for about half an hour. Observing the trees, he wound up discovering a stream bordered by willows and birches. The grass was not very thick yet, but it was already green; with the bucket and the saddlebags on the ground, Walden, tied to a branch, began to eat, lifting his head occasionally to listen to the sounds of the undergrowth. When Bowman returned empty-handed to his camp after a two-hour hunting trip, night was falling and the air was growing cold. He lit a fire, put some water in a saucepan, stirred in the cornflour, made a pancake, and started to cook it. He found flora and fauna that he recognised on this new continent, like that peppery watercress that grew by the stream, which they used to give to the soldiers after long sea-crossings, a cure for the ravages of scurvy. While he knew the plants, though, he was not yet ready to eat the meat. His talents as a huntsman were not up to the mark. A deer and two rabbits had escaped him. Too heavy, too noisy, his reflexes too slow. The animals had fled before he'd even spotted them.

After finishing his meal, he stretched out the raincoat on the grass and lay there fully clothed, pulling the blanket up to his neck. With his head resting on his travel bag, he listened to the crackle of the fire and looked up at the stars in the sky. Unable to sleep, he kept the fire going until dawn. Walden slept leaning against a birch, indifferent to his master's insomnia. Bowman splashed his face in the stream and, after cooking another pancake and eating a bit of salted meat, he opened his bag, put the Thoreau book on top of it and used it as a desk. On the page he had half filled during the *Persia*'s crossing, he noted:

> I went to Reunion, but there was nothing there. Some men from a convoy in El Paso said in Dallas that there'd been a horrible murder near Fort Bliss and I set off again. In New York, soldiers fired at women and there was one who died in my arms just after I'd got off the boat. I bought a rifle.

He reread his notes, let the ink dry, and folded the page back. Then he took out the block of letter paper he'd bought in Fort Worth, dipped his pen and slowly traced the letters, making them as neat as possible.

> *Alexandra,*
> *I left Reunion one day ago and I slept by a stream with Walden. I didn't manage to kill any game and the coffee I made was not as good as yours. I have decided to write to you regularly. Because it's like having company, like Walden, only prettier, and because soldiers always do that, write letters to the most beautiful woman in the world.*

He hesitated, then added a few words before closing the block of paper and tidying up his things:

> *I hope you will receive this letter one day or that I will be able to bring it to you.*

The first inn he reached was called Sweet Water. Around the Butterfield building, a nascent village was taking shape: three huts and a tent. A farrier had put his anvil by the side of the track and, opposite the transport company's inn, a German couple had set up four chairs and a table under a tarpaulin, serving food to travellers. The competition must be fierce between the inn and this little restaurant, thought Bowman, reading the hand-painted sign by the Germans' tent: *Best food in Sweet Water*. Bowman took his horse to the Butterfield stable and sat down under the tarp to eat. The afternoon was almost over, but he decided to push on a little further and to sleep in the woods. For a dollar, man and horse set off once again with bellies full and thirst quenched.

Finding another stream proved no more difficult than it had the night before. Bowman did not try to hunt; he just prepared his fire for the night and, in the last rays of daylight, lay his head down on his travel bag to read a few pages of Thoreau. He began a chapter entitled "Solitude". The descriptions of nature and Thoreau's moods meant nothing to him. Seeing the title, he had thought he would learn more about what was happening to him, but the words were foreign to him. All that stuff about a poetic and spiritual fusion with the world went straight over his head. Looking at the forest around him, he did not understand how it could soothe him, how he might, like Thoreau, become one with it. Nature and landscapes, he thought, were just things that men crossed through. Over there, in the camp, the Burmese jungle had never been a source of comfort. He thought again about the green hills he had imagined when he was reading Irving, thinking that perhaps they were like those impossible dreams Alexandra Desmond had talked about: images that must be kept in mind in order not to lose hope, but that did not really exist; like Thoreau's idyllic cabin, which Bowman finally realised, from the pompous, impassioned descriptions of it, was merely a sort of imaginary ideal. That night, he fell asleep and, when he woke up, he saw Walden leaning down over him, eyes closed, as if the mustang had wanted to sleep while breathing in his odour. Bowman did not write down anything about his journey, but continued his letter to Alexandra. Fighting against the disappointment of writing to someone who would never read his words, he forced himself to write clearly and legibly.

> *Thankfully there's only one road crossing this country, because otherwise I think I'd get lost. It's only been two days since I left but already I don't know where I am anymore. Walden slept next to me. I think he's a good horse.*

Until he reached Pe'cos, he had to stray further and further from the track to find streams, meaning that his journey took a day longer than the two weeks that a carriage, transporting water, would take to reach El Paso. He avoided the little farms along the path, staying clear of habitations, and began to kill some game. A partridge, a hare and, another day, a young deer of about fifty pounds that he butchered, cooking as much of it as he could in order to keep the pieces for later in his journey. After cutting up his prey that night, Bowman suffered nightmares and woke with a start, shouting so loud that he frightened his horse.

About fifty people lived in the village of Pe'cos. Bowman passed through it without stopping, knowing now that he would have all the water and meat that he needed. For five days, he followed the river north-west, towards the Guadalupe Mountains, and his bad dreams continued. He stopped only once to buy some food and a bottle of whiskey. The Pe'cos river continued northward, but the track to El Paso turned off towards the West. Before entering the arid zone, he stopped at the last inn on this part of the track, buying two extra wine-skins and a peck of oats. Dirty and stinking, his back bent by two weeks on a horse, Arthur Bowman entered the white, rocky plain. On the horizon, sixty miles further on, he could make out the silhouettes of mountains. The Butterfield stagecoaches, pulled by a train of fresh horses, crossed the distance in less than a day; he would have to go pretty fast to manage that. Walden broke into a trot as soon as they entered this desert, apparently guessing that the next drop of water he would taste was to be found at the other side of this desolate landscape.

Bowman had crossed deserts before, but with the logistics and resources of an army. If Thoreau had undertaken this ride, maybe he wouldn't have forgotten to talk about the kind of solitude in which nature too can abandon you.

Walden kept going as long as he could before slowing down. Bowman gave him just a small amount of oats in order not to make him thirsty, and shared the water with him. Three wineskins for the horse, one for his rider.

Night had fallen long before they arrived at the mining camp. After 90-degree temperatures during the day, the mercury suddenly plunged. The Butterfield inn, signalled by a lantern over their sign, was located amid the miners' barracks: long buildings with no lights or windows. Bowman, sunburnt and shivering with cold, knocked at the door of the inn. A young boy took care of his horse, then led him to a tiny room full of icy draughts. Bowman collapsed on the soft bed and took the bottle of whiskey from his bag. He drank it slowly, sip after sip, down to the last drop. He was not fighting only against the cold. One day on horseback separated El Paso from Fort Bliss. If Penders or Peavish had gone there, they must have spent the night here. When the nightmares woke Bowman, his sore, reddened face was covered with sweat that the cold air froze to his skin. Wrapped up in his clothes, his blanket, and the inn's blanket, he shivered and fought against sleep until dawn. He had not felt this bad since leaving London. His old pains returned, familiar whispers in his thoughts, which he began carefully surveying once again. With two bottles in his saddlebags, he set off as soon as the sun was over the horizon.

The salt mine was open-air, in the bed of an old, dried-up lake whose contours, dug into terraces by shovels and pickaxes, grazed the side of the mountain. A raised track, its verges also terraced, crossed over towards the West. At the bottom of the basin, so white it dazzled his eyes, Bowman saw men loading blocks onto carriages; several hundred men. Short, with bow legs, dark skin, cotton clothes, working barefoot on the harsh, burning salt. In summer, these men – who Bowman supposed were Mexicans – must die like sepoys in the hold of a ship. Cool in the shade of carriages and sentry boxes, white men watched the miners, occasionally greeting the horseman who was crossing the mine.

Walden advanced slowly on this white embankment, ears flat, leaving Bowman time to think. The sight of this place reminded him of other places. Construction sites in India, negroes building a bridge, thousands of yellows digging a canal, the muddy building site at Millwall. After the desolation of Reunion, the salt mine was another image in a fresco depicting the interior landscape of Arthur Bowman. He took a bottle of whiskey from his saddlebags as he entered another desert plain, this one not ending in any mountain, with the track still arrowing wide and straight ahead of him. Walden quickened his pace.

Halfway to El Paso, they passed a Butterfield stagecoach going in the opposite direction, filled with mail and passengers. As Bowman watched it speed past, he thought that if he threw a letter inside it, it might reach Reunion before Alexandra Desmond could leave.

—ᴍ—ᴍ—ᴍ—

El Paso was as big as Fort Worth, the size of an English hamlet. Before entering it, Bowman stopped near the river on whose banks the town was built. The famous Rio Grande that the Paterson men all talked about – the border with that unknown land of Mexico – was as wide as the Thames, as powerful as the Irrawaddy, and as muddy as the Ganges. On the other shore, more spread out and populous than El Paso, he saw a white town with the figures of people in it, and a small crenellated fort, on the water's edge, facing the American town. Walden plunged his head into the river and Bowman, sitting next to the horse, finished a bottle of whiskey. He had not drunk so much in a long time and he felt nauseous.

In town, he asked the way to Fort Bliss, leaning down from his horse towards the citizens he questioned. There were other sorts of Mexicans in the streets, men with long black hair, wrapped up in blankets, walking in twos, sitting in the dust outside saloons. Maybe they were Indians, even if they didn't correspond to the idea he had of them: savage warriors running all day long under a hot sun, the fleet-footed hunters described by Irving, or the colourful horsemen that Cooper wrote about. As in the streets of Reunion, Walden snorted hard as they passed through El Paso, confirming Bowman's impression that this place stank.

Unlike Fort Worth or Fort Smith, Fort Bliss was not a town that had taken the name of a military camp: it was actually the headquarters of the Eighth Infantry Division, one mile north of El Paso. Bowman came to a halt two hundred yards from the stone fortifications and observed the patrols of horsemen, the columns of soldiers coming and going through the wide gates in their blue uniforms, just like the ones the soldiers in New York had worn. He took out his second bottle and finished it while observing the incessant to-and-fro of the troops.

Sentries on passageways watched him approach, and two guards at the entrance to the fort ordered him to stop.

"What do you want?"

Bowman was drunk. He looked down on them from his nervous horse. His lips stuck together and his words got mixed up in his mouth. Seeing that the soldiers were young and lacking in confidence, he spoke to them tersely:

"I have to see the commander."

"The commander? Who are you?"

The two soldiers glanced at each other.

"He's completely plastered."

"What do you want with the commander?"

"I have to talk to someone."

"Civilians can't just enter the fort like that. You need an authorisation or a good reason."

Walden stamped his hooves and Bowman let him.

"Let me pass."

"What did you say?"

Walden moved towards them, shaking his head. The two youths stepped back and grabbed their rifles. A sentry aimed at him from his post. Bowman spoke loudly:

"I have to see the commander, about the man who got chopped up."

Walden whinnied and moved further forward.

"Halt!"

The other young soldier called out:

"Corporal! There's a problem at the gate!"

He was shoved in a cell, a small building next to the officers' quarters. Through an arrow slit, he saw his horse, tied up, kicking with all its strength until the load it had been carrying was scattered all over the courtyard of the fort. No-one could calm it down, and Bowman watched while waiting for someone to fetch him. He smiled as he saw the soldiers and the officers in their usual agitation, stiff-backed and close-shaved, their weapons polished and their uniforms worn with pride. By the time a sergeant told him to leave his cell, his nausea had diminished, as had his desire to see Walden crush the soldiers under his hooves. He was led to an office belonging to a young captain with a moustache, whose nose wrinkled as soon as he entered.

"Guard, leave us. Sit down, please."

Bowman sat on a chair.

"Could you give me some water?"

The officer poured him a glass from the pitcher on his desk. Bowman drank it and handed back the empty glass. The captain poured him some more.

"Thank you."

"So you do have manners, despite the way you arrived at the fort."

"I'd been drinking."

"Your body odour is rather strong, sir, but it's true that I can still smell the alcohol on you. Are you in a fit state to tell me what you are doing here?"

"Sergeant Arthur Bowman, East India Company. British."

"Your accent testifies as much, Sergeant. But not your uniform."

"I'm not a soldier any more."

The captain smiled.

"I guessed that much. What are you doing in America, Mr Bowman, and more particularly at Fort Bliss?"

Bowman would have really liked to drink a bit more water.

"In Dallas, I heard talk of a murder here, something horrible. I wanted to find out if there was a connection with what happened back in London, several months ago. Another murder."

The captain's expression was strange: a mixture of disgust and fear. He was one of the few – along with young Slim, the cops in Wapping, Mrs Desmond and old Brewster – who had seen it. The two men exchanged a look, then the captain poured himself a glass of water.

"Why are you interested in that case?"

Bowman scratched his beard with his three fingers.

"The victim in Dallas, Richard Kramer, was a friend."

The officer made a suitable face and offered his condolences.

"This country is still badly organised, so it is the army that has the task of investigating and judging. Too many people think they can mete out justice themselves. Is that why you came to Fort Bliss?"

"Whether you or I do it makes no difference."

"And if you did it, I don't suppose any judge would send you to prison. But that's not the point. Anyway, you were wrongly informed, Mr Bowman. The case you've heard about did not occur here but in Las Cruces, about fifty miles north of here."

Bowman smiled.

"I was part of an army that meted out justice too. It did such a good job of it that it ended up with an entire country on its back."

"So you understand what I'm saying."

"No, it's you that does not understand."

In the fort's courtyard, Walden was still whinnying fiercely. Bowman looked out of the window.

"In the Company's army, I was the executioner. I'm not sure I would do it again."

The captain smoothed down his long moustache and observed Bowman for a moment. Then he opened a drawer of his desk and took out a leather briefcase, from which he drew two sheets of paper.

"Mr Bowman, I have no reason to provide you with this information. If I do so, it's because I believe there is no connection between these two cases. On the other hand, if you have any information that might aid us, please let me know. From one soldier to another. And I hope that, after that, you will calmly make your way home."

Bowman nodded.

"I hope so too."

Captain Phillips read out the investigation report. During those ten minutes, Bowman did all he could to memorise the facts – date, place, witness, identity of the victim – while waiting for the most important one: the description of the corpse. When Captain Phillips had finished reading, he was pale. The pitcher rattled against the glass when he poured himself more water.

"Given the conditions of the death, we concluded that it was an Indian ritual. I fought against the Comanches and the Apaches, and what I saw in Las Cruces . . . No-one else is capable of that. So, is there a link with your friend's death?"

Bowman thought for a moment.

"None at all."

The captain stood up.

"I suspected as much. And I think it's better this way. As for you, Mr Bowman, go back to Dallas and get on with your life."

Bowman stood in turn, dizzy from the alcohol he had drunk and the words he'd just heard. The captain accompanied him to the door and shook his hand.

"Go home, Mr Bowman."

Bowman tried to smile and looked outside, where his horse was still terrorising the fort.

"I don't think Walden likes this place. And I'm not going to be able to change his mind."

A guard gave him his belongings and he went outside to untie the mustang, which finally stopped bellowing. When Bowman sat in the saddle, he held his legs tight around the horse's body, well aware of what was about to happen. Walden charged through the fort's wide gates, with one final whinny.

He headed towards El Paso until he was out of sight of Fort Bliss, then turned back. Circling around the camp, he went north until he was back on the track to Santa Fe. About fifteen miles north of Fort Bliss, the road forked. A sign indicated New Mexico and Santa Fe to the north, and another, perpendicular, announced simply: *West*. Bowman continued northward. He spent the night in a rocky shelter in this half-desert landscape, leaving Walden untethered so he could wander off and find some dry bushes to feed on.

Bowman found only a few branches to burn. He was out of alcohol and the night was freezing cold. His clothes and blanket were not enough to protect him. Woken by a coughing fit, he discovered that he was feverish. Hands trembling, he drank a mouthful of Brewster's decoction, then he took out his papers and his pen and hastened to write down everything he remembered.

> *I found their scent again at Fort Bliss. They were at Las Cruces a month ago and the soldiers think it was the Indians who did that but it's them. The dead man's name was Amadeus Richter and he was a travelling salesman who worked between Mexico and the United States and also with the Comancheros – white men who trade with the Comanche Indians. It was the people in the village who found him one morning in a barn and they only recognised him because of his things. Nobody saw anything and as he thinks it was the Indians Captain Phillips has not even asked if Richter was with any white people before being killed or if there were any white strangers in Las Cruces. I'm going there to ask the questions he didn't ask.*

Bowman did not open his block of letter paper. Instead of continuing his letter to Mrs Desmond, he simply wrote to her on the same page.

> *The captain told me I should go home and if I had a home where you are now, I think I would go there. I've been in the same places as them and now I am only one and a half months behind them.*

Brewster's potion was having an effect now. Bowman felt floaty and kept writing anything that came into his head.

> *I don't feel good and when I got to Fort Bliss I thought I was going to have a fit. I don't know if you will be pleased but when I crossed the mines in Guadalupe I thought about what you said. About what I should hope for and what is more important than the things I imagined. It made me think of something I heard from Peavish, the preacher I'm looking for. He said we keep only what we give to others. He said that to the men in the Company who gave others death.*

*

By the time he entered Las Cruces, the effects of the potion had mostly passed and his fever was reduced. The town resembled the one he'd seen on the other side of the Rio Grande. Wattle-and-daub buildings with rounded corners, earth-coloured or painted white, were stuck to each other in a way that seemed prettier than the Americans' wooden constructions. Unlike Fort Worth or Dallas, the streets of Las Cruces were sheltered from the wind. In place of a central building like the one created by the dreamers of Reunion, the heart of the town was a paved square surrounded by shops. The inn where he asked for food – for himself and his horse – had a Mexican name: *Cantina de la Plaza*. The customers, too, were Mexican, and for the first time since his arrival in New York, Arthur Bowman had the impression of being in a foreign country; for the first time in even longer, he was the only white in a crowd of natives – men who looked like the miners he had seen in the Guadalupe Mountains: stocky, dark-skinned and black-haired.

Bowman paid for his meal, leaving a good tip for the landlord, and asked if he knew where the white man had been killed the previous month. The man recoiled and began stammering rapidly in Spanish while crossing himself several times, his hand making uninterrupted circles from his forehead to his chest.

"I don't understand what you're saying. The barn – where is the barn?"

"Burned, *señor*. Someone burned it down. All that's left is the gravestone in the cemetery. Nothing else, *señor*."

Bowman walked up to the hill that was scattered with gravestones, all of them as white as the town. Floral tributes to the Virgin Mary, candles and pieces of pottery decorated the monuments that lay under the sun, unprotected by any wall. Out of breath from the climb, Bowman crouched in the shade of a vault and took off his hat. At the far end of the cemetery, a group of graves without crosses caught his eye. They were just planks stuck in the earth, some of them anonymous. Bowman examined them until he found the one belonging to Amadeus Richter, the most recent of the banished tombstones.

Someone had at least taken the time to write his name. Bowman did not stay long to meditate over this mound of earth. The grave told him nothing about Richter's murderer, and he was not very interested in the idea that he, too, might end up with a plank over his head, without anyone to write his name on it.

He walked back down to the town and ordered a drink at the cantina. The landlord put a bottle of perfectly clear alcohol on the table. The bottle had no label. Bowman tasted the tequila and did not let go of the bottle until he had finished it.

When he woke up, he was lying on a pile of straw, his boots in a trough where Walden was placidly chewing hay and staring at him. He filled his buckets with water and his saddlebags with flour, lard and a few vegetables, and spent forty cents on two bottles of that Mexican alcohol. A shopkeeper recommended the fruit of a cactus, which, he said, helped against thirst, hunger and hangovers, and – if necessary, *señor* – gave you back your strength and vigour in bed. Prickly pears, identical to the ones Bowman had eaten in Africa. The Mohammedans, on the other side of the Atlantic, also claimed that these fruits gave a man the strength to walk a dozen miles without drinking water but that no well-made man needed them to honour a woman. Everything that the desert produced was a gift from God capable of curing death. Bowman bought a pound of them.

The track to Santa Fe was the path of gold. Colorado – the place dreamed of by the employees on the Paterson ranch – was now four hundred miles ahead of him. The next towns on his route were Albuquerque and Rio Rancho, a five-day ride away, before Santa Fe and the New Mexican border. Between Las Cruces and Albuquerque, the path crossed the Chihuahuan Desert, two high plateaus divided by the Rio Grande valley. The inns no longer belonged to Butterfield, but to the American Express Company. Bowman continued to stop at them for as short a time as possible and, when he could, crossed the Rio Grande to ride along the bank opposite that of the main track, which was frequented by stagecoaches and convoys of carriages. The traffic on the track grew ever busier. Traders or migrants, almost everyone was headed north, and in the inns, one name was on everyone's lips: Pikes Peak.

Bowman's hunting expeditions did not go well and he had to buy most of his food at the inns, along with his alcohol. He was no longer able to fall asleep or get up without a sufficient dose. When he had no alcohol, he drank some of old Brewster's potion.

After six days, he came within sight of Albuquerque and decided to spend the night by a river before going into town. He lit a fire and cooked his last ration of flour. Leaning against the fallen trunk of a dead tree, his rifle beside him and a bottle in his hand, he watched the traffic on the other shore: covered wagons pulled by cattle, tired women and children, men walking next to their animals to keep up their pace. The convoys, whether they had left as a group or come together by chance, often numbered two, three or four loaded carriages. Furniture, tools and barrels, with a cow or a workhorse tied behind them, they all looked the same, from the goods to their owners. While their slow, painful progress made Bowman smile as he sipped his whiskey, their grim determination to reach their goals made him lower his head. He uncorked the little bottle of potion. Walden pricked up his ears and snorted. Bowman glanced over the trunk, grabbed his rifle and tried to aim it despite the numbing effects of Brewster's plants. On the shore where he had taken refuge, coming from the north, a cart drawn by a mule had stopped about thirty feet away. A tall, skinny man in a black suit, a bowler hat on his head, raised his hand in greeting.

"Good evening!"

He had a strange accent. The man looked around him, at the river and the trees, the nook where Bowman had lit his fire.

"I have a few things to eat. And some fresh coffee."

He was smiling and unarmed. Bowman signalled him to approach. The mule advanced a few steps and stopped in front of the camp. The man got down from the cart. He was about fifty years old, with a greying beard on his chin and a face as long as his arm. He unloaded a wooden crate, which he put down near the fire. The first thing he took out of it was a jug of hooch.

"We don't have to eat right away. The weather will be fine tonight."

He raised his bottle and Bowman, still in a haze, did the same.

"Vladislav Brezisky. American for five years. I'm seeking my fortune around these parts. I'll return your hospitality one of these days, in a big house or maybe even in a town I've built myself. In the meantime, I make good coffee, and if you have any aches or pains, I can look after you, because I'm a doctor. I can't do anything against alcohol, though. I have too much respect for that passion. What are you looking for, my friend? Gold or oblivion?"

Walden snorted and stamped. Brezisky looked at the mustang.

"Not an easy-going kind of horse, is he? Sarcastic too, I bet. My mule, typically for that barren species, practises irony and silence. But I didn't give you time to introduce yourself."

He was just as drunk as Bowman was high on his decoction. Dry-mouthed, Bowman slowly articulated as he leaned his rifle against the dead tree:

"Bowman. I'm from England."

"Well, nobody's perfect. And I don't like drinking alone."

Brezisky watched a carriage go past on the other shore, the canvas cover quivering in the colours of the sunset.

"Truth be told, the company of those goody-two-shoes makes me sick. If you have no objections, I think I will start preparing dinner while I am still able to stand up straight."

From his crate, he took some mess tins, a bag of black beans, some lard, some bread and three eggs. He got the fire going again and put a pan of water to boil, continuing to speak as he did all of this, pausing occasionally to have a drink. He told Bowman about his hometown and his native country, Poland; he described the quality of Polish delicatessen products, the university where he studied medicine and discovered morphine, how he almost kicked the bucket in the hold of a third-class ship, what his wife died of, over there in Warsaw, before he decided to come to this nation of savages, madmen, heartless bastards and overly pious women. He served Bowman beans and fried eggs, with little bits of lard and a slice of bread.

Night fell. When they had finished eating, the doctor warmed up some coffee.

"And you, Mr Bowman . . . What brought you here? Because that is, ultimately, the only question one can ask in this rotten country."

Bowman wiped his beard on his sleeve. The alcohol, added to Brewster's plants, was weighing down on his half-closed eyelids. He smiled as he watched the flames.

"I'm searching for a killer."

"Very interesting, but I already have a job, Mr Bowman."

"Someone who always kills in the same way. He's murdered three people so far."

The doctor sat up in the firelight.

"Are you serious?"

"In London, a man whose name no-one ever knew. An engineer near Dallas, a year and a half later. And, two months ago, a travelling salesman in Las Cruces, which is five days' ride from here."

Brezisky burst out laughing, then, seeing that the Englishman was still serious, changed his expression. Hoping perhaps that the hooch, though drunk with another intention, would wake him up, the Pole wiped out the bottom of his jug and took another from the crate.

"You're not joking? You mean he does this in a repetitive fashion? Like a ritual?"

"That's what the soldiers at Fort Bliss said. They think it's an Indian ritual."

"Murders that are exactly alike . . . from one side of the world to the other . . . Never in my life have I heard such a thing. But, Mr Bowman, are you some sort of international policeman?"

Bowman swallowed his whiskey the wrong way and coughed.

"Not really."

Brezisky leaned back against the trunk, staring at his jug and apparently meditating on the usefulness of an extra mouthful.

"It's mathematical."

"What?"

"A sequence."

Bowman looked at him.

"A mathematical sequence?"

"Elements that precede and follow each other in accordance with a constant law, Mr Bowman. It can be infinite or finite. It is the repetition of a function, but in this case a human function."

Bowman had no idea what he was talking about.

"I met an old man in Dallas who said it was not a science but a passion."

"A 'passionate series' . . . And you're here to arrest him? That is by far the best reason for coming to this country that I've heard in the past five years."

Brezisky drank to that. Bowman joined him.

"For now, I'm just following him. Nothing else. I don't even know if I'm on the right track anymore."

"And the army thinks it's Indians?"

"Because they say a white man couldn't do such a monstrous thing."

Dr Brezisky sat up straight.

"And what do you say?"

"They say it's Indians. Because whites aren't that cruel."

Bowman laughed and the effect of the plants made him laugh more. His head was spinning. The Pole turned towards him, visibly panicked.

"My God."

"What's up?"

"The negro they're going to hang . . ."

"What negro?"

"There was a murder in Rio Rancho, a few weeks ago. Something no-one dares talk about."

He stared at Bowman, wide-eyed.

"It's your killer."

Bowman grabbed his lapels. Walden shivered and the mule opened an eye.

"Where?"

"Rio Rancho . . . The town's sheriff had arrested a black man and was getting ready to hang him when I passed through. Just like with your Indians, the inhabitants claimed that only a black could have done that."

Bowman stood up, holding on to the dead tree, and then ran over to the river. He stuck his fingers down his throat and made himself vomit. Then he splashed cold water on his face for a minute. Brezisky was pacing around the campfire.

"There's no point now. He must be dead already. You'll never get there in time!"

Bowman, struggling with dizziness, shoved his things in his travel bag and saddlebags. He threw the saddle on Walden's back.

"Mr Bowman, Albuquerque is an hour's ride from here, and it's another two to get to Rio Rancho. The gallows was already up . . ."

Bowman strapped on the travel bag and the blanket. The Pole started throwing his own belongings into his cart.

"I'll find you there!"

Bowman urged his horse into the black water of the Rio Grande and reached the other shore.

"Giddy-up!"

The mustang galloped along the main track to Santa Fe. Thirty minutes later, when he entered Albuquerque, they were still making good time. The town was asleep, flecked with a few lights. He sped through it.

"Giddy-up!"

They reached Rio Rancho in two hours, Walden, now trotting, covered in foam and pumping huge lungfuls of air through his nostrils, Bowman's body paralysed with cramps. He could see the entrance of the village in the pale night, the outlines of the wooden houses, recent constructions, that came before the traditional earthen buildings. Like Las Cruces, the centre of Rio Rancho was a paved square. Walden, with his shoes cracking against the paving stones and his laboured breathing, moved through the village like a noisy ghost. The moonlight was reflected on the white façades, illuminating the gallows and the immobile body suspended six feet above the ground. The horse snorted and its rider, still numb from the journey, contemplated the hanged man, grey in the moonlight. The negro's face was swollen like a drowned man's, his massive tongue dangling over his chin.

Bowman got down from the horse and walked over to the arcades that surrounded the square. There, he sat on the ground, his back against a pillar, and waited for sunrise.

Doors and windows opened. Rio Rancho awoke in silence and the inhabitants walked past without daring to cross through the square, glancing up at the gallows and crossing themselves. They also avoided going too close to the white horseman, sitting on the ground, who was staring at the negro's corpse swinging in the breeze. The body's smell, in the warming air, reached his nostrils now. Given the state of the body, the hanging must have taken place the day before. The Americans had maintained the European taste for early-morning executions and Bowman had arrived twenty-four hours too late. The time he had spent getting drunk in Las Cruces.

He stood up, entered the nearest cantina and asked for someone to look after his horse, for a table to be put outside, and to be brought a bottle of tequila. Bowman had just started drinking when Brezisky arrived in the square in his shaky cart. After waving to Bowman, the Pole rode around the gallows, his eyes never leaving it, and brought his mule to a halt in front of the table. Then the doctor sat down next to the Englishman.

"I know the justice system in my own country is far from perfect, but it's still better than the one in this country. Here, Mr Bowman, let me tell you, the judges are as hasty as an angry crowd."

Bowman looked at the hanged man.

"How long will they leave him up there?"

"I am not acquainted with the local customs, but it seems rather unusual to have left him up this long already. Besides, most of the hangings I've seen before now have not taken place in the centre of town, but on the outskirts. A warning for new arrivals, I suppose. This one seems to be addressed to the townspeople themselves."

In the time it took him to finish this little speech, Brezisky drank half the tequila. When the bottle was empty, Bowman stood up, walked over to the gibbet and climbed its steps. He took the dagger from his belt and cut the rope. The corpse fell like a bag of potatoes on the paving stones. The villagers watched him in shock. Bowman returned to the cantina, called the landlord, stared at him and put two one-dollar coins in his hand.

"Bury him."

Not daring to refuse the money, the Mexican ran off to the back of his restaurant.

"Mr Bowman, I have a feeling your company will become more and more interesting."

An hour later, three terrified men loaded the corpse on a mule and took it away.

Brezisky watched as two white men walked towards them from the other side of the square. Metal stars gleamed on their waistcoats and pistols hung from their belts. One of them looked tough, a moustache dangling over a square jaw; the other was much younger, beardless and nervous. The bigger man stood in front of the table.

"What the hell is all this? Who are you?"

The Pole stood up.

"Vladislav Brezisky, doctor. We rushed here, my friend and I, thinking we still had a chance to save that negro."

The sheriff turned to look at the gallows, suppressing a snigger.

"You cut him down to save him?"

"Ah, no. That does not lie within our jurisdiction, alas. We hoped to arrive before the execution."

The sheriff stared at Bowman, who was still sitting. The policeman's tone of voice changed after their eyes met.

"By whose authority did you cut him down?"

There was something off about this man. Bowman, without understanding why, saw Collins again, in the Irish bar, putting his hands to Bowman's throat to strangle him. Sergeant Bowman said through gritted teeth:

"The black you hanged. It wasn't him."

A nervous tic pulsed in the young deputy's face. The sheriff spoke in a muffled voice:

"What the hell do you know about it?"

Leaning on the table's edge, Bowman stood up, his head heavy with fatigue from the alcohol and his sleepless night. The deputy leapt backwards and his hand moved to the butt of his gun. Bowman stared at him, then at the sheriff, then opened his waistcoat and began unbuttoning his shirt. The sheriff did not move.

"What are you doing?"

Bowman continued opening his shirt, tearing off the last few buttons by yanking at the fabric. Brezisky muttered something in Polish and the deputy covered his mouth.

"The corpse you found, did it look like this?"

The Mexicans who had not fled at the sight of the sheriff now took off at a sprint. The tall man with the moustache did not react at all.

The lawmen escorted Bowman and Brezisky to their office, a hut in the middle of the wooden houses. White people on the sidewalks watched them go past.

"You, doctor: stay here and don't move. You, go inside."

The sheriff sat in his armchair. The deputy pulled out a chair for Bowman.

"No chair. Let him stand. Name?"

"Bowman."

"Where did you come from, Bowman?"

"When did you find the corpse?"

The sheriff put his hat on the desk and cracked the joints of his fingers by twisting them.

"Why do you need to know that?"

"If you want me to tell you what I know."

"What you know?"

The young policeman, leaning against a wall, was watching the sheriff, and that was the second thing that seemed wrong to Bowman. He was scared of his own boss. The man with the moustache smiled unpleasantly.

"We found Rogers three weeks ago, in an old Indian house on the edge of town. Rogers' specialty was acting as a guide for pioneers. We were able to identify him because there was still a handful of hair on his head. Rogers was half-black. He had a negro's hair, but blond as straw. That bastard always used to keep his hair hidden under a hat so people'd think he was white. Funniest thing was that he hated blacks even more than the rest of us."

The sheriff glanced over at his subordinate, whose face was deformed by the tic again.

"Half the inhabitants of Rio Rancho are Mexican. The other redskins came down from the mountains to beg in our streets. We also have some negroes, a Chinese family, and some white folks from God-knows-where, just as poor as the niggers and who don't speak a word of English. The folks who pay me to do my job are the others, the Americans, those who try to live their lives honestly. After Rogers' murder, everyone started getting uppity."

He turned to his deputy.

"How many fights did we get after Rogers' killing?"

The boy blinked.

"At least twenty."

"At least twenty. And when the Mexicans get their machetes out, it's not so they can slice up beans. Never in my life had I seen such a mess in our little village. And in the middle of all that, last week, Willy showed up in town with Rogers' hat on his head and his waistcoat on his back. Rogers was a card-player too. He used to wear that waistcoat when he sat down at a poker table, said it brought him good luck. Willy was completely drunk. When I asked him where he'd found them clothes, he just went crazy. He started talking about the Devil, how he'd met him, and the Devil had entered him. That kind of shit. Them negroes take religion too serious, and on top of that they get it mixed up with their African bullshit. Willy said he'd put the dead man's clothes on so that Lucifer wouldn't recognise him. When we tried to arrest him, he stripped buck naked. And it was . . . He'd cut himself all over his chest, like Rogers."

The sheriff shuddered. He spat in a saucepan that was placed at his feet, looked up at Bowman and stared at his open shirt as he wiped his mouth.

"Like your scars."

Bowman glanced outside. Brezisky was waiting on his cart, Walden beside him. The Henry was in the holster that hung from Walden's saddle.

"Did you ask him what his devil looked like, or did you just hang him?"

The deputy moved in his corner. The sheriff raised a hand towards him without looking away from Bowman.

"Stay where you are, kid."

But the boy had not been about to move, he'd been about to speak. The sheriff had just told him to shut his mouth.

"In the house where we found Rogers, there was nothing but his body, not a single one of his belongings. Willy was wearing them. And he'd always been a bit crazy. Rogers had even kicked his ass once or twice. Because he was black, you know."

"So you didn't ask any questions."

"It was an open-and-shut case."

"But it wasn't him."

The sheriff sat back in his chair and put his hands on his thighs.

"It wasn't a good idea to cut Willy down. Up to now, everything was going fine."

"And the judge agreed with you?"

"Bowman, I don't understand what you're doing here. You didn't know Rogers, and you didn't know Willy neither. In fact, none of this is any of your business. The closest judge must be in El Paso, unless people have been telling me lies. And even if I did make a mistake by sending Willy to the gallows, don't imagine that any judge, from here to New York, would blame me for it. So now, either you tell me what you know, or . . . I find myself with a second man in Rio Rancho who has the same scars as Rogers, and that would be a serious problem."

Bowman had pins and needles in his legs. Not as if he was about to have a fit. This was more like something trembling in the depths of his flesh. Bowman thought of Brewster and his passionate attraction.

The man sitting across from him was like them: Peavish or Penders. And the deputy, in his corner, leaning against the wall, was shit-scared of him. The boy watched Bowman face up to his boss and waited to see what would happen.

Bowman spoke slowly.

"I know the man who did that."

The sheriff blinked.

"The man who did that?"

He looked again at Bowman's open shirt. Bowman glanced at the deputy.

"The negro had nothing to do with it. But he saw him and you hanged him for it."

The sheriff slid a hand under his desk. The young deputy had also put his hand on his gun and his hoarse voice surprised them both:

"We beat him up and never even asked him a question!"

The boy was angry and, for the first time, this anger was perhaps stronger than his fear. His fingers tightened around the butt of his revolver as he stared at the sheriff.

"We hanged Willy and it wasn't him. And the other man got away long ago."

"Shut your mouth, kid."

Bowman almost screamed:

"The other man?"

The deputy was still staring at his boss and his gun was half out of his holster.

"The other Englishman. The one who came to town with Rogers."

Before the sheriff had time to move, the young policeman had unholstered his pistol. He wasn't really aiming at the older man: his gun was half raised towards the desk, his hand trembling, his face pale.

"We didn't do anything, but he could find him. You have to let him go."

Keeping an eye on the sheriff, Bowman continued questioning the deputy:

"What did he look like?"

"An Englishman. Light hair. He came in with a convoy of other pioneers. Rogers acted as their guide. When . . . when we found the corpse, he was the only one who wasn't in town anymore. But we never asked Willy anything, we just beat him up and hanged him. He wasn't even in town when it happened!"

The sheriff shouted louder than the boy:

"Shut your mouth!"

The deputy raised his gun and aimed at the sheriff's chest.

"Let him go! He'll find the killer."

Bowman was going crazy.

"What was he like? What was his name?"

"I don't know! No-one in the convoy knew. Just an Englishman, and they said he was blond. He'd left town by the next day."

Bowman took a step back and began to turn towards the door.

"Don't move! Stay here, Bowman!"

The sheriff was yelling. The boy cocked his revolver and cut him off:

"Let him go. I won't tell you again."

Bowman opened the door and turned back to the deputy. The boy nodded at him.

"Go on."

Bowman closed the door behind him. Walden stamped on the ground. Bowman got in the saddle, one hand on the butt of the Henry. Brezisky, on his cart, asked what was happening.

"We need to get out of here."

Forcing the pace, they reached the outskirts of Santa Fe in the afternoon and decided to avoid the town. Brezisky said that the mountains of Sangre de Cristo, a few miles further on, were a good place to stop. As they approached the mountain peaks covered in forest, Bowman pushed ahead, driving between larches and pines. He followed a winding path, navigable by carriage, until he reached a little lake, a few acres in area, nestled in the hollow of the mountain like the palm of a hand. He went back down the path and waited for Brezisky. It was too late to go hunting, so the two men dined on pancakes and beans, then started drinking. The doctor waited until they were both quite drunk before speaking.

"What happened at the sheriff's office?"

The name of Penders had been circling Bowman's head ever since they left Rio Rancho. Nothing but his name and the memory of the smile that went with it. Sergeant Erik Penders had been in Rio Rancho. When Bowman did not reply, Brezisky tried another question.

"How do you feel?"

Bowman looked at him.

"How do I feel? I don't feel anything."

"Mr Bowman, can I ask you something?"

"What?"

"Your scars . . . Was it this murderer who gave them to you?"

Bowman took Brewster's flask from his pocket and handed it to the Pole.

"What is it?"

"Dunno. Just plants, but it works. Like laudanum, but stronger."

Brezisky accepted it eagerly. Bowman drank some too.

"Without this, I couldn't tell you anything. And it'll help you sleep afterwards."

—⁓—⁓—⁓—

Bowman rose with the sun, his dagger in his belt and the Henry in his hand.

The animals of this mountain, ignored by the pioneers because it contained no gold, were not mistrustful of humans. Bowman was able, without difficulty, to approach a small group of deer grazing in a clearing. The males, the size of bucks, had short, curved antlers and black heads. Their coats were fawn and they had white speckles on their bellies and necks. They smelled his odour but, not associating it with danger, merely went back to grazing. Bowman spotted a young male, maybe eighty or ninety pounds in weight. There were bigger targets to aim for, but he and Brezisky did not have the time or the means to salt the meat. Shoulder leaning against the trunk of a pine tree, he lifted his rifle and lined up the animal's head in its sights. The gunshot startled the troop, which remained where it was, heads raised and ears pricked, while the young male collapsed. Bowman lowered his gun, moved away from the tree and took a step into the clearing. Their tails sweeping the air, their big round black eyes following him, he continued moving forward until, at last, a large male took a first step and then ran off, the others following it.

Bowman slung the dead deer over his shoulder and walked back to the lake. He hung it from a branch, slit open the belly and removed its innards. He cut the skin around the hooves and then sliced it up to the thighs. He pulled the skin over its head and threw the fur on the grass. Then he untied the carcass and lay it down on a rock by the water. Breaking the joints, chopping the thoracic cage in half, he separated the quarters, the legs and the shoulders, then rinsed his hatchet, his dagger and his blood-covered arms in the lake. Fish came to the surface, drawn by the scraps of flesh.

Brezisky had got the fire going again and was cutting branches from a larch tree. As Bowman sliced up the pieces of meat, the Pole stuck them on stakes around the fire. Soon the odour of thirty pounds of roasting flesh rose through the air. Bowman cut out the heart and the liver, put a flat stone on the embers and waited until it was hot. He tossed bits of offal onto the stone and stirred them with the end of his dagger; while they cooked the meat, he and Brezisky chewed mouthfuls of it.

"What kind of animal is this?"

Brezisky, while picking at his teeth, told him that the Americans called them "pronghorns" or "antelope". Bowman smiled.

"In Africa, antelopes have horns about three feet long. Some of them weigh nearly five hundred pounds. They run twice as fast as a horse and can leap over almost anything. It takes several lions or tigers to catch one."

"American antelope are not in the same league, but the meat is excellent. We've got enough food to last us quite a while."

Bowman stabbed a piece of heart and trapped it between his teeth.

"You'll have plenty to eat, Doc. But you're going to go your own way after this."

The Pole smiled at him.

"Is it because you told me your story that we have to go our separate ways?"

"What?"

"I'm not going to try to change your mind, but I do wonder: have you ever stuck around with someone who knows you?"

Bowman turned a piece of shoulder on a spit, walked away from the heat of the fire, and sat in the grass.

"I've always lived alone. Even before. And what I'm doing now . . . that's nobody's business but mine."

Brezisky rummaged about in his crate in search of some hooch.

"Anyway, your company may well be dangerous. My arteries are no longer in the first flush of youth, but I still hope to build that big house one day. I'll go my way, dear friend, don't you worry. But you must ask yourself that question."

"It might happen. But for now, it's impossible."

The doctor thought for a moment.

"There's an island in Japan where the men and women all live to a hundred years old. Bloody fish-eaters! Our lives and our world use us up much faster than that. You're not as old as me yet, but life has been hard to you. Don't wait until you're my age, Mr Bowman, because solitude becomes difficult to fight. Having said that, I am not in your skin."

Brezisky coughed and looked at Bowman.

"Excuse me. That's not what I meant."

The sergeant hesitated for an instant, then smiled at the Pole. The doctor smiled back at him and started laughing, his mouth almost toothless from too much alcohol.

"On the other side of the mountains, you have the choice between taking the Denver track, which goes through a few towns where the gold-panners go, or following the Rio Grande. On one bank, you'll find the same convoys you've been seeing recently; on the other, just desert plains. Water isn't a problem if you don't move away from the river. You can do some hunting, but you have to like rabbit or wild horse, no offence to your mustang. If you want to be alone, the Rio Grande is the best route for you."

Brezisky gave him a bag containing beans, wheat flour and the rest of his coffee.

"I'll be passing through a town soon, and, as I think I know where you're headed, you'll need this more than I will."

Bowman offered to pay him for the food.

"A bit of generosity wouldn't hurt this country, Mr Bowman. Nor would a bit of friendship. Thank you again for that marvellous decoction. I don't know what the old herbalist added to the hemp, but it was definitely a success. Did you know that Mr Washington, the first president of the United States, himself grew that excellent psychotropic? Although I imagine he preferred it in the form of fabrics and American flags."

Bowman smiled.

"Probably better if you don't go back through Rio Rancho."

"Thank you for your concern, but that was not my intention."

"Good luck."

"Mr Bowman, there are still only a few roads in this damned country. I hope we will meet again. Although it is probably absurd to drink to your success, I wish you good luck at least. And when the war comes, try to get as far away from it as you can."

"The war?"

"Lincoln and the northern businessmen will certainly win the next election. The South has just announced that it will secede if Lincoln is elected. The country will be cut in half."

"I don't make war anymore, Doc. No chance."

Brezisky raised his jug of hooch and his mule started away.

Arthur Bowman rode into the woods of Sangre de Cristo. From the northward slope he saw two paths: the green line of the Rio Grande crossing the grey plains, straight ahead of him, and, further west, the pale line of the main track rising towards Pueblo and the Colorado mines. He turned towards the river but did not leave the mountain straight away. He stopped near a spring, unloaded the bags from his horse, and let it graze freely. Then he took his rifle and followed the tracks of antelope. He brought a forty-pound female back to the spring. Once he had chopped up and quartered the animal, Bowman sharpened his knife and cut the meat into thin slices, which he laid out to dry in the smoke from the fire. Walden stood dozing by the stream. Bowman took out his writing materials.

I have described journeys that lasted weeks in ten words. Now I have to write pages to describe a few hours that I spent in Rio Rancho. I found him. It's Penders.

I don't know what to think. If I'd rather it had been Peavish.

In Rio Rancho, a sheriff had hanged a negro in the middle of a village and I sat there watching the body swing. The negro had not done anything except for seeing Penders, and maybe even the murder. Captain Reeves said it wasn't my fault, that the murderer wasn't his fault either. So what about that hanged man? The sheriff in Rio Rancho saw my scars and for the first time I saw someone who thought they looked good. I think he admired them. I discovered that other men, who did not come from the same place as us, can also be as mad as Penders.

Today I said goodbye to a Polish doctor who wished me good luck and told me he was a friend.

Walden is standing in the grass by the stream and that's the first time I've seen him like that. I wonder if he misses the Pole's mule.

I passed the point I was scared of when I left Reunion. The point of no return. Because I can't let blacks die in place of Penders. This started in Burma eight years ago and now I am only three weeks behind him, on the other side of the world.

That's a summary of everything that's happened to me but I also have to write something else. My friend the Polish doctor, he said that I could choose to live with people who know me. I thought of you even if we don't really know each other that well.

It was dark now. Bowman moved close to the fire to trace the last words on a page that was as red as Alexandra Desmond's hair, then folded the letter he would not send. He fell asleep in the grass, thinking about the desert into which he would descend the next day.

8

It was as if no-one wanted this water. The Rio Grande flowed amid rocks and thorny bushes, tracing its route between the plains and the plateaux, digging channels in the soft rocks without a single tree growing on its banks. It seemed to pass over the earth rather than being part of it, seeking its path, always lower down, on this vast, endless brown slab. No tracks except those of wild animals. The river was all his.

In the large gorges, the echo of Walden's hooves mingled with those of stones rolling down cliffs, pushed into the void by big lizards scurrying away at the sound of his arrival. The mustang slowed down as they went on, not finding any food nutritious enough to revitalise it. Whenever Bowman spotted a dash of green in the landscape – even the smallest plant with its roots in an irrigated crack – he led his horse straight over to it.

The nights were no cooler than the days. Like the river water, the sun seemed to pass over this place without belonging to it. The rocks produced their own heat and their own light. If these dry plains had any kindred, it was the moon, which gave them back their true colours. The same colours as the hanged man in the plaza. In the grey and blue of the night, desert dogs, invisible during the day, ran and barked after rabbits. Insects, turtles, lizards and snakes were the daylight inhabitants, their colours, shells and carapaces blending with the rocks.

There was no shortage of antelope meat. To make a fire, he had to spend an hour looking for twigs, which burned for a long time in little yellow flames that gave no heat. As he had coffee, Bowman continued collecting wood as he walked during the day. Then he stopped. He had nothing left to cook, the nights were hot, and those cold flames, rather than offering him the comfort of company, reminded him of will-o'-the-wisps rising from mass graves on battlefields.

Instead of the green hills he had been dreaming of since he left London, he had found a desert.

Bowman did not write during his crossing, and when he reached Alamosa, after five days and five nights, he would have struggled to say what he had thought about during all that time. He retained the memory of only a few words, repeated like the echoes of Walden's steps, like the sound of stones rolling to the bottom of the Rio Grande's riverbed. "Alexandra." "Arrive." "Peavish." "Penders." "Reunion." "Sharks."

Although he neither wrote nor spoke, he did reread Thoreau's chapter on solitude.

> *What sort of space is that which separates a man from his fellows and makes him solitary? I have found that no exertion of the legs can bring two minds much nearer to one another. What do we want most to dwell near to? Not to many men surely, the depot, the post-office, the bar-room, the meeting-house, the school-house, the grocery, Beacon Hill, or the Five Points, where men most congregate, but to the perennial source of our life, whence in all our experience we have found that to issue, as the willow stands near the water and sends out its roots in that direction.*

On the afternoon of the sixth day, he rode past an immense sandbank, sculpted by the wind into dunes. The Rio Grande had shrunk; its shores were greener and more wooded. When he saw the lights of Alamosa, he stopped to let Walden eat, taking the time to conclude this stage of his journey. Arthur Bowman, beard dangling down to his chest, the lines in his face filled with dust, felt good when he entered the little town.

Alamosa was nestled in a forest of trees that he did not recognise, with pale, smooth trunks, their branches covered with little white balls that looked like exploded grains of cotton. There were a dozen buildings, each constructed in a small clearing made by pioneers. No shops, no inns, nothing but white farmers and livestock owners who had gathered to work together, or at least to live close to each other. Bowman's arrival was met with curiosity, firstly from the children, then from the men on the doorsteps of their houses, and lastly from the silhouettes of women at the windows. It was the cleanest and most peaceful village he had seen up to now. On the opposite bank, facing houses with brick chimneys, was another village. Or rather a camp. Cabins made of branches, fires on the ground, chickens and dogs running free, scruffy children playing with them. The Indians who lived there were strangely dressed, wearing only bits and pieces of European clothes – a top or a pair of trousers – mixed with their traditional cotton garb. At first sight, there appeared to be two or three times as many as Indians as whites, separated by the river in which some rocks had been rolled to form a sort of bridge. Bowman advanced slowly between the houses, turning his eyes from one side to the other of this two-faced village. The contrast between the perfection of the whites and the messy informality of the Indians was striking, like a military garrison located next to a refugee camp.

A solid-looking man with a chinstrap beard and red cheeks came over to Bowman with a smile. Bowman pulled on the reins and Walden reluctantly came to a halt.

"God bless you, my son. Welcome to Alamosa, the Lord's own country."

The first words he had heard in six days.

Bowman decided not to stay, asking simply if he could buy some food and how to find the road to Pueblo. Each loaf of bread, each bean and each ounce of flour he received in exchange for his money was twice blessed. He asked if he could buy some alcohol and received only advice about the benefits of abstinence. After that, the negotiations became more difficult and the tone of the exchanges less friendly. Bowman felt sure that, if he'd crossed the Rio, he would have got what he wanted from the Indians. The only other things he was able to obtain were some tobacco and directions on the best way to get out of the village. He left Alamosa with strange images in his mind. Of women and girls staying behind closed doors, lurking behind windows, while all the men came out of the houses. Of Indians wearing hand-me-down clothes from the whites. The wild children, only just evangelised, with their skin of many colours, from the dark skin of the Indians to the paler skin of the Mexicans and the white children running around the campfires after chickens. And of that stone bridge that connected and separated the evangelists, all those good, dignified fathers, from the Indian women. He left this green, fresh paradise behind him, but before continuing east towards Pueblo, he stopped one last time by the river.

After removing the load from Walden's back, Bowman took all his clothes off and, pulling on the halter, led the mustang into the middle of the river. He splashed and rubbed it until the horse had had enough and left the river at a gallop, rolling itself in the dust as soon as it could. Bowman pulled out a few handfuls of grass, folding and twisting them together to make a sort of flannel. Leaning his head against a rock, he let the cool water flow over his body. Then he used stones to build a little dam against the shore. On the smooth surface of this tiny pond, bent over his reflection, Bowman trimmed his beard with his knife. He shaved himself the best he could in this sky-coloured mirror and cut his own hair. He washed his clothes on a stone, stretched them out to dry in the sun and lay in the grass to take a nap, waking in the early evening and lighting a fire close to the water.

The next morning, his flasks full of water from the Rio Grande, he got back on the road. He rode steadily and spent two nights near springs that the inhabitants of Alamosa had told him about. Each evening, he wrote to Alexandra Desmond, describing his journey to her, the silent desert and his bath in the river, the increasingly disturbing presence of Penders, the distance he kept stretching every day between himself and Reunion. On the third day, he reached the main track, with its convoys of carts heading towards the gold of Pikes Peak. Late that afternoon, he arrived in Pueblo, a crossing point between the northern road and the path to Santa Fe, joining the Oregon path in

Independence, on the Missouri river. Though grandiloquently calling itself a "town", Pueblo consisted merely of a few huts, all of them shops this time.

The real activity took place around these buildings. Dozens of carts and tents were gathered, with hundreds of pioneers walking in a cramped space filled with bulls, mules, horses and cows. People traded, sold and haggled over everything, from nails to foals to information. Guides offered their services, and so did women. There were country brothels next to open-air masses and baptisms, and preachers bellowing to be heard over the din. Blacksmiths hammered horseshoes and wheel hoops. Old women sold stews, baked bread and read palms. You could hear twenty different languages being spoken. At every third tent and every second cart, someone – on a plank and two crates – was selling alcohol.

Walden's ears were pinned back. Bowman crossed the camp towards the centre of town, looking for a stable, and then for the saloon. The bar was packed to the rafters and he doubted he would discover any information at all here. He elbowed his way to the counter and ordered a drink. The atmosphere was festive and violent. Some of the pioneers had brought their children with them, and they watched with wide, worried eyes as the head of their family got drunk. A female singer hollered in a corner while a pianist attacked an out-of-tune keyboard with half its keys missing. Mugs of beer were passed over people's heads. Men rolled around on the ground.

The saloon's landlord, standing on a chair behind the bar, banged a hammer against a cracked bell.

"Next round's on the house!"

The announcement was met with hurrahs. Hats, thrown into the air, landed on chandeliers or fell on other people's heads.

Bowman was given a free whiskey, like everyone else. After the landlord's round, the drinkers, presumably thinking they had saved themselves some money, started ordering more and more drinks. They paid for four or five and handed them around to total strangers. The saloon's customers were united by a fierce joy and a determination to celebrate.

A man put a drink in front of Bowman, and they clinked glasses.

"What are we drinking to?"

"Haven't you heard?"

Bowman downed his whiskey.

"What's happened?"

The man, speaking in a strong Irish accent, turned to the crowd and shouted, laughing:

"He doesn't know!"

No-one paid any attention to him and he moved closer to Bowman to yell in his ear.

"They got 'em! Them fucking redskins! The lads from St Vrain got their hands on 'em! Three ropes for them sons of bitches!"

"The Indians revolted?"

The Irishman stared at him seriously, his eyes crossed in a drunken stupor.

"A revolt? What the hell are you talking about, lad? It's the three Indians from the track. They found 'em and they're gonna make 'em wear the hemp tie."

"The Indians from the track?"

"Fucking hell, where have you been? You didn't know that Indians have been attacking pioneers?"

A sudden crush separated the man from Bowman. He yelled something else, but a scrum of Irishmen had dragged him over to a table, where they were singing. Bowman had heard only a few words of his last sentence. He shoved his way through the crowd, grabbed the man by the shoulder and turned him round, shouting at him over the drunken chorus:

"What did you say?"

The man stopped singing.

"Bloody hell, go have a drink! Let me sing!"

Bowman picked him up by his lapels and carried him over to the counter.

"What did you say about the Indians?"

"Give me a drink!"

Bowman ordered three whiskies and lined them up in front of the Irishman.

"Tell me."

He downed the first one.

"The Comanches who were attacking pioneers to rob them, they're for it!" And he drew his fingers across his throat.

"What did you say, before?"

"That them bastards are gonna get what's coming to 'em, after what they did to all those poor men!"

Another glass vanished.

"What did they do?"

"Torture, lad! The horrible things they did, corpses all the way to Mexico. Apparently, they killed about twenty white men! For weeks, everyone on this track has been scared shitless! Well, not anymore!" And again he drew his fingers across his throat.

He downed his third glass, thanked Bowman with a bow and told him that everything would be alright now, that there was no need to worry anymore, that the gold of Pikes Peak awaited them and that he was going back to sing with his mates.

"The hanging. Where does it take place?"

"Bent's Fort, on the Independence track. Hell, we'll all be going to see that!"

The Irishmen were singing something about a road leading to Liverpool, passing through Dublin, waving shillelaghs above their heads. At the other end of the room, some Englishmen had also begun to sing, trying to make more noise than the Irish. A brawl was taking shape.

Bowman shoved and elbowed his way out of the pub as nostalgic songs were belted out with ever greater fury. Outside he caught his breath, hands on his knees, then stood up and ran over to the stable to pick up Walden. He crossed the pioneers' camp, stopping to ask for directions to Bent's Fort from four men who were playing cards.

"It's on the other side of town. It's not complicated, there are only two tracks. Take the eastern one."

"Sixty miles."

"The hanging's not till tomorrow afternoon. There's no need to rush off!"

Bowman galloped away. He bypassed the town, the tents and the carts, making a circle around campfires and finding the crossroads where the two tracks met, before taking the eastern one and setting off into the night. A half-moon shone from the sky. He rode on. One minute longer might have finished off his horse, but Bowman arrived in Bent's Fort in the early morning and Walden was still standing.

—⟋⟋⟍—⟋⟋⟍—⟋⟋⟍—

As in Pueblo, there was a camp of carts around the fort. Bowman passed between the just-waking immigrants and a crowd of travellers who looked slightly different. Some were curious onlookers already in town for the hanging, and there were also a number of tradesmen there to sell their products, drinks and food, plus gun salesmen, funfair attractions, magicians and games of chance. Hucksters, red-eyed from last night's drinking session, chased nosy children from coloured tents. Whores washed out their mouths in buckets. Men lay on the ground, snoring, dressed in dusty clothes, with bottles in their pockets. As he approached the fort, Bowman heard the sound of hammering. Bent was not a town, not even a village, simply a large, traditional fort, built in earth and brick, with three-foot-thick walls and arrow slits. There were one-storey buildings, ochre-brown, that acted as big inns designed especially for war and commerce. Stable, warehouses and offices, houses for the employees. Above the main door, a sign was hung: *Bent and St Vrain Trading Company*.

In the middle of the large courtyard, a team of carpenters were putting up the gallows, big enough to hang three men at the same time. The wood was not new: clearly, the gallows was not used every day, so it had to be assembled for the next day's execution.

Bowman went over to the stable. An old Indian man took Walden's reins.

"Tired. Good horse. Two dollars. Lots of people for hanging."

Bowman dismounted, untied the holster containing the Henry and put the strap over his shoulder. Outside the only door of a small building, three men armed with rifles and revolvers stood guard. Bowman walked towards them.

"Who's in charge here?"

"Don't stay there, sir. Move along."

"I'm just looking for whoever's in charge."

"In charge?"

"The sheriff, the judge. Whoever's responsible for all that."

Bowman pointed at the gallows.

"There's no sheriff here, just the manager. He's in the office."

"The manager?"

"Of the company. He's in charge of everything here. Now move along."

Bowman walked away, glancing back at the door. Thick oak, with a small, barred opening at its centre.

Some men were coming and going through the open door to an office. Bowman mingled with them and waited for his turn to pass before a man sitting behind a table. He was reading lists, signing papers, giving orders, checking and writing down figures in notebooks.

"What can I do for you?"

"Are you the manager?"

"He won't be long. Are you looking for work?"

"No. Where is he?"

"If you want to see him, wait here. Next!"

Bowman went back out and waited in the shade of a wall, observing the gallows and the door guarded by the three armed employees. Other guards were posted at the main entrance and checked everyone coming through, pushing away children and gawkers who were gathering to see the gibbet. They let a man past on a little cart. On the carriage's canvas covering, the man's name and profession were painted: *Charles Bennet, photographer*. Bowman watched him walk around the courtyard in search of the best viewpoint, then unload his equipment from the cart. He assembled a little stage in front of the gallows, put a tripod on top of it, and lastly his photographic chamber. He peered into the lens, moving the camera around until he was satisfied by the composition of the picture, then marked the position of the tripod in chalk before dismantling it.

The guards at the entrance let another man pass on a horse. He was well-dressed and armed and he did not respond to their salute. This man, who Bowman presumed was the manager, stopped in front of the cell to take a look inside, exchanging a few words with the guards, and then continued towards the office.

Bowman stood up and walked over to meet him. He had been fooled by the man's height and stockiness; up close, he realised that the manager was older than he had thought, maybe sixty years old.

"Can I speak to you?"

The manager did not stop.

"If you're looking for work, talk to the foreman."

Bowman followed him.

"It's not for work. It's about the Indians you're going to hang."

The man stopped and looked at Bowman.

"Who let you in? Who are you?"

"Arthur Bowman."

"I don't know who you are and I don't have time for this. If you're selling furs, talk to the . . ."

"I'm not selling anything, but I have to speak to you."

"Sorry, not now."

"The Indians didn't kill the pioneers."

The manager stopped again.

"What?"

"In Las Cruces, they hanged a negro, saying it was him. It's not the Indians."

The manager thought this over for a moment.

"I wasn't aware of that."

*

John Randell's office was a little haven of luxury and calm in the middle of the fort. A rug on the floor, hunting trophies. On the wall above the table were photographs, showing Randell standing next to two men in dark suits: Bent and St Vrain, the directors of the trading company. Another of him, alone in a pine forest, with his foot on the belly of an impressively large bear. The portrait of a woman sitting on a sofa, a baby in her arms. Another of a young army officer standing to attention, probably his father.

Bowman held his rifle by the barrel, standing in front of the solid wood desk.

"Bowman, people talk a lot of horseshit about these murders, and it doesn't surprise me that a black ended up on the gallows. Everyone was frightened and the rumours were getting ridiculous all along the road. The less people know, the more they imagine. You seem pretty sure of yourself, but I have to tell you you're not the first man to turn up here with a new theory. I couldn't even tell you all the stuff I've heard in the last few weeks. And I'll spare you the apparitions of the Devil on the Santa Fe track. But this time we have proof. I'm sorry about that man they hanged in Las Cruces, but I know how to keep a cool head and I would not send these men to their deaths unless I was certain about what I was doing. Why do you say it wasn't them?"

Bowman stayed calm because Randell was calm too. He addressed him as if he were delivering a report to an officer:

"The man who killed people on the track, he started in England. His name is Erik Penders and he was under my command when I was a sergeant in the India Company. He killed a man in London, another closer to Dallas, called Kramer, and a third, Rogers, in Las Cruces. I didn't see the last two, only the one in London. But I know that he killed them in the same way and I also know where he learned to do that because I was with him at the time. When we were soldiers in Burma. I've already seen the negro hanged. I know it's not your three Indians either."

Randell lit a pipe and blew the smoke towards the ceiling of his office.

"Bowman, I don't have much time, but I do want to explain this to you. Despite what you say, you're misinformed. People say they've killed about twenty men. I don't know about that, but there are at least two others than the ones you mentioned. One in Mexico, a few months back. I wasn't down there, but the testimony comes from a man I know and trust, a partner in our company. And another, which happened less than a week ago, a bit further along the Independence track."

Bowman wavered, trying to organise his thoughts.

"But you didn't know about the murder in Dallas. So you don't know everything either."

Randell continued in the same serious tone of voice:

"How long is it since you slept, Bowman? Please, sit down."

Bowman pulled a chair in front of the desk.

"What happened a week ago?"

"Fedor Petrovitch . . . I had him here in this office just a few days before, sitting exactly where you are sitting now. Petrovitch was an inventor who was looking for financial partners to launch a new method of gold-panning that used cyanide. He came to speak to me, to ask if Bent and St Vrain were interested. My employers do not want to invest in gold mining. That is what I told him."

Randell lowered his head and stuffed the tobacco into the chamber of his pipe.

"It was the Comanches. The last warriors of a tribe who refused to give up their arms and join the New Mexico reserves. The Indian Affairs office already knew about them. They were roaming the road for nearly a year, regularly crossing the Mexican border. Their group was reduced, along with their resources, as the tribes were brought into the reserves. I am not an enemy of the Indians, Bowman, and the success of this company is due in no small part to the trade we have carried out with them. I have gotten to know them. I know they are not the savages that people claim they are, and that they cannot bear hope-lessness. Their constitution is no better at resisting alcohol. Those men are capable of going to war for months and living like animals in caves if they know they will be reunited afterwards with their land and their children. But if you take that away from them, they are already dead and they might do anything. How would you behave, Bowman, in a world that destroyed your own world?"

Bowman could feel pins and needles in his hands, dizziness, his dry tongue swelling in his mouth. He took Brewster's flask from his pocket and swallowed a few drops so he could carry on without collapsing. Randell watched him do it, smiling at the thought that it must be alcohol, and went on:

"Our company has been in charge of maintaining a semblance of order in this place, and will go on doing that until the government has representatives here. Ceran St Vrain, who co-founded this company with Bent, fought with his men alongside the army and personally subdued the revolts in New Mexico. But, like me, he is no warmonger. We believe it is our responsibility to deal with this task. The three warriors who are going to be hanged tried to attack a company convoy. But they were drunk and there weren't enough of them. They were taken prisoner and brought here. One of them was riding Petrovitch's horse. We found other things belonging to him in their possession. And his scalp. We questioned them and they ended up confessing the whereabouts of his body. I sent a team there and they brought it back here. Fedor Petrovitch is buried in Bent's Fort. I saw his remains, Bowman, and I can find no other way of telling you this: it was the corpse of a world without hope."

The manager of Bent's Fort smiled bravely at the man sitting across from him.

"Once again, I am saddened by the news you brought me, Bowman, of an innocent man executed for these men's crimes. I am sickened by this circus and all those gawkers who've come to watch the execution, but unfortunately I have no doubt about their guilt."

Bowman felt the symptoms of his fit calm down, though at the same time he had to struggle to control his senses as they came under the influence of the hemp.

"It was the same thing in Rio Rancho. The negro just found the dead man's things."

Randell shook his head wearily.

"There is no doubt."

"But the Englishman I'm looking for ... Wasn't he here?"

"The soldier you mentioned? Apart from an absurd day like this one, the fort is a quiet place with very few visitors we don't know. My family is English, and even though I never lived there, I have a particular amity for your countrymen. The only British man I have met recently was just before the murder, but he wasn't a soldier. Quite the contrary. He was a preacher, a very friendly man, who stayed with us for a few days. I thought about him when we buried Petrovitch. Perhaps he would have found the words that I couldn't."

Arthur Bowman leaned forward and began to slide from his chair.

"Peavish?"

John Randell's face lit up.

"You know him?"

Bowman closed his eyes so he wouldn't have to see the room spinning around him anymore.

"It's Peavish ... He killed them."

Randell stood up.

"What did you say? Bowman, you're white as a sheet! What's happening to you?"

Bowman reached out with one hand towards the desk and collapsed on the rug.

He woke up again, surrounded by horses. He was lying in fodder in the shade of the stable roof. The old Indian was drawing water from a well and pouring it from buckets into the troughs. He walked past Bowman without looking at him, slowly continuing his task.

It took Bowman a few seconds before he was able to look over at the too-bright courtyard. The fit had not been too violent, he could feel it in his body, and he quickly felt normal again and remembered everything. Brewster's herbs had helped.

"Old man, give me some water."

The Indian stopped, looked behind Bowman, put a bucket next to him, and moved away. Bowman turned around.

"Who's there?"

No-one replied. A figure was visible in the shadows. The man was leaning against a post. The old Indian walked past him, head down. A white man with a sunburnt face, pale eyes, a rifle pressed against his leg.

"Stopped dreaming yet?"

"I'm not sure."

"It'll come back to you."

"What?"

"Everything you don't want to see."

The man had turned his head back towards the courtyard. Bowman followed his gaze towards the gallows and came to his senses.

"Are you one of Randell's men? Are you here to keep an eye on me?"

The man smiled.

"No. Just here for the show, like everyone else."

"Yeah, watching redskins die always draws a crowd."

The man smiled and walked past Bowman. He left the stable and went straight into the sunlight. Bowman turned his eyes away.

"Old man, who is that?"

The old Indian dropped his bucket into the well without responding. Bowman stood up, shook his head and went out into the courtyard. He entered the foreman's office again and asked to see Randell.

"Aren't you the man they threw in the stable? Mr Randell doesn't have time to talk to you. In fact, he said he didn't want to see you again. So get out of here before things get complicated."

An armed man was guarding the manager's door.

"Where's my rifle?"

"You'll get it back when you leave the fort."

"I have to speak to Randell."

"He doesn't want to see you anymore, and neither do I."

The foreman made a sign and the armed man advanced towards Bowman.

"Better leave now."

Bowman turned on his heel.

After eating and drinking, Walden had regained his strength. Bowman walked beside the horse to the main door and stopped in front of the guards.

"I have to pick up my rifle."

"The Henry?"

The employee handed him back his gun after admiring it for a moment.

"I prefer the Winchester, it's lighter. But this is a nice gun. What do you hunt with it?"

Bowman attached the holster to his saddle and left the fort, entering the fairground next to it. Standing by a rudimentary counter, in the shade of a tarpaulin, he ate some beans in mutton fat and drank some industrial-strength whiskey. He had been unconscious for several hours. Or maybe he had just slept after his fit, catching up on the sleep he had lost during his ride? Walden, his backside in the sun, had put his head under a corner of the tarp and fallen back asleep in the shade. The camp was calm: all those who had been drinking that morning were now lying in shade, taking a nap before night fell and they started drinking again.

Bowman looked over at the main door of the fort.

"Another one."

His glass was filled.

"You gonna get me something?"

Bowman turned around. The man from the stable was scratching Walden's head. The mustang, eyes half closed, made no protest.

"Why would I do that?"

"Because I watched over you while you slept."

"I don't see what difference that makes."

"It doesn't. Except I didn't just watch you sleep – I also listened to what you said."

His eyes were almost as grey as Alexandra Desmond's; his face was sharp, tanned and without a single line. Bowman ordered two more glasses.

"And what did you hear?"

"You were talking about a priest. You kept saying his name."

"I don't know any priests. I was just dreaming and I don't remember anything."

"You said it was him. That the Indians weren't to blame. You also said another name – Penders. And the priest's name was Peavish."

Bowman turned towards the man and moved his face closer. Lowering his voice, he hissed:

"I was just babbling. Now fuck off."

The man finished his whiskey without grimacing and put the glass down. He was missing part of the little finger on both his hands, severed at the first knuckle. He looked up at the sky, over to the north, where a line of clouds was drifting towards the fort.

"It's going to be a cloudy night."

He touched the brim of his hat with one hand and walked off between the tents. Bowman stayed there the rest of the afternoon, drinking steadily, one glass after another, until night-time.

When the camp grew lively again and the crowd around him began to drink and sing, he walked about a hundred yards away from the tents. He didn't unload his horse, he just rolled himself up in the blanket and closed his eyes to get some rest. Letting his body relax while he remained on the lookout: an old sentry's habit. He monitored the camp and the fort, without needing a watch to know what time it was. First, he listened as the noise from the camp died down – the last drinkers, the vendors closing their stalls, about three or four in the morning – and then silence, insects buzzing and animals scurrying. Finally came the moment, just before dawn, when the Bent's Fort guards were at their most tired. The hour when a good sergeant makes his round to kick the arses of any dozing sentries.

Walden was softly scratching the ground with his hooves. Still Bowman waited. The better he felt, the less vigilant the guards were becoming. He had managed to master the flow of his thoughts; no longer were they crashing over him. He had examined them as if reading a book.

Penders in Las Cruces.

Peavish in Bent's Fort.

One month in between. Ten days on horseback.

Another murder in Mexico. The rumour, the legend of murderers on the Santa Fe track while he was crossing his deserts, following his path. Not the same as the path the two others had taken, but which kept crossing it.

Were Peavish and Penders travelling together?

Coyotes howled. The moon was hidden behind clouds. Bowman just needed a bit more light. His eyes, rested, would see clearly when the guards' tired eyes no longer distinguished anything. Just that first line of brightness on the horizon. He remembered the courtyard, distances, the number of men, hiding places, the photographer's cart against the wall, very close to the stable, the place where the old Indian kept his things and must be sleeping.

No. He would not sleep. The old warriors always wake up at the hour of the attack.

He knew where the shadows would be if the moon came out from behind the clouds and which doors the fort's employees would leave through if the alarm was sounded. He had also spotted the well, when he passed the doors of the fort the previous morning. Bowman stood up.

He rode back towards the camp, going past the tents and the carts, listening to the noises and the snores. He got down from the horse, lit some tinder with a match, threw a few twigs on top and pushed the little fire under a tent where whiskey was stored. Then he jumped back in the saddle, galloped away and rode around the fort. In no time, he was on the other side, far away from the camp and the main entrance. There was an explosion. A barrel of alcohol. Very quickly, the red light of the fire rose into the sky. He heard the bell ringing inside the fort and the first yells.

"Fire! Everyone out!"

The panic spread. Bowman rode Walden fast towards the battlements and jumped down from the saddle. Pressed against the wall, he listened hard, waiting for the moment when the chaos was at its height. Just above him, a sentry shouted:

"My God! The camp's on fire! Come on, lads, we have to go out there!"

The screams of animals, men and women echoed over the plain. The foot of the battlement was shadowed by the fire, illuminating the sky over his head. Bowman began to run, dragging Walden behind him. He counted the arrow slits. The one in the foreman's office, the one in the room where he'd spoken with Randell. Three more. And the fourth was the one in the stable. He stood on his saddle and pulled his hatchet from his belt, then started smashing it against the wattle and daub as hard as he could. The arrow slit was about eight inches wide; he needed twice that space to slide through. Under a first layer of dried mud, he unearthed a wooden support and began to chop at it. The wood, a tree trunk about eight inches in diameter surrounded by earth, was full of knots. When the hatchet's blade hit any of these, it made a muffled thud.

Through the arrow slit, he could see the panicked horses, the courtyard, the gallows and, behind the wide open doors, the furiously burning camp. The stable's well was the furthest away from the exit and, as he'd hoped, the chain of buckets was organised next to the entrance and the other wells. The blade got stuck in the wood after being buried more deeply. Bowman levered it upwards and heard a crack. He pulled out his hatchet, put it back in his belt, and dug into the earth with his bare hands to make a passage around the wood.

Once he had attached his rope to the upright, he tied it to the pommel of the saddle and spurred his mustang. One movement from Walden was enough to pull the trunk to the side, though it remained part of the wall. Bowman tied the reins to it, took the Henry from its holster, and hoisted himself inside the stable, where he rolled in the fodder, jumped over the troughs and weaved between the horses. He hid himself at the corner of the wall, cocked his rifle and did not forget to check it. Turning his head towards the old Indian's corner, he aimed the barrel in his direction. The old man, sitting in front of a coffee pot, watched him and put a finger to his lips. Bowman crouched down and looked out. If he passed behind the photographer's little cart, he could run to the door, where only two guards remained. Fifty feet out in the open.

Slowly, he opened the barrier of the stable, picked up a handful of hay and lit a second match. He threw the flaming hay into the stable and the horses, already nervous, began to rush in all directions before running out into the courtyard. As the flames touched the main door of the fort, the horses grew crazy and started racing around the courtyard. The chain of men attempting to control the fire was broken, the cell's guards fled from the maddened horses, and Bowman sprang into action. He reached the oak door without being spotted, leaned his rifle against the wall and took out his hatchet. With three furious blows, he broke open the padlock, then picked up his gun, entered the cell and closed the door behind him. He could not see anything. The only light was that of the flames through the small, barred opening in the door. His pupils dilated and he made out the three figures sitting on the ground.

"Follow me. I'm going to open the door and you're going to come with me."

They did not react.

"Do you understand what I'm saying?"

The three Indians had blankets over their heads. They watched him without moving. He went over to them, speaking louder than he would have liked:

"Don't you understand me?"

He saw a head move. One of the three was nodding: he understood.

"Then fucking move! If we go now, it won't be too late!"

Bowman bent down and started whispering:

"We have to go now. Follow me."

The one who understood shook his head: no. Bowman stared at those three pairs of dark eyes, each reflecting the light from the small, barred window. The Comanches watched him.

Bowman aimed the barrel of the Henry at the one in the middle.

"Get up."

He didn't even blink. Outside, close by, a man said:

"What's going on here?"

Another voice answered him:

"The door . . ."

Bowman rushed over to the wall and raised his rifle. The Indians were still watching him. Bowman closed his eyes. A guard kicked open the door. The light came in with him and he saw the three prisoners, who had not moved.

"Shit, they're still there!"

His colleague followed him inside.

"Who smashed the padlock?"

They turned around at the same time as the door was banged shut behind them. Plunged into darkness, their eyes were useless for a few seconds. Bowman opened his. He knew very few men capable of keeping their eyes closed when they were in danger, but those few seconds of terror, when you wanted to see and you had to fight against all your instincts, gave you a big advantage. He knocked out the two guards with the butt of his rifle. The guards never saw a thing.

He approached the Comanches again.

"This is your last chance. Come with me."

The dark eyes gleamed dimly. The three Indians did not move.

"Fucking stupid monkeys! I'll have to drag you out myself!"

Bowman grabbed one by his clothes and tried to lift him. The Indian was as heavy as stone. Bowman pulled him towards the door; he let himself be dragged like a sack of potatoes, and finally Bowman gave up.

"You're going to die like dogs for something you didn't do!"

He couldn't wait any longer. He half opened the door, looked outside, and turned one last time towards them. The Indian he had dragged across the room was still in the same place. Bowman spoke loudly:

"Fuck it, if that's what you want . . . I'm not going to die with you."

He closed the door behind him. The horses were still running wild, but the fire had died down, whether because it had been contained by the men outside or because there was nothing left to burn. Daylight was colouring the sky. Bowman crossed the distance that separated him from the photographer's cart, slid behind it and entered the stable.

"What the hell are you doing there?"

The voice at his back was loud, a yell of surprise and fear.

"Hands up!"

He raised his hands and his rifle. The guard who had caught him screamed at the top of his lungs:

"Sound the alarm! Shit, get over here! The cell is open! There's someone in the stable . . ."

There was a flash through the arrow slit that Bowman had widened and the explosion made him jump. He turned around. The guard was curled up in a ball on the ground. A voice called out to Bowman:

"Hurry up!"

Bowman had not even taken a step when there was a burst of gunfire in the stable. He charged towards the arrow slit. A blow to his back threw him forward and his head banged against the wall. Conscious but incapable of moving, he felt his hands being grabbed and pulled, then there was nothing else for a fraction of a second – nothingness, weightlessness – before hitting the rocks. Hands grabbed him.

"You're heavier than a coffin!"

He was thrown across Walden's saddle. In a flash, his wrists and ankles were tied up with a rope. There was more gunfire and, before losing consciousness, his head hanging low, he saw rocks rush past before his eyes and the frenzied blur of Walden's black hooves.

9

The man with grey eyes stared out over the valley, the rifle resting on his arms. Black clouds rolled over the plain, bolts of lightning struck the earth and the thunder rumbled.

"We have to get going."

He threw the water from the saucepan over the little fire, rolled up the blood-stained strips of cloth and shoved them in his pockets, then covered the ashes of the fire with stones.

"You gonna be O.K.?"

Bowman, supporting himself with the barrel of the Henry, got to his feet and buttoned his shirt and jacket over the bandages wrapped tightly around his chest.

"Yeah, I'll be fine."

He groaned as he climbed into the saddle and put on his long rain-coat to protect himself from the wind. The man grabbed Walden's bridle.

"Hang on."

Steering his own horse with one hand, pulling the Englishman's mount behind him, he continued climbing the hill, moving slowly up the rocky, back-breaking slope. The animals had not yet recovered from their flight and they stumbled in the scree. When Walden slipped, Bowman had to clench his jaw to hold back the yells of pain. The rain caught up with them as they were crossing the first mountain pass. Before them lay a little chain of eroded hills, like a field of rocky dunes. The first drops fell on the stone and stuck to the dust. The wind blew in violent gusts. The sky turned black and the rain beat down on them. Bowman lowered his head and let the man guide him, shivering with cold and listening to the sound of the water drumming on his hat and his jacket.

They crossed tiny valleys, climbed over other hills, hour after hour, until they reached a peak slightly higher than those around it, ending in a rocky tip. The rain was no longer falling on them: they were walking in the shelter of an overhang, following a narrow path along the rock wall. It sloped down almost vertically on the other side. The man halted the animals and got down from his saddle.

"Lie down on your horse."

Bowman lay down over Walden's shoulders and put an arm around his neck. His silent guide entered a passage between the rocks and the light vanished. For a minute, they followed a dark corridor, coming out in a cave with a crack in its vault. Through this crack, a feeble ray of light fell, and a thin line of raindrops.

The man helped Bowman to get down from his horse and lay him on a blanket.

Bowman watched him light a fire that had already been prepared. There was a small reserve of wood there and, lifting his head, he saw that the vault of the cave was blackened by soot. When Bowman felt the heat reach him, he closed his eyes.

The smoke rose towards the crack in the vault. The rain had stopped, but the cave was still damp. The smell of the horses and the fire mixed with the humid stink of their soaked clothes. The man was not there. Bowman was leaning against his saddle. There was a new reserve of wood beside the hearth. He sat up and the pain ran down his spine like venom in a vein. He drank earth-tasting water from a flask that lay nearby, then poured some on his hand and rinsed the saliva-encrusted corners of his mouth. The two horses were sleeping, one leaning on the other, their heads touching the ceiling of the cave.

The man had put fresh bandages on him. Bowman slid a hand behind his back, feeling for the wound. Eight inches beneath his shoulder blade. The bullet had not gone through him; it had ricocheted off his ribs. The cracked ribs took his breath away whenever he moved. He tossed two branches on the fire and leaned back slowly against the saddle again. He would have liked to drink some of Brewster's potion to soothe the pain, but he preferred to wait until the man returned. He made do with the bottle of whiskey.

When he heard footsteps, Bowman put the Henry across his legs.

"Who's there?"

"Calm down, Englishman. It's me."

He came back with flasks filled with water hanging from his shoulder and, in his hand, holding them by their tails, a big rodent and an iguana.

"For us, but we can't stay here too long. The horses haven't eaten anything for two days."

"There's some oats in my saddlebags. Two days?"

"I already gave them the oats. You slept nearly twenty-four hours, Englishman. I'll take the horses out later. I'll go look for some bushes."

Bowman put his rifle down.

"My name's Bowman. Arthur Bowman."

The man removed his hat. His hair was black and straight.

"John Doe."

"In England, that's the name given to unknown people during a trial."

John Doe looked at him, curious.

"I didn't know that came from you. Here, it's the name we give to unidentified corpses."

John Doe leaned on an elbow and sat up.

"It's not your real name?"

"It's the name I chose. My white name."

"Mixed blood?"

John Doe smiled at Bowman.

"The Mandans have pale skin and eyes. There's a German who came to our land a long time ago, to study us. He said we were the descendants of a Welsh prince who came here with the Spanish. We are not only Indians, we are also bastards."

He gave a little nervous laugh, took a knife from his belt and began butchering the creatures he had brought with him.

"Why do you have a white name?"

"I was raised by Protestants who thought it was a good idea to adopt a little Indian orphan. But I didn't keep the name they gave me."

Bowman looked around the cave and asked what this place was.

"A hideout where I come sometimes."

"Do many people know about it?"

"Only Indians."

The Mandan had gutted the two animals. He threw their intestines on the embers.

"John Doe is my criminal name."

"Criminal?"

"I'm a thief. But the Indians are not even allowed to be outlaws like anyone else. We are renegades, those who are not even part of the white world."

He smiled again.

"I want to be treated like a real criminal, so I chose this name. And you, you have an Indian name. 'The Man of the Bow'. Where did you get your scars, Bowman?"

Bowman tensed up, realising that John Doe had undressed him while he slept. He looked at the Mandan's hands, with his two severed fingers.

"In some of the countries I've been, they cut off thieves' fingers. Is that what happened to you?"

John Doe put the meat to grill over the fire and stopped for a moment, to look at his hands.

"When I left the white people, I went back to my tribe's land. I wanted to have my true Indian name too."

"And they cut your fingers off?"

He turned towards Bowman.

"I did it myself. It's the Okipa."

"The Okipa?"

"The rite of passage. To take your name and your place in the tribe, to become a warrior."

Bowman shivered.

"You cut your fingers off to have a name?"

"The fingers, that's only at the end."

"The end?"

"No white man must know – it's a secret ceremony. But you, too, have done the Okipa, Bowman, so I can tell you. Afterward, you must tell me what you did."

"I didn't cut my own fingers off."

Bowman lowered his head and gripped the bottle of whiskey tight in his hand. John Doe had smiled at him like Alexandra Desmond. With an intimacy that he did not yet understand. The Indian spoke slowly.

"First, you sit outside in the middle of the village and you fast for four days and four nights. When the fasting is over, you go into the big hut with the other men and they whip you until your skin is torn to pieces. When they're done, they drive stakes under the muscles of your shoulders. They tie ropes to them and hang you from the ceiling of the hut. They attach bisons' heads to your feet and then they use poles to swing you from side to side and spin you round."

The Indian smiled at Bowman.

"During all this time, you must not stop smiling."

Bowman almost spat out his mouthful of alcohol. The Mandan watched the flames and the smile disappeared from his face.

"When you faint, the elders untie you and wait to see if the spirits bring you back to life. If you wake up, you must leave the hut and run five times around the village. When you have finished running, you cut your two little fingers off with a hatchet and then you are welcomed into the tribe like a Mandan worthy of remembrance."

He turned back to Bowman. His smile had reappeared.

"Four Bears, the greatest chief of all the Mandans, did the Okipa twice in a row. I managed it only once and I was lucky, because small-pox killed nearly all of my people. There are only about thirty Mandans left in the whole country. So the village was small and it was easy to run around it."

Bowman rolled onto his side, got on all fours and lifted himself up by gripping the wall of the cave. He staggered over to a dark corner and leaned forward, trying to vomit. All he threw up were a few mouthfuls of bile mixed with whiskey. Bent double, he waited to get his breath back.

"You did the same thing, Bowman. Why does it scare you like that?"

Bowman wiped his mouth. He was breathing hard and each inhalation made his broken ribs ache.

"I didn't do the same thing. I didn't want this to happen. You'd have to be mad to choose to do something like that."

"Mad?"

Bowman went back near the fire, trembling from head to foot.

"I've never heard anything so sick in my life. You can't choose that."

He collapsed onto the blanket. The Mandan stood up, shook out his own blanket and draped it around the Englishman's shoulders.

"Do you think I chose to see my family and my tribe die of small-pox, poisoned by the blankets of the fur traders who wanted our land? The Okipa is a ceremony of life, Bowman. The strength I needed to bear the pain, I keep that with me. You did it too, and the spirits kept you alive."

"It was torture. And so was what you did."

The Indian sat near the fire to cut the rodent and the lizard into small pieces.

"The spirits brought me back to earth, and it is on earth that I walk now. When you turn in the air, hanging from the ceiling of the hut, the only thing you think about is going back down to earth and living there. Afterward, you know where the spirits are, where you are and what your place is, among the living. The memory of suffering remains only in the body; the spirit is free. You, Bowman, you remained suspended in your pain and you are still seeking the earth."

"You don't know me. And I didn't choose it. They did it to me."

John Doe looked at him with an amused expression.

"What good does it do to continue feeling anger towards them? You cannot be the victim of your own life, Bowman. That is the Okipa too: understanding that you cannot choose."

Bowman pulled the blanket tight around him, watching as the white Indian slowly chewed his meat.

"What's your real name?"

"Inyan Sapa. In your language, that means 'Little Black'. The whites will never find me, because I'm an Indian hidden inside the skin of one of their own."

He was still smiling, but Bowman didn't feel he could trust that smile, given that the Indian had learned it while being hung from the ceiling of a hut.

"Why did you help me, if you hate the whites?"

"That is a question to which I have, as yet, no answer. Maybe because you wanted to save those Comanches, but I'm not sure about that. Sometimes it's John Doe who chooses. Sometimes it's Little Black. They do not have the same reasons. The white and the Indian do not see things in the same way, but occasionally they agree to do something together."

John Doe gave Bowman some food.

"The Comanches didn't want to follow you?"

Bowman swallowed some of the juice from the meat and shook his head. The Indian stood up and his voice rose inside the cave:

"I am not like them. The whites kill us because we are Indians. I will not die because I am one of them. They want to force us to change, so I hid the Indian deep inside me. They won't find him. The whites invented America as a country without a past so they could have a new life. But this land has a memory. That is why they kill us, to erase that memory. What do you think about this?"

"What do I think? That it's the same bullshit everywhere I've been."

The Indian slowly inhaled.

"The Okipa is the meeting of the two men that are inside us. The warrior and the man who walks the earth in peace. You have to live with both of them, Bowman."

Bowman smiled in turn.

"Which one of them revolted, John Doe or Little Black?"

The Indian turned towards him.

"Revolted? The smallpox killed us. There are only a handful of us left. What do you want me to revolt against? I steal because I want money, like the whites."

Bowman stopped smiling.

"My tribe is even smaller than yours. There were ten of us after the Okipa, if that's what you want to call it. Three are already dead and two have come over here. The ones who killed on the track. The Comanches were hanged because of what those men did."

"I heard about murders committed by your brothers. I understand now. They are like you, suspended in the air."

"My brothers?"

"How do you want to call them?"

Bowman did not reply. The Mandan sat back down.

"I have to sleep now. Rest, Bowman. Tomorrow, we must leave."

"The man in Bent's Fort . . . Did you kill him?"

"No, but I shot at him and some people were injured in the fire you started. They are searching for us."

John Doe fell asleep a few minutes later and his body began to tremble, shaken by nervous spasms.

The light burned his eyes for a long time before he was able to recognise the landscape. It was still the same: little rocky mountains. The horses, weakened, struggled beneath their weight. It took them three hours to reach the last mountain pass, which opened onto a dry plain with the green line of the river in the distance. Before leaving the shelter of the mountains, John Doe stared out far ahead, sniffing the air for several minutes.

"Fort Lyon is only forty miles from here, but we have to take the horses to the river. We'll be there by nightfall. We can't stay long."

The sky was cloudless, the moon large and the stars pale. The sound of the river became increasingly loud and soon the silhouettes of trees grew visible before them.

They tethered the horses, leaving them enough rope to graze all they wanted, and the two men walked to the riverbank, rifles in hand.

Bowman washed his face and drank, while the Indian remained standing. He did not touch the water. When Bowman saw this, he stopped moving and looked around him.

"What's the matter?"

John Doe, or Little Black, did not reply straight away. Strangely, the moonlight, which whitened his skin, also seemed to bring out his Indian features.

"This place. Something isn't right here."

Bowman continued scanning the darkness beyond the bright current of the river.

"It's just a river in the middle of a plain."

"You don't like rivers?"

"Why do you say that?"

"Your voice."

Bowman moved away from the water. He was moving more easily. The wound was beginning to scar. Only his broken ribs hurt him now. He sat in the grass and watched the Indian, who was still immobile.

"Where are we?"

"Sand Creek River. A hundred miles north of Bent's Fort. You have to decide where you want to go, Bowman."

"The men from the Bent and St Vrain, they don't know who was with me. You can go now. I'll be alright."

"Not yet."

"Not yet?"

"We must travel further."

"I don't know where I'm going. You already rescued me, and you don't owe me anything."

John Doe turned towards him.

"The two brothers you're looking for . . . Are they different from other men?"

"What?"

"Are they different?"

Bowman looked out at the black river, flecked with moonlight.

"Maybe not that different. Or only because of what happened to them. Before, we weren't the same."

John Doe smiled and Bowman caught the gleam of his white teeth in the darkness, like the reflections on the surface of the Sand Creek River.

"If your brothers are not different from other men, then we know where to go."

"What are you talking about?"

"If the whites were here for anything else, they would have come to see us and they would have listened to us."

Bowman slowly got to his feet.

"I don't understand what you're saying, Indian."

Little Black smiled again and this time his eyes shone in the moonlight.

"Gold, Bowman. Gold."

———ᗱ—ᗱ—ᗱ———

At daybreak, they entered a desert.

John Doe found his way like an animal, following an itinerary engraved in a memory older than his own, without any landmarks that Bowman could see. When Bowman began to feel thirsty and worry because he could see nothing but rocks all the way to the horizon, John would stop at the foot of a rock where there was a trickle of water. Anyone else would have died there without knowing that salvation was at hand. For the horses, they always managed to find a little nook where bushes grew. The animals devoured them, even though they were as dry as rocks. There was something erratic but necessary about the course they took, following incomprehensible detours that led them, at evening, to a little spring that burst through a crack, vanishing three feet further on under the rocks. Sometimes it took them two hours to fill the flasks from a miraculous trickle of water on the surface of a stone. But there was water, food, and wood to cook snakes and lizards. John dug holes at the foot of dead bushes, cutting off bits of roots to chew. They had a sour taste, but they created saliva in the mouth and staved off hunger. Every evening, the Indian changed Bowman's bandages. He took some herbs from his saddlebags, crushed them, mixed them with ash from the fire, and rubbed them into the wound. John Doe and Little Black continued to coexist in the Mandan's head. Without warning, he would switch from English to a strange language that sounded like that spoken by negroes living in contact with the British. A well-bred Christian, a thief or a nostalgic Indian? Bowman could not tell who was the real John Doe. But whoever he was, he knew the right way and found them food.

Always heading southward, they safely navigated a vast labyrinth whose invisible walls were death in every form offered by this desert: thirst, hunger, exhaustion, pursuit, ambushes. They travelled three times the distance that separated them from the track between Pueblo and Denver, but it was the only way they could get there. On the last night, they slept very close to the track. They did not light a fire and left the horses saddled.

"Here, where there's no-one, we must hide. But when we get to Pikes Peak, surrounded by other people, we won't have to anymore. Sleep now. I will wake you."

"John?"

"What?"

"What do you do with madmen, in the tribe?"

"Those who walk on another earth live among us."

"And my brothers?"

"Sleep. Tiredness is home to deceptive spirits."

"I don't think I will sleep."

"See you later."

John Doe rolled up in his blanket and a few moments later his body was shaken by spasms again. Bowman lay down without closing his eyes. Three hours later, he was startled when Little Black shook his shoulder.

"The moon is with us. It is the moment to cross the white man's track."

The right moment, when everyone was asleep, even Sergeant Bowman. Annoyed, he got to his feet and rolled up his blanket. The Indian had tied cloths around the horses' hooves and, under a line of clouds blacker than the night, they walked the path under the Devil's nose. They moved slowly for a few miles and then stopped to remove the cloths that had served to muffle the sound of horseshoes.

"The horses want to gallop to the forest. How is your wound, Bowman?"

"What do you mean, they want to gallop?"

"This part of the land is theirs. Many of them were born here."

Bowman smiled.

"What are you on about?"

He had not finished asking his question when the two horses began stamping on the ground. He got back in the saddle and felt Walden's muscles trembling between his legs. The Indian jumped on his horse.

"Brother Bowman, do not touch the reins."

Bowman clung to the pommel.

After three days of detours and precautions, the horses set off at a fast gallop, tracing a perfectly straight line through the night, faster than trains, not even slowing down when the land began to climb. John Doe looked up at the sky and spread his arms wide. Bowman let go of the pommel with one hand, and then with the other, opening his arms to feel the air on his body.

He yelled:

"When will they stop?"

Little Black burst into laughter.

The air grew colder as they climbed up through the woods. The horses went their separate ways, each following its own itinerary for a while before coming back together, leaping over a stream, running through thick-grassed clearings. The riders picked up the reins again and finally slowed them down. John Doe led them to an overhang, a rocky mass suspended like a jawbone over the void, its peak covered with high grass, between pine trees with their roots in the stone. They removed the packs from the horses' backs and let them graze. They did not light a fire, knowing that it would soon be daylight. When Bowman woke, the shadows cast by the pine branches were dancing on his face and the sweet smell of resin filled his nostrils. He stretched out to the limits of his pain, feeling rested and breathing calmly.

The Indian was not there.

Bowman picked up his rifle and walked to the edge of the peak, searching for the source of the noises he could hear. Below him, in the valley, a convoy of carts was following a track past a waterfall. The bells on the cattle and the yells of the drivers rose up to him and, at the same time as the uninterrupted procession of pioneers, lifting his head, he discovered Pikes Peak and its still-snowy summit. The mountain was a few dozen miles away, towering over the first foothills of the Rocky Mountains. In the distance, to the east, he saw the desert plains he had crossed with John Doe. All around him lay the green mountain, criss-crossed with rivers, where high-altitude flowers were blooming.

Bowman did not hear the Indian arrive. When he turned around, John Doe was just behind him, smiling, a young pronghorn draped over his shoulders. They lit a fire, chopped up the animal, putting the quarters aside to dry and smoke, and putting a thigh on a stake over the flames to grill it for breakfast. The two men swallowed the meat in small mouthfuls, trying not to eat too much after all those days of hunger. When they were full, John Doe took a handful of cranberries, slightly sweet and sour, from his pocket. Bowman opened the bottle of whiskey and they shared the last few drops.

"Are they all going to Pikes Peak?"

"The first big camp on this side is Woodland. Maybe it's become a town since my last visit? The biggest camps are on the other side, on the northern slope, where they found the first gold. Idaho Spring, Black Hawk, Mountain City and, over towards the plain, Denver. The deposits are starting to run dry, and there are more and more people working the same lodes. Concessions are more expensive and gold is rarer. The money has already been made. These men are going there for the crumbs, or because they took too long to get here."

They sat with their feet in the void, watching the incessant ballet of immigrants climbing the mountain. After the rocky plains and the company of snakes, this absurd transhumance gave the impression that the world had become too small.

Bowman had imagined Pikes Peak as a huge bare rock in the middle of a desert, covered in men with pickaxes. Pikes Peak was a majestic and peaceful mountain, the southern gateway to the Rockies, transformed into an anthill by gold-diggers whipping their cattle while, above them, the lodes were almost exhausted.

"If your brothers are mad, Bowman, it won't be easy to find them among all these others."

Bowman smiled and tossed a stone into the void, watching it crash down the slope before coming to a stop in the grass.

"I don't want to make it sound like I believe in your spirits, Indian, but them and me, we will always find each other."

Little Black smiled at him.

"Let's just call it luck then."

"Yeah, amazing bloody luck."

John Doe patted his shoulder.

"We must prepare the meat. We'll need plenty in reserve for the journey. We can leave tomorrow morning."

At sunset, the anthill changed into a volcano. The lanterns on the carts looked like thin lava flows at the bottom of the valley, accumulating in bright craters as the pioneers came together and lit their campfires. The entire mountain was scattered with points of light, sketching a galaxy of yellow stars, an ephemeral mirror of those in the sky above. The sound of singing and musical instruments, distorted by the wind and the shape of the land, reached the two men lying in their rocky nest.

"Brother Bowman, we must go our separate ways at Woodland."

Bowman laughed softly.

"So you decided together, you and the white?"

"Our meeting was good. It is the reward for those who travel alone. But I must also continue on my way."

Bowman tried to think how to respond, but he couldn't put into words what he wanted to say to John Doe.

"Thank you."

The white Indian replied in his native language. Bowman did not understand.

Bowman took Brewster's flask from his pocket.

"In England, I used to smoke opium when I wanted to end my nightmares. Over here, an old man gave me this. It stops pain, but it also has plants that make you dream. That old man, he lived in a town called Reunion, which he'd built with other immigrants. A town where they were all trying to be happy together. Maybe those are the whites you should have met, the ones who could have listened to you. There was a big communal house in the middle of their town. You couldn't even run around it now because it doesn't exist anymore. Their dream is at the bottom of this bottle now."

The Indian sat facing Bowman. He took the bottle from him, drank some of the potion, and handed it back to the Englishman.

"Our village, too, had a big hut where we all came together."

Little Black, sitting cross-legged, smiled and closed his eyes.

Bowman leaned against his saddle and watched the gold-diggers' fires as they were born and died out in the valley. Following the lines and the dots, after a few minutes he began to make out shapes, patterns that altered with his thoughts. A strand of red hair, the fire in the abandoned house reflecting from old Brewster's glasses, the brightness of the sun rising over the Trinity River when he arrived in Reunion at dawn.

The Indian began to sing.

IO

All day long, staying in the highlands, following the ridge paths, they advanced towards the snow-covered mountain. They walked a few hundred yards above the line of carts before having to descend to the valley. Located at the foot of Pikes Peak, in the middle of a brown circle of cleared forest, Woodland was not yet a town, merely a vast stretch of tents, set up close to one another, without much logic that could be seen from this distance.

Crouching in the grass of a steep clearing, Bowman and the Indian observed the camp, holding the horses' bridles. John Doe smiled inscrutably as he chewed a root.

"I bet Reunion doesn't look like that."

"At least they had planks to make coffins for the last inhabitants. Here, they probably just throw you to the pigs when you're dead."

John Doe slid his rifle from its holster and loaded the magazine. Bowman watched him do it, then picked up the Henry, used the lever to open it, listening to the gun's mechanism, and loaded it. Sixteen bullets.

He climbed into the saddle and the Mandan came over to him.

"Indians don't shake hands. That may be the only thing we should have learned from you. Unfortunately, so many lies were sealed by a handshake that we have become reluctant to adopt this tradition. It should only be done between friends."

Little Black held out his left hand. Bowman did the same, wrapping his three remaining fingers around the Indian's four.

"You're not going into town?"

"I have no intention of missing that, but I would rather say goodbye here. Oh, and one last thing: when we're down there, let me do the talking. You may be white, but you don't know these places."

"I shouldn't say anything?"

"Just be yourself. You scare people and I'll do the talking."

John Doe spurred his horse, and Bowman urged Walden into a gallop behind him.

Woodland was like a cross between the Pueblo pioneers' camp and the Paterson ranch in construction, but its atmosphere was closer to the frenzy of St Louis, multiplied tenfold. There were ten times more alcohol vendors, ten times more shops, ten times more whores and preachers. The camp was growing as fast as the lumberjacks could cut down trees. There was no time to build anything with more than one storey, and most of the dwellings were merely tents of various sizes, including saloons big enough to hold two hundred customers. The streets were rivers of mud and the carts sank down in them to their axletrees.

Outside the few permanent constructions, made with wood and nails, armed men stood guard. The traders' offices. Along with the gold merchants, the most flourishing businesses were those that sold gold-extracting equipment. Pickaxes, shovels, sieves and pans arrived on carts and were piled up in their hundreds inside the tent shops. While some men came out of these tents with new equipment, others went in to sell their old gear. The ambience in this mining town was febrile but not happy, tense rather than serious, and definitely more aggressive than welcoming.

Among all those who'd had no luck, the few men with gold to spend were easily spotted, and Woodland existed purely to empty their pockets as quickly as possible. To the music played by orchestras under the tents, the fortunes of a season of gold-digging were squandered on drinks for everyone, and the last night in a dry bed, before going back to work the lode, was paid for on credit. The landlords of the bars, the pimps and the pickaxe-sellers had hired bouncers who worked calmly but steadily, picking up drunkards by their belts and gently throwing them outside, while those who put up any resistance were thrown a little harder and further, landing in the mud.

When they decided on a saloon that also offered rooms, girls, first-class steaks, cold beer, gold-panning equipment, second-hand guns and a stable for the horses, Bowman felt reassured that his Indian companion could pass for a white man. The dominant emotion in Woodland was not gold fever but disappointment, numbed by large quantities of alcohol. The presence of a redskin at the bar was probably the worst news for these luckless gold-diggers.

There was still room to move around inside the tent, a sign that the busy period had not yet arrived. They asked for two rooms and the landlord led them to the dormitories, telling them that they would have to share one.

"There's not enough space for everyone in this shithole, so you'll have to squeeze up. And pay in advance."

Under a roof that offered no shelter from sunshine or rain, bits of cloth hung down from ropes: these were the walls. On the floorboards full of holes lay some dirty sheets, sewn together and stuffed with hay: these were the beds. Even for the modest sum of fifteen cents per guest, it was daylight robbery.

"Where do we put our things?"

For ten cents each, their personal belongings would be securely guarded in the saloon's special room: another space with cloth walls, watched over by a bearded old man armed with a flintlock rifle and a bottle.

"So if someone steals my things from here, can I be reimbursed in fat from your belly?"

John Doe smiled and the landlord, who was indeed rather plump, burst out laughing,

"In that case, take the advice of a friend, gentlemen, and look after your own things. It'll save you twenty cents, and if you buy a drink, I'll give you the next one free."

The landlord shooed a few barflies away from the counter – the only solid piece of furniture in the entire saloon – and poured them two whiskies.

"Is this the good stuff?"

"There's always something better, sir, but it's not what we give the Indians, if that's what you're worrying about."

John Doe laughed along with the landlord and drained his glass. The barman glanced down discreetly at the hands of the two men, the one with tanned skin and the big one with a scar on his forehead.

"You don't look like gold-diggers. What brings you here?"

"We work for the Bent and St Vrain."

Bowman nodded, silent, and lifted his glass.

"And what are good folks like you doing in our mountains?"

"We're looking for someone. Two men, in fact. English."

John Doe had leaned his head down as he spoke, giving a mysterious look from under the brim of his hat.

"Why are you looking for them?"

Doe stared at the landlord with his grey eyes.

"We have to take them back to Bent's Fort. If possible."

The landlord filled their glasses without being asked.

"I know everyone here. If I get you some information, will there be anything in it for me?"

"Maybe."

"What have they done, your Englishmen?"

The Mandan looked around him and spoke even more quietly.

"They set fire to carts and they tried to help some prisoners escape."

The man puffed his cheeks out.

"Jesus Christ, the ones who wanted to free those four Indians? The ones who killed two men in Bent? Everyone's talking about that round here. There's even a detachment of cavalry who came through here a week ago, looking for them. You're too late, lads!"

Bowman and Doe exchanged a look. The landlord generously served them a third glass.

"Hell, I didn't know it was Englishmen. Doesn't surprise me, though. There's only them and those French bastards who associate with redskins. Say, is it true they cut the heads off pioneers? I heard they massacred a whole family, women and children, down near the Mexican border."

"Are there any Englishmen in town at the moment?"

"Yeah, there's always some hanging around here."

Bowman tried to mask his London accent, imitating John Doe's speech patterns.

"There's one who's pretending to be a preacher. Tall man, with black hair and no teeth. The other's a big blond man."

"Well, there's no shortage of preachers or blonds here. Are they travelling together?"

"Maybe."

"I'll ask around."

The saloon was filling up. By the time they left, it was packed solid and night had fallen.

Woodland was in a frenzy. Under each lantern hung to a tent, groups of men crowded around to drink, their feet in the mud, exchanging information on the latest lodes or gambling their earnings in poker games. Most of them had abandoned gold-panning on their own account and were working for the large mining companies. Bowman and the white Indian mingled with the crowds, moving from one bar to the next, seeking out groups of Englishmen. They put their saddle-bags at their feet by the counters, rifles on their shoulders, and ordered drinks while listening to the conversations around them, asking a few questions about where the pioneers were headed to, where they were coming from, if there was a Methodist preacher among them. Many were not planning to stop in the Rocky Mountains, but were simply passing through, via Wyoming and the Oregon path, on their way to California. Once they got here, it didn't take them long to realise it was over, or even that it had never begun, and that only the companies now had the means to hire and finance extraction. So they left Pikes Peak, swapping the gold of the mountains for the sunshine of the West, the dream of fortunes buried under the earth for that of idyllic farms by the Pacific Ocean.

They hung around in the camp for several hours, accruing no useful information but tons of stories that all seemed like versions of a single story, sharing the same departures and arrivals, the same difficulties and determination. The alcohol made John Doe increasingly taciturn and aggressive. By the end of the night, he was hardly speaking at all anymore, so it was down to Bowman to ask the questions. The night wore on, and the greatest tenacity of all these brave souls was revealed in their unwillingness to go to bed. The two men headed back to the main saloon, the Indian still sure of himself but staring around him with malice in his eyes.

"We should leave, sleep in the mountains. We'll be better off up there than in this filthy room, and I'm not going to find anything here."

John Doe's voice was altered by the whiskey, slow and slurred:

"I have to spend some time with my kind. Go to the mountain, Bowman. I'm going to stay with the whites."

"I'm not leaving without you."

"You scared of being alone, brother?"

"It's you I'm worried about. Where has Little Black gone? I think he's the one I need to talk to."

"When I'm with whites, he doesn't come out. He hides because he's a coward."

"You've got too much Dutch courage. You're going to get us in trouble."

"I want to drink another glass with my white brothers. After that, we can go and hide out in the mountains if you want."

Bowman went with him into the saloon. John Doe stood at the entrance to the big tent, brought a hand to his mouth and gave a wild yell, an Indian horseman's shrill war cry. Half of the drinkers in the bar turned around. The Indian took off his hat, revealing his black hair, then made a sort of wobbly bow and smiled.

"Good evening, civilisation!"

A few people laughed. Slowly, faces turned away and John Doe walked through the room to the counter. The landlord was no longer there. Another barman served them drinks. People around were still observing them, and Bowman downed his whiskey quickly.

"You're off your head. I'm getting out of here. I'm going to get the horses."

"I'm going to have one last drink."

"Do what you want. I'm off."

Bowman hoisted his saddlebags over his shoulder and held his rifle tight against him. At the entrance to the tent, he saw the fat landlord, who was returning accompanied by three armed men. He was standing on tiptoes, trying to spot someone over the crowd of heads.

Bowman crouched down and rushed back to the bar, where he grabbed John Doe's arm.

"Time to go."

The Indian remained leaning over the bar and yanked his arm free.

"Don't touch me, Bowman. I told you, we're going our separate ways here."

"Stop fooling around and come with me."

The landlord and his escort were pushing through the crowd, headed in their direction.

"What are you playing at?"

"Beat it, Bowman. I'll find you again, one of these days."

"The landlord wasn't fooled. You know what'll happen to you, you bloody idiot? You'll do another Okipa at the end of a rope, and I've never seen a hanged man smile."

"I've done my part, white brother. Just go."

Bowman tried to drag him from the bar. John Doe turned around and, in a single movement, freed himself from Bowman's grip and loaded his rifle. For a fraction of a second, his grey eyes met Bowman's and a wide smile cracked his smooth face.

A few yards away from them, the landlord pointed towards the bar and shouted:

"It's them! Jesus, they're here!"

The Mandan raised his gun and fired a shot in the air, piercing a hole in the canvas roof. Around him, men scattered, while others cheered. He lowered the barrel of the gun and aimed just above the bellowing landlord's head. The bullet whistled through the saloon and this time the crowd panicked.

"Go, Bowman! I'll see you again on the road, somewhere or other."

John Doe aimed at the ceiling again and fired three shots, shattering some oil lamps and sending them crashing to the ground.

"Come with me. We can still get out of here!"

The Indian no longer heard him. He jumped over the counter, resting his elbow on the bar to aim his rifle. His bullets skimmed close and all the drinkers started screaming, tearing off the cloth doors of the tent in their desperation to escape. The three men who had come in with the landlord fought against this movement, trying to fire back. Bowman ran into the crowd, shoving his way through to the cloth walls, where he took the knife from his belt and sliced the fabric open.

He heard a burst of gunfire before he'd had time to jump into the mud. John Doe was whooping and the bottles and glasses on the shelves behind the bar were exploding. Bowman thought about turning back, but instead he cursed and leapt outside, running all the way to the stable. There, he waited for the grooms to leave so they could see what was going on in the saloon, and when they had gone, he rushed inside and strapped the saddle to Walden's back. The gunfire continued. He could still hear the sound of rifle shots. He cut the cloth wall of the stable, slicing it in two, climbed on the mustang and rode away.

He galloped straight to the mountain, urging the horse up steep slopes and not stopping until the lights of Woodland had disappeared behind him. Avoiding the gold-diggers' camps, sleeping on his horse, Bowman made his way around Pikes Peak, progressing through ever deeper snow. On the fourth day, after crossing over the mountain and heading back down the northern side, he stopped to spend the night in a forest, above a small town nestled at the bottom of a valley, the only viable passage for continuing on his way. Wearing his raincoat with the collar turned up and his hat pulled down over his head, he entered the empty streets of Idaho Spring the next morning, riding through town without stopping and coming to a crossroads on the other side. He headed towards Mountain City, about fifteen miles away, at a trot, and turned off the road before he reached any houses, leaving the valley behind to ride up the hillier ground.

The pain in his back was getting worse and worse. He came to a halt and curled up against the enormous stump of a redwood, putting his hand under the bandages that he had not changed since separating from John Doe. When his fingers touched it, he cursed: the wound had opened up again and become infected. He emptied his pockets and counted the money he had left. Thirty-seven dollars and a few cents. Bowman also inventoried his ammunition – twenty bullets, plus the sixteen in his gun – and decided to sleep far away from town and to come back the next day to buy the medical supplies he needed. There was still an hour of daylight left before nightfall. Arthur Bowman, trembling with fever, opened his bag and took out his pen and ink.

Alexandra,

I don't know what day it is or how long ago I left Reunion. A month, maybe two now. Tonight I am hiding on a mountain and I have an infected wound. A man shot at me while I was trying to free some Comanches but they were hanged anyway. Another Indian helped me escape. We separated in Woodland four days ago. He was the strangest man I've ever met but we talked quite a lot. Because he went through something that was similar to what happened to me in Burma. He said I wasn't looking at my past in the right way. That I could be a new man and I thought of you when he said that. I'm sad that he stayed in Woodland, because the people there will finish him off. He was mad and I think that is what he was looking for, but he didn't deserve to end up like that. I hope he managed to escape. I am walking the earth, as he said, but only to escape and hide because I am a wanted man. I am searching for Peavish and Penders, and the others are searching for me.

I've still got a little bit of Brewster's potion left. I'm keeping it until after my letter, so I can write to you without falling asleep.

Tomorrow I have to go to Mountain City to buy some medical supplies. I hope I won't have any trouble and that I'll be able to write to you again.

This reads like a letter written by someone who is going to die. I'm not going to die.

I would have liked to introduce you to my white Indian friend. I told him about Reunion and I said that the Indians should meet people like you.

It's dark now and I can't see the paper anymore. For the first time in a long time, I feel alone.

Sleep well.

———⁓——⁓——⁓———

Beneath the sign announcing the entrance to the town, a sentence had been added: *The world's richest square mile.*

Mountain City was abandoned. The lone gold-panners had all left and nothing remained but the gold traders' empty offices, doors boarded up and shutters closed. The town looked like Woodland after all the tents had been cleared away and all the buildings evacuated. Nature was stealing back its territory in the vast clearing, grass and young trees growing around the derelict constructions. The few tents still standing near shacks were full of Chinamen cooking over camp-fires. A few carts belonging to white people formed distant, isolated circles, and after stopping here for the night they were already preparing to leave again. Bowman rode past a large pile of broken shovels and pickaxes, rusted pans and ruined sieves. Plants were also beginning to grow on this monument to the memory of gold-panners who had given up and moved on, a cemetery of abandoned tools.

The Chinamen appeared tiny in their tight-shouldered tunics, the sleeves too short and the fabric frayed by work. Pale and thin, they lowered their heads when the horse rider passed them. Only one general store remained open. Bowman tied Walden up in an alley near the shop, walked hesitantly to the door, then stood still before entering, wiping away the sweat that was trickling down his forehead and pulling his hat brim further down towards his eyes. Behind the small counter, standing on a chair, a barrel-hipped woman was decorating a shelf with tins of food. She turned around when she heard the bell ring, greeted the customer, and continued her work. It was hot inside; a large earthenware stove was purring, and Bowman walked slowly past it.

"What can I do for you?"

Bowman cleared his throat.

"I need medicine for my horse. He was injured on the rocks and the wound's getting infected."

The woman turned around again to observe him. Leaving the tins where they were, she got down from her chair. She was about forty years old, with round pink cheeks and curly blonde hair, and she looked incongruously healthy amid all this decay. She leaned forward and her large breasts overflowed from her low-cut dress.

"You don't look too good yourself."

"I caught cold in the mountains."

She looked at him too insistently and Bowman attempted to divert her attention by turning towards the store's window.

"So, everyone left?"

She gloomily followed his gaze.

"Yeah, it was like a stampede. A year ago, there were ten thousand people here. Now there's just a few Chinks and Gregory's men, but even they don't come here anymore. They're at the mine up on the hill, on the Black Hawk road. That's the last mine that's still active, apart from a few crazies who are still in the mountains and who might well be dead by now."

She put some terracotta pots on the counter, unfolded a few newspaper pages, and began to pour a few spoons of powder and seeds into them.

"Business was booming for a few years, but it's over now. It won't be long before I sell up, if anyone even wants this pile of planks. Hell, if someone asked, I'd probably give it them for nothing. My husband is buried on the outskirts of town. He got a fever and didn't want to take anything for it. I don't need your medicine, he told me, there are customers waiting! Well, those customers all trampled over his grave on their way out of here."

She folded up the sheets of newspaper.

"For your horse, you boil these flax seeds and spread them on the wound. Twice a day. After three days, you continue with the clay poultices. For you, rub this alcohol on your chest and your forehead before you go to bed. And as we know it doesn't do anything but everyone believes in it anyway, I'll put some whiskey in here for you. You boil these herbs three times a day, let them infuse for ten minutes and then swallow it – and try not to think about the taste. Believe me, it's the most disgusting thing you'll ever have drunk."

Bowman opened the bottle of whiskey straight away and drank a mouthful.

"What was I saying? Here's another one who doesn't believe in medicine! Well, say hello to my husband as you go by the cemetery. Where are you off to, anyway?"

"California."

"You don't say. Get to Denver and out of these mountains as fast as you can, my lad, because the cold will get you if you don't. Around here, the springtime doesn't arrive until the summer's already over. Here, I'll give you some syrup too. It's mostly just alcohol, but apparently there are a few plants in it too. On the house."

"I need bandages too."

She went into the back room and returned with a sheet, which she bit into pieces, smiling as she stored the strips of cloth in her cleavage.

"I never get a chest cold!"

She burst out laughing.

Bowman handed over three dollars and told her to keep the change.

"The quickest way to Denver?"

"The Gregory mine and then Black Hawk, ten miles from here. After that, it's all downhill. Sixty miles to Denver."

Bowman gathered up his purchases.

"Good luck."

"You too. If your horse wasn't hurt and I weighed sixty pounds less, I'd jump in the saddle with you."

She laughed again and Bowman walked over to the door.

"If you're too cold out there and you change your mind, I'll be ..."

She stopped, mid-sentence.

"You're bleeding like crazy!"

The blood had soaked through the bandages on Bowman's back, through his shirt and jacket too.

Bowman rushed outside, grimacing as he ran to his horse. He loaded the medicine into his saddlebags and left the town at a gallop that almost made him faint.

Snowflakes fell over Mountain City and the valley filled with fog. As soon as he found a path off the main track, he rode away into the pines, lit a fire, put some water to boil and threw in a few flax seeds. The pain paralysed his neck, and he was so dizzy that he couldn't stand up. He drank a mouthful of the syrup, followed by some more whiskey, then took off his clothes and began to undo the bandages. The last roll of fabric around his chest was glued to the wound. He took a deep breath and yanked it off. The pain was like a blow to the head and he collapsed on the carpet of pine needles.

When he came to, the water in the pan had evaporated and the flax seeds had burned. He cleaned out the saucepan and started over. He held the blade of his knife in the flames and then, contorting his body, used it as a spatula to spread the poultice over the wound. He wound the strips of cloth around him, put his clothes back on, and threw as many bits of wood and pine needles as he could on the fire without having to move too much. When his shivering was less violent, he got back in the saddle and started to ride again. The mountains were still impracticable and he had to follow the road to the Gregory mine. The fog was getting thicker and at first all he could see was a few scattered shacks. He heard the sound of a river flowing nearby. The snow was starting to settle on the track and the roofs, muffling all noises. He could go through the settlement without being seen. He passed carts and bigger buildings, without glimpsing a single miner. Walden pinned back his ears and moved aside. A man on a horse appeared suddenly, coming forward at a gallop, whipping his mount and not even glancing at Bowman. Bowman had put his hand on the butt of his rifle. He paused until his heartbeat returned to normal, then held the reins more tightly and continued along the path, his senses alert now. The sound of the river grew louder. He rode alongside the rails of a small train track that passed above the roofs. On the track were carts full of ore. He thought he glimpsed something between two hangars. Bowman stopped and listened. Walden was nervous. The mustang snorted and the river drowned out the other sounds, but Bowman was certain he had seen and heard something. He made a U-turn, going under the little viaduct and around the buildings.

All the miners were there, under the lights of torches and lamps that glowed in the fog. Perhaps a hundred men, all silent, shoulder to shoulder, massed in a circle around something he couldn't see. Bowman listened again and started to believe that he was hallucinating, that it was the sound of the water playing tricks on his mind, or that his fever was returning. He got down from the saddle, walked noiselessly along a plank wall and moved closer to the miners. The silence of all these men, gathered in a corner of the deserted mine, made him afraid. He stopped, listening, but could not prevent himself moving further forward. Bowman was now just behind the closest row of miners. Nobody turned around. He put a hand on one of the men's shoulders and pushed it aside, insinuating his body between those of the men. They stood with their chins on their chests, lips moving, silently repeating the prayer being intoned in the middle of the circle.

Bowman reached the centre. The lamplight illuminated the thick, milky mist. On the snowy ground, a body lay, covered by a blood-soaked sheet.

The cold air made his throat tight. Bowman concentrated on breathing.

It was not an intuition that had made him turn back, and it was not a fever either. It was not Brewster's passionate attraction or Little Black's spirits that had led him to guess at the presence of the corpse. Something in him had remembered as he was passing through the mining settlement, a sound mingled with the rush of the river, even before he had seen the lights. A voice.

Bowman tore his eyes away from the corpse and lifted his head, looking for the man who was reciting the prayer. Standing amid the miners, in shabby clothes, as pale as the mist, eyes closed, hands together, Edmund Peavish was intoning an *Our Father* in the same fragile voice that Bowman had heard for a year from inside his cage. The preacher ended his litany and opened his eyes, contemplating the corpse.

Some miners brought a hand-cart over and loaded the body on it. One scarlet, skinless foot slid out from under the sheet and a man rushed up to cover it.

Peavish lifted his head.

Bowman retreated through the ranks of the miners, returned to his horse, took the Henry from its holster and stood pressed against the wall of the hangar. The cortège of miners moved away, following the hand-cart, torches in hands. Peavish had remained alone, standing where the corpse had been. The sergeant slipped through the mist, passing behind him and watching the preacher's tall figure for a moment, his head lowered, his narrow shoulders and thin arms, as he prayed over a yard of American earth. Bowman took a step forward and shoved the rifle's barrel into Peavish's back.

"Move and I'll kill you."

Peavish froze and then slowly, ignoring this order, turned around. The preacher's face was streaked with little wrinkles. Swollen veins encircled his hollow eyes, and his thin lips trembled, purple with cold. Arthur Bowman felt his legs sway beneath him.

"What are you doing here, preacher? What's going on?"

The rifle slipped from Bowman's hands. The preacher's sunken eyes filled with tears.

"Sergeant?"

Slowly he lifted an arm, hesitated, then put his hand on Bowman's shoulder.

"You're here?"

Peavish, a black-and-white ghost in the fog, seemed almost afraid to touch the sergeant, fighting with his reason.

Bowman was paralysed.

"What's going on, Peavish?"

"Was it you?"

"What?"

"Did you do that?"

Bowman took a step back.

"What are you talking about?"

The preacher leaned his head to the side.

"It's not you?"

"Peavish, where is Penders?"

"Erik?"

II

Sitting under the awning of a hangar, the two men, numb with cold, could not bring themselves to look at each other. Bowman handed the bottle of whiskey to Peavish. The preacher took a gulp and coughed.

"I got here yesterday with a convoy of pioneers. They found him this morning."

Bowman had placed the Henry on his thighs, the barrel turned towards the preacher, who seemed not to notice.

"He died last night?"

"Huh?"

"Did it happen last night?"

"The cold preserved him, but he died a while ago. They were looking for him."

"Who was it?"

"A foreman in the mine. Someone had stolen some gold. They thought it was him because he disappeared at the same time as the gold, about ten days ago."

Bowman looked around him at the deserted mine, barely visible in the mist and snow.

"We have to get out of here. Have you got a horse?"

The preacher said no.

"You need one."

"I don't have any money."

Bowman took three five-dollar coins from his pocket.

"Find something. We have to go."

"Sergeant?"

"What?"

"Were you here to kill me?"

Bowman lowered his head.

"I don't know. I don't know what's going on anymore."

The preacher stood up, took a few steps and turned around.

"He was here too."

"Who?"

"Penders. The miners saw an Englishman here. A blond man who said he'd been a soldier. He came through here not long before the foreman disappeared."

For fifteen dollars, Peavish could not even find a donkey for sale. Animals were too precious at the mine and the workers did not want to be separated from them, no matter what the price. For ten dollars, he bought a flat cart in poor condition, and another two dollars got him a patched-up harness, the leather dry and cracked. They fitted it to Walden.

As the snow fell harder and harder, Bowman and Peavish left the Gregory mine and set off into the fog.

The cart was no more comfortable than his horse and Bowman suffered as it jolted over the stones on the track, though he tried not to let it show in front of the preacher. More than anything, without the warmth of Walden, he felt much colder. Peavish wore frayed clothes and no coat, a dog collar black with grime and a hat with holes in it, but he showed no reaction to the temperature. After a few mouthfuls, he even refused any more whiskey. Bowman had given him the reins, and he held his arms tight around his body to protect his ribs. His saddle and saddlebags were tied to the cart, along with the preacher's battered old suitcase. Bowman had put the Henry between his legs, and in the chaos the barrel ended up pressed against his cheek.

"It was Pastor Selby who told me you'd come over here to preach. In New York, I met Ryan, at the church on John Street. He told me you went through St Louis, and at the Methodist church there, they said you were out West."

Peavish turned towards the sergeant.

"I don't understand."

Bowman drank some whiskey and held the bottle tight in his arms.

"In London, I saw an article about a murder in Texas."

"In Texas? What are you talking about, Sergeant?"

Bowman looked at the preacher.

"The man in the mine . . . where did they find him?"

"In an abandoned tunnel. Why did you say there was another murder?"

Bowman pressed his temple against the Henry's barrel.

"Was there anything else, apart from the corpse? Anything written?"

The preacher started to tremble.

"On a beam. In blood."

"*Survive?*"

Peavish's eyes widened. He stared at the track ahead of him. Snowflakes fell into his eyes, but he didn't even blink.

"When Selby told me that you'd gone over here . . ."

"You thought it was me."

"You left just after my visit. I hadn't found Penders, but you were in America, and there was a second murder."

"There have been others?"

The two men listened to the noise of the horseshoes and the cart's wheels, neither of them knowing how to fill the void that had opened between them.

"I found his trail at Rio Rancho. He was travelling with a man who was killed. For a few days, I felt sure it was him. And then the manager of the Bent and St Vrain told me that you had passed through there, before they found the body of that man with a Russian name . . . Petrovitch. Peavish, why did you leave Plymouth after my visit?"

The preacher pulled on the reins and lifted the cart's brake, coming to a halt in the middle of the path.

"I'd wanted to leave England for a long time, but I didn't have the courage to do it. When you came to see me, and you told me about the list of the survivors, about Penders who had disappeared and the murder in the sewers, I made my decision. You had mentioned America, and our Church is well established here. I think I was afraid after your visit, Sergeant, afraid that it would all start again, that the nightmares would return. I packed my suitcase and I took a boat."

He turned to Bowman.

"Sergeant, I've been in America for nearly two years, but when I went through Bent's Fort I knew nothing about all this. I was on my way back to St Louis. On the Independence track, I met a convoy of employees from the Bent. They were very upset and they asked me if I could say a prayer for them and listen to their story. They told me that some Indians had killed a man and they'd brought his body to the fort."

The preacher reached out and grabbed the bottle of whiskey.

"I saw the corpse."

He drank a large mouthful.

"For two days, I had a fever. I remembered what you'd said at the chapel, about the sewers. I knew it couldn't be anything else. But for it to happen here, thousands of miles from England, when I thought I'd finally escaped it . . ."

Peavish almost finished the bottle.

"I'd heard all those horrible rumours on the road, but I thought they were exaggerations, superstitions. I couldn't bring myself to believe them. After all this time, so far from London . . . When I was able to stand again, I did the same thing as you: I followed his tracks, trying to find him . . ."

He tried to smile at the sergeant.

"I thought of Penders, of course, because you said that he might have come here. And I thought of you. The police in London believed you were the murderer. Erik or you, Sergeant . . . there was no other possibility. So I was looking for you, too."

Bowman got down from the cart and took a few steps. He had a hot flush and couldn't breathe. He took off his hat, lifted his face to the sky and let the snow fall on it. Peavish joined him, putting a hand to his chapped lips.

"So it's true? It's really him?"

Bowman put his hat back on.

"He's the last one."

It was slightly less cold in Black Hawk. It was no longer snowing and the fog had dispersed. The town did not look like a mining camp. Quieter and better constructed, it had survived the gold fever and its end and it had managed to endure in another form. There were dwellings, a few shops. Lamps were being lit behind windows.

Bowman was at the end of his strength. His wound burned his back and he swayed as the cart advanced, shivering and gripping tight on his rifle. Peavish came to a halt outside a house and knocked at the door. A man opened and, seeing the white collar, came out to shake his hand. Bowman heard them speak, then the preacher returned to pick up the reins and steer the cart into a neighbouring barn.

"We can spend the night here."

Bowman stumbled as he descended from the cart. He walked over to a pile of feed and collapsed.

"What's the matter with you?"

"I was shot in Bent's Fort?"

"What?"

"I tried to free the Comanches that they hanged."

"Why didn't you tell me you were wounded?"

"There's medicine in the saddlebags."

Peavish brought him a flask.

"Drink this. I have to go and bless our hosts' dinner. I'll come back to look after you. It won't take long."

He ran off. Bowman levered open the Henry, put a bullet in the chamber, placed the rifle on his belly and waited for the preacher to return, trying to stay awake.

Walden was tied to a trough. Peavish had found the flax seeds, the bandages and the syrup. He stirred a steaming saucepan with a pocket knife and smiled at Bowman. The preacher did not have a single tooth left in his mouth.

"It's nearly ready, Sergeant. Can you take off your clothes or do you need me to help you?"

Bowman wanted to undress himself, but the pain was too much. He managed to remove his jacket, but then the lamplight began to dance before his eyes. When the preacher reached out to move the rifle out of the way, Bowman gripped tight to the Henry and clambered backwards into the hay.

"Sergeant, I'm not going to hurt you."

They looked at each other for a few seconds. Bowman put the rifle down next to him and Peavish, moving cautiously, started to unbutton his shirt.

"I'm used to looking after the sick, Sergeant."

When he pulled on the sleeves, the preacher froze and closed his eyes. Bowman waited for him to continue.

"It's not the first time you've seen that."

Peavish began removing the bandages.

"I haven't seen them for a long time. I got used to washing myself in my underwear. People think it's because I'm a preacher."

He tried to smile. So did Bowman.

"It's true that you smell worse than me."

"I shave, though. That makes me look cleaner."

Peavish threw the dirty bandages away and opened the bottle of alcohol.

"For a long time, I couldn't shave."

He soaked a strip of bandage and cleaned the wound. The flesh was yellow and swollen. He paused for a moment, examining it.

"It was always more difficult seeing the others. I didn't hear my own screams, only yours."

He finished bandaging Bowman and they ate some meat and soup given to them by the owners of the barn. The broth ran between the preacher's lips and dripped down his chin when he drank from the plate. Peavish was younger than Bowman, but since the visit to the chapel in Plymouth, he seemed to have aged a hundred years.

"Nice job you have there, preacher. Do you always eat for free in return for a prayer?"

"Sergeant, no-one ever feels robbed."

"Soup isn't expensive, though."

Bowman finished his plate and lay down on his side, one arm under his head, back turned to the preacher.

"Peavish, it wasn't you who killed them, was it?"

"Sergeant, the men were afraid of you because you always knew when they were lying. Anyway, I never managed to make you believe anything."

Peavish laughed softly.

"I wasn't afraid of you because I don't lie. I have not killed anyone since we fought under your command."

"We fought to stay alive."

"That doesn't alter what we did."

Bowman stared at the rifle in his hands.

"Preacher, I don't hear my own screams in my nightmares either."

"I know, Sergeant."

Bowman lifted his head. Peavish, sitting next to him, knees up to his chest, was looking at him.

"You've changed, preacher. You haven't even tried to make me say confession or to convince me that I'm walking in God's footsteps."

There was a silence between them. The first one, since the Gregory mine, that did not separate them.

"Sergeant, I don't know if you will understand this because you have always been solitary, but these last few weeks, I was alone for the first time. I mean that God was no longer with me. I almost went mad."

Bowman thought again about Thoreau's book, about his interrupted reading in the desert of the chapter on solitude, about the last words he wrote to Alexandra Desmond.

"Solitary isn't solitude. Me too, I've gone crazy."

Bowman heard Peavish turning towards him.

"Without you, Sergeant, no-one would have survived. The reason we are not all dead is that you never gave up. Even . . . even if it was you they treated most harshly. But without you, we wouldn't have been in that situation. After the village was burned, we would have rebelled if you hadn't been there. We would never have gone that far upriver. We owe you our lives, Sergeant, but you are our worst nightmare."

Bowman, hidden under his blanket, did not move.

"I think you've changed a great deal too, Sergeant."

Bowman let go of the rifle, pushed it away, and closed his eyes.

"Peavish, even if it was you I was looking for, I'm glad not to be alone anymore. I need to sleep now, so if you have to do it, kill me quickly and don't screw it up."

The preacher laughed softly, but Bowman remained silent.

Peavish stood up, blew out the lamp and lay back down on the hay.

"Good night, Sergeant."

"Good night, preacher."

The news spread that a man of God was in town. They could not leave Black Hawk before Peavish had given a sermon, standing on the steps of a grocery store, in front of half the town's inhabitants. The others – whether because they belonged to a rival faith, or because God did not interest them enough to spend an hour in the rain with their feet in the mud – had stayed at home. The audience for the sermon was a motley crew. Deaf old men, curious children, dutiful bigwigs, unforgiving bigots, Chinamen with flexible beliefs or who did not understand a word he was saying and were waiting to see what this man in rags was selling. A few prospectors and drunkards were also waiting around for the doors of the grocery store to be opened so they could do their shopping.

Bowman had harnessed Walden. Sitting on the bench of the cart, sheltered from the rain outside the barn, he listened to the preacher's sermon. Within a few minutes, Peavish had metamorphosed, transforming himself from a sickly scarecrow to a black-and-white flame moving wildly from one side of the steps to the other. His voice grew clearer and more powerful. Never had Bowman seen anything like it. The women crossed themselves and sighed with dread when Peavish mentioned the hell hidden beneath their feet, the temptations and debaucheries, the terrible sins that God would judge pitilessly if they did not repent in time. There were a few laughs when he talked about alcohol, but silence fell again when he roared against greed, the lure of profit and wealth that drew us away from mercy. And his entire audience – mostly good people who had come to the Rocky Mountains to make their fortune – chorused their heartfelt amens.

"Our difficulties are the tests of our faith."

"Amen."

"Forgive and you shall be forgiven."

But the apotheosis came when Peavish explained that, while this country had as yet no government worthy of the name, and while perhaps, deep down, free Christians like them did not really need to be governed, God had already taken America in the palm of His hand. Under His divine governance, the nation of pioneers would find its path and its most perfect fulfilment.

Peavish knew his audience.

We must never despair.

Amen.

We will never be alone.

Amen.

"And remember, my brothers, that if God did not live in our hearts but in a house, there would be a portrait of each one of you on the wall of His living room!"

"Amen."

A drunkard, realising that the preacher was about to come down the steps, fired a shot into the air and shouted hurrah. The women, with rouge on their cheeks, lined up in front of the toothless former soldier, hoping for a minute of privacy with this great man, pressing coins and banknotes into his hands. Peavish made the sign of the cross above each person's forehead and moved on to the next one.

Bowman waited for another quarter of an hour while the preacher freed himself from his admirers and came over to join him. He rolled up the collar of his jacket, snapped the reins, and Walden ran through the mud. People waved to them all the way to the outskirts of the town.

"How much did you get?"

The preacher waved and smiled at a small child perched on his father's shoulders.

"I don't count it."

Still smiling, Peavish turned to Sergeant Bowman.

"Not until we're out of town."

The Denver track was wider and in better condition. Bowman urged Walden into a trot and they made good progress. The sun grew warmer and they re-entered the forest. For a moment, exhilarated by the wind, they said nothing, content simply to breathe, and then finally the preacher pronounced the first words:

"How are we going to find him?"

Bowman felt irritated by this pointless question, by the end of the silence that he wanted to enjoy a little longer.

"Same way I found you. Providence."

Peavish did not rise to the bait.

"We can't just follow leads and wait for another death."

"That's all I've done since I left London."

Bowman glanced over at Peavish, as if in apology for his aggressive tone.

"After Pueblo, I followed the path to the gold mines. But that makes no sense, after what happened at the last mine."

"You think he'll continue heading west?"

"Or go north. Or make a U-turn and go to Mexico. There was a murder down there. He could also head back east."

The speed at which they were travelling suddenly seemed futile. Bowman pulled on the reins to slow Walden down.

"But there's something else."

The preacher turned towards him.

"What?"

"The victims."

Peavish's shoulders tensed, a nervous tic.

"I only know about two. Petrovitch and the foreman of the Gregory mine."

"The one in London was never identified. We also don't know if there were any others before that."

Peavish's shoulders spasmed again. Bowman pursued the train of his thought.

"But the important thing is what happened here. As with London, we don't know if it's the first murder, but the man in Reunion – Kramer – was an engineer."

"Reunion?"

"In Las Cruces, Richter was a travelling salesman. Rogers, in Rio Rancho, was a small-time conman who acted as a guide on the path. Petrovitch was trying to sell an extraction procedure to the Bent and St Vrain. At the mine, he killed a foreman and stole some gold. In Mexico, I don't know who the victim was."

Peavish was concentrating on Bowman's words, trying to be rational in order to distract himself from his body's reaction. He took off his hat and tapped it back into shape with his thin fingers.

"It's not completely random."

"I met an old man who said it was a passion, that he couldn't stop. And another man who said it was a mathematical sequence. Something that repeated."

An acid belch rose up Peavish's throat. He covered his mouth with his hand as if to push the nausea back.

"Are you saying there's been a logic to this since the beginning?"

"How much did he steal?"

"Quite a lot, apparently. The mine is offering five hundred dollars to whoever catches the thief. The army was informed about it too. We're not the only ones looking for him."

"Gold, a conman, and travelling salesmen."

Bowman gritted his teeth.

"And Penders was a soldier. He has a plan."

"He wants to start a new life."

Bowman lowered his head.

"Survive."

The preacher's tongue flickered over his dry lips.

"The victims . . . It's as if he's looking for a partner."

"Going into business."

"Or maybe he's just like us. He can't stand being alone anymore and he kills the people he meets."

Bowman looked at the preacher and continued as if he hadn't heard this:

"Everyone who wants to go into business is headed to the same place."

"Out West."

"And if he has money, he won't hang around here. Now everyone who's searching for him knows it wasn't the Indians."

Walden advanced slowly as the two soldiers thought through this theory. Peavish took off his dog collar and scratched his neck.

"This is all conjecture. Maybe he's already on the way to St Louis. Maybe he's headed back to England."

"He won't go back."

The two men glanced at each other. Peavish put his collar in his pocket and put his hat back on, pulling it firmly onto his head. Bowman raised his arms and snapped the reins.

"Giddy-up!"

Two hours later, they entered Denver, the biggest town Bowman had seen since St Louis. The dried-up lodes had left enough people behind that the town had a reason for its existence: customers to keep the shops going, artisans to build them, savings for buying land, children to justify the opening of schools, money for building churches, a sufficient number of citizens to pay for a police force and to fill the dozens of taverns and saloons in town. On the sign, beneath the name of Denver, was a proud, round number: *5,000 inhabitants*. The town was as densely populated as a popular district of London, the only difference being that the houses were made of wood. For the rest, the streets and back alleys were, like those in the English capital, open-air sewers. Most of the constructions were raised up on stilts so as not to soak in the mire, and the inhabitants walked around on wooden sidewalks.

Only animals, carts and Indians used the streets.

While Bowman looked like he'd just come down from a mountain after a long retreat, Peavish – despite his gaunt and prematurely aged face, his toothless mouth and his madman's eyes – inspired trust. The power of his filthy dog collar was impressive. People greeted him politely, then gave a suspicious nod at Bowman.

"I didn't realise it was so big. I'm not used to towns anymore."

"In general, I get a good welcome wherever I go."

"In general?"

"I have been thrown out of a few farms and saloons."

Bowman smiled at the preacher's dignified expression, the way he humbly accepted that some people would rather give a priest a good kick up the arse than listen to him preach.

"Anyway, we won't find anything here."

Peavish frowned.

"Are you sure this is the right decision, Sergeant?"

Bowman brought the cart to a halt outside a grocery store.

"We don't have any other choice. We were close to catching him. Now he has money, we need to speed up."

He got down from the carriage and tied the reins around a post.

"We have to stick to what we said."

"And what if he went east?"

"Then we turn around. We have to eat, and we have to find you a horse. The cart is too slow."

They bought reserves of flour, lard, coffee and bandages, and asked where they could go to buy a horse. The shopkeeper gave them directions to a corral in the north of town.

After haggling, the horse merchant agreed to buy the cart for seven dollars and offered them an eight-year-old gelding, a piebald horse with strangely shaped markings on its face that made it look stupid. It was a good animal: Bowman had patted it and observed it. Healthy feet, solid back, teeth that backed up the assertion of its age, and its shoes were good for quite a few miles yet. It was not as fast as the mustang, of course, but it was a strong, muscular horse.

The merchant wanted thirty dollars for it. After buying food supplies in town, Bowman had thirty-three dollars left, plus another three that Peavish had earned by preaching in Black Hawk. The corral owner agreed to lower the price to twenty-five.

"Not that it's a bad horse, but it looks so dumb that no-one wants it."

"What's it called?"

"The man I bought it from never told me a name. I just called it the piebald."

They spent two of the five dollars they had saved on an old, worm-eaten saddle. When the transaction was over, they had nine dollars left. If they had ever intended to sleep in town, it was now out of the question.

As soon as he put his foot in the stirrup, the leather broke and Peavish ended up on his back in the mud. When he was finally in the saddle, his horse tried to approach Walden, who bit its ear.

"I have to christen this animal. He can't remain nameless."

Bowman contemplated the preacher for a moment. He was as thin and straight as an I, his old suitcase strapped to the saddle of the black-and-white horse, which was stocky and apathetic-looking.

"Apart from its colour, the two of you don't have much in common."

Peavish smiled his black-gummed smile.

"This is the first means of transportation I've ever possessed."

"You still owe me twenty-four dollars. You'll have to preach to pay for our food. And, until you've repaid me, I reserve the right to eat your transportation."

After passing the last buildings in Denver, they crossed the South Platte River behind a large convoy of pioneers en route for Wyoming. There were about thirty carts, together raising a cloud of dust so high it looked like a sandstorm. On the other bank, they moved away from the convoy and set off at a canter. The piebald did not give it his all and Peavish was too squeamish to use his heels. Bowman came behind the preacher and kicked his horse's backside. The piebald immediately launched into a gallop, perhaps also to escape Walden, who was trying to chew its tail. Peavish's horse clearly had the capacity to move quickly, given the right motivation. They passed the convoy and got back on the track. After a few kicks from Walden, the piebald fell in line obediently behind the mustang. After an hour of this, Walden let the other horse walk alongside him, though not even an inch ahead of him. As night approached, they started looking for a place to sleep and set up camp near a stream. Before dark, Peavish cut a strip off his suitcase to patch up his stirrup leather.

They had continued descending ever since they left Denver, riding past the foothills of the Rocky Mountains, and at dusk, it was still warm. The vegetation grew lower to the ground, but the grass and bushes were dense enough to feed the horses. The trees, smaller and sparser than in the mountains, also provided firewood.

The two former soldiers sat in silence around the campfire, eating the last pieces of Bowman's pronghorn and watching the lanterns of the large convoy as it rode past. The carts, having caught them up, continued moving forward until late at night, coming to a halt half a mile further on and setting up their own camp. Bowman watched the pioneers' fires while Peavish, exhausted from his first ride, lay down with his head on his saddle.

Bowman took his oilskin from his bag and tossed it to the preacher.

"We need to get you a blanket."

"Thank you, Sergeant."

Bowman lit a pipe with his last few scraps of tobacco.

"Preacher, will you stop calling me 'Sergeant'?"

Peavish sat up.

"What do you want me to call you?"

"Bowman. Or Arthur. As you like, but I'm not a soldier anymore."

Peavish crossed his arms behind his head and stared up at the sky.

"The first time I saw your Christian name was on the list of prisoners in Rangoon. After a year in the forest, I still didn't know what you were called."

Bowman bit the mouthpiece of his pipe.

"Call me Bowman."

"As you wish."

"I don't remember your name."

"Edmund."

Bowman blew out a cloud of smoke.

"Alright, I'll try. But no promises."

12

They passed the pioneers' camp; the horses in the convoy had been pushed too hard the night before and they needed more time to recover. Peavish rode to the circle of carts and Bowman saw him talking with a few men before waving to them and coming back.

"They're not interested."

"Not even for a blanket?"

The preacher did not look downhearted.

"They're Mormons. They're heading to Salt Lake City."

Bowman glanced back at them.

"Ryan mentioned them when I went to John Street. What are they going to do in Salt Lake?"

"That's their capital."

"Ryan said they had an army."

"They had a lot of problems in the east, so the Mormons decided to move to Utah. It's still deserted over there. But three years ago, the American army sent an expedition there because they were afraid the Mormons would secede. They'd elected their prophet as the State governor."

"Their prophet? What do they believe in?"

"The founder of their church, and also their first prophet, Joseph Smith, was murdered by dissidents from his own cult. He had an eventful life before becoming a prophet. Money problems and trouble with jealous husbands. That's what his detractors say, anyway. Apparently, Smith met the angel Moroni at the foot of a tree in New York State, and the angel gave him some golden plates engraved with an unknown language. But he also found some magic glasses that allowed him to translate the words, and from that he wrote the Book of Mormon. That became their Gospel. They're polygamous. I mean, the men have several wives. Their church is a great success. But that's also why they've had problems with other Christians here."

Bowman smiled.

"Not because of the magic glasses?"

"No."

"How did it end, the army expedition?"

"Since the California gold rush ten years ago, the road to the West has gone through Salt Lake City. They control the passage through the Rocky Mountains. The government had to negotiate and the only thing that changed was that the governor is no longer a Mormon. That church was stronger than the American government."

"You sound pleased about that."

"I understand the battle they're fighting to defend their faith."

"Maybe you haven't changed so much after all, preacher."

Peavish smiled, and so did Bowman.

"All the same, you'd better find some good Christians sooner or later, because you still don't have a blanket and the nights are cold."

They trotted on for a few miles, to put a bit of distance between the convoy and themselves.

Peavish did not know this part of the path, but he had already travelled along the Platte River to outposts about a hundred miles further on along the road to Salt Lake City, the main track to the West taken by pioneers, stagecoach companies and the Pony Express.

"When I was there before, there were no towns, just temporary camps, and some farms and inns. I don't know what it's like now. Towns here can be born in a few weeks. We should reach that track tonight."

"Is that the stagecoach road?"

The preacher guessed at Bowman's concern.

"From the Platte River, if you get in a stagecoach, you can be in San Francisco in two weeks, in St Louis in one."

"Shit, I shouldn't have left all that money."

"What money?"

"I had two thousand dollars. I gave it to someone in Texas."

Peavish spurred his horse so it drew alongside Bowman's.

"Where did you get all that money? And who the devil did you give it to?"

"I figured that you and Penders wouldn't have any, so to find you I should travel in the same way."

Peavish scratched his cheek.

"I suppose that made sense. But it doesn't explain who you gave it to. Nor where it came from. Did you really say two thousand dollars?"

"It was Reeves' money."

"Reeves?"

"The captain of the *Sea Runner*."

Peavish reflected for a moment. The name rang a bell. He frowned, then his smile disappeared and he muttered to himself:

"The fishing village."

Bowman did not look at the preacher and was careful not to break this silence. It was as if a fuse had been lit, and Peavish had gone back there again. The boarding of the *Sea Runner*, the village in flames, the river, the rain, the deaths on the junk, the forest, the cages, the screams.

Peavish did not say another word all day, even after they set up camp.

In the middle of the night, Bowman woke up and grabbed his rifle. Peavish had come out of a nightmare and was yelling his head off. The screams of one woke the other. Just as they had over there. Seeing Bowman's scars made it impossible for Peavish to forget his own.

At dawn, when the preacher had finally fallen back asleep, sweating and mumbling as he dreamed, Bowman took out his papers to quickly write a few words.

> *Alexandra,*
> *I found the preacher I was looking for. It wasn't him and we are travelling together now. We're looking for the other one, Erik Penders, who is somewhere ahead of us and who must be having the same nightmares as us every night.*
>
> *Together, we cannot escape what we are and who we were.*

It is an illusion to believe that anyone can change.

We are going the wrong way but we don't have any other way to go and it's going to cost us our lives or drive us crazy.

I think about you and I believe you were right to leave. There's nothing to find here.

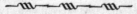

They avoided the first inns they came to on the Pony Express road. Bowman began hunting again. The track went straight on along high plateaux crossed with ancient rivers that had left behind rocky peaks in the shapes of sentries and cathedrals. About fifty miles south, the jagged summits of the Rockies stood out on the horizon, reflecting the colours of the rising and setting sun.

As long as they had food and could find animals to hunt, Bowman and Peavish remained far away from the track, seeing only the line of dust raised by a convoy or a stagecoach, following the hills by the side of the plateau, seeking out water and the cover of trees. They drove their horses on, waiting for nightfall before they stopped and setting off again before daybreak. Bowman's wound had healed, and his ribs no longer hurt so much. They could have continued like that, contenting themselves with game and picked fruit, but their parallel itinerary cut them off from all news, so they had no idea if they were still going in the right direction, if Penders was already far ahead of them or if they had perhaps overtaken him.

On the fourth day, they drew close to an inn. Peavish went in alone to buy some food and to try to find out some information. Bowman waited for him, hidden in the woods. The preacher returned four hours later; he climbed down from the saddle and began unloading his purchases. Tobacco, flour, some coffee and two bottles of whiskey.

"No-one has seen an Englishman travelling alone. Nothing has happened on the road."

The sergeant looked disappointed.

"No murders?"

"No. There's a small town, two days' ride from here. Rock Springs. Maybe we'll have more luck there."

The preacher's tone was gloomy. Bowman opened a bottle and started drinking.

Peavish's face darkened.

"I didn't find out anything about Erik, but . . ."

"Stop calling him that."

"Why?"

"We don't know him anymore."

The preacher stood up.

"I'll call him whatever I want. And although I didn't learn anything about him, the inn's employees did talk about you."

"What?"

"A group came through here two days ago: half a dozen men from the Bent and St Vrain, others from the Gregory mine. The companies are now offering a thousand dollars for the capture of the man who set fire to the pioneers' camp, tried to free the Indians and stole the gold. They think the two cases are connected."

"And?"

"It's starting again, Sergeant. Like in London. They think you murdered the foreman and that you were the accomplice of the Comanches who were hanged."

Bowman did not react. Peavish drank a mouthful of whiskey and put the bottle between his legs. He did not put the cork back in it.

"They don't know where you are. That group was heading west; others have gone east and south. But as far as everyone else is concerned now, there's only one Englishman, and Erik has your face."

Bowman balled his fists.

"Stop calling him that."

"On the road, there's only one name on people's lips, Sergeant: yours."

"Stop saying that. I'm not like him."

Peavish raised his bottle. The alcohol disgusted him, but he kept drinking.

"If you're asking me not to feel compassion for him, I'll have to stop feeling it for you too."

"You should go back to preach in your churches, Peavish. You're not cut out for this job."

Bowman turned on his heel and walked away.

"You're wrong, Sergeant. I won't give up. But you won't be able to escape this logic."

"What logic?"

"The sequence that began when you chose me on board the *Joy*."

The preacher lay down and rested the bottle on his belly.

"That was my first scar. Bufford's knife wound."

Bowman looked over at the track. It was too late to start riding again today. The two men remained where they were, sipping the whiskey until it was all gone and falling asleep drunk, with dry mouths and heavy heads, without having lit a fire.

For two days, they continued on their way, keeping close to the hills and only approaching the road again at Rock Springs – a few shacks built around an inn. From the shelter of the trees, they observed the main path, bathed in sunlight. They saw a stagecoach stop, long enough for its three passengers to eat a meal, and a little later, a Pony Express horseman galloped hard to the inn, where he swapped his horse for a fresh one and left at once.

The small town seemed to come alive only when couriers and stagecoaches passed through. There was only one main building, adjoining the inn and the stable, and workmen were still finishing its roof. The other houses, about ten of them, were shabby wooden huts. This was the end of the Wyoming plateau. After Rock Springs the road began to climb up to the Rockies. The final stage before the mountain, the town was returning to life now that the winter snows had melted and the mountain passes were open again. For them, it was a mandatory stopover before they headed towards Salt Lake City.

"You go first. If all is well, give me a sign."

Bowman watched the preacher join the road, cross through town and stop outside the half-built construction next to the inn. Peavish looked inside, turned around and, pretending to greet the workmen on the roof, shook his hat at Bowman, who left the woods and went into town. When he crossed the empty street and passed the saloon, hotel and general store of Rock Springs, the roofers hailed him. He saw figures in the windows of houses, and outside the inn's stable a negro was currycombing the dust-covered horse left behind by the Pony Express rider. The black man glanced at Bowman. Instead of continuing on his way, Bowman pulled on the reins and tied up Walden a few yards away from Peavish's piebald. It would probably have been more suspicious to ride through Rock Springs without pausing than to stop and have a drink here.

The counter of the shop had been extended to become the bar of the saloon, and the tables where people drank were also those of the hotel's restaurant. There was an unlit stove, some furniture that didn't match, and half-empty shelves; rays of light passed through the gaps between the planks that formed the walls. The main room smelled of spices and alcohol.

Peavish was leaning on the bar, talking with the landlord, a glass of water and a foamy beer in front of him. Two tables were occupied. Three men were in discussion, seated around a map; one of them, well dressed, was talking to the other two, dressed in work clothes, about land, surface areas and prices per acre. An old man sat alone, drinking coffee and turning the pages of a smudged, creased old newspaper. They looked up when he entered. Bowman pulled out a chair and touched his hat with one hand.

The landlord excused himself with Peavish and asked the new arrival what he wanted to drink.

"Whiskey."

Peavish had stared, wide-eyed, when he saw Bowman come in, and now he turned back to the bar, his shoulders hunched.

The landlord brought him his glass.

"Well, you're today's second visitor to Rock Springs, after Father Peavish there, who's sitting at the bar! So where are you headed to?"

Bowman nodded at Father Peavish, who gave him a tense smile, and told the man he was going west. His American accent was not very convincing, but his attitude was cold enough that the landlord left him alone and went back to the bar to chat with the preacher.

"Well, of course we've heard about Bowman! But if you want my opinion, they'll never catch him. In this country, a man who can hunt can hide out for two or three centuries before anyone finds him! Especially a man who's lived with Indians. If Bowman had been through here, we'd have seen him, no doubt about it. The men who are searching for him for the reward money will go all the way to the Pacific and back again if they have to, believe me. I did hear rumours that him or a man who looks like him went over the mountains, but you hear stories like that all the time and the men from the patrol didn't believe it. After two weeks of riding all the way here from Bent's Fort, they were starting to lose heart a little bit. There's even one who fell off his horse and is staying here at the hotel."

"You mean he's still here?"

"Well, yeah! He broke his leg."

The landlord, pleased with himself, leaned towards Peavish and spoke so loud that all the other drinkers could hear his secret:

"And he saw the killer in person, because he was at Bent's Fort when Bowman tried to help the Comanches escape!"

The landlord stood up tall and turned towards the staircase.

"Oh, Mr Nicholson! We were just talking about you . . ."

A man came down the steps, holding on to the banister, a crutch under his arm and a splint on his leg. He hobbled over to the bar and sat down. The landlord poured him a glass.

"I was telling Father Peavish what happened to you while you were pursuing the killer along the track, and how you saw him in person."

The man with the crutch turned towards the preacher.

"As you can see. I was guarding them damn redskins and Bowman walked past me, as close as you are to me, Father. And a little later, I saw him escape after he'd knocked out two of my colleagues. A real savage, he was, firing at everything that moved. But there was another Indian with him and they managed to get away."

The man drained half his glass and slammed it down on the counter.

"They found the Indian in Woodland. They gave him the treatment but he wouldn't say a damn word. Tough as hell, that one, too."

"Is he in prison?"

Nicholson smiled to himself as he looked at the preacher, then changed his mind.

"Not that I want to sound happy about it, Father, but they hanged him right away. Four inches from the ground, and he took a good two minutes to die with his feet almost touching the earth. Never saw anything like it, Father, because he didn't shake or anything. In fact, he managed to stare at us and smile while he was choking to death. He was either tough as hell or totally crazy, that damn redskin."

The Bent employee picked up his glass again, perhaps to chase away the memory of that Indian who smiled as he died, but he froze before he had brought the glass to his lips. For a second, he smiled, as if thinking it was a joke. The landlord was pale, his hands in the air. Nicholson turned around and his crutch fell to the floor. He clung to the counter. Peavish moved out of Bowman's line of fire. When he moved the lever of the Henry, the men at the other tables pushed their chairs back, without daring to run away.

"Don't move."

Bowman aimed at Nicholson and walked slowly towards him, until the mouth of the barrel was touching his forehead.

"Drop your pistol."

Nicholson pissed himself. The urine made a quiet rattling noise as it landed on the floorboards.

"Don't kill me, Mr Bowman."

When Nicholson pronounced his name, the customers and the landlord fidgeted nervously, but did not move from their positions.

"I'm going to blow open your belly and tie your guts round your neck. I'm going to sit on a chair and watch you die while you try to put your innards back where they belong."

Peavish slowly approached him.

"Don't do that. Go, my son. Leave this place."

Nicholson slowly drew the pistol from its holster and let it fall to the floor.

"Preacher, pick that up and put it in my pocket."

Peavish obeyed. The barrel of the Henry was trembling. Bowman's hands were white. He took another step, pushing Nicholson's head backward, making him bend his back over the counter.

Peavish reached out and put a hand on the rifle's barrel.

"Leave, please. This would do no good. Just leave this place."

Bowman turned towards Peavish. The preacher started to cry.

"Please."

Bowman stared at Nicholson and pressed the barrel into his throat.

"You and your race – slaves who think they're upholding the law – we should shoot the whole fucking lot of you."

Peavish closed his eyes.

"Mr Bowman, leave him. I beg you."

Bowman kicked Nicholson's broken leg, smashing the splint and bending the knee backwards. The Bent employee collapsed, screaming. Bowman walked backwards through the room, sweeping his gun from side to side, pressed down on the door handle with one hand and kicked it open.

"The first man out of here gets a bullet in the head."

He continued to aim at them through the window as he untied his horse, then he climbed into the saddle and set off at a gallop. At the end of the street, he stopped and pulled on the reins to make Walden face the way he had just come. Then he raised his rifle and waited. When the door of the inn opened, he unloaded the Henry's magazine: sixteen bullets, one after another, shattering the shop window and exploding the wooden façade. Sergeant Bowman let out a war cry, yelling like John Doe, dug his heels into Walden's sides, cut between the shacks and sped away along the path. On the outskirts of the town, he left the road and disappeared into the forest, making a semi-circle several miles wide and returning to a spot about a hundred yards from the road. There, he got down from the horse, hid behind a rock and reloaded the Henry.

Three hours later, Peavish rode slowly past him. Bowman got back in the saddle and followed him at a distance, waiting for dusk when the preacher would move away from the track and make his camp for the night. When the fire began to glow in the darkness, he waited another hour and then joined the preacher. The two men exchanged a look. Peavish climbed onto his horse, the saddle still strapped to its back, and they rode until morning.

If the posse that was hunting Bowman had been on the verge of giving up their search, news of the incident in Rock Springs now spread along the western path at the speed of a Pony Express horse. He and Peavish slept during the days, taking turns to keep guard, and moved forward at night, continuing this way for the whole week it took them to reach Salt Lake City. They stayed away from the track, seeking smaller passages through the mountains. Several times, forced to turn back from dead ends or crevasses, they had no choice but to follow the track for a few miles through the darkness, before riding away from it as soon as they could. For one whole day, trapped in a narrow pass, they had to camp a few hundred yards from the track in an icy wind, without making a fire, without any water, listening as convoys of pioneers drove past.

After four days, they reached the mountain pass separating the two sides of the Rockies, crossing the dividing line between East and West in the middle of the night, exhausted, starving and stinking. After drinking from springs that flowed towards the eastern rivers and the Atlantic Ocean, they now went down slopes following streams that ran towards the Pacific. Bowman shot a wild sheep with a single bullet and they ate it half raw, ending their journey with stomach pains and diarrhoea. Their clothes were shredded from climbing over rocks, and the horses were on their last legs. They had to walk beside them for half of the descent.

Their scars and old wounds ached and their fatigue was the kind no-one ever recovers from. They aged years in days, draining their bodies of an energy they would never get back. The two men felt no relief as they reached Salt Lake City. A few miles from the town, near a mountain spring, they collapsed and slept for a whole day and a night. The next day, they were able to stand again and that was their only source of contentment.

The preacher cut off his beard, shaved, washed his clothes and dog collar. Holding his long johns in the stream, he rubbed at them without soap until his odour had diminished slightly. Bowman had decided to bypass the town to the south, circling far from any dwellings and passing on to the mountains on the other side of the valley, where he would wait for Peavish after he had ridden along the main track.

The preacher, having cleaned himself up as best he could, counted their last few dollars.

"You'll have to wait a couple of days. I'll bring you some food."

The two men looked out over the valley and the straight lines of the town, twice as big as Denver. For a moment, they were silent, gathering their courage. They did not exchange a word, but they knew that, after a week of shivering with cold, pressed close together, they would be simultaneously relieved and terrified at being separated.

Bowman crouched down. He thought, again, of John Doe, a root between his teeth, observing the town of Woodland before going down there. *I would rather say goodbye here.*

"Preacher, if you don't make it back, if you have any trouble, save your own skin. Tell them what you know about me. Do what you have to. And if you decide that you've had enough, I'll understand. I reckon it'll take me two days to reach the pass and I'll stay there another day after that. Then I'll go on, with or without you."

"I'll be there, Sergeant."

"You might think differently when you're in a bed, eating a steak paid for with my money. But do what you want. You don't owe me anything, Peavish. I'm the one who's in debt to you."

Peavish crouched down next to him.

"Sergeant, I'll come back."

The preacher smiled, exposing his rotten gums. Bowman looked at him, and then looked away.

"You didn't have to follow me. You never should have done. Not you or any of the others. I can find him on my own."

"I know, Sergeant."

Bowman stood up, walked over to his horse, and untied his travelling bag. He opened it and handed Peavish the little leather briefcase from the English bank.

"If you don't see me again, you have to look after this."

"What is it?"

"Everything I've done in the last two years, since the murder in the sewers, and some letters. You have to remember this, Peavish: Alexandra Desmond in Reunion, Texas, near Dallas. If we never see each other again, you have to send this to her. Alexandra Desmond in Reunion, Texas."

Peavish put one hand on the worn leather briefcase and tried to hand it back to Bowman.

"No need, Sergeant. I'll come back."

"I don't want this to disappear with me. You can still make it through."

"You know more than you're saying. You always make it through, Sergeant."

Bowman pushed the briefcase back at him.

"Take care of it, Peavish. This is all I'll leave behind me. I didn't think there'd be this much."

The preacher shook his head. Bowman smiled at him.

"This is the last thing I'll ask of you."

Peavish put the briefcase in his old suitcase, tied to the piebald's saddle, and turned back to face Bowman.

"Sergeant, who is that woman?"

"Someone I met. I told her I'd come back too. But that's not possible anymore."

The preacher tried to smile.

"Was it to her you gave all Reeves' money?"

Bowman did not reply. Peavish held out his hand. Bowman looked at him, this old ghost, and saw again, in the preacher's eyes, a little of the light he had seen there, on board the *Healing Joy*, when he had asked him if there was anyone on the boat he trusted.

"I'm glad we made it through together. Now clear off."

Peavish climbed into the saddle, spurred his horse forward, and turned around.

"I'll see you in three days."

"In three days."

13

Bowman found some bushes and dug out their roots, cutting them off and shoving them in his pockets. The valley, flat and pale, was hot, catching all the sunlight between the mountains. He walked out in the open after hiding for days in the Rockies, but he no longer felt threatened. Fifteen miles from the town and the track, there was no-one around and, for the first time in weeks, he no longer sensed the presence of any pioneers around him. He went down the rocky bank of a river, attached the rope to Walden's halter, tied it around a rock, and left the mustang to eat and drink while he went off hunting.

He crouched behind a bush, on the alert, for half an hour, and finally shot a hare, then returned to the river to cook its meat. He stripped off and dived into the water, soaked his clothes and put them out in the sun to dry, and lay down on a flat rock where he fell asleep. When he woke up, his skin was red and his scars hurt. He ate the remains of the hare then opened his bag and put his things out on the rock. His writing materials and the end of his block of paper. Thoreau's book. Some underwear, just as shabby as what he was wearing. A shirt in better condition, which he put on. It was too big around his arms and shoulders now. He probably looked more like the preacher than he imagined. He unfolded a pair of work trousers without any holes and the powder horn fell onto the rocks. He turned it in his hands, watching the sunlight reflected from its mother-of-pearl inlays. The silver had oxidised and turned black. For an hour, rubbing at it with a corner of his old shirt, he polished it until it shone again and placed it on top of a stone. Then he took out his pen and sharpened it, and sat down to write, without taking his eyes off the powder horn.

Bowman tried to remember Thoreau, the way he expressed what he felt and experienced. He didn't want to write anything so complicated or poetic, he just wanted to tell his story. The letters and the notes he had given to Peavish were for Alexandra. What was left of the block of paper was for him. He traced the first words.

Letter to the white Indian and all my other ghosts

I am in the sunlight in a valley in Utah, next to a town filled with people who believe that salvation comes from magic glasses and murdered prophets. I watch a powder horn shine in the sun. I had it made in Bombay, in silver and mother-of-pearl. I've been carrying it with me for a long time, but I have the impression that it has followed me. It was a gift I got for myself after a victory, back when I was a killer for the India Company. I became a soldier because, in the part of London where I was born, poverty killed children of my age faster than cholera. The horn followed me even after I left it on a boat, in a little bay near the Burmese coast where a fishing village was burning. Since then, it's as if the screams of the women and children were trapped inside it. Like, much later, I was given a bottle containing the last dreams of a vanished town.

My name is Arthur Bowman and I never had a nickname when I was a child. They always called me Bowman. When I became a ship's boy and I discovered the sea, I was sick. But I stayed on the deck and watched the ocean until the nausea stopped and I went cross-eyed from staring at the waves. I decided I would never stop travelling and here I am in America, twenty-five years later, trying to escape from a powder horn where I've been held prisoner for eight years.

I've talked to it a lot before. Now I'm listening to it.

―――――――

On the morning of the third day, Bowman woke up long before sunrise and threw stones over the last embers of his fire. He had spent two days writing, the powder horn placed in front of him, with the Salt Lake stretching out endlessly behind him. He went back down from the mountains and found a hiding place among the rocks allowing him to watch the road. The sun came up behind the Rocky Mountains and its colours were reflected on the dried-out lake. All day long, he waited for the preacher to arrive, mechanically counting the carts heading to California. In the evening, he climbed back into the hills to set up camp. The next morning, he returned to his surveillance post. The preacher should have arrived the previous evening. When the sun reached its zenith, he still hadn't gone past on the road. Still Bowman waited. The afternoon came to an end.

He had prepared for Peavish's absence. He had even made it easy for him, but if the preacher was crazy enough to join him, Bowman thought it only fair to give him some extra time to make his decision. And anyway, he had needed time to write his story.

Other groups of travellers, stagecoaches and carts filed past. Bowman did not recognise Peavish's figure nor the colours of his horse. The sun went down in the west, it grew dark: there was no longer any reason to wait. He watched another two horsemen ride past, going slowly, pulling packhorses. He watched one last convoy pass, then he stood up, tightened Walden's girths, and climbed into the saddle.

Bowman came down from his hiding place and joined the path, which would soon be under cover of darkness. He headed in the direction of some trees and prairies that he had seen from his mountain viewpoint, a little oasis a few miles from the desert lake. Walden seemed to accept this renewed solitude with the same calm as Bowman; the horse's footsteps were soft and it lifted its head in the darkness, snorting quietly. They had once again taken their place under the moon and the first stars. The path gradually peeled away from the lake, and Bowman silently rode between the fires of pioneers who had stopped for the night.

Walden's ears pricked.

"What is it?"

Bowman stopped to listen. Nothing but the sounds of insects and the moan of the breeze. He started up again. Again, Walden's ears went back and again Bowman stopped. Thinking that he heard his name carried by the wind, he realised he was dreaming. Maybe he and the horse both needed some more time, after all, to get used to solitude again.

"There's no-one there. Walk on."

Walden shivered and this time they heard it at the same time. Bowman pulled on the reins to make a U-turn and froze in the middle of the track. The sound was fighting the wind in an effort to reach him, but there was no longer any doubt: a horse was galloping behind him and someone was calling out his name. He climbed down, pulled on the mustang's bridle and led it away from the road. Then he picked up the Henry and put a bullet in the chamber. Walden shuddered at the noise of the gun's mechanism.

"Shh. Calm down."

Bowman rested his arms on the saddle and aimed at the night, listening as his name was repeatedly yelled. The sound of horseshoes grew ever louder.

"Bowman!"

He made out a figure in the darkness.

He knew that voice, even if he couldn't identify it, hoarse and distorted by the horse's movement as it was. He aimed at the horse's legs as they came into view and put his finger on the trigger.

"Shh. Don't move."

Then he saw the white markings, illuminated by moonlight, and recognised the piebald. He raised his gun an instant before firing.

"Sergeant Bowman!"

Bowman ran over to the track, yelling:

"Peavish!"

The preacher, surprised by Bowman's apparition, pulled hard on the reins. The horse, its back legs stiff, came skidding to a halt on the stones. Peavish lost his balance, fell off, and landed on the ground.

Bowman helped him to his feet.

"Bloody hell, preacher, I almost shot you."

The piebald was panting like a locomotive. The preacher began shaking Bowman, while gasping for enough air to speak.

"I missed him. He was there, Sergeant. At the same time I was. I was searching for you. I didn't know where you were."

"Calm down!"

The preacher shouted:

"Erik was in Salt Lake three hours ago! He's just ahead of us!"

Now all he could hear was the jerky breathing of Peavish and his horse. Bowman turned in a circle, sweeping the blackness with the barrel of his rifle.

"Where is he?"

"I . . . I don't know . . . He took the path three hours ago."

Bowman stammered:

"I was watching it. I've been watching the path since this morning. I didn't see him. Damn it, Peavish, I didn't see him!"

"He went with someone. Two men on horseback and some animals to transport equipment."

Bowman climbed in the saddle. Peavish clung to his leg.

"I'm sorry, Sergeant. I wanted to stay there. I didn't want to anymore. But I asked questions. Just like that. And some people had seen him in the guesthouse. An Englishman. Blond hair. With money. Heading west with another man. Businessmen. Other people said he was alone and not so well-dressed. But they saw him. A former soldier . . . I didn't want to come back. But I found him, Sergeant. I found him."

"Let me go. For fuck's sake, let me go!"

Bowman kicked out at Peavish's chest and set off at a gallop.

He reached some houses. A lantern to guide visitors was hung over a sign: *Grantsville*.

Some of the houses still had lights on.

Bowman searched the stable and enclosures, looking for pack-horses and other animals, trying to remember the colours of the last two horses he had seen on the path. The horses started neighing and kicking. People came out of their houses, holding lamps. In the middle of the village, Bowman rode Walden in a small circle, yelling:

"Penders!"

He charged from one end of the street to the other, passing the torches held up by the inhabitants, seeing their faces terrified by this furious spectre.

"Penders!"

Men and women began to shout from windows:

"Go away!"

Bowman was growing enraged.

"PENDERS!"

A man came from his porch with a rifle and fired a shot in the air.

"Go away! Leave this place!"

Other armed men came out of their houses. All the windows were lit up now. Bowman tried to calm his horse, sent into a frenzy by his shouting and the threatening circle of Grantsville citizens. Women in pale dresses emerged from their houses, three or four in each one. A Mormon community.

"Leave or we'll open fire!"

There was an instant of silence. Walden had frozen. The men had stopped moving. Bowman, his face lit up by the torches, no longer knowing what to do, started edging his hand towards his gun and, in that moment of silence, a gunshot rang out.

Everyone turned towards the outskirts of town, towards the west. The shot had been fired a few hundred yards away, maybe even a mile. Bowman spurred his horse. Walden reared up and charged, knocking Mormons out of the way, sending them flying in the dust.

Still yelling, leaning forward on his horse, he heard another gunshot ahead of him. And again, someone calling him:

"Sergeant!"

Bowman turned around. Peavish had caught him up. The piebald had almost killed itself chasing the mustang. The two men continued side by side. There was a light ahead of them. A little yellow dot below the moon. On the roadside, fences and trees rushed past. It took them another two minutes to reach the light. A barn.

They jumped off their mounts. Bowman put Nicholson's pistol in Peavish's hand.

"Take this."

He stepped over a fence and found himself in the middle of a herd of cows, Peavish just behind. Bowman pressed his body against the barn wall. The light was coming from a window, under which a saddled horse waited, its reins dangling on the ground. They went around the building, pushing through the crowd of cattle, which began to moo and jostle nervously. The doors of the barn were half open and a stain of light illuminated the ground.

Bowman signalled Peavish to remain where he was, then he bent double and ran past the light. He positioned himself on the other side of the double doors and slowly breathed in.

"PENDERS!"

There was no sound.

"Throw your gun on the ground and come out of there!"

Peavish cocked the hammer of his pistol and called out in turn:

"Erik, it's Peavish! Come out of the barn! I'm with the sergeant. We came to find you. It's over, Erik."

The preacher's voice broke. With a surge of courage, he yelled at the top of his voice:

"It's over, you hear? We came to find you!"

Sergeant Bowman stood up straight, walked towards the beam of light and raised his rifle.

"Peavish, open the door."

The preacher crawled over to Bowman's legs.

"Don't kill him, Sergeant. Don't kill him."

"Open the door."

Peavish lowered his head and sobbed into the dust. Then he reached out his arm, caught hold of the door and pulled. Bowman rushed inside.

The oil lamp was placed high up on a beam. A saddled horse and two others with packs on their backs stamped their feet and moved around in front of him, preventing him from seeing beyond them. Bowman crouched down to look between their legs. He squeezed past the animals, moving along the wall. As soon as he was out of their way, the horses spotted the open door and ran outside. Bowman stood with his back to the wall. Peavish entered, arms dangling, holding the pistol without any intent, and fell to his knees.

Still Bowman aimed his gun. His lips moved. The preacher had dropped the pistol, joined his hands together and closed his eyes.

Between two posts, one arm tied to each of them, was a bare-chested man, covered in blood, his head drooping over his chest. Just as before.

Lying on the ground, arms by his sides, head back, Erik Penders had his eyes open. His back was arched, his throat cut, and he lay in a pool of his own blood, a rifle next to him and a pistol in his hand.

Two corpses.

Bowman dropped his rifle and moved towards Penders. Then he too fell to his knees and crawled through the dust. After yelling so loud his voice broke, he repeated one more time in a whisper:

"Penders?"

Sergeant Penders had been dead for only a few minutes or seconds. Bowman could feel the warmth of his body and blood was still flowing from his throat. Perhaps he had even heard Bowman and the preacher. Perhaps he had tried to call out to them.

Like Bowman, his beard was blond and grey; like Peavish, his face was prematurely aged, his wrinkles deepened by a grimace of pain. The man who had watched the Burmese coast rush past from the deck of the *Sea Runner*, with the marks of the Company's fetters on his ankles.

Sergeant Bowman sat back on his heels, his head fell forward and he began to weep. The preacher approached them. His long, thin fingers touched Sergeant Penders' eyelids, closing them, then he walked over to the hanging corpse, made the sign of the cross, wiped his tears away and began to pray in his calm voice:

"Lord, receive unto You the souls of these two men . . ."

Behind him, Bowman started speaking:

"It's not you."

". . . so that beside You they may know the peace they did not find on earth . . ."

"Why didn't you wait for me?"

". . . none deserve to die like this, but they are with You now . . ."

"I was looking for you, Penders."

". . . and will remain there for eternity."

"I didn't want to believe it was you."

". . . where we will join them soon to celebrate the beauty of what we will leave behind us."

"What am I going to do?"

The preacher's voice suddenly changed, becoming hard and cold:

"And now, Lord, let me do what I have to do. You can turn your back if you want. This does not concern you."

Peavish went out of the barn and returned a few minutes later with all the horses. They started sniffing the floor for the remains of their feed, indifferent to the corpses and to Bowman, who was incapable of moving. He unloaded the equipment strapped to Walden's saddle and did the same thing with Penders' horse, which had remained outside, waiting, while the others had fled. He searched Penders' body and emptied his pockets, then those of Bowman, who, paralysed, let him do it. Once all the belongings were spread out in front of him, Peavish sorted through them and began redistributing them.

Everything that might identify Bowman was given to Penders: his clothes and the powder horn. Everything that might identify Penders went to Bowman. Then he filled the saddlebags on the dead soldier's horse with all the food and money he could gather, and he went through the pockets of the stranger's corpse, the killer's last-known partner. Finally, Peavish went over to Bowman and helped him to his feet.

"You have to take off your clothes, Sergeant."

"What are you doing?"

"Look at me."

Bowman's eyes rolled in their sockets, staring all over the barn.

"You have to trust me."

Bowman managed to concentrate and looked at the preacher's face.

"Do you trust me, Sergeant?"

Bowman nodded.

The preacher helped him to undress, then took the clothes from Penders' corpse and dressed it in Bowman's.

When they had swapped clothes, Peavish picked up the pistol and approached Penders' body.

"What are you doing, preacher?"

Peavish looked at Bowman.

"No-one knows Erik here except us. There is only one name on the track now. You become Erik Penders. Sergeant Bowman died today. I killed him."

The preacher raised the revolver, aimed at the corpse's chest and fired twice. The bullets went through the body as through straw. He raised his sights, aimed at Penders' face and fired the last four bullets from the cylinder. Penders' head exploded.

All that was left on the ground was a body the same height as Bowman's, with his clothes on his back, and some blond hair.

Bowman collapsed unconscious beside the disfigured corpse.

When he came to, Peavish, with his tall frame, thin fingers and calm voice, was lifting him onto Penders' horse.

"What's happening?"

"Hang on, Sergeant."

Lying with his arms around the horse's neck, Bowman articulated:

"Who is it? Answer me, Peavish. Who were we looking for?"

"I'm not looking anymore, Sergeant. It's over. It all ends here. I won't go any further. And you should save yourself too. This is your last chance. It is easier to live with God than with ourselves, Sergeant. You've known that for a long time and I discovered it only a few weeks ago. But it's over. There is only one thing left for you to do."

Peavish smiled, eyes shining.

"What should I do, preacher?"

"Hang on to this horse and don't let go until it has taken you far from this place. The villagers will be here soon. You must be gone when I tell them my story."

The horse stamped at the ground.

"You think it wants to gallop?"

"I'm sure of it."

The preacher took the horse's bridle and led it outside.

"Peavish, I'm not going to make it."

Edmund Peavish whispered in Bowman's ear:

"Your letters are in your bag. The only thing that remains of you, Sergeant Bowman. You'll bury them yourself."

Bowman had enough strength to put his hand on Peavish's shoulder. Peavish put his on the sergeant's back.

"Goodbye, preacher."

"Save yourself, Arthur. Go."

Peavish hit the horse as hard as he could, giving a war cry worthy of a Mandan Indian.

Erik Penders' horse was large, with a good stride. It ran hard along the black road.

IV

1860–64

Sierra Nevada

I

Arthur Bowman left the road and followed the traces of vegetation, a few yellowed bushes along a dried-up creek, until he reached some tufts of grass and a trickle of water flowing down a slab of rock. The horse licked the water from the stone and Bowman let himself fall from the saddle. The water was lukewarm. He splashed some on his face and lay down on his back. He didn't know how long he had ridden from Grantsville, nor what distance he had crossed in the hot sun, but the plain around him was just a long, pale desert and the next line of hills, at the horizon, were at least thirty miles away. For an hour, he did not move a muscle, staring up at the blue sky, letting his thoughts evaporate in the heat. He took off Penders' jacket, which he soaked in water and rubbed at with all his strength to remove the bloodstains. He left the clothes to dry and untied the horse's saddlebags. The horse was a mare, about the same age as Walden, with calm eyes, a light chestnut that did not seem to suffer too much in the sun.

Bowman opened the saddlebags and spread out their contents on the ground. Cornflour, dried meat, a little flask of rum, black beans, three apples, coffee and some cooking utensils. He focused on inventorying these objects, aware that his survival no longer depended on food but on his will not to let himself die. He put the food aside. As well as clothes, a flint lighter, a purse containing about thirty dollars, ammunition for the rifle, a bar of soap, a razor, a pipe and some tobacco, he also found a book among Penders' things – a large, leather-bound notebook – and a little tin box. He opened the box: inside were some pencils and a small penknife to sharpen them.

The book was wrapped in paper, dirty where Penders' hands had touched it. Bowman read the flyleaf. *The Blithedale Romance* by Nathaniel Hawthorne. He thumbed through it, then put it down and looked at the notebook again. The name of a bookshop and its address in London were printed on the leather. He undid the strap that held it closed. There were only a few blank pages remaining; the others were covered in a tightly spaced handwriting, the letters more regular than Bowman's clumsy scrawl. The pages were covered with paragraphs of varying lengths, sometimes preceded by a date, sometimes containing only a single sentence.

He read the first page.

> London, 16 February, 1857
> Today, it took all my strength to keep standing.

Bowman skimmed the other pages without reading the words, just looking at the lines of writing. He closed the notebook, put it on top of his clothes, and sat on a stone without taking his eyes off it.

The powder horn.

Bowman was no more. He now had a whole life before him, a life with a new identity. Bowman reached out to the journal, opened it again and found the last page. He closed his eyes, took a deep breath, opened his eyes and read the final paragraph. The letters were bigger and the lines less straight. It had been written in a rush.

> Salt Lake City, 22 April, 1860
> Bowman was here at the same time as me. Never, in all these weeks, have I been so close to him. I will get back on the track to catch him up in the coming days or hours. The end of my journey is near. The end of his crimes, too, and perhaps of my nightmare.

Bowman felt his stomach turn. He threw the notebook away as if he'd been holding a snake in his hands, uncorked the flask of rum and drank it down in one. Then he ran to the stream and lay down on the slab, his face against the stone, letting the water flow over his body.

*

Back on the road, he rode slowly for four hours in the hot sun, hatless, draining his two flasks without worrying about where he would next find water. In late afternoon, throat swollen and face burned, he caught up with a convoy that had stopped for the night and headed towards the carts without responding to the greetings of the pioneer families. He asked a young couple if he could buy water from their barrel. The man and the woman exchanged a nervous look before accepting. Bowman filled his flasks. The husband, a man of about twenty-five, smiled at Bowman while glancing back at his wife and the other pioneers who were watching them.

"Where are you headed?"

"Erik Penders."

"Sorry?"

Bowman looked at him.

"My name is Erik Penders."

He took some coins from his pocket and put them in the man's hands.

"Is that enough?"

The young man saw the two one-dollar coins and lifted his head.

"No, that's far too much."

He tried to return the money, but Bowman refused and walked away. The woman called out to him:

"Wait!"

She gave a hat to her husband, who walked over to the Englishman and handed it to him. Bowman refused, and did the same again when the man tried once more to give him his money back.

"It's far too much. We can't accept it."

Bowman finally took the old hat from him, then walked away from the camp, stopping a little further on. He poured the two flasks into the mare's mouth, and on the white earth in front of the horse he laid out the bag of flour and the apples. Then he lay down on the rocks and opened the journal.

London, 23 February, 1857
I look at them and wonder how they do it. They get up, go to

work, bring children into the world. The fathers who will go off to die in the war or the factories smile sweetly at their children, their future already set out before them from the slums to the grave, and they strive to believe that their descendants will have a better life. This is not confidence or hope, it's madness. If I'm mad, then they are absolute lunatics and somewhere, in the boards of directors and the corridors of Parliament, other men are sniggering along with me.

London, 11 March, 1857
The gangs on the docks rob anyone who sleeps in the street. Last night I got into a fight with three children who tried to steal from me. I knocked two of them out and the other one ran away. They'll come back in greater numbers. I have to move to a different part of London.

The workers' charities won't let me in the dormitories anymore or give me any food. Too many problems with the other tramps, and my screaming wakes everyone up at night. A noisy madman. A pastor wanted to talk to me. He reminded me of Peavish, with his gentle voice while I wanted to rip his head off. I would have liked to make a confession, slide a knife over his belly until he denied his God and admitted that omnipotence exists on earth. I would have told him about Min's soldiers and about Sergeant Bowman. But he would have refused to believe that they were men. He would have said they were agents of the Devil. My ghosts are not demons. They are men, and a priest in London should meet them once in his life before asking anyone to repent. He had no idea what he was talking about, that madman.

Yesterday, I fell down in the street. My legs gave way and I collapsed.

I went to see the Company's boats in the port, the goods being unloaded and the soldiers disembarking. I shouted at them, asking how their trip had been, if they'd killed lots of people and how many of their comrades they had thrown overboard on the *way home. I shouted until some soldiers fell on me and beat me up. But I saw at least three soldiers who were terrified by what I shouted. I'll see those men again one of these days, sleeping on the same pavement as me.*

Bowman read until nightfall, then he closed the journal and looked over at the pioneers' fires. He fell asleep without eating or drinking, next to the mare, who he hadn't tied up.

At dawn, Penders' horse was still there, rummaging under stones in search of dry grass. Lying in the sun, Bowman watched as the convoy broke camp and passed him on the road.

London, 18 May, 1857
I've been working on the docks for three weeks. My muscles ached to begin with and I feel disgusted as I sense my body gaining strength again. This machine is relentless and has a life of its own. It demands food to stay alive. It demands health and couldn't care less about the mind that lives inside it. Like the companies want to become rich and powerful. But I still manage to revolt. With the money I earn, I drink as much alcohol as I can, and when I'm drunk I take control again. I make my legs stumble and slam my shoulders against walls. I make my body fall down, my body that thinks it can stand straight without me. I also get it into fights. In the taverns, I always find someone to fight with, to help me tame my muscles' arrogance.

I wonder where the others are. What they're doing. If any of them live here in London, and if we could talk. I wonder what I'd do if I met Bowman. In fact, he's the one I think about. I'd like to know if he's managing any better than I am. I don't know if I'd want to see him again. Thinking that he's still stronger than us — that's something that hurts me. Because he deserves to be destroyed, but if a man like him can't make it through, that means we have no chance.

How many are dead already?

Who still has the strength to keep going?
Where is Sergeant Bowman?
I have to leave this city.

Portsmouth, 1 September, 1857
What difference does it make?

The streets are just as filthy. The docks stink just as bad. The faces are the same. Here too I work, I drink and I fight. But I like looking at the sea.

There was a storm. A boat ran aground on the reefs and I went to the beach to walk amid the wreckage. Blue, swollen corpses rolled in the waves. I slept down there. Fifty tons of goods were lost and seventeen men from the crew were killed. It was strange to see corpses again. Among the living, you forget too quickly the importance of death. This association of the body and the mind is a problem. We learned that over there. You can't abandon your body to the waves or to the hands of Burmese soldiers, you can't separate yourself at will. Because if you do, you can't put yourself back again.

I want to escape my skin.

It took me a while to remember their first names.

Arthur
Edmund
John
Peter
Edward
Christian
I don't remember the last three.
Erik.

London, 4 October, 1857
I come out of the hospice tomorrow. The cuts on my legs have scarred over and I can walk. The doctor and the sisters think I'm getting better. I reassure them. I lie because I couldn't make them

understand that it's normal for a man like me to want to die.
There's this barrier between us and it's not just a religious thing.
What they lack is experience.

I listen to the noises of London outside and I'm almost happy
to go back there after having to put up with the nauseating solic-
itude of these people. Malice is much safer than generosity,
because its motives are less suspect.

I can't quite remember the exact reason why I wanted to do
it. I think my reasoning was solid, but my hand was not precise
enough, or else it betrayed me.

I am very tired and dejected. Surprisingly, this deep melan-
choly seems to calm my dreams. I manage to sleep a few hours
each day and I have fewer nightmares.

The sun was high, the heat sweltering. Bowman put the journal away and strapped the saddle to the mare's back. After a few miles at a walking pace, he dug his heels into the horse's sides. Four hours later, they caught the convoy, which had stopped by a half-dry river. He passed the carts and stopped a little further on by the water.

When he led the mare there, it drank only a few mouthfuls before sinking to the ground, breathing heavily. Bowman watched it curiously, lying there in its death throes. He drank some water and listened to the animal's lungs roaring as if they were filled with gravel, then sat down next to it.

"So you're tired too?"

Bowman turned around. The young man from the previous day, the one he had bought water from, was walking towards him. Hat in hand, with his thin moustache, he looked like a child. In his other hand he held a folded cloth.

"Mr Penders? Are you well?"

"What?"

"Is everything alright?"

Bowman did not reply. The man looked at the mare.

"Your horse is dying, Mr Penders. She's too weak to drink."

Bowman turned to face the mare.

"Yeah, you're right. She doesn't look too good."

The pioneer put down the cloth and his hat, filled a flask in the river and slowly poured it into the mare's drool-filled mouth. The animal drank it. The young man kept glancing up at Bowman, who sat on the ground, turning a stone in his hand.

"You should bring her some food. She doesn't have the strength to get up."

Bowman looked up.

"What?"

The young pioneer went over to the circle of carts and came back with a bucket. He reached inside and shoved handfuls of oats mixed with water into the horse's mouth.

The mare was breathing more easily now. She ate the whole bucket of oats and closed her eyes.

"That's a good horse you've got there, Mr Penders. She'll be alright, but if you keep on like that you'll lose her. My name is Jonathan Fitzpatrick."

The pioneer held out his hand to Bowman, who did not move.

"Erik Penders."

"Yes, you told me yesterday, Mr Penders."

He put the cloth in front of him.

"I brought you some porridge."

"You wouldn't have anything to drink, would you?"

"Yes, of course."

He filled a flask with water and brought it to Bowman, who stared at it uncomprehendingly.

"Whiskey?"

"Sorry, Mr Penders, but I don't drink alcohol. If you like, I could ask one of the others."

Bowman rummaged in his pockets, took out the purse and gave it to Fitzpatrick, who waved his hands in refusal.

"With what you gave me yesterday, I have plenty already."

When he came back fifteen minutes later, Fitzpatrick put a jug in front of Bowman and placed the cloth back on top of the untouched porridge, which was beginning to attract ants. He helped the mare drink some more water.

"Your horse needs to rest. And you should eat something too, Mr Penders. If you need anything, we're just over there."

When he had walked away, Bowman opened the saddlebag that was tied to the prostrate horse, then lay down with his head on the animal's belly. Listening to its irregular breathing, he started to read again.

London, Lavender Hill, 1 December, 1857
It wasn't really a decision to come here, still less to find work. I went for a walk because I wanted to get out of town. When I reached the fields and farms, I felt good and I fell asleep on the building site of the new park in Battersea. Finally, I asked if there was any work, and for a while I shovelled earth and pushed carts. And then they told me there was work in the porcelain factories by the Thames.

I went to work there.

I like this place.
I feel better.
The work with the porcelain is delicate and it does me good to concentrate.

London, Lavender Hill, 11 February, 1858
I found a room to rent in a widow's house, just over a mile from the factory. Her husband worked there. Some people who knew her told me about the room. Her name is Mrs Ashburn. She is elderly. She used to be a schoolteacher. She has books in her house.

I still don't really understand what is happening to me. Maybe I finally hit rock bottom, like I'd been trying to do, and maybe I'm starting to get better.

I came back to England more than four years ago and suddenly I have the feeling that I am seeing the world as it is, not merely through my own hallucinations.

I'm not under any illusions. I may be healing, but I'm definitely not healed. The forest is still part of the world as it is. But I can look at the other side.

I see the other side.

London, Lavender Hill, 3 June, 1858
It's getting hotter and hotter at the Battersea factory. I suffer in the heat and I've had fevers, but I still feel good. I hardly dare to write this, but the books I'm reading are starting to give me ideas. I surprised myself at the factory by thinking about a journey. Going away again.

Mrs Ashburn looked after me when I was ill. I hide my scars from her.

Mrs Ashburn did not have any children and I think I'm a sort of son to her. A son returned from the war. I lie to her. I pretend I'm fine whenever I feel bad. And pretending, although it's difficult sometimes, also helps me feel better. I don't lie to myself, only to her, and each time is a little step towards a small new remission.

She's not fooled. She listens to my lies like a mother to her child's. We pretend when it's difficult, so most of the time we talk about the books we are reading.

London, Lavender Hill, 11 July, 1858
Today is Sunday. I've just come back from a walk in town. The situation is taking on biblical proportions. The Thames is now just a trickle of shit and all of London seems spooked by the threat of a catastrophe. I am not giving into the panic of those people who are terrified by the toxic air, but it's true that the atmosphere in the streets is enough to make you imagine the strangest scenarios. As if the bad weather and the technical problems in the sewers

have become signs of something that has been rotten for a long time. I walked along the empty docks. On the way back to Lavender Hill, I made my decision. As if being able to bear this horror had confirmed that I was ready and that I had the strength to go through with it. I don't know where yet, but I have to leave. What worries me most is having to announce my decision to Mrs Ashburn. Coming back here, I wondered again what had become of them. If they were in London, hiding in houses to escape the stink. If they were like me, finding something calm and soothing in this deserted city. And I wondered what he was doing. Bowman. The sergeant would be at home in filthy, rotten London. And I shuddered as I imagined that I might see him, wandering the empty docks like me.

London, Lavender Hill, 18 July, 1858
In a few days, the rain swept away all the city's fears. The Thames began to flow again past the factory. But since the Great Stink began, my nightmares have come back. Several times I woke screaming and Mrs Ashburn is worried. And yet I interpret it differently this time, the return of my ghosts. They are telling me that I have to get away from here. I am going to work for a few weeks longer and put some money aside. I know now where I will go.

Bowman could no longer make out the tiny letters. The mare had fallen asleep and her belly rose and fell in a steady rhythm. The pioneers' campfires glowed. He lifted up the jug of hooch, looking up at the stars over the desert, listening to the howls of the coyotes come out from their dens to hunt.

In the morning, he let the convoy go. The mare was on her feet and had found some food along the riverbank. He unfolded the cloth and ate some porridge, then opened the journal while he waited for the horse to finish its meal.

*

Pacific Mail Steamship Company, SS California.
18 September, 1858
I didn't believe them until I was actually on board the boat and out at sea. Never could I have imagined that a ship of this size could move so fast. I walk on the main deck and the sea air reminds me of my first voyage on a Company vessel. But this time, I am not a soldier. Unlike Bowman, Collins and Bufford, I never was. It was normal that I ended up with the Company's chains around my ankles. Now I am leaving them behind me. In four days, I will land in New York.

I like this city, but I am waiting for only one thing: getting on the road.
I've thought of something. A real job. I am trying to find contacts.

New York, 2 October, 1858
The newspaper editors I met seemed interested in my idea, particularly when I explained that it was time to describe this country in a different way to Cooper and Irving. My accounts might be of interest to readers on the coast and could appear in the form of a regular column, which I would send east from the road. I've been told that the mail is increasingly safe and takes only a month to cross the country from east to west.
In my pocket is a train ticket to New Orleans. I leave tomorrow morning. I can't sleep.

The convoy had been gone for two hours when Bowman set off again. This time, he spared Penders' mare, letting her go at walking pace. She was faster than cattle anyway, and would catch up to the carts before night. He finished the hooch and shoved the empty jug into a saddlebag. That night, he passed an inn without stopping or worrying. Arthur Bowman, the notorious killer, was dead, and he was Erik Penders, an Englishman who had come to America to remake his life, a wandering correspondent for New York newspapers, a happy man without night-mares.

—⁓—⁓—⁓—

The camp was located at the foot of some round, arid hills. There was no water, so the pioneers made their animals drink from the barrels. Bowman passed alongside the carts until he found the one belonging to the Fitzpatricks. The other travellers greeted him cautiously, recognising him as the lone horseman who had been following them for the last two days. The young wife said hello to him and Bowman noticed that she was pregnant. Her husband walked over to him, caressed the mare's head, and led it to the barrel, where he let it drink, then filled Bowman's flasks.

"My wife would like to invite you to dinner, Mr Penders. Would you care to join us?"

Bowman shook his head. From his pocket, he took the cloth that had covered the porridge and handed it to the man. The woman rushed over, took the cloth and brought it back after wrapping some more food inside it. Bowman took out his purse and put a one-dollar coin on the bench of the cart, next to the empty hooch jug. He climbed up the nearest hill and stopped a little closer to the camp than he had the previous day.

Fitzpatrick brought him the alcohol and a bucket of oats for his horse.

"Your horse is looking better. That's a good mare you've got, really. I love horses. We used to have three on our farm in Cork. What's her name?"

Bowman looked at the mare.

"I don't know yet."

New Orleans, 1 November, 1858
This town is the strangest I've ever seen. A colonial capital trying to pass for a European city, in a semi-tropical climate.

I am working for the Southern Traveller, *which appears three times a week in Lafayette. I am their New Orleans correspondent. I sent my first article to New York, describing my train journey and I am awaiting a response.*

New Orleans, 28 January, 1859
I think again about the sepoy revolt which brought the India Company down . . . generations of soldiers certain that giving food to slaves was too good for them and that those savages were grateful to learn their masters' language. I am in New Orleans, amid colonists, and I feel worse and worse.

The commercial cynicism of the Americans is every bit as bad as that of the British. The plantation owners sell the children of their slaves to other rich owners as if they are horses or cattle. But behind this cruelty there is another logic than the market value of negroes. They separate their families to protect themselves from them. There are six times as many blacks as whites here. Even if the rich people in New Orleans think the place they have grown up is completely normal, they know that something is wrong. No guilt, no. But they do have doubts about the durability of their system, a formidable crucible of wealth. A flaw in their reasoning, which taints this hot, humid city with a sombre mood of menace. Just like London at the time of the Great Stink, the end of impunity seems inexorable. The city is beautiful. Here, the men speak softly, in even voices, and laugh in the same way. The madness shows beneath their laughter. They are as steeped in certainties as they are in fear.

Memphis, 13 April, 1859
I found some temporary work in an office of the Butterfield Mail. My latest articles on the South were rejected in New York. Only one appeared in the New York Tribune. *Since I left New Orleans, I have decided to buy a horse to explore the country. As soon as I have everything I need, and I have put some more money aside, I will get back on the road.*

Memphis, 5 May, 1859

I am leaving. My mare is a magnificent beast and my only regret is her name, Trigger. She does not answer to any other and I do not share the enthusiasm of her former owner, who was proud to say that she set off at a gallop like a bullet from a gun. I also bought a Winchester rifle because I will need to go hunting. I have everything I need now, and I leave tomorrow at dawn.

Bowman looked up from the journal and watched the mare sleeping beside him.

"Trigger?"

The horse opened its eyes and turned its head.

Little Rock, Arkansas, 15 May, 1859

After these first weeks of travelling along the Butterfield road, I am staying just one day in Little Rock. I leave tomorrow for the Ouachita Mountains.

Ouachita Mountains, July 1859

I have lost track of the days. I have been in the mountains for more than two months. I have not written anything about the Indians and the fur traders I've met and with whom I have lived. I am going to stay here until the first snow. I want to see the autumn and another season in these mountains. Then I can leave in peace, because I know that this place exists. I do not need anything else.

Fort Worth, Texas, December 1859

How disappointing to be back on the track with all its agitation, to be in soulless towns like Fort Worth. I will continue heading west, but now I go forward thinking only of the distance that separates me from the Ouachita Mountains. The track is a toxic place, full of rumours and suspicion. In Fort Worth, everyone is talking about a murder in a small town a few dozen miles from here, and the chatterboxes go on and on about the sordid details to captivate their credulous listeners. I will leave as soon as Trigger has had enough rest and food.

Pe'cos, Texas, 2 January, 1860
The river is beautiful and after the dry plains I have found some good hunting and a bit of solitude. I will be in El Paso in a week and, because I have heard so many people talk about it, I think I will cross the Mexican border.

It was night. Bowman put down the journal, ate some dried meat with the porridge, then leaned back against the saddle and started drinking. The next day, he went on, riding behind the convoy like a shadow, and in the evening he camped close to their carts, paying them for water, food and alcohol.

Penders described the Indians, the villages and the mountains of Mexico, his mood wavering between euphoria and disappointment as he stopped in various places and continued on his journey. He wrote more than he had in the United States and Bowman guessed that he was growing bored, in spite of those repeated phrases: *I feel good. I am going to stay here.* He noted details and impressions that Bowman recognised but had never been able to express. Bowman remade his own journey through Penders' eyes. The way he felt good in wide open spaces, the miles he travelled and the less and less often he thought about what he was leaving behind. Except that Penders was not yet travelling in pursuit of the killer. His itinerary illuminated only part of what Bowman had been through.

The next evening, when they stopped, Bowman spent a few minutes with the Fitzpatricks. The couple were heading towards the San Francisco area to meet up with other Irish people – family members who were already established there – in order to work with them. The young man admitted that he dreamed of raising horses. They tried asking their guest questions. They just wanted to know more about him, because the other pioneers in their convoy were worried by his presence. Their curiosity and their kindness troubled Bowman, who wondered if it was the result of his new identity, if Penders was a man who inspired more trust than Sergeant Bowman.

Bowman let Trigger graze with the cattle and made his little camp about sixty feet from the carts, leaning against some rocks, from where he could keep an eye on the animals and the convoy. He read the journal, continuing with Penders as he visited mountains, followed rivers and spoke with Indians he met on his journey, until the date of 17 February, 1860, in the town of Chihuahua, where his handwriting suddenly became confused and full of crossings-out.

For four days I have not been able to get up and even now I can barely write.

I don't know. It's impossible.

There was a murder in the town.

I saw a corpse pass by me on a cart, pulled by wailing men. All I remember is collapsing in the street. I woke up in the room of a guesthouse.

The screams and the visions have returned. I think I am mad. I thought I was healed. I saw a corpse pass like the ones in the forest. In Chihuahua, Mexico.

I do not have enough strength to keep writing.

I still can't stand up and I don't know how long I've been here. I tried to ask the owners of the guesthouse, but they speak only Spanish and don't understand me. I still don't know what happened and I still doubt that I really saw what I saw. My hallu- cinations are a daily event. I see them all again. They file past my bed at night, the Burmese sailors and the English soldiers.

Some Mexican soldiers came to interrogate me. One of them spoke English but they didn't understand anything I said to them. What I said made no more sense to them than it did to me. I do not let anyone approach me. They must not see my scars. The nightmare has started again. The murder really did happen. In

*the same way. The local authorities are clueless. My presence,
and what I told them, have made me a suspect. I am not mad and
I must get away from this place.*

The border is only one day's ride away.

El Paso, 19 February, 1860
*Physically, I feel a little better, but I dare not sleep anymore
because I wake up screaming. I spend my nights trying to understand and the less I want to believe it, the more I am forced to
surrender to the evidence. I saw the corpse in Mexico. I am not
the only one to have come this way. There were ten of us. One of
the others must have crossed the Atlantic.*

This was followed by a list of ten names.

Bowman's was at the top of it, underlined. Below were those of
Collins and Bufford, also underlined. At the bottom, he had added:
"One of those three." And again written down the names of Bowman,
Collins and Bufford. Strangely enough, Penders had written his name
among those of his former fellow prisoners, as if he too were a possible
suspect. He didn't know that Collins and Bufford were dead.

Penders had stayed in El Paso for a week. He was still there in late
February. Bowman remembered that he had been hired at the Paterson
ranch back then. It was not until three weeks later that he had heard
about the murder in Las Cruces, whereas Penders, living close by, had
heard the news almost immediately. When Penders went to Las Cruces,
Bowman was going back and forth between the Paterson ranch and
Reunion, where he was visiting Alexandra.

He read one last entry before the letters started getting mixed up
with the night. Penders' handwriting was tightly spaced and regular
once again.

The Santa Fe track, March 1860
*They killed another man in Las Cruces and now I am on the
northern road. I have only one hope now, the last thing keeping*

me going: to find the killer and put an end to the slaughter that is starting again. I cannot presume anything. Nine other men survived along with me. Collins and Bufford were already capable of this before our captivity, that's for sure, but I can't imagine them travelling alone across the world.

Who else could it be but Bowman?

Tonight, I am thinking again about Edmund Peavish, the one they called the preacher. Of all the men I knew, he is the one I would like beside me now.

That's not true.

There is another.

Peavish could comfort me, but in my situation the presence of only one other man could really reassure me – Sergeant Arthur Bowman himself.

I must find his courage within myself. So I can find him.

The next morning, Bowman saddled up Trigger as the pioneers were breaking camp. When the carts set off, he rode alongside the convoy, caught up to the Fitzpatricks' equipage and let his horse walk next to them. They looked at him: the pregnant young woman blushed and placed her hands over her belly, while her husband smiled and touched his hat before turning back to the road, sitting up a little taller.

Penders had explained it to him, so Bowman understood what they wanted from him. The Fitzpatricks were scared. The presence of this man reassured them. Having the strength to pretend, Penders wrote, was the beginning of remission.

2

Colorado, April 1860
I am two men.

*One flees his nightmares and at the same time chases them
away. The other, hidden, pursues his dreams in silence and does
not want to give up.*

*I pass through towns with reasons to be fragile, temporary
camps in the mountains. I do not pass through them, I pass above
or below them. I am the flood of pioneers, without being able to
tell anyone where I am going.*

The families, about thirty people in all, were travelling without a guide,
and they had accepted his presence. After riding beside the Fitzpatricks
for one day, Bowman had moved towards the front of the convoy. The
pioneers were neither lost nor incapable, but this horseman was of
another kind altogether, armed with a good rifle and scanning the horizon with a sentry's concentration that made them feel safe. At night,
Bowman continued to sleep at a distance from the camp. They brought
him food and drink and looked after his mare. In the mornings, he
went back to the head of the convoy, riding a hundred yards ahead of
the others, choosing the best paths, looking for places to camp for the
night. When they encountered other travellers, it was to him that
the travellers spoke. Some of the pioneers avoided looking at him or
speaking to him, but they all accepted his new position. The anxiety he
inspired went hand in hand with his usefulness. And he did not ask
for any money.

Whenever the environment was conducive, young Fitzpatrick
borrowed a horse and went off hunting with Bowman. He was a good
shot and had an old American army Springfield, a percussion-cap rifle,

more modern than the muskets Bowman had used in India but rudimentary compared to Penders' Winchester. They saw packs of wild horses on the plains and the young man pursued them for the thrill of galloping with them. He explained to Bowman how to capture them, how to recognise a well-built foal and choose the best females. He watched the packs and amused himself by matchmaking the horses, choosing the stallions and mares and describing what their foals would be like, then selecting from among these imaginary horses, constructing genealogical trees in order to produce, from fifty horses seen in a little valley, the best animal that the pack could possibly produce.

"That would be a magnificent beast, Mr Penders. The rich people in the east and the west would pay a fortune for it."

Bowman listened to him. Fitzpatrick smiled, joking about his wife and their future child, his very own foal. They brought back antelope. The pioneers cooked and shared it in the evenings, taking Bowman his ration, which he ate alone.

Wyoming, April 1860
The beauty of these places is cruel. I cannot stay here or look at them for too long without being overcome by the desire to give up. And yet I am the only one forcing myself to go on. This country would not change any more if a murderer died than if a man decided to live in one of these deserted forests.
The road to the Ouachita Mountains is forbidden to me now.
Damn you, Bowman. I exist only for you now.

The dark line of the Sierra Nevada barred the convoy's horizon now. After leaving St Louis three months before, the pioneers' savings were dwindling. At inns, the families began to trade their possessions – clothes, tools, sometimes a piece of jewellery – for a few rations of vegetables, a packsaddle, or the repair of a cart. When they stopped, Bowman remained apart and sent Fitzpatrick to buy alcohol for him, adding a few extra coins.

"If you find something nice for your wife."

Aileen Fitzpatrick was increasingly tired and in the daytime she rested in the shade of the cart, swayed and shaken by the bumps and holes of the track. Her husband worried about her and began to suggest that they should maybe stop in Carson City, the next big stopover at the foot of the Sierra. Maybe they should even let the convoy go without them, give his wife time to recover, then wait for another convoy before they started on their way again. Maybe even wait for the baby to be born before they continued . . . But for the others, their savings did not allow them to stop for very long. His wife repeated that she was fine, that it was just the heat, and that they must keep going, that the cool mountain air would get her back on her feet. And yet every day she grew weaker. The child was due in two months. Other women from the convoy looked after her during the stopovers, but their skills would soon not be enough. As the Fitzpatricks sadly admitted, their journey was in jeopardy.

> I crossed over the last pass in the Rockies. Now I am heading west as if into the void. Along the path, I find traces of his passage. No new corpses, but the vague memory of a blond-haired Englishman travelling alone. Sometimes behind me, sometimes ahead. Perhaps we have already passed each other several times. His itinerary makes no sense. He slows down and I pass him, then he leaps ahead and I suddenly learn that I am several days behind. Soon I will be in Salt Lake City and I wonder where he will stop. What event or place will decide that his voyage is over? He will go to the Pacific and I sometimes think that Bowman is a giant, that he will dive into the ocean and swim all the way to Japan, China, India, going all around the world back to our forest, and that only there will I find him. What force can oppose Bowman? Who is capable of stopping him?
>
> If that monster is still a man, then something will stop him. I am that force. I have to be. Because death is not enough: Bowman is eternal, he has never been afraid of it. But neither have I. We are no longer alive.

Come back to life, Bowman. Die. Or wait for me.

Today I am going to Salt Lake. This town is too big for me to pass by. I must go in and search for him.

I would like to give up now. Go back to my mountains.

Salt Lake City, 22 April, 1860
Bowman was here at the same time as me. Never, in all these weeks, have I been so close to him. I will get back on the track to catch him up in the coming days or hours. The end of my journey is near. The end of his crimes, too, and perhaps of my nightmare.

——— ⋙ — ⋙ — ⋙ ———

Carson City had only one doctor for a few hundred inhabitants. Fitzpatrick borrowed Penders' mare and went off to look for him as soon as the convoy stopped on the outskirts of the town, with all the other pioneers preparing to cross the Sierra Nevada. He came back with the doctor, perched on a mule, as night was falling. People brought lamps to the Fitzpatricks' cart.

Jonathan waited, pacing around, while Bowman, for the first time in months, stayed outside the town without doing anything – neither hiding, nor seeking information – in the middle of a camp that resembled the one he set fire to at Bent's Fort. Like the young Irishman, having nothing better to do, he waited for the doctor's diagnosis. Half an hour later, the doctor emerged from the cart, wiping his forehead. The town was barely any cooler than the plains, and more humid. Clouds of mosquitoes buzzed around them, drawn by the heat of their faces.

"There's no reason to worry too much, young man. No complications, no infection. But it could happen if your wife doesn't get some rest. She will give birth normally, on one condition: you must stop travelling until the baby is born."

Jonathan went to join his wife. Bowman offered money to the doctor, who refused.

"I only ask for money from people who can afford it. If I needed a doctor, I hope he would extend the same courtesy to me."

He got back on his mule.

"Are you travelling with them?"

Bowman shrugged his shoulders in a non-committal way, like a sort of hesitation or a silent question.

"If you could try to convince them, that would be helpful. I know these pioneers: they never want to stop. You wouldn't believe how many of them have died because they didn't want to stop and recover for a week. If they don't listen to reason, those young folks will lose their child, and I can't guarantee the mother's safety either. She is very weak."

"What should they do?"

"Nothing. Apart from going up into the hills, where the air is better. Up by the lake is a good place, and she shouldn't go any further than that in her condition."

"The lake?"

"They can't miss it. The road goes right past it and it's twenty miles long. This time of year, that's the best place for her."

The convoy joined with some others and, the next morning, forty pairs of cattle left Carson City in unison – nearly two hundred pioneers, following a line of horsemen who had agreed to clear their way and escort them. The Fitzpatricks' carriage was the last to leave, going as slowly as possible in order to spare Aileen. Behind them came Arthur Bowman. The line of carts began to spread out in the curves of the track, like a column of ants moving its eggs. At each bend in the road, the air felt a little cooler. Jonathan led his cattle cautiously, letting the other carriages move ahead into the distance.

After the first pass, they came to the vast Lake Tahoe, its miles of blue water reflecting the clouds up above. Aileen refused to listen to her husband's protestations and insisted on sitting next to him so she could see this landscape. The abundance of colours and water, after crossing the plains from Salt Lake City, were beyond comprehension, and none of the other carts ahead of them – just like the thousands that had already passed by – stopped here. The convoys continued their way westward, refusing to be diverted from their objectives by the beauty of the mountains. Bowman thought about the Mormons who had built their town in the hollow of an arid valley, about the citizens of Reunion living in the scree of Texas and desperately seeking water for their farms, about all those villages and camps chosen for absurd reasons in places without any resources or attractions, and compared them with this place, where everything seemed ready-made for human habitation. He wondered if Penders' mountains resembled these.

In the middle of the day, the carts that had been travelling with the Fitzpatricks since St Louis came to a halt by the side of the lake. In a rush to join the rest of the pioneers and the line of horsemen, the families took only a few minutes to say goodbye to the young couple. Aileen Fitzpatrick gave a letter for a friend to pass on to their family in Rio Vista, in the San Francisco area, explaining the reason for their delay and promising to see them after the birth of the child and before the end of summer. Everyone wished them good luck and soon, all that remained by the waterside was their cart. Aileen and Jonathan Fitzpatrick looked at Bowman on his mare.

"You should join them, Mr Penders."

Bowman climbed down from the saddle, led Trigger to the lake and let her drink, then walked back to the cart, putting the old hat back on his head.

"What are you going to do?"

The young man stood up tall.

"It's a good season. We'll find a place to live for three months. There's good hunting round here, and plenty of plants and berries to pick. We're used to this kind of life, Mr Penders, we'll be fine. If we hurry, we could even have a garden by the start of the summer. It'll just take a few weeks."

Bowman looked at the last few carts disappearing up the path.

"A few weeks?"

Aileen turned to her husband.

"And there are a few camps around the lake. We could live with other people, so you won't be on your own when I can't do anything anymore."

She smiled, her forehead and cheeks still pale. Her husband looked at Bowman.

"You see? We're in the clear. This place is perfect. Aileen will give birth by the lake and afterwards we'll be on our way with another convoy. We'll make it to San Francisco long before the autumn. If you're over that way, you'll have to come and see us once we're settled in."

Bowman looked at the young man, who was trying to maintain a firm, unwavering voice in front of his wife. He got back in the saddle. His eyes lingered on Aileen Fitzpatrick's swollen belly.

"I don't need to follow the convoy. I'll leave once you're settled."

—ᗣᗣ—ᗣᗣ—ᗣᗣ—

The seekers of gold and money from Mount Davidson, about forty miles east of the lake and Carson City, had not yet made it here. In the little camps that they visited, local inhabitants, before even saying hello, asked if they were prospectors, then spat on the ground, hoping that no-one would find any gold in this region. The land had been bought from the Paiute Indians by the government of the Utah Territory, which in itself meant nothing as the Indians did not consider themselves the owners of the land and the sums paid were ridiculous anyway. An office in Carson City registered plots of land, marked off their borders, fixed the prices, delivered the ownership deeds, and banked the money.

An old man, who stank of rotting meat and said he had lived in the Sierra for more than fifteen years, told them not to worry and to tell the representatives of the State to go screw themselves.

"Just settle down wherever you want. The people who run the

Territory are a bunch of varmints who'd be better off if they just left the mountain alone. I came here in '44, with Frémont and Carson. I haven't moved since and I'd like them to come ask me for my deeds of ownership. I melted it down to make bullets, if anyone wants to read it with their own eyes!"

On the eastern shore of the lake was a series of log cabins, spaced at intervals of one or two miles, filled with dogs and children, cooking pots over fires, drying hides and furs, and all along it the smell of rotting carcasses. The families and the solitary trappers were dressed in a mixture of hides and cloths; the children had long hair and the men beards; the women wore knee-length dresses. Half wild, silent and suspicious whenever the cart passed, they were like something halfway between Indians and white people, an intermediate race in the process of adapting to its environment.

They headed towards the southern part of the lake, passing by one last camp. They greeted a woman with children clinging to her legs, who responded with a hostile stare, and then rode another two or three miles without encountering anyone. They began to look for a place to set up their camp. A little further ahead, they spotted a stretch of green. A stream flowed into a little cove, about fifty yards in diameter and not very deep. The water there was transparent; sunlight illuminated its bottom, where fish swam between aquatic plants. At the end of the cove, the blue became darker and the water suddenly much deeper.

Reeds grew all around the cove, then a thick grass, and then the first trees, before the slope got steeper and the dense forest began. Redwoods, junipers, aspens and, higher up, sequoias. Fitzpatrick pulled on the reins and the cattle halted. Bowman crossed the stream with Trigger, riding in a wide circle up to the trees, as if he were simultaneously tracing and following the border of a plot of land. On the slope, between tree trunks, he came to a halt and looked at the clearing and the little peat bog around the cove. He stayed there for a few minutes while Jonathan and Aileen got down from their cart and approached the water. Bowman joined them, climbed down from the saddle and took the Winchester from its holster. He used the lever to arm the rifle.

Aileen and Jonathan watched him, uncomprehending. Bowman lifted his gun, pressed the butt against his shoulder and aimed at the mountain, setting his sights on the trunk of a giant redwood three hundred yards away. He took his time, put his finger on the trigger, and fired. The sound of the gunshot ricocheted from the mountain, seeming to turn around and come back to them before disappearing over the lake. Bowman lowered the Winchester and, with Jonathan and Aileen, looked at the pale mark on the trunk of the tree where the bark had been removed. He swivelled northward and, in a single movement, took aim at another tree near the lake. He fired again. Aileen Fitzpatrick gave a little cry of surprise and fear. Another pale mark on another tree two hundred yards away. Bowman handed the rifle to Jonathan, who smiled, turned to the south and aimed at a fir tree on the edge of the clearing. He, too, sent fragments of wood flying, and all three of them admired the triangle they had just traced, in the middle of which they stood. Aileen took the gun from her husband's hands.

"What are you doing?"

She moved the lever, turned to the water, put the butt to her shoulder and aimed at the sky.

"Aileen! Not in your condition."

She smiled and fired a fourth gunshot, at a forty-five-degree angle, straight into the blue above Lake Tahoe.

They took down the tarp and hoop from the cart and transformed them into a tent, in which they put the couple's equipment and belongings. The Fitzpatricks possessed almost nothing. Apart from an old wool mattress, they had no furniture at all. They arranged the bed for Aileen, who refused to lie down and insisted on helping to set up the camp. There was only one thing in their cart of which Jonathan was proud: an old saddle. His wife mocked him:

"He bought that in Independence. It's no use at all and he paid far too much for it."

Jonathan paid no heed. He looked at Bowman.

"It's a good saddle. I can repair it."

"He bought that before he even found a mattress!"

Jonathan continued speaking to Bowman:

"Mr Penders, when we have finished setting up camp, a few days from now, I'll have a favour to ask you."

Bowman rolled a barrel over to the tent and returned.

"You can take the mare. But don't break your neck trying to bring a horse back when your wife is going to give birth two months from now."

Fitzpatrick grinned.

"They're magnificent, Mr Penders. I have to take one with me to San Francisco."

The tent was ready. They took the cart and the cattle to the edge of the forest, loaded some stones onto the bed of the cart and then dug a hole in the earth, large enough to cook big game and smoke meat. Around this they built a hearth with the stones and then dragged over some dead trunks, which they cut up with an axe.

It had been a long day. Lying on her bed, Aileen watched the sun set over the lake. Jonathan and Bowman washed their arms and faces.

"I'm going to take a look around, see if I can shoot something before nightfall."

Jonathan rushed ahead of him.

"I'll take care of it, Mr Penders. You've done enough already."

"You don't know the area and it's nearly dark. I just want to take a look around."

"There's a good hour of daylight left. I won't go far, and anyway we have enough to eat for tonight."

Jonathan kissed his wife, and Bowman handed him the Winchester.

"At least take this."

Jonathan walked off towards the mountain, stopped at the edge of the woods and yelled while waving his hand before disappearing between the trees.

Bowman lit the fire and sat next to it. He started to take apart the Springfield to clean it. The air was growing cool and, in the dim light, above the rushes, insects fluttered. Frogs came out of the water and fish swam to the surface, chasing dragonflies. Aileen came out of the tent, a blanket over her shoulders, her hair dishevelled and her face drawn. She sat on a stone next to Bowman. She was silent for a while and Bowman, glancing up from the dismantled rifle, looked at her on the sly. Her hair must have been blonde when she was a child. The roots were dark and only the tips, in the light of the setting sun, still appeared pale. She still had the smooth, round face of an adolescent.

"It was kind of you to stay with us while we found this place, Mr Penders. When I saw it, I even wondered why we have to go to Rio Vista. But in any case, we'll be fine here until the birth."

She might not even be twenty years old.

"Why are the two of you travelling alone?"

Aileen pulled the blanket up to the back of her neck.

"Jonathan's parents are dead. We're going to join his uncle and aunt. They left Cork five years ago. My parents were too old and they didn't want to leave the farm. Jonathan worked in a factory every day for three years to save up the money for the trip. His uncle sent us a bit of cash too."

"Your husband is a brave boy."

"Yes."

She looked up at the mountain. Shadow was spreading over the lake and their clearing, rising up the slopes.

"Mr Penders?"

Bowman put the rifle back together and glanced up. She looked at him, hesitated, and turned towards the fire.

"I was a bit suspicious of you to start with. I wanted to apologise. I just had trouble trusting you."

Bowman put the rifle down and took a little tobacco pouch and Penders' pipe from his pocket.

"No need to apologise. It's normal."

She smiled at him, but Bowman could tell there was something else. While he waited for her to go on, he stuffed tobacco in his pipe and lit a match.

"Can I ask you a question?"

"Of course."

"When you arrived on the first day, you looked like you were in a bad way. Lost or something. You kept repeating your name."

Bowman said nothing. The young woman wriggled on the stone, searching for her next words, her arms wrapped around her big belly.

"As if it wasn't really yours, and you wanted to get used to it. And then you went off to read. And there's your hand, and that scar on your forehead."

"What do you want to know?"

She looked down.

"We haven't asked you any questions, and if you don't want to talk, we respect that. But I wanted to know if there's something you're hiding."

The peaks of the Sierra were turning red in the sunset and the lake had darkened. The ballet of insects and amphibians became frenetic.

"What I'm hiding is not important. When I'm gone, it won't do you any good to know. The only thing I can tell you is that Erik Penders is not my real name."

She looked at him shyly.

"What is your real name?"

"Arthur Bowman."

"And the other name, why did you keep repeating it?"

"It was the name of someone I knew. He was killed."

Aileen stood up, one hand on her belly.

"I have to go and lie down now. Thank you, Mr Bowman."

"I didn't kill him, if that's what's worrying you."

"I'm not worried anymore."

She went into the tent and lay down. Bowman looked up at the mountain. It was almost night now.

Bowman took Penders' journal from his pocket and thumbed through it. Peavish's little magic trick did not change anything. Erik Penders had died in vain. Arthur Bowman would follow the same path and fall into the same error.

He threw Penders' journal on the embers and watched it burn, then threw all the wood on top of it that he could. The flames rose ten feet high. They could probably be seen from the other side of the lake and far off in the forest. He moved away from the heat of the blaze. Aileen's voice reached him from the tent.

"Isn't he back yet?"

Bowman tried to smile and the light of the flames painted a disturbing mask on his face. The young woman shivered and did not hear what he said:

"He'll be back, don't worry."

Two hours passed.

There was no point going out to look for him in the middle of the night. Nor was there any question of leaving Aileen alone. Bowman stood guard near the fire, keeping it stoked all night.

One hour before dawn, he saddled Trigger. Aileen was up. She hadn't slept a wink either and Bowman did not know what to do to soothe her fears.

"You should go and lie down. You can't do anything in your condition. I'm going to look for help and we'll find him. I'll be back soon."

He climbed into the saddle and left at a gallop, following the shore of the lake to the last camp they had seen the night before. It was still dark when he knocked at the door of the cabin. A man's voice answered from the other side:

"Who the hell is that?"

"We passed by yesterday with a cart. The family with the pregnant woman. Her husband went out hunting and he didn't come back last night."

"I'm going to open the door. But if there's any trouble, I've got a rifle in my hand. You'd better not be armed!"

"I don't have a gun. I'm stepping back. You can open it now."

The doorframe creaked. Bowman made out the outline of a man in long johns and saw the gleam of a rifle barrel.

"What is all this?"

"It's the young lad you saw go past yesterday. He went out hunting last night and he hasn't come back. His wife is at the camp, a bit further on. She can't move because she's pregnant. I need some help. Someone who knows the mountain."

A woman appeared behind the man, holding a lamp. She lit a match and the light illuminated the cabin's interior. She shoved her husband out of the way and moved in front of him.

"And you left her all alone?"

"I didn't have any choice. I need a guide to go into the forest. I have money."

"Don't be ridiculous!"

She turned to her husband.

"Joseph Ervin, saddle your horse and get a move on. I'm going to look after the girl and you'll go with this gentleman. Put your rifle down now!"

Ervin leaned his rifle against the wall.

"Where did you set up camp?"

"Three miles from here. There's a stream and a little cove."

The man spat on the ground.

"It's full of crevasses around here. We should go and get old MacBain – he knows it best."

"MacBain?"

"He's the oldest man here, and his damn dog will be useful."

The old man they had met when they arrived, who had told them to settle wherever they wanted.

"Can you go to the camp? I'll fetch the old man."

The woman told him not to worry, and Bowman climbed back in the saddle.

By the time they left the camp – Bowman, Ervin and old MacBain with his dog – it had been daylight for several minutes.

The day was over and the sun had vanished behind the mountains when they returned, with Jonathan Fitzpatrick's body lying across Trigger's saddle. Aileen did not stop screaming until the middle of the

467

night, when she collapsed with exhaustion. The next morning, Mrs Ervin found her motionless on her bed and lifted up the blood-soaked sheet. They harnessed the cart as quickly as possible, but when Bowman arrived six hours later in Carson City, there was no point looking for the doctor. Woman and child were both dead.

—ɯɯ—ɯɯ—ɯɯ—

Ervin helped Bowman dig a grave for the two bodies, by the side of the clearing, facing the same way as the gunshot Aileen had fired over Lake Tahoe. Joseph Ervin had forgotten his prayers a long time ago, but he said a few words, throwing in the word "Lord" whenever his mind went blank. His wife threw a bouquet of mountain flowers on the pile of earth, and soon Bowman was the only one left by the side of the lake, with the cart, two cattle, his mare and a stained mattress with hundreds of flies swarming over it. He relit the fire and threw the mattress on top. Then he sat next to it, put his papers, pen and ink on his legs, and contemplated the flames and the column of black smoke rising from the burning wool. The smell was unbearable, but he stayed there, unmoving, holding all his letters, the corners of the pages lifting up in the heat.

Then Bowman abandoned the camp, went back to Carson City, entered the office of the Express Mail Company, and headed back east to Salt Lake City, armed with an old percussion-cap Springfield rifle. He slept the first night by the side of the road and, when he woke up, saw the Express Mail stagecoach speed past, drawn by ten horses. Inside it was his little saddlebag and about fifty pages: everything he had written, from his little hut in London until his last letter to Alexandra Desmond:

> Alexandra,
> Rather than burning everything I've written, I'm sending it to Reunion. I don't know who will find these letters one day, now you're no longer there. Maybe there's one last citizen there and

he'll send them on to you or read them before burning them, like I should have done. But I didn't want to know where the ashes were.

I arrived on the shore of Lake Tahoe, in the Sierra Nevada. If you had continued travelling across this country and you had seen this place, I feel sure this is where you would have stopped.

I just buried another dream. That of a young woman, her husband and their unborn child.

My road ends here. I won't leave again. The killer has disappeared. I won't disappear by going after him. You are somewhere in France and all I have to offer you is an image, before I send these pages along the road, so that they can make the exact opposite journey to the one I've made since I first met you.

We are two dreams who each retain a memory of the other.

I borrowed the name of the man I was looking for, while I came to understand that I was still alive. That miracle is of a sadness I cannot yet measure. I owe it to a young man who liked to gallop with wild horses, and to his young wife who didn't care what I was called. The only ones left who know my real name are you and the preacher.

I have loved you since I first saw you.

Your old soldier

When he reached the plains where he had gone hunting with Jonathan Fitzpatrick, Bowman left the track and went in search of the pack of wild horses.

3

Joseph Ervin, who was washing himself in the lake, looked up when he heard the sound of horses. He walked up to the path and greeted the Englishman who had disappeared two weeks before. Bowman was as dirty as his mare, tired and covered in dust. Behind him, in a line, were two horses, a male and a female. Bowman nodded to him.

"We took care of the cattle. Where did you go?"

Bowman raised his hand without turning around and continued on his way to the camp. Ervin's wife came out of the cabin and watched Bowman ride into the distance.

"He came back?"

"He won't leave again."

"How would you know?"

"You can tell."

"Go and finish cleaning up, Mr Know-It-All."

Nothing had moved. The cattle were in the clearing by the waterside, kept there by the thick grass more than by the ropes tied to trees. The empty cart, the sagging tent, the cold hearth and the two graves. The flowers had been blown away by the wind or eaten by animals. The little hills of earth were starting to level off.

Bowman tied the two mustangs to a juniper and set to work. First he fashioned two cross-beams from some branches, then cut down two young trees. It took him three days to build an enclosure big enough for his three horses. That evening, by the fire, he started repairing Fitzpatrick's old saddle. Near the enclosure, he chose a spot for his hut, leaning against a rock that would form the first wall.

Joseph Ervin gave him advice – and a helping hand when he had the time. He and his wife were tanners, and they had been here for seven years. First, they had tried to sell furs, but the big companies like the Bent and St Vrain and the Western Fur Trade Company had monopolised the market. So Ervin had specialised in the fabrication of leather, which he tanned with white oak bark, not as strong a tannin as black oak, but one which made the leather more supple. Their cabin was rudimentary, but the quality of their leather improved and they started selling their products at a good price to a trader in Carson City. Third-generation Americans, Ervin and his wife had met and married in Pennsylvania before trying their luck in the West. Joseph had no interest in farming, and he did not share his contemporaries' dreams of making a fortune from gold. He looked out at Lake Tahoe and said:

"Hell, if this isn't the only wealth that matters, they can hang me."

Seeing the Fitzpatricks' graves, he scratched his head.

"Better to die here than at the bottom of a mine, digging gold. At least they saw it before they passed away."

In exchange for their help, the Ervins were allowed to use the cattle whenever they needed. In the end, Bowman offered to sell them the animals. As the tanners could not pay him, Bowman made a deal with them: they would help him build a bigger corral and, before the end of the summer, Joseph would go with him to capture more horses.

"What are you planning to do with all these horses?"

"A stud farm."

"Here?"

The hut resembled a small fort, a dozen feet wide, with thick walls made from trunks with the bark stripped off that gave the impression that there must be no space left inside. There were two windows: one looked out on the horses' enclosure, the other on the lake. The roof was also made of logs, covered with bark strips and earth. Soon, grass began to grow on it. Bowman built another little shelter against his house – four posts and a bark roof – under which he put the cart and the tools. In his hut, he kept all the Fitzpatricks' more useful belongings, most of them for the kitchen, with a few other objects that he had decided to keep arranged on a shelf. A framed photograph of the couple, posing proudly in front of their new cart, taken in St Louis before their departure. Aileen's sewing things, an old razor that smooth-faced Jonathan could not have used very often, a medallion, an embroidery, their wedding rings which he had not wanted to bury with them, a trousseau of clothes and cloth nappies for a newborn. He hadn't been able to bring himself to throw that out either.

He gave the clothes to his neighbours. A shirt of Jonathan's to Joseph, a skirt of Aileen's shortened for Mrs Ervin, a pair of shoes for Vernon, their eldest son, who was twelve. The tanners had three children – two boys and a girl – little savages who didn't speak much and who hung around Bowman's camp, worked with their parents and spent the rest of their time in the woods. Vernon was already a good hunter and set traps all over the mountain, bringing in a bit of money with his mink and sable furs.

Once he was settled, Bowman began to take care of the horses. For several days he observed them. Their behaviour, their reactions to Trigger, the way they had accepted captivity. He had chosen the stallion and the mare by trying to remember Jonathan's advice. Although his main intention for the animals was reproduction, he still wanted to train them.

The male was not the dominant stallion in the pack – he was still too young – but he seemed destined for this role when Bowman spotted him among the other horses. His physical constitution seemed to push him naturally towards that status, and Bowman felt he had the ambition too.

The mare was as calm and indifferent as Trigger. When Bowman had captured her, she had not put up much resistance once she had been separated from the pack, but she had faced him in order to understand his intentions. It was not that the horse was resigned to its fate, but it had gauged Bowman's determination.

The stallion had to be tamed, albeit gently. With the mare, he had to make a deal.

Penders' horse let them eat beside it. Trigger had become used to the comfort of not having to find her own food, and she no longer sought to defend her territory. And the stallion liked Trigger.

In mid-June, Bowman began working with the stallion on a lead rein. He had been living next to Lake Tahoe for almost two months and he had got into the habit of washing in the lake every morning. He had set up a wooden block next to the cove and he hung his clothes on it and threw himself naked into the water. On this piece of tree trunk, he had put a mirror he'd found among the Fitzpatricks' belongings, and he used Penders' razor to shave himself.

His letters had reached Texas long ago. If Alexandra Desmond were still in Reunion, with the money he had left her, she would already have had time to take a stagecoach and come here. Perhaps she needed more time to make her decision and settle her affairs before leaving. As when he had waited for Peavish on the Salt Lake road, he kept giving her more time until he no longer believed she would come, postponing his departure for the plains. He began to cut down trees for the second enclosure. Once he had all the wood, stripped of bark and neatly stored, he hammered in the stakes and put up the first crosspieces. Joseph had told him that, with the heat, it would soon become impossible to capture mustangs.

They prepared to leave, Joseph with his workhorse – a half-breed, still young enough to gallop, heavy but robust – and Vernon on Trigger, who was less difficult to handle than the newly broken mare, which Bowman rode. They were armed with the Springfield and the Ervins' Colt rifle. The Winchester had been lost in the crevasse where they found Jonathan's body. They left Mrs Ervin in charge of looking after the animals and keeping an eye on Bowman's property.

With his remaining five dollars, Bowman bought all the food he could in Carson City, some extra flasks and some rope. They left the town in early July and, on the road, Bowman offered to pay Joseph half of what he received for the animals during the first two seasons. Ervin was taking a risk. The capture of horses was dangerous and even if Bowman seemed to have a good eye, he still knew nothing about stud-farming. Ervin did not think about it for long, but held out his hand.

"A few weeks away from my wife . . . that's the best contract I've signed since our wedding day."

When they met a stagecoach speeding towards Carson City, Bowman stopped and watched it go past, glancing inside. Three days later, they reached the land where the wild horses roamed. Their objective was to bring back one more male and at least five mares. For two horsemen – plus Vernon to look after the animals they captured – the task was possible but ambitious. They thought it would take them about three weeks. They were not only going to capture horses; they had to closely track the pack in order to spot the best animals. Because it was not just a question of taking whichever ones they could get. They had to select them according to Fitzpatrick's methods.

"Some men shoot them. They injure their necks and wait until they're tired before capturing them. If you're a good shot, it saves time, and if you kill them . . . well, there are always other horses."

Bowman refused point blank and Joseph never mentioned it again.

The pack's territory extended over many hundreds of acres. First they had to find where the horses were, going back westward towards the mountains, where the mustangs found their food. While the heat and dryness made this task more difficult, the horses could not stay away for very long from grassy areas and watering holes. Once they were on the horses' tracks, they found a place to set up a base camp. They needed water and enough land to build a makeshift enclosure, which Vernon would take charge of looking after. They had been away from the lake for a week when Bowman and Joseph got up one morning to capture the first animals. Vernon remained behind at the camp with the new mare, who was not yet tame enough to pursue mustangs.

Bowman did not find the pack he had followed that first time, but he came across other, larger groups that came together and separated as and when they happened to meet or when they fought over a grassy area. The rolling hills made their task more arduous, but as they had hoped, when a pack ran away from them, all they had to do was wait until it returned in search of food. Ervin, while he didn't know much about horses either, was a good hunter. He knew how to use the wind, follow tracks, read passages and choose the right spot to ambush an animal.

Four days later, they returned to the base camp with three mustangs, all of them mares. After one day of training them with a lead rope, the horses, which had struggled furiously during their capture, followed docilely. They had also killed an antelope, stayed with Vernon long enough to get their strength back, then left the boy alone again. They had to move quickly now. In a few days, the captured animals would have recovered from their fear and their fatigue, and once they became really hungry, Vernon and a few ropes would not be enough to prevent them escaping. If they became too nervous, he would have to lead them out one by one, tie them carefully to the saddle of the new mare, and take them to find some grazing land.

On the fifteenth day, they captured two more mares.

"Let's take them back to the camp. We'll come here again to get the male. We can't stay here too long."

The heat was becoming overpowering, food and water too rare; their exhausted mounts risked injuring themselves. And despite the confidence he felt in his son, Joseph was starting to worry about Vernon. On nights when he heard wolves, Ervin didn't sleep, even though they had left the Springfield at the camp and though Vernon was capable of shooting a sparrow at a hundred feet.

When they got back to camp, they had captured only two more mares and still had no stallion. The boy was waiting for them. He had a big bump on his head, a black eye and his shirt was in tatters. Sitting by the campfire, he explained to them how he had gone out with a mare, which had tried to escape. It had dragged him over the stones for twenty yards, but he had not let go of the rope.

"She hadn't eaten yet, so I reckon she was tired, and she just gave up."

Joseph hammered on his son's back with his fist, laughing loudly and proud as could be. The next day, they decided that Bowman would leave on his own. If the mares escaped, they would have done all that work for nothing, and Bowman did not have a single dollar left to stock up for a new expedition. The mustangs were everywhere on the plains, but it cost money to hunt them. It would take him a whole year to save up the money, and he'd have to find work in Carson City.

Bowman went out alone in pursuit of a stallion and found a pack two days later. He followed this pack for another day. He needed a well-built male, but with a character different to the one he already had. A strong horse with a calm temperament. A humble mustang, to balance the pride and arrogance of his first stallion.

This is what Jonathan Fitzpatrick had told him: *You have to choose opposing characters, Mr Penders. To breed racehorses, you always follow the same line: size, muscles and speed. But to breed the best horse in the world, what matters is its character. So you have to build a personality. Pride, because that's important, and also humility when necessary. You have to mix them, Mr Penders.*

In the end, he chose an Appaloosa with a coat like the negative of a night sky: white with a scattering of black stars. Bowman watched it for another day, following its movements, memorising its reactions when the pack went into a gallop or went to drink or stopped to eat.

He waited until the end of the day. The pack had roamed a long way and the mustangs were tired. They were gathered in a little valley around a half-dry watering hole. Before the Appaloosa went over to drink, waiting its turn after the first males, Bowman galloped down the slope, hollering war cries.

The horse ran in exactly the direction he had anticipated and soon found itself separated from the other animals, galloping alone towards the mountain, with Bowman in pursuit.

—⁂—⁂—⁂—

The six horses followed the path without difficulty. Their riders tried to keep up a good pace to tire them out without exhausting them. That evening, when they stopped, all the mustangs cared about was eating and drinking.

When they reached Carson City after three weeks in the plains, the three of them stank as badly as old MacBain. Ervin and Vernon rode through the town like returning war heroes. Joseph had wanted to stop in a saloon to celebrate their success, but Bowman insisted that the animals get some rest as early as possible.

Ervin made do with buying whiskey in a shop where he already had a tab. They agreed to advance him the bottle when he told them he was the owner of half of everything that would be born from these mares' wombs. Before the first mountain pass, he had drunk half the bottle and let his son taste some too. Vernon smiled and his father sang his head off. Bowman dropped them at their cabin, where Mrs Ervin welcomed home her men with a salvo of curses and sent them to take a bath in the lake.

When Bowman reached his camp, the stallion started whinnying and the new mustangs responded. He put the animals in the large enclosure and filled the two barrels with buckets of water. He let them drink, then led them over to the grass, where he tied them to trees. At nightfall, he took them back to the enclosure, went into his hut and fell asleep fully clothed.

The next morning, he swam across the cove to the place where the bottom fell away almost vertically, and continued into the dark water.

Bowman shaved in front of the mirror, smiling, regularly turning to look at the horses, which stared back at him while they waited for their food. Clean and changed, he went to visit Jonathan and Aileen's grave.

"I can't give them Christian names, otherwise I'd name them after you, the stallion and the first mare. But that's not done. And besides, I wouldn't really like that. So I thought of something else. The male, given that I've already got a mare called Trigger, I'm going to call him Springfield. They like each other. And for you, Aileen, I called the new mare Beauty."

Bowman cared for the mustangs and started training Springfield. After three weeks, the stallion became resistant to the exercises. Then Bowman began to prepare for the impending autumn and winter.

In exchange for the cattle, the Ervin family had extended its vegetable garden, creating reserves of cereals and potatoes for Bowman. It was too late to reap fodder for the animals; this winter, he would have to lead his pack to low-lying pastureland. He still did not have many horses and there was enough food for them there. After that, he had to dry some meat, construct a stable, gather firewood, and build an oven and a fireplace in the hut. He also had to learn to fish on the lake. When the wild animals were hibernating under the snow, he would still be able to catch fish.

In early September, he had an oven and enough meat, so he started the construction of the stable. Beauty and two other mares were already in foal.

In three weeks, he built the framework, sometimes helped by Vernon and Joseph, sometimes by old MacBain. As they had neither the means to buy planks nor the time to saw them, they covered the building with bark and filled in the gaps with mud from the bottom of the cove. Bowman took two days to cut down a giant redwood and pull the chopped-up trunk to his ranch, then he hollowed out the blocks to make troughs. Hollowing out young pine trunks in the same way, he created gutters and diverted part of the stream to provide the building with water.

Before starting on his reserves of firewood, he hammered two stakes in the ground next to the northern boundary marker – the tree into which he'd fired a bullet. He split one last block of redwood and fabricated a thick, ten-foot plank, which he sculpted with a hatchet and on which he engraved letters with an iron heated up in the embers. Above the two stakes, high enough for horses to pass beneath, he fixed the sign for the Fitzpatrick ranch. The Ervins and old MacBain came to his place that evening to celebrate the official inauguration, five months after the arrival of the Fitzpatricks and the man they called Erik Penders. The old man brought a bottle of alcohol that he had distilled himself. No-one asked him for the recipe.

The next morning, Bowman took a bath and felt the cool air on his skin when he emerged from the water: the first shiver heralding the change of season. October began and the trees' leaves turned brown and yellow. In front of the mirror, he rubbed soap on his cheeks. The horses now roamed freely around the ranch, going ever further to find grass on the ground. Beauty, for the most part, remained close to the buildings. The mare walked over to him, smelling his still-wet hair.

Bowman caressed her head, waiting for her to go away so he could shave.

"Leave me in peace. I'll cut myself."

The mare retreated. He opened Penders' razor, lifted up his chin and put the blade to his throat. The mare pricked her ears and suddenly turned her head, knocking Bowman's hand. The blade nicked his throat.

Bowman leaned down to the water, rinsed off the soap and stood up in front of the mirror. It was a deep cut. He pressed his fingers to it firmly.

"Shit! Look what you made me do!"

The mare was staring at the entrance of the ranch. Bowman followed her gaze.

On an uncovered cart, a driver and his passenger were approaching. As if to signal her presence, the traveller lifted a hat. A bright spot of colour shining in the sunlight. Bowman walked to meet the carriage without bothering to put his shirt back on. The driver pulled on the reins and froze, seeing this big, half-naked man standing there, covered in scars and with blood pouring down his chest.

Alexandra Desmond got down from the carriage, shook the dust from her dress, and moved towards him.

"Were you afraid I'd be more interested in the landscape than in you, Mr Bowman?"

Putting a hand to his throat, Bowman stammered:

"It was Beauty. She nudged me."

"Beauty?"

"The new mare."

The driver cleared his throat.

"I have to get going now. Shall I leave your things here, ma'am?"

She turned towards him.

"Yes, you can unload them."

While she spoke to the driver, Bowman lost sight of Alexandra's eyes and his heart almost stopped. He shivered when she turned back to him.

"Let's go and clean up that wound. And you can tell me what I don't know yet."

———◦◦◦——◦◦◦——◦◦◦———

Naked, Alexandra came out of the hut, walked past the horses' enclosure and entered the lake. Her hair floated on the surface for a moment like red seaweed and then she dived under the water.

With a blanket on his shoulders, Bowman approached the cove.

She swam far off towards the deep waters and lay on her back, letting the current take her for a moment before coming back towards the shore. Her wet hair fell over her shoulders and her breasts, water ran down to her belly, and she stood there looking at Bowman. She waited for him to smile before she emerged from the lake. Bowman opened up the blanket and she pressed herself against him, streaming with cold water. They lay on the grass and let the sun warm them up.

"Alexandra?"

She turned onto her side and leaned her cheek against his chest.

"I know this is probably a stupid question, or one I shouldn't ask because it's not very nice, but I wanted to know if you're going to stay here."

"Arthur?"

He looked down at her.

"What?"

"I'd like you to ask me."

"I already asked you."

She smiled. Bowman stroked her hair with his three-fingered hand.

"Alexandra, do you want to stay here with me?"

"Yes. On one condition."

"What?"

"That you tell me what you wrote to me."

She leaned away from him and rested her head on her arm. Bowman rolled onto his side and looked her in the eyes.

"Are you afraid it was just a soldier's letter?"

"No. I just want to hear it from your own lips."

"Why?"

"So that this place becomes the place I dreamed about."

"I've loved you since I first saw you."

She put her hand on his cheek.

"Where was that?"

"On the staircase of the hotel in Fort Worth."

"That's not true."

Bowman reflected for a moment, staring into her grey eyes.

"Yes, it is. But I didn't realise it straight away."

"When did that happen?"

"Later, when you opened the door of your room to that young man."

She smiled.

"You saw me?"

"I was downstairs, in the restaurant."

"Why at that moment?"

"Because you saw me too, before you let that man in, and we both thought the same thing."

She burst out laughing, pushed him over onto his back and lay on top of him, slowly rubbing her breasts and her belly against Bowman's body.

"Do you need me to love you?"

"No."

"Alright, so I won't tell you when it happened for me."

"I know."

She sat up, putting her weight on his belly, and with her fingertips she stroked the wound on his neck and the scars on his chest.

"You can't know."

"When I went inside Kramer's house. To chase the ghosts from

481

your town. I opened the window and you were standing on the other side of the street, in front of the black barn."

She stopped stroking him.

"I didn't understand straight away."

Bowman put his hand out towards her breasts. Alexandra's belly tensed. He caressed her thighs and her buttocks, she lifted herself up on her knees, took his erection in her hand, guided him inside her and slowly slid down on him, her eyes never leaving his.

"There won't be any more ghosts."

"Just one."

Alexandra closed her eyes and bit her lips as she lifted herself up and slid back down him.

"Your name?"

"Arthur Bowman no longer exists for anyone but you."

4

Bowman ordered a branding iron from the forge in Carson so he could brand his horses, and another, bigger one for marking the boundaries of his property. Alexandra Desmond and Erik Penders bought land and received their ownership deeds from the town's Territory Office. The Fitzpatrick ranch extended from the shore of Lake Tahoe to the border of the Ervins' property, one mile wide and just over four miles long in an eastward direction. Over two thousand acres, stretching from the low prairies in the foothills, above Carson City, to the lake, including a wooded peak. The boundary markers were put up at the end of the autumn. Next to each stake in the earth, they made a fire to heat up the large branding iron and burn the sign of the ranch into the wood. A vertical diamond, with its top and bottom crossed by a line. Two As, reflecting each other.

Young Vernon Ervin was hired as a farm boy and, before the first snowfall, Bowman went off on a three-week expedition in the plains of the Utah Territory, this time with six men recruited in town. To the initial group of seven horses, another twenty new mustangs were added.

Joseph Ervin was, in turn, hired by the Fitzpatrick ranch as a foreman, with his son the only other employee. Dividing his time between the ranch and his leatherwork, he began to draw up plans for a large tannery. The ranch, in exchange for a two-year employment contract, advanced him the money he needed for the creation of this new building.

The construction of an enclosure and a temporary shelter, on the eastern prairies, was the last the thing they were able to accomplish that winter before the earth began to freeze. In early December, they had a thousand dollars remaining from Captain Reeves' fortune. The cove iced over. Alexandra and Bowman spent their first winter together in the hut. Bowman's reserves of food, insufficient for two, obliged them to make several trips into town. Thankfully, that year, there was not too much snow. From their territory, it took them three hours to reach Carson.

The Fitzpatrick ranch quickly acquired a strange reputation. Mrs Desmond's appearance as she rode her mare, dressed in men's clothing, her long red hair falling down over a fur coat – not to mention her arrival in the region with so much money – set tongues wagging. She sometimes went to visit Henry Mighels, in the office of the *Carson Daily Appeal*, and it was said that she met the journalist to order books and have discussions with him.

On two occasions, she also went into town accompanied by Bowman. When he rode beside her, they were greeted with the respect due to such wealthy owners. Equal partners in the ranch, they lived, it was said, in a house too small to contain two beds. And they weren't married.

No-one knew anything about them and, despite the immorality of their conduct, they paraded shamelessly through town, her with her hair worn long and him with his distant gaze, his broad shoulders, and the scar in the middle of his face. Their stud farm in the mountains was another topic of discussion, this time in a comic vein. No-one wanted that land for farming of any kind, least of all a stud farm. The winters were too harsh. It was a place for trappers, tanners and reed-eating Paiutes. The men who had participated in the capture of the twenty mustangs told people how Penders had chosen the horses for their "personalities". No-one had ever heard such ridiculous nonsense. Others said that Penders and Desmond were not mad at all, and that the slopes of the ranch made good pastureland. It was even admitted, in the end, that the Fitzpatrick ranch was not such a bad piece of business. The land was three times cheaper than that around Carson City, and in the long term, the ranch might even prove profitable. Some swore they would never work there, but already certain builders had signed contracts to construct buildings there in the spring.

When, in February 1861, on his way through town, Bowman was greeted by Abraham Curry, owner of the Eagle Ranch and founder of Carson City, the negative comments about the Fitzpatrick ranch were toned down definitively. Not to mention that none of the town's eight hundred inhabitants had any desire to get on the wrong side of Erik Penders.

"I saw him trap a stallion on his own, and believe me, that horse was fierce. I wouldn't have gone near it till I'd put two bullets in its head, and another one in its heart, just to make sure."

If the redhead had been a witch, even in the old days, they would have hesitated to burn her for fear that the flames would have had no effect on that devil Penders.

In November, the Republican candidate Abraham Lincoln was elected the new president of the United States. Very soon, South Carolina, Mississippi, Florida, Alabama, Georgia, Louisiana and Texas seceded from the Union. In February, the Confederate States of America were officially formed. Lincoln took power in March, and in April a civil war blew up between the North and the South.

The first three foals on the Fitzpatrick ranch were born as the new government in Washington was initiating a system of conscription to raise an army of eighty thousand men. Alexandra went to Carson City every week where she met Henry Mighels of the *Daily Appeal* in order to keep informed of events.

Abraham Curry of the Eagle Ranch and other influential figures in Utah decided that the western part of the Territory should secede, creating the new Nevada Territory and thus freeing it from the authority of the Mormons of Salt Lake City. The American troops stationed in Utah, called away for the conflict in the South, left behind them a void that the Mormons filled in order to re-establish their authority over the promised land of the Church of Jesus Christ of Latter-Day Saints. Rumours of Indian attacks on the California road, no longer protected by the army, grew stronger and stronger in Carson City.

In May, the builders erected a large construction on the eastern prairies, capable of sheltering about thirty horses and reserves of feed for the hardest winter months. In early June, Bowman hired a dozen men for another expedition on the plains. He had to offer bonuses to overcome their fear of encountering Indians. They left Carson heavily armed and returned to Fitzpatrick at the end of that month with thirty mares and seven stallions.

All of the first batch of mares had given birth to foals, in addition to the progeny of Trigger and Springfield, and of Beauty and the Appaloosa. Bowman began selecting the stallions and females, reserving enclosures in different parts of the ranch for each of the males, and, with Alexandra, sketching the beginning of genealogical trees, noting down the dates of coverings, spotting the mares and choosing the right stallions for them on the basis of character and morphology. In July, three more men were hired; they established their seasonal camp in the forest, on the eastern border of the land.

The builders had begun the construction of the Ervin tannery. Joseph's wife was worried about conscription. The government was recruiting in ever greater numbers and her husband, a third-generation American, was going to end up on the Union's volunteer list. All the shops in the area saw their activity boosted, directly or indirectly, by the war, with goods for the army sent east on a daily basis. On the plains, during the last expedition to capture mustangs, Bowman and his men had encountered three teams of hunters who shot the wild horses, following the method Joseph had explained to him, on behalf of companies that had contracts with the army. The mustang hunters left half of the horses dead, killed by bullets that lacked precision. In August, applauded by the citizens of Carson City, eight volunteers left to swell the ranks of the North's army.

In September, in an Express Mail stagecoach, a letter left Carson City, signed by Erik Penders and addressed to Pastor Edmund Peavish, Grantsville, Utah Territory.

In October, Alexandra and Bowman paid their last wages to the three seasonal workers. The brown leaves fell from the trees. The reserves of meat, wood, feed, cereals and dried fish were almost exhausted and

Reeves' money was all spent. All they had left was about a hundred dollars to get them through the winter and cover the first expenses of the following spring. The hut had not been extended. They were preparing to spend their second winter as they had spent their first, with Alexandra reading books out loud. The first one she had read, the previous year, was Hawthorne's *The Blithedale Romance*. In it, the author told a story that took place in the imaginary utopian community of Blithedale, which bore a strong resemblance to Reunion. She read the whole book while Bowman lay next to her and listened.

"Was your friend Penders interested in that subject?"

"No idea."

"Blithedale, in fact, is Brook Farm. A community founded in 1840 in Massachusetts."

"What happened to it?"

Alexandra's face darkened.

"The same as Reunion. Poverty and sickness. Power struggles."

By late October, the mountain peaks had already been white for three weeks and snow was beginning to fall on the lake. Before retreating into their hut, they lit a large fire on the edge of the cove and jumped into the water one last time. They only stayed in there for a minute, hugging each other tight and shivering with cold, then ran over to the fire and wrapped themselves up in blankets.

"That's it, we've got rid of it."

She turned towards him.

"Rid of what?"

"Reeves' money."

Alexandra nestled close to him.

"Look at me – I came to America to build a socialist community, and I end up the prisoner of a misanthrope on a mountain and a partner in a two-and-a-half-thousand-acre ranch funded by the British India Company."

Bowman put his arm round her shoulders.

"There's not enough room in the hut for anyone else."

"I'll last another winter."

A few days later, as the snow was settling in a disturbingly deep layer, a young Express Mail employee left Carson City, cursing heaven. He took the path to the Fitzpatrick ranch and rode under the first boundary markers. He saw the horses gathered around the big barn or sheltering under the trees. He went over the mountain pass and headed down the western slope towards the lake. After four hours, he reached the prairie, the little corral and the small, snow-covered stable, and stopped at a prudent distance from the hut, where he called out to Mr Penders. The horse, held by the lead rope behind him, started to snort and stamp its feet.

Bowman opened the door of the hut, rifle in hand.

"Who is it?"

"It's Ricky from the Express Mail, Mr Penders! I have a horse and a letter for you!"

Sergeant,

Your letter, which reached me a month ago, came as such a surprise that it took me a long time to get over it.

A year and a half has passed since our last encounter and never would I have imagined all that has happened to you, nor believed that you would find peace in those mountains. Whether you like it or not, my dearest prayers for you have been granted. I had been hoping to hear from you, but I could never have believed your news would be so good or that it would represent, for me, such a liberation. Since the tragic events that brought us back together and then separated us again, I have been living my life like an impostor, unsure whether I had made the right choice, not knowing if you were still pursuing the search that I had abandoned.

Today, thanks to you, I know that we did the right thing.

So I stayed in Grantsville, firstly because I was incapable of leaving for a long time, weakened by fever and bad dreams, and then because the sad renown I acquired after the death of the killer had turned me into a sort of celebrity. The community of Jesus Christ of Latter-Day Saints welcomed me as one of their own.

I converted to these men's religion. Primarily because I wanted to stay here and live with them.

I am a little ashamed to admit this to you, Sergeant, but I have taken wives in Grantsville. I have two at the moment.

The reward money was under lock and key for a long time, as I had resolved not to touch it. But since your letter, I have decided to invest the sum in a farm in Grantsville, one of the few areas of pastureland around Salt Lake. The demand for meat – between this war that has broken out and the convoys of immigrants – is increasingly significant. I am becoming – like you, if in a rather less wild way – an American citizen taking care of business, and a priest who now has a real parish and a real community. Here, among my kind, I feel safe.

As promised, I have taken care of your horse. That animal has an impossible character – it often made me think of you. I hope it will have made the journey without carrying a burden; I was promised that it would be very well treated. So the horse will be my messenger to your mountains, where I hope, one day, to come and visit you.

It sometimes seems to me, when I am tired, that we are a hundred years old.

Dear old friend, my thoughts are with you.

Kind regards to you, and to your lady friend too.

Edmund

Despite the snow and the wind, Bowman saddled up Walden and took the horse on a ride around the Fitzpatrick ranch, showing it every boundary marker, as if the horse were a new business partner. He led it to crevasses hidden by snow, so that it would remember them, including the one into which Jonathan had fallen, and where Erik Penders' Winchester now lay rusting. He took his mustang back to the little stable, looked after it, and left it for the night with Beauty, Trigger and their foals.

The winter of 1862 was the harshest that old MacBain had known in his fifteen years in the Sierra Nevada. One third of the Fitzpatricks' animals died: some of cold, some of disease, some eaten by wolves, some fallen in crevasses while they foraged for food beneath the snow. The horses sheltered in the big barn emerged after the winter all skin and bones. Alexandra and Bowman crammed about a dozen horses into the little stable near the lake, and they all somehow survived. Throughout January and February, the weather alternated bizarrely between torrential rain and snowfall, decimating the game on the ranch and flooding the plains all the way to Owens Valley, in the south of the Sierra. The Paiute and Shoshone tribes, starving, began to kill cattle from the mining camps, which strayed onto their land in search of food. The conflict escalated, and some miners were killed. In March, a detachment of cavalry left Aurora, north of Carson City, with a mission to pacify Owens Valley. The first clashes took place and the renegade Indians fled into the mountains.

In spring, the mountains slowly came back to life and the Fitzpatrick ranch recovered from the damage inflicted by winter. The *Carson Daily Appeal* reported increasingly violent battles between Union troops and Confederate troops in the south of the country. In Shiloh, Tennessee, four thousand soldiers died in two days.

In June and July, eleven mares gave birth, two of them dying along with their foals. It was a beautiful summer and the ranch's forty horses returned to good health. Alexandra and Bowman no longer had money to hire people and they negotiated a line of credit with the Eagle Ranch for horse feed if the need arose. If the following winter proved as difficult as the last one, they would leave a few of their horses there to be looked after. The Fitzpatrick ranch, specialising in the breeding of prize horses, would take at least two years to move into profit, and the army did not care about the animals' characters: it needed as many horses as it had cavalrymen, and their only requirement was to charge for a few minutes before being killed by bullets and shells. But Abraham Curry, of the Eagle Ranch, believed in their project and agreed to help them after visiting their ranch and seeing the promising yearlings.

In September, 75,000 Northern troops and 50,000 Southern troops clashed in Antietam, Maryland. Twenty thousand men were killed or injured during a single day of battle, and both sides claimed victory. The factories and large farms of the United States were booming, and the country had emerged from the economic crisis that had gripped it since the great drought of 1857. As soon as winter was over, the flow of immigrants continued increasing, and the California track – which passed through Carson City – became a ceaseless flood of convoys headed to the Pacific. The city grew and, while a dozen other volunteers left farms devastated by the winter weather, two hundred new inhabitants moved there within a year.

From Grantsville, Father Peavish exchanged a few letters with Erik Penders, the owner of the Fitzpatrick ranch. Peavish had been luckier than Bowman. His business was already going well, and the bad winter in the Sierra had only boosted his meat trade even further. He offered to give Bowman money, if he needed it: "I owe you that money." Peavish now had three wives and as many children. "It is customary, in our community, to have a family as large as our means allow. Believe it or not, Sergeant, but I have, with my bony frame and rotten gums, become a very eligible man."

The last pioneers crossed over the mountains in October and the snow returned. The ranch was ready for another winter. Joseph Ervin's new tannery was operational now, and when the season ended at the Fitzpatrick ranch, he and his wife set to work, refining their method of white oak bark tanning. As he no longer had time to go hunting, Ervin ordered hides from the Sierra's trappers, who became accustomed to camping on the ranch's land when they visited.

Alexandra and Bowman lit their big fire by the waterside and swam one last time. Under the blankets, they were silent for a moment, looking at their hut, their horses in the enclosure and the bare forest.

Alexandra pressed herself against him.

"Do you remember what you said last year?"

"No."

"You said there wasn't enough room in the hut for anyone else."

Bowman looked at her.

She smiled.

"How old are you, Arthur?"

"Forty-one."

"I'm thirty-seven."

She had sounded strange when she said this. Bowman lowered his eyes.

"You're bored here, aren't you?"

She burst out laughing.

"Not at all."

Alexandra looked over at the hut.

"We'll have to make it bigger."

"If that's what you want, we'll do it next year."

She took Bowman's hand, placed it on her belly, and stared deep into his eyes.

"I was wondering why it didn't happen earlier. Maybe we needed time to prepare ourselves."

He did not understand.

"Are you ready, Arthur?"

His face showed surprise, then he frowned: an expression of worry and fear that Alexandra had never seen before. He opened his mouth but could not pronounce a single word. Big, tough Bowman was struggling to breathe. His eyes did not leave Alexandra's, and his hand, on her belly, was trembling.

She kissed him and stood up.

"I'm going inside to get warm."

On the doorstep of the hut, she turned back. Arthur Bowman had stood up and moved away from the fire, draped in his blanket. He stopped at the water's edge and watched the sun disappear behind the mountains. The sky was grey, ominous with snow. The sunset lasted only an instant, casting an orange glow on the naked forests and the ripples on the lake. He stayed there for a moment, standing tall and motionless in the cold, blowing little clouds of steam until night had fallen. Before going to the hut, he paused by the Fitzpatricks' grave.

"This time, I'll use one of your names."

He shivered. His bare feet ached on the cold earth.

"Sleep well."

The fire crackled. He threw his blanket on the bed and warmed himself before the flames, which soothed his painful scars. He rubbed the stumps on his bluish hands, then got into bed with Alexandra. Her body was already warm. She wrapped herself around him.

"You O.K.?"

"Yeah."

He buried his face in her hair.

"Sorry."

"Why?"

"Because I can't speak."

"That doesn't matter."

As winter went on, Bowman anxiously watched Alexandra Desmond's stomach swell. He often left the hut, going for long rides in the snowy mountains with Walden, coming back to sleep with her in the evenings, placing his hands on her belly to feel the child move beneath the skin. Sometimes he had nightmares. He dreamed about the fishing village, women throwing themselves in the flames with their children in their arms.

—⟋⟍—⟋⟍—⟋⟍—

The winter was mild and the Fitzpatrick ranch did not need to go into debt to buy fodder. By March, the snow was starting to melt.

Alexandra Desmond gave birth to a little girl on 8 May, 1863.

Aileen Penders was born in the hut by the lake in the middle of the afternoon, under the blue sky and bright sun of the Sierra.

Although Mrs Ervin protested, having given birth to her three children without anyone's help, let alone her husband's, Alexandra had refused to let Bowman leave. He almost fainted as he held her hand, fascinated by the sufferings of labour and Alexandra Desmond's fierce determination to bring a child into the world. Mrs Ervin handed Aileen to him, her body covered in white grease and blood, looking tiny in his hands. He dared to hug her for a few seconds, but when she screamed for the first time, he placed her, terrified, on her mother's breast.

When Alexandra was able to get up and walk again, she went to swim in the lake's cool water, where Aileen took her first bath. Carrying her daughter on her chest, wrapped in a blanket, Indian-style, she took Aileen everywhere, and rode with her, on Trigger, around the Fitz-patrick ranch.

The Eagle Ranch ordered two three-year-old males for the following year. In June, a breeder from Aurora came to visit them, having heard about their horses, and he too bought an option in three future stallions and four mares. The advance fees, though far from huge, were the first dollars they had earned in two years. Bowman used this small profit to fund another expedition in Utah. In September, the ranch's population was back to the levels it had had before the terrible winter of the previous year. Sixty horses, a dozen of them male. Springfield, now seven years old, was a magnificent stallion. Within a year, his and the Appaloosa's progeny would begin to interbreed, the branches of the genealogical tree growing more numerous.

In early July, 160,000 thousand soldiers fought for three days in Gettysburg, Pennsylvania. Forty thousand died on the battlefield.

Bowman went swimming every morning with his daughter. At three months old, she already had curly hair as red as her mother's and Bowman watched her grow up, searching for signs that she resembled him too.

"She just looks like you."

Alexandra took the little girl in her arms and spoke to her, making fun of Bowman:

"Did you hear that?"

Aileen had Alexandra's hair, but she had Bowman's thin, serious mouth, his cheekbones, his blue eyes and his expression.

After the birth of his daughter, Bowman's nightmares ended.

He took her into the mountains, riding Walden, telling her about what he saw, describing the landscape, the horses, telling her about his memories of grand hotels and wide rivers and deserts, describing London and the ships sailing up the Thames, telling her about sea-fishing and those steam liners crossing the Atlantic faster than trains. Aileen, her head on Bowman's chest, fell asleep listening to his voice.

A trader in Carson City bought all of Joseph Ervin's stock of leather for the year. Some of it was sent to sewing workshops in New York, to be made into gloves for the Northern army's senior officers. Ervin lent the Fitzpatrick ranch two hundred dollars for the construction of a new, three-bedroom house on the edge of the lake. Alexandra drew up the plans, while Bowman went to town to hire builders and take care of the business that took him there twice a month. He went to the offices of the *Daily Appeal* to buy the week's copies for Alexandra and give her response to Henry Mighels. The journalist had asked Mrs Desmond to write a column for the newspaper. Alexandra had agreed.

She waited until late at night for Bowman to return, but it was early morning of the next day before he did. She found him sitting on the roof of the half-built house, on the beam that the workers had just put in place, staring out at the lake, red-eyed and stinking of alcohol and vomit. At his feet was a copy of the *Carson Daily Appeal*, dated 7 July, 1863.

Carrying Aileen in her arms, she sat down next to him without a word, watching the sun rise over the mountains. Aileen wriggled and grabbed Bowman's sleeve. Bowman made a nest for her in his arms, leaned over her and whispered:

"You're nothing like your father."

Aileen smiled and tried to grab his lips as they tickled her ear.

Alexandra got up and left Bowman alone with his daughter. She went back into the hut and lay on the bed, hands on her thighs, trying to control her breathing and hold back her tears.

The next day, an envelope left Carson City for Grantsville, containing a page from the *Daily Appeal* and a brief note from Arthur Bowman for Father Peavish.

For three weeks, Bowman had been locked inside a monstrous silence, not speaking a word to anyone except his daughter, whom he took for horse rides. He told her about the India Company army, its battles, Africa, the lost garrisons, Godwin's fleet and the white sloop, the war in Burma and the monsoon, the forest, the drought in London and the sewers of St Katharine's Dock.

In early August, a letter arrived at the ranch. Inside the skeleton of the new house, its construction interrupted, Bowman opened the envelope.

> *Sergeant,*
> *I have not slept since I got your last letter. I spend my nights with a lamp lit in my house. I can't bear the darkness of the night anymore. During the days, I wander around, unable to speak to anyone, and as much as I've been able, I've tried to think about what we should do.*
>
> *I don't have the strength anymore.*
>
> *Now that we know, it will probably be impossible to live normally. Our scars have opened again, after we had managed to forget them. Both of us have children. A life. And even if we are lying to ourselves, I want to continue living that lie. The pain might fade away with time. I will forget. That is my choice and I ask you to make the same one.*
>
> *We have too much to lose now. We have achieved the impossible. Why destroy what we have built?*
>
> *That man's life must not ruin ours anymore. You said he was dead. Let him stay that way.*
>
> *I can hear you saying it through gritted teeth, Sergeant: "Coward."*

This is not cowardice. We have already paid a high price for our guilt and carried out duties to which the rest of the world was indifferent. We do not owe anything to anyone anymore, apart from ourselves.

We have changed. I don't know what man he is today, the one hiding behind the photograph and article in the newspaper, but it is possible that his homicidal madness is at an end. He wanted to remake his life. Survive. Perhaps that is, like us, what he has achieved? He killed for reasons we know all too well, Sergeant. To steal, to get rich. The way he did it is another story altogether – our story – but what does that change in this country where the North's businessmen send tens of thousands of men to their deaths in order to settle their differences with the South's businessmen? What are his crimes in comparison, apart from a few nightmares that I had managed to stop?

If he has found what he was looking for, why would he continue?

That does not erase his crimes, but why should we continue to suffer for what he has done?

I ask you to reconsider your decision, for the love of your daughter and your partner, in the name of all I possess now that is most precious to me. Don't go there. Let us live and let God judge this man.

He will be dead soon, like all of us.

I beg you to give up, and to forgive me: I want to keep my remaining strength in order to live. Those who commanded us no longer exist. We are not soldiers anymore. This battle no longer makes any sense.

That was the first thing you said to me, Sergeant, more than ten years ago now: "The one who refuses to fight sometimes wins the war."

Give up.

If you start this hunt again, the man who died in that barn to save you will have been killed in vain. You now bear his name, and

so does your daughter. Don't let it die with you. Don't become
your own nightmare again.
The Preacher

Bowman had saddled Walden, and the mustang was waiting, tied to one of the posts in the small enclosure. He shoved food into his saddlebags, along with a blanket, a few tools for the journey, and ammunition for Jonathan's old Springfield rifle. Into his pocket he put part of the money that should have been used to finish the construction of the house.

He untied his horse, not daring to look at Alexandra.

"I'll be back."

Bowman put his hand on the pommel and climbed into the saddle, breathing heavily. Walden smelled Alexandra and Aileen's hair. The little girl tried to caress the animal. Her mother pushed it back with her hand.

"Stay here. You'll be killed."

Bowman picked up the reins.

Aileen lifted up her arms to him; she wanted to climb up on the horse and go into the mountains.

Bowman rode under the sign for the Fitzpatrick ranch without turning around. He followed the shore until he reached the northern point of Lake Tahoe and the main road. There, he wove between the pioneers' carts, heading in the same direction as them: West.

5

CARSON DAILY APPEAL
7 July, 1863

The mayoral elections in San Francisco, California, ended on July 1 with the resounding victory – by nearly a thousand votes – of Henry Perrin Coon, the candidate for the Vigilance People's Party, who defeated the Republican candidate Robert C. Delauney.

During a campaign marked by the concerns of the war, the two candidates chose very different programs.

Henry Perrin Coon, of the Vigilance People's Party, focused his on the issue of safety in the streets of San Francisco, institutional corruption, and the defense of Americans' rights in the face of the ever-growing wave of immigration in the town and in this area of California. Coon, originally from New York State, has lived in San Francisco for ten years and is a father of four. In his acceptance speech, the new mayor declared: "This is not my victory, but a victory for the American citizens of San Francisco. Together we will work to make this great city a safe and prosperous capital, and we will support with all our might the Union in its battle and its coming victory over the Confederate rebellion."

Robert C. Delauney, of the Republican Party, while supporting the Union's war against the South, had based his campaign around the town's economic prosperity, its openness to trade with Asia and its financial independence from the federal government. An ambitious entrepreneur, specialized in the import and export of chemical products, Robert Delauney has lived in Sausalito, close to San Francisco, for three years. However, the *much-envied example of his rapid fortune and the money invested in his campaign proved insufficient to win the election.*

In this period of war and ever-spiraling immigration, it was Coon, betting on the issue of security and other topics closer to the hearts of San Francisco's citizens, who came out on top. Delauney saluted his adversary's victory by declaring that he would remain a citizen with an investment in the political and economic future of the city, and that if his help was required, he would support Coon in any project that would profit San Francisco.

An election, and two candidates, worthy of a great democracy.

At the end of the article were the photographs of the candidates. Coon looked like a belli'cose pastor, Delauney like a wealthy lumberjack, with his shirt collar buttoned up to his chin.

—⫯—⫯—⫯—

In Stockton, after crossing the Sierra and spending five days on the main track, Bowman moved away from the pioneers and headed northward, bypassing the vast network of lakes and rivers, the labyrinth of earth and water where boats were already leaving for the San Francisco bay. The region had been invaded by prospectors and miners, who for two days had been spreading from the track towards gold-digging sites and the large mines, where they would look for work.

The excavation sites were bigger than those Bowman had seen in the Rockies. Water from huge hydraulic pumps sprayed down hills and valleys, transforming the earth into rivers of mud that were gathered and sifted by prospectors. Railways and high, fragile buildings were under construction – or in a state of permanent repair. Around the mines, workers lived huddled in slums made of tarps and planks, while the ground was strewn with rubbish and destroyed vegetation. A mine became a village, and villages became towns, or disappeared completely, leaving only disfigured valleys and scraps of abandoned constructions. On this side of the Sierra, the large valleys were better irrigated and slightly less hot than in the plains of Utah.

For all those who did not continue towards the coast, this was the end of their journey. Outside the offices of mining companies, lines of men waited in the hot sun to be offered a job. Between the mines, small farms sometimes joined forces to give rise to other villages of a few families. The war was as far away from this place as it was from Lake Tahoe.

Bowman arrived at the Sacramento River and paid for his passage on a ferry, which deposited him on the pontoon for the little town of Rio Vista. In the general store, he asked where the Fitzpatrick farm could be found. The shopkeepers explained how to get there: it was a few miles north of here, on the banks of the river. Yes, they knew the Fitzpatricks. They came here regularly to do their shopping.

Night was approaching. Bowman asked if he could leave something for them. He wrote a short letter and, in a knotted piece of fabric, left on the shop's counter the photograph of Jonathan and Aileen, a razor, an embroidery and two gold wedding rings. The shopkeeper asked Bowman who he was, bringing a message for the Fitzpatricks.

"It's in the letter. There's nothing else to add."

Bowman went on his way. He rode slowly for part of the night, until he reached a forest of giant sequoias. He stopped at the foot of a tree as wide across as his log cabin, and slept for a few hours. When he woke up, he lit a fire to make some coffee. Shrouds of light fell between the trees, painting stains of light on the ground. The sergeant drank his coffee and slowly chewed some meat. The forest was like an abandoned sanctuary, guarded by motionless giants, each one a hundred and fifty feet tall, like a petrified army from an ancient myth. Bowman listened, as if he might hear the trees whispering to each other. They had been growing here together, next to each other, for centuries. They must know each other, and the idea came to him that they must have learned to communicate silently, that they were able to exchange ideas.

Their bark was soft and warm. Their immobility and their imposing presence led Bowman into a slow meditation. He began to feel oppressed. The air was humid and heavy, as if there wasn't enough of it between the massive trunks. The sequoias did not leave him enough to breathe and their high arms hid the sky above him. He put out his fire – perhaps it was disturbing them? – and got back on Walden and left the forest, taking care not to wake the giants from their sleep. Bowman felt he was being watched; his intrusion into this sanctuary was no longer tolerated.

The next night, he slept near a little lake, and in the morning he stripped off to go for a swim. He had forgotten the smell of his body and clothes, when sweat and grime had become encrusted in his skin after days spent travelling. He thought about Aileen, about the baths he took with her in the mornings. He made his hands into the shape of a cup and filled it with water, holding his fingers tight together to hold it in. But the water trickled through the holes left by his stumps, and he was left empty-handed.

By noon, he had reached the shores of the wide bay of San Francisco. He continued southward, on that increasingly narrow tongue of land, until, from the top of a hill, he saw the bay to his left and the ocean to his right. He decided to spend another night under the stars before crossing the last few miles that separated him from Sausalito, on the northern point of the strait, which he could see from his camp. The ocean wind brought the sound of the breaking waves to him. When night fell, he watched as San Francisco lit up on the other side of the strait. Ferries and boats wove across the bay, their lanterns advancing slowly over the black water. He lay down, facing the Pacific. The last frontier. A dead end. In his first life, Bowman had found himself on the other side of this ocean. His tour around the world was coming to an end.

Perhaps he should have written one last letter. To Alexandra, Aileen, or Peavish. But he had nothing else to add. And the words would just kept going round in circles. He looked out at the black mass of the Pacific and the stars above: more eternal guardians, he thought, remembering the sequoias. The ancient trees knew that flight was futile. Bowman remembered already having breathed the air of this forest. On the deck of the *Healing Joy*, by the Burmese coast, after coming out of Wright and Cavendish's cabin. The air of a coffin closed around him. Listening to the waves in the distance, Bowman realised that he had not passed through all these places with impunity. Each time, he had left part of himself behind, in time spent and life disappeared. Sergeant Bowman was now scattered all over the four corners of the world. There was not much of him left.

He woke at dawn, saddled up Walden, and descended towards Sausalito.

A little fishing village on the bay, with houses on stilts and pontoons, and on the hills above, overlooking the strait, more luxurious residences, the holiday homes of wealthy San Franciscans and the first homes of a few rich citizens who preferred the peacefulness of the village to the agitation of a big town. Ferries took people to the capital, three miles away on the other side. Among these high, white houses was one, bigger than the rest, which Bowman recognised without difficulty. The first time he had seen it, in London, he had thought he was mistaken, that the house was a century old. This time it was new and it overlooked Sausalito, perched on the peak of the hill, at the end of an unpaved cul-de-sac.

Bowman rode up to the gate of the stable. It was open. A black man was sweeping the driveway. He stopped what he was doing.

"Can I help you, sir?"

"Is Mr Delauney there?"

"In the house, sir. Would you like me to fetch someone?"

Bowman grimaced as he climbed down from the horse. He was exhausted after days on the road, and his knees ached.

"No need. Can you look after my horse for me?"

The black man took Walden's bridle. Bowman caressed the mustang's breast and patted it gently.

"Take good care of him."

"He's a beautiful horse, sir."

"Yeah, he's got a nasty temper, but I haven't seen many as brave as him."

"I'll take care of him, sir. He'll be waiting for you here."

Bowman walked through the narrow garden in front of the house, reaching the main driveway that led from the entrance gates to the front door. He lifted up the knocker – a capital "D" wrought in iron-work – and let it fall. A young black woman in a servant's outfit opened the door to him. On her cheeks, three lines of scars ran across her face. They looked like tribal incisions, but were more likely an owner's mark or a form of punishment.

"Can I help you, sir?"

"I'd like to see Delauney."

"Do you have an appointment, sir?"

Bowman smiled.

"Yes."

She moved out of the way to let him past.

Despite the British style of architecture, the *décor* in the entrance hall resembled that in the Paterson ranch. Dark furniture, a mixture of the rustic and the refined. Rugs and paintings were badly arranged, and there were too many clashing colours. In various genres and formats, the canvases represented landscapes from America and from Asia, battle scenes, ships, windmills and horses.

"What name should I announce, sir?"

Bowman turned distractedly towards the servant.

"Tell him it's his old friend, Richard Kramer."

Bowman stayed near the door while she crossed through the entrance hall, its large glass doors opening onto a white stone terrace. She opened of one of these doors and disappeared.

He waited next to a painting showing an Indian market, perhaps in Bombay or Madras, where the painter had obviously never been in his life. He must have worked from a photograph or someone else's memories. Among the Hindus in turbans were a few American Indians in feather headdresses.

The servant returned. She came to a halt a fair distance from Bowman and informed him that Mr Delauney was waiting for him on the terrace. She watched him walk past as she remained where she was in the middle of the large entrance hall. Bowman turned back to her.

"You should leave the house."

She started trembling.

"Mr Delauney already told us we should all leave."

"Good."

He walked to the glass doors and went onto the terrace. The sun glinted from the pale stone slabs. He squinted in the glare. The house's grounds stretched out in front of him, at the foot of a short stairway. Some saplings had just been planted in a piece of land that was still without grass. At the far end of the grounds was a long, single-storey brick building, like an English cottage. The servants' quarters.

Bowman recognised the place, in spite of the increasingly numerous differences. Not in the design, but in the execution. The recreation of the *décor* had doubtless proved too time-consuming for the house's owner, as there were signs of haste and imperfections everywhere he looked. The trees were planted in a disorderly fashion, the cottage seemed too low, the windows too small.

A metal pergola had been erected on the uneven stone slabs of the terrace. In all four corners of the terrace, climbing plants grew from earthenware pots, but they were still too young to give any shade. Bulrush reeds had been worked through the metal framework. The main house's western façade was also a flawed copy. Whereas the original model had possessed an elegance, a refined presence, this one was austere, and its unbalanced dimensions made it look pretentious. This facsimile of a grand English residence lacked the original's patina of years and its architectural expertise. As with the painting of the Bombay market and its American Indians, it was the fruit of a distorted reminiscence. Money and imagination had not been enough to fill the gaps in memory.

*

Delauney was sitting under the reeds in a wicker chair, at the end of a wooden, white-painted table, with a plate and a pitcher of alcohol in front of him. He put down his glass, removed the napkin that had been tied around his neck and put it on his legs as he watched Bowman approach.

Bowman pulled out a chair and sat facing him, at the other end of the table.

In the photograph printed in the newspaper, Delauney had appeared to have a round head, squeezed into a shirt buttoned up to its collar. But he still had the same square face that the sergeant remembered. The years had not left their mark on him as they had on Bowman or the preacher. His skin was still smooth, even if his hair was starting to thin at his temples.

A man of about forty, in good health, dressed in a tailor-made white cotton suit, his shirt collar open, his hands large and strong, his little blue eyes sunken under blond eyebrows, his chin close-shaved, his lips taut and thin, his face blank. He looked at Bowman as if through a thick layer of time, his square head held slightly backward on his bull's neck.

Is there anyone you trust on this boat? Peavish had pointed a finger. *Him?*

As Christian Bufford observed Sergeant Bowman, not a single muscle in his face or body moved. Bowman sat back in his chair and stared into Bufford's eyes. He did not really see him either. Slowly he reconstructed his memory of Private Buffalo, from the *Healing Joy* to the junk, from the forest to the widow with whom he drank tea in the cottage at the end of the grounds of the house in Walworth. He had given her money for her husband's gravestone.

His face was perhaps a little softer – money had given him a layer of fat, and his shoulders were rounder – but his animal-like neck was still just as thick. Bowman would have liked Buffalo to look ridiculous in his suit, exposing his coarseness and making him look like a man in disguise, the old untutored soldier clearly visible beneath his expensive clothing. But Robert C. Delauney, sitting at the other end of the table, had the sleek assurance of a real businessman. Bufford could have shared a drink with the customers in the pub across the road from the East India House, could have walked with a cane in the City Hall Park in New York, could have sat around a table with Paterson or negotiated a price for gold in an office of a large Colorado mine.

Bowman turned again towards the grounds and the servants' quarters.

"You didn't have a well dug?"

The serial killer, the San Francisco mayoral candidate, did not react.

"Your widow was inconsolable. She said it was the Great Stink that got you. She was right, even if she didn't know it. She also said that you'd left. Not that you were dead, just that you left."

Christian Bufford's lips opened slightly. His voice was hoarse:

"Hello, Sergeant."

"Hello, Buffalo."

Bufford was still deep in his visionary mist, eyes staring, face blank.

"No-one calls me that anymore."

"I imagine. No-one dared, even back then."

"Except you, Sergeant."

"I was the one who gave you the nickname, Buffalo."

One of Bufford's shoulders rose and fell in a nervous movement. Bowman looked at the house's façade.

"So you're the boss now. Did you pay for this with the gold from the mine?"

Bufford frowned.

"The gold?"

"The Gregory mine."

The subject seemed not to interest him. He replied as if he were thinking of something else:

"It's the fertiliser that brings in the money. The formula that Kramer discovered."

"The fertiliser that was supposed to save Reunion."

"Why did you use his name, Sergeant?"

"What's the name you're using, Delauney?"

Bufford answered mechanically, his mind occupied with other thoughts:

"My wife's maiden name . . . I have three ships now, making trips between San Francisco and Asia. Four hundred employees working in the factories. How did you find me, Sergeant? Was it Penders who told you?"

"In England, he was the only one I couldn't find after the murder in the sewers. He was the one I was looking for here."

"Erik?"

Bufford tore himself slowly from his dream. A wrinkle deepened in his forehead.

"I remember the night he came to that barn. He tried to speak to me, but . . . we didn't have time. He panicked when he saw the other one, who wasn't dead yet. I wasn't able to ask him how he found me."

"Who did you throw down the well?"

"What?"

"Who did your widow bury?"

"Some tramp who thought the world was ending because the city was full of shit."

"After the death of your son."

"Elliot?"

Bufford leaned forward.

"Why are you talking about him, Sergeant?"

"Your wife said you went mad after your son died."

Private Bufford looked suddenly concerned. His mouth shrank and he spoke slowly:

"Why aren't you armed, Sergeant?"

"What good would it do?"

Bufford thought for a few seconds, strangely concentrated.

"It wouldn't."

He slipped a hand under the table, pushed his plate back and put a revolver in front of him in a casual gesture, as if he had taken a pouch of tobacco from his pocket, or money to pay for his meal.

"I don't understand why you're here, Sergeant."

"Who was it, in the sewers?"

"A former colonist. When Elliot died . . . I don't like remembering that, Sergeant. Why don't you tell me what you're doing here?"

"Was he the first?"

"The first?"

"Of your partners."

A smile crept across Bufford's face.

"Yes. I needed his money so I could leave."

"And then there was Kramer. And six others."

His head tilted slightly sideways.

"You've come a long way, Sergeant, but you haven't been everywhere I went."

"I'm sure. You were on the road for a long time, Buffalo."

He frowned.

"No-one calls me that anymore, Sergeant."

"I know. Mr Delauney."

"Yes."

"I changed my name too. Because they thought I was the killer. They accused me of being you."

"What's your name, Sergeant?"

"Erik Penders."

Bufford shivered. His neck muscles moved beneath the skin.

"He already died once. He's the only one I saw again, Sergeant, before you."

"Why didn't you die in your bosses' well, Buffalo?"

Bufford's shoulders rose more violently.

"Don't call me that, Sergeant."

"I don't understand how I could have made that mistake."

"That mistake?"

"None of the ten committed suicide. How could I have believed that you would have the courage to do it? You, who ate your shit to make them laugh, who fought for a ration of rice, and who cut off my fingers when they told you to."

509

Bufford looked saddened and offended by Bowman's tone.

"It was so I could make it through, Sergeant."

"I know."

"We all did the same."

"No."

"Not you?"

Bowman looked at the gun on the table.

"Not like you. Why wasn't I looking for you, Buffalo?"

Bufford blinked.

"Stop calling me that."

"Bufford died in London, and I don't know Delauney. What should I call you?"

"I don't know, Sergeant, but not that."

Christian Bufford sat back in his chair and wiped the sweat from his chest with one hand. In the lines of sunlight and shade thrown by the reeds, Bowman saw the scars on his torso.

"I don't have another name for you, Buffalo, since you tried to kill the preacher. Twelve years ago."

Again, his shoulders rose and the veins swelled in his neck.

"I don't like the memories you keep bringing up, Sergeant."

"What else do you want to talk about?"

Bufford sat up, a sort of ferocious joy lighting up his face.

"The future, Sergeant."

Bowman smiled.

"The future?"

"This country . . . it was waiting for me. I am going to build it, Sergeant. It's mine."

"I know. But it's also mine now, and I am an objection to your plan."

"An objection?"

"As long as there's someone – even just one person – to come and look you in the eyes, Buffalo, your plan will remain a dream. It will never be carried out."

Bufford's mood changed again, and he fell back into that misty trance, wavering between concentration and absence.

"You don't have the guts anymore, Sergeant, same as Penders. I saw it when you came through that door. I've met loads of men like you, men who fell into my arms because they were so scared, when I looked them in the eyes and they could have run away. You too, you'll beg me to finish you off."

"Is that why you killed them? To prove they were as cowardly as you?"

"When I told them to, they cut off their own fingers. I could sit down and watch them do it."

Bowman stared into Bufford's eyes.

"But you kept all your fingers."

"You think you're already dead, Sergeant, but you don't know what it is yet. Your act won't work on me anymore. There's no point looking at me the way you looked at Collins on the junk."

"You haven't proved anything yet, Buffalo. You haven't proved that I'm afraid of you, and you haven't proved that the rest of the world is as cowardly as you."

"That is the last time you will call me that. I've sent all the monkeys away – there's just you and me in the house now. What do you think is going to happen, Sergeant?"

"That depends on you."

"On me?"

"You haven't changed, even with your suit and the newspaper articles and your crooked house."

"Oh, I've changed, Sergeant. You just want me to become the way I was before, but I'm not afraid of you anymore."

"You still don't understand, Buffalo."

There was the sound of a gunshot and Bowman fell off his chair. He rolled onto his side and then got on all fours. The bullet had gone through his arm. Bowman slowly got to his feet, put the chair back upright, pressed his fingers to his wound, and sat down facing Bufford again. Private Bufford stared at him, pistol in hand. Grimacing, Bowman put his elbow on the table and looked up at the house's lopsided façade. Sweat ran down his face. His mouth was dry.

"Why did you have that house rebuilt? It was because of this house that your son died."

"You don't have a child, Sergeant. You couldn't understand."

The image of Aileen and Alexandra playing in the lake flashed through his mind. Bowman immediately pushed it away and stared at Bufford, who was leaning forward, smiling.

"You have a family, Sergeant? Is that it?"

Bowman shuddered. He closed his eyes for a second and opened them again. Bufford was still smiling. His teeth looked like a single tooth: a long piece of ivory embedded in a bed of wood.

"So you abandoned your family to come here too, eh, Sergeant?"

Bowman balled his fists. The pain in his arm took his breath away.

"What did you say to Feng's little slave, Buffalo?"

Bufford cocked the revolver and aimed at Bowman's other arm.

"What?"

"I saw you on the junk. You kissed him and spoke to him before you threw him in the river. What did you say?"

Bufford slowly lowered the pistol, pulled himself together, aimed again, then tilted his head sideways and lowered the gun again.

"Why are you talking about that?"

Bowman's head was spinning. He increased the pressure on his wound, to try to stop the blood loss.

"You remember Reeves, the captain of the sloop that took us to the fishing village? He gave me money so I could come here and search for you. And he told me that if I found you, I would have to explain to you that it wasn't your fault. He asked me not to kill you. He thought he was to blame – him and the officers who gave us our orders. He was wrong, but he gave me the money and he died afterwards."

Bufford burst out laughing.

"You think I'm going to kill myself because you found me, Sergeant? Are you expecting a confession?"

"There's no need. I've known it all for a long time, Bufford. I just didn't understand it until I read that article and saw your photograph in the newspaper."

"I don't understand what you're saying anymore, Sergeant. You're starting to rave. You've lost a lot of blood."

Bufford looked at the table. The red stain was spreading, flowing towards him, passing between the pitcher of alcohol and his glass.

"It's because you haven't told me yet."

Bufford looked up.

"What?"

"The little slave."

"Why are you talking about that again, Sergeant?"

"Did you think about him when your son died, Buffalo?"

A vein throbbed in Bufford's forehead, from the roots of his hair to the top of his nose.

"If I fire again, you'll lose too much blood and I won't be able to do what I want, Sergeant. You'll be too weak. Is that what you want? To die quickly, before you tell me where your family is?"

Sergeant Bowman's eyelids kept falling, ever more slowly over his eyes.

"Did you tell him about your son?"

Bufford put his hand to his neck again to wipe away the sweat. Bowman knew that itch, when the salt from the sweat ran into the scars. Christian Bufford's lips trembled.

"I told him he was called Elliot."

"What else?"

Bufford tried to smile, but he was losing his self-assurance.

"Why does that interest you, Sergeant? You think you're going to soften me up, is that it? That I'll start blubbering and hand you my gun?"

"What did you say to him?"

The tone of Buffalo's voice changed.

"That I became a soldier so my son could go to school, so he wouldn't end up begging in the streets or working in the sewers with the other children in London. I have three ships now, Bowman. And four hundred workers. I did what I had to do to succeed, that's all."

"But Elliot is dead. It's too late. What else did you say to him?"

Bufford gritted his teeth.

"I told him it was over, that I was going to drop him in the water and he could leave. I asked him for forgiveness and then I threw him in the water."

"Forgiveness?"

Bufford sat forward in his chair and yelled:

"I asked him for forgiveness because you'd wanted to cut his throat in front of us! I told him it was over and he could leave!"

Bowman looked down and his head fell towards the table.

"I would have killed him. I wouldn't have hesitated. And you asked him for forgiveness for me, Buffalo?"

Bufford stood up and pointed the revolver at Bowman's head.

"When I'm done with you, Bowman, I'll go and find your family."

Bowman tried to sit up straight, but instead he fell backwards, collapsing against the chair. He smiled.

"Reeves couldn't have known."

Bufford looked lost.

"What are you talking about, Sergeant?"

Bowman extended his injured arm. The pain almost made him faint, but he lifted his three-fingered hand, covered with blood, above the table.

"I've already saved you twice, Buffalo. Reeves couldn't have known."

Bufford leaned over the pool of blood, dropped his pistol, and put both his hands on the table.

"You saved me?"

"When you cut off my fingers to save your own skin, Buffalo. I could have killed you, torn out your throat with my teeth."

Bufford wiped his eyes with the sleeve of his suit.

"You didn't do anything because you wanted to survive too, Sergeant. You're no better than I am."

"Survive? Is that what you're doing here, in your big house? Are you fighting to survive, Buffalo?"

"If you'd tried to defend yourself, they'd have killed you like the others."

"But I looked you in the eyes, Buffalo, and I didn't move, both times, when you attacked my hand. You can't have forgotten. I looked at you the way I'm looking at you now, Buffalo. Not to scare you, but to help you find the courage not to do it, not to become their minion, the way you've become the servant of the rich people you want to resemble. The world is cowardly, Buffalo. Men like me murder children to earn their wages, others like you kill to take revenge on their masters, but they thank you for it, Buffalo. They thank you. You've become their manservant, in your rickety house, with your paintings and your negroes."

Bufford shouted:

"You were begging me not to do it, Sergeant, that's all you were doing! If you'd tried to touch me, they'd have killed you. They would have protected me!"

Bowman snorted.

"They were waiting to see who would kill who. They wanted us to do their work for them. Like when they threw one ration of rice for two men, and you bit off Briggs' ear so you could steal his food. I didn't kill you, even though it could all have ended there. I looked you in the eyes and I sought the strength not to attack you while you were cutting off my fingers. You know how I did it? I thought about you on the junk, kissing that child that I almost killed. Reeves couldn't have known . . ."

Bufford screamed:

"Known what?"

Bowman slowly stood up, holding onto the table with his uninjured arm. He grimaced with pain and looked Bufford in the eyes.

"That I'd already forgiven you, Buffalo. I had to come here to tell you. That I was still there, that you weren't rid of me, even at the other end of the world, hoping that poor sods like Penders, Peavish or me would pay for your crimes."

"Stay where you are, Sergeant. What are you doing?"

Bowman staggered and grabbed hold of one of the pergola's posts.

Bufford pulled a dagger from under his jacket and caught up with Bowman in two strides.

"Nice try, Sergeant, but there's no point anymore. And if you're still here now, that's because you too are a bastard capable of surviving anything."

Bowman looked over at the far end of the grounds, the widow's cottage where he had drunk tea while thinking that she was too pretty for Bufford.

"I just had to know if you remembered the little slave."

Christian Bufford put his hand on Bowman's shoulder, gently striking the blade of his dagger against his trouser leg.

"Is that all you wanted to know, Sergeant? You left your family behind just for that? So you could come and tell me that you'd already forgiven me? What good is that going to do you now?"

Bowman looked him straight in the eyes. His voice was calm.

"To be able to keep going. To live an honourable life."

Bufford raised his eyebrows.

"What are you on about, Sergeant?"

Bowman smiled at him.

"Courage. That's still me, Bufford."

"Because you came here and looked me in the eyes?"

"No, because I'm going to turn my back on you."

He feebly pushed Bufford's hand from his shoulder and closed his eyes. He could smell his own blood, and Bufford's odour, a few inches away: his sweat, his breath, his clothes. For a moment, he listened to the two of them breathing, suppressing the fear of darkness, then he opened his eyes again. Bufford had not moved.

"On the *Joy*, I didn't want to choose men who were like me so I wouldn't have to face them. In the end, it was the preacher who chose you."

Bowman smiled one last time.

"You can stick your knife in my belly. It'll only take a second. But do you have the courage to do this, Buffalo? To turn your back on someone like you?"

Bowman took a deep breath, let go of the pergola's metal post, slowly swivelled on his heel and took a step towards the glass doors.

"Stop, Bowman."

Bowman stopped for an instant, to get his balance, and then took another step.

"Don't turn your back on me."

He kept moving forward.

"BOWMAN!"

He was five yards from the doors.

"You were begging me not to do it. You saved your own skin just like the others!"

He put his hand on the door handle.

"BOWMAN!"

Bowman opened the door and spoke quietly, too quietly for Bufford to hear:

"You're saved, Buffalo. I'm leaving."

He went into the entrance hall, and Bufford's yells, repeating his name over and over, followed him to the front door. Bowman supported himself against the wall of the house as he walked over to the stable driveway and pulled himself onto Walden's back. He stopped in the middle of the unpaved street, tore off his shirt and tied the strip of cloth around his arm. He squeezed his legs together, and the mustang started down the hill to the village.

A horseman in a broad-rimmed hat rode towards the Delauney house. He was wearing a black suit and the horse he rode was as black as his clothes. The chain of a gold watch hung from his waistcoat pocket. His horse breathed heavily as it climbed the slope. It was covered in foam, its mouth full of thick drool. A rifle, in a worn leather holster, flapped against the horse's side. Bowman pulled on the reins and Walden stamped the ground. The man lifted his head and stopped next to Bowman. They exchanged a look. The preacher smiled, then his face looked gaunt and drawn once again.

"I'm glad to see you, Sergeant."

"Why did you come, preacher?"

Peavish stared ahead of him, at the house at the top of the sloping street.

"When I sent that letter . . . I realised I wouldn't make it, Sergeant."

He squinted at the house.

"Is he still there?"

Bowman lowered his head.

"Don't go."

Peavish patted his horse's neck and wiped the animal's sweat on his trousers.

"It's fear, Sergeant. I don't have a choice."

He dug his heels into the horse's sides and it started walking forward again.

Bowman remained in the middle of the street, looking up at the bay and the trade ships in full sail as they moved towards the ocean.

———◈——◈——◈———

It was August by the time Arthur Bowman arrived at the Fitzpatrick ranch after one final week-long journey along the road.

While he managed to hug his daughter, it took him several days to exchange words with Alexandra. The two of them remained mute for a long time, driven by contradictory emotions that they tried to suppress. Then, one morning, when Bowman was bathing in the lake with Aileen, Alexandra joined them in the water and he kissed her.

Work on the new house had recommenced in his absence. The builders had started on the cladding. In mid-August, while the Penders family was returning from the eastern prairies through the forest, a man in a black suit waited for them outside their hut. Bowman got down from his horse, carrying his daughter in his arms, and shook Edmund Peavish's hand. His new businessmen's clothes were covered with dust. He took off his hat to greet Alexandra Desmond and pay his respects. The preacher seemed to have aged even more. The sleeve of his jacket was torn and the fabric was stained with dried blood. Beneath his shirt, dirt-grey bandages were strapped around his shoulder. The two men made their excuses to Alexandra, who took Aileen from Bowman's arms and watched them walk away towards the cove. The preacher washed his face and hands in the water, then they went along the shore until they vanished from sight.

When they returned to the hut, Bowman and Peavish were silent, walking slowly together. Their faces were grave, and the same deep wrinkles marked their still-young foreheads. Peavish spoke to Alexandra Desmond without being able to raise a smile.

"I hope that we will see each other again, ma'am. Take care of your family and yourself."

He climbed into the saddle, untied the rifle holster and looked at it for an instant before handing it to Bowman.

"You'll need it more than I will in these mountains, Sergeant."

They shook hands one last time. The preacher rode away. When he passed under the ranch's sign, his back sagged. Bowman sat in the grass and watched him disappear. Alexandra hugged him and watched Aileen crawl straight ahead.

"What did he say?"

Bowman watched as his daughter reached the fence of the enclosure. She clung on to a post and pulled herself upright. Walden poked his head through the bars to smell her hair. The little girl let go of the post so she could try to caress the horse, gave a little yelp of excitement, then fell backwards onto her bottom.

"It's over."

On 19 September, 1863, in Chickamauga, Georgia, twenty thousand soldiers died in a battle won by Confederate troops.

The house was finished in October and the family moved its few belongings from the hut to its new home, with the terrace on stilts overlooking the water of the cove. They took one last bath before winter, this time with their daughter, and warmed up around a big fire. Bowman jokingly asked Alexandra if she didn't have any announcements to make to him this year.

"Not yet."

The next morning, while the ashes of the fire were still smoking, snow started falling onto the lake. The snow fell heavily that month, and they feared they were in for another harsh winter. But in early December, the weather grew milder and they had two weeks of sunshine. In places on the prairies, the snow melted and for several days the horses were able to eat some more grass. As Christmas drew closer, the snow returned.

Arthur Bowman grew unhealthily silent and wrote letters which he sent to Grantsville. He seemed to be suffering, in the middle of his family, from a strange form of solitude. The peacefulness of the mountains was sometimes too painful for him, but he hardly ever went to town anymore. Alexandra Desmond left him alone when he drifted towards other times and places in this way. She could imagine those places and times, but did not want to know more about them. In these absent moments, Bowman walked around the ranch, stopping near the hut or the sign, as if he were following a track, gathering his scattered memories. Then he came back to her or their daughter and managed to smile, each time for a little longer.

On New Year's Day, 1864, Arthur came out of the house in the middle of the night and cocked his rifle. In the stable, the horses had begun to whinny and kick the walls. A lamp in one hand, his rifle in the other, Bowman approached in silence, expecting to find wolves roaming nearby. Then he heard voices inside the building, someone trying to calm the horses. He blew out the lamp, put it down on the snow and continued to move forward. The moon was big and its light, reflected by the snow, illuminated the night. He closed his eyes to adapt them to the darkness, skirted around the stable and half opened the manure hatch, at the back of the barn, so he could take a look inside. Walden and Trigger were rearing up, kicking the walls. Bowman moved away from the hatch and held the rifle in both hands.

"Come out or I'll shoot."

There was no response.

"If you come out now, I'll let you go. Move away from the horses and leave."

Someone answered from inside:

"We'll leave. Don't shoot. We're going."

Bowman heard the main door creak open on the other side of the building. He ran through the snow and fired a shot above the two figures as they climbed over the enclosure's fence.

They froze.

"Don't move."

"You said we could leave. We're going. We didn't want to steal anything, sir. We just wanted to sleep in the barn."

Bowman found his lamp in the snow and lit it again. He lifted it up at the same time as he raised the barrel of the rifle. Two dirty-faced boys in patched-up rags, with scraps of military uniform visible beneath the patchwork. They were standing in line like prisoners next to the fence.

"Are you armed?"

They shook their heads.

"Where have you come from?"

They looked at each other, their chests still swollen from running, breathing out big clouds of steam in the lamplight.

"We were on manoeuvres with our squad, sir, and we got lost in the mountains."

Bowman lowered the lamp that was dazzling them and observed them for a moment.

"Deserters?"

One of them took a step back against the fence, while the other dared to raise a hand in protest.

"No, sir, we got lost. We're looking for our squad and we're lost. We just wanted to spend the night in your barn."

Bowman lowered his rifle.

"Walk in front. If either of you tries anything, you'll get a bullet in your back."

He pushed them forward with his gun until they reached the hut. Then he made them go inside and blocked the door and the shutters over the windows. Alexandra was waiting for him on the doorstep of the house. He led her inside and put wood in the stove, and they sat either side of the table. The next morning, Bowman went back to the hut and knocked at the door.

"Can you hear me?"

"Yes, sir, we hear you."

"I'm going to open the door and you're going to leave without making any trouble. I'm still armed."

He unblocked the door and took a few steps back, his gun by his side. The two boys came out, one after the other, hands protecting their eyes from the daylight.

"Where are you from?"

"We were in Aurora with a convoy of recruits, sir, headed south."

The two boys looked alike. One of them – the one who had spoken – was a bit taller and more muscular than the other.

"Are you brothers? What are your names?"

The bigger one crossed his arms over his chest in an attitude of defiance. The other looked at Bowman.

"I'm Oliver, sir. Ferguson. And he's Pete. We're from near Portland, in Oregon."

"Why did you desert?"

The elder brother uncrossed his arms.

"We didn't desert because we weren't volunteers. They forced us to join, so we didn't desert. We freed ourselves."

They had not eaten in several days and they were both in a weakened state. The younger brother had a fever. His sibling, Pete, had taken a step forward as he spoke and now raised his voice:

"If you want to take us to Carson City, go ahead. Whether they shoot us or send us to the slaughter, it's the same thing anyway."

The Ferguson brothers stood tall in front of Bowman, as if he were a firing squad.

"How did you get here?"

They did not understand the question.

"Did anyone see you?"

They exchanged a look. Oliver turned to Bowman.

"We passed the town at night. We've been in the mountains for two days. No-one in Carson saw us."

Bowman hesitated for a moment, then turned towards the house and made a signal with his hand. Alexandra came out on the terrace. She walked over to the hut, greeting the two boys as she passed between them, put some food inside, and came out again to stand next to Bowman.

"Where are you going?"

"We don't know, sir."

"You're not going home?"

The big brother spoke:

"Our parents are dead. There's just my brother and me."

Bowman looked at Alexandra. She was pale. Neither of them had slept that night.

"Go inside and eat. We'll see what we can do afterwards."

They hesitated, no longer daring to look at the man or the woman.

"We'll leave the door open, but I'd advise you not to go outside. It's better if no-one sees you for now."

"We'll leave tonight. Thank you for the food, ma'am."

Bowman lowered his head and looked at the rifle in his hand.

"Sleep here tonight. I'm going to saddle two horses in the stable. If someone turns up, jump on them and head for the mountains. And if you get caught, you'd better tell them you stole the horses, otherwise I'll kill you."

The threat made them shudder. Oliver took his brother by the arm and led him inside. Before closing the door, he spoke to the ranch's owners:

"Thank you."

"Go inside."

Alexandra and Bowman stayed near the house all day long, never taking their eyes off the hut. In the evening, Alexandra brought more food to the Ferguson brothers.

The snow began to fall again. Wrapped up in a blanket, his gun in his hand, Bowman stood guard on the terrace. Alexandra joined him and snuggled under his arm.

"Will they find them?"

"Almost certainly."

"And shoot them?"

Bowman did not reply.

"The youngest one's not even seventeen."

"I know."

"What will happen if they find them here?"

"Nothing good."

She looked up at him.

"Arthur, when you were a soldier, did you . . . When there were deserters . . ."

He looked at her.

"It happened."

"You did it yourself?"

He turned towards the hut.

"Sometimes."

He felt Alexandra press herself a little more tightly against him. She spoke in a soft voice:

"We have to hide them."

Bowman thought for a moment.

"Until the end of the war."

"But not here?"

His arm squeezed her shoulders.

"In the forest. We'll build another hut."

"In the spring, can we say that they came to work here, that they're part of your family?"

He leaned down to her.

"They'll stay at the ranch."

Inside the house, Aileen had started crying. Alexandra took his hand.

"Come on."

He kissed her forehead.

"I'm going to stay out here a bit."

She did not let go of his hand.

"No-one will hurt them?"

"No."

She closed the door behind her and Aileen's crying stopped. Bowman leaned his shoulder against a post and watched the sun go down behind the white mountain peaks and the sky darken above the lake. Night was falling on the Fitzpatrick ranch.

Sergeant Arthur Bowman turned towards the little hut where the deserters waited, pulled the blanket over his neck, and crossed his arms over the preacher's rifle.

"No-one."

ANTONIN VARENNE was awarded the Prix Michel Lebrun and the Grand Prix du Jury Sang d'encre for *Bed of Nails*, his first novel to be translated into English. His second, *Loser's Corner* was awarded the Prix des Lecteurs Quais du polar and the Prix du Meilleur Polar Francophone.

SAM TAYLOR is an author and translator. His translations include works by Laurent Binet, Hubert Mingarelli, Joël Dicker and Maylis de Kerangal.